S0-ACC-080

THE ERRAND OF THE EYE

A NOVEL

THE ERRAND OF THE EYE

A NOVEL

HOPE NORMAN COULTER

Hope Norman Coulter

August House / Little Rock
PUBLISHERS

Published by August House, Inc.,
P.O. Box 3223, Little Rock, Arkansas, 72203,
501-663-7300.

Printed in the United States of America
10 9 8 7 6 5 4 3 2 1

LIBRARY OF CONGRESS CATALOGING-IN-PUBLICATION DATA

Coulter, Hope Norman, 1961-
The errand of the eye.

I. Title.
PS3553.0844E77 1988 813'.54 88-6233
ISBN 0-87483-056-7 (alk. paper)

First Edition, 1988

Cover illustration by Robert Weathersby
Production artwork by Ira Hocut
Typography by Lettergraphics
Design direction by Ted Parkhurst
Project direction by Liz Parkhurst

This book is printed on archival-quality paper which meets the guidelines for performance and durability of the Committee on Production Guidelines for Book Longevity of the Council on Library Resources.

For Nate

Whether my bark went down at sea—
Whether she met with gales—
Whether to isles enchanted
She bent her docile sails—

By what mystic mooring
She is held today—
This is the errand of the eye
Out upon the Bay.

—Emily Dickinson

1

In 1966, when Allie McCain was six years old, her Great-Aunt Amalie asked her family to move back to Louisiana and help manage her plantation. Great-Uncle Hudson had just died and the place was going to seed.

Plantation! Frank McCain thought at first, uneasily. Me run Green Isle? It was not exactly the scenario he had pictured when he daydreamed about returning.

"Plantation!" the Bostonians at Frank and Lillian's dinner parties always said, whenever one of the McCains mentioned Green Isle. "You've been telling us the South has changed."

"It *has* changed," Frank would say hastily. "It just means 'farm.' You're awfully knowledgeable about the South, for people who've never even been there." But inside he wasn't so sure they were wrong.

The letter was not the only thing Great-Aunt Amalie had put in the big, lumpy manila envelope postmarked Edgewood, Louisiana. When Frank up-ended the packet over the coffee table Allie and her older brother laughed to see its contents tumble out: a hodgepodge of papers, some upside down, some back to back, some folded and some not, either stiff with age and coffee rings or slick with a blur of new copy fluid. They included an aerial photograph of Green Isle, a blueprint of the dairy barn, a funeral home fan with several genealogies sketched on the back, last year's tax return, a smashed boll of cotton, some figures and charts on crop production from two years before, in Uncle Hudson's writing, and a brochure on tourism in the central Louisiana area, with a cryptic note clipped to it: "Mr. Skinner's wife sends this, she works for the Highway Dept. It came out last year but I'm sorry I ever let them put Green Isle in it. You can keep this but send everything else back, or bring it with you, except the cotton of course, With love, your loving Aunt, Amalie Rand."

This miscellany seemed out of place among the spare Scandinavian furnishings of their third-floor townhouse apartment. Lillian raised her eyebrows and smiled with one corner of her mouth. "Tourist brochures about *Edgewood?*" Frank picked up the aerial photo.

He could see which part of the farm was the original tract, a narrow strip of land that ran westward from the river for three or four miles, because the drainage canals that marked its perimeter were the oldest and deepest on the farm. In the photo the scoring was clearly visible, like chalk lines around a football field.

"Look," he showed his family, drawing with his little finger. "This is the oldest part of the farm, the original land grant. Made by the King of Spain," he added, mainly for Fayette's benefit. The boy peered over the map with greater interest then.

Years ago, Frank had done a report on the place for eighth-grade Louisiana history. He vaguely remembered swaggering in front of his friends about it; the fact that his father never owned real estate had made him arrogant about his great-uncle's.

"What are those?" Fayette was saying.

"Oh—those are houses for the people who work on the farm."

"They look like Monopoly-game houses," said Fayette.

"Monopoly houses are probably better built."

"You remember," Lillian said, "where Miss Corey lives. Remember visiting Miss Corey last time we were in Edgewood, when we went out to see Uncle Hudson and Aunt Amalie? That black lady who let you pick strawberries out of her garden?"

"Sort of."

"Well, one of these houses is hers."

"I remember," said Allie. "We went to this place where there were baby-cows and we could feed them out of our hands and there was this big tree in the back with limbs that came down to the ground."

"Calves, stupid. Not baby-cows. Calves."

"Fayette, don't let me hear you call anyone stupid."

"That's the place," said Lillian. "That's the place where we might move."

"Oh," said the children.

The irregular row of little houses—cottages rebuilt in the 1920s from original slave cabins—was in a curve of the bayou that wiggled across the farm. The road to town hugged it close. A little farther to the southeast, down a long thin scar of a drive, were a matrix of trees like tufts of yarn, and Amalie's farmhouse. Frank squinted to see its yard, some sheds and a barn, and the workshop, smokehouse, muscadine arbor, and dog pen. Near the house were pastures—smooth silver plains freckled with cattle—and row crops that looked like corrugated cardboard.

"This picture must have been taken just after planting," muttered Frank. Already he felt he needed to show he wasn't *that* ignorant about farming.

"Hunh?" said Fayette. "Hunh?" Frank shot him a look. "Sir?"

"I said it looks as if these fields were just plowed up for planting."

"Did you ever plow when you worked on this farm?"

"No, I only worked in the summers, when the crops were already up."

"Someone took this picture from an airplane?" Now Allie was chiming in.

"That's right, sugar."

"So it still goes all the way to the river on the east," said Lillian.

"I believe so. Uncle Hudson used to worry all the time about losing the land by erosion. See this sandbar? It used to be a good bit wider. Of course that cuts both ways, though—look, a little farther down, there's beach where there used to not be any at all." White sand like an uneven cuticle joined the river to the wild, uncleared part of the farm, which showed up in the photo as dark and wiry as a tract of steel wool.

Lillian started to marvel. "You know, this is really gorgeous. You could hang it on the wall. Look at the different textures. Look at the contrast in darks and lights. It looks like abstract art."

"Well, it ain't abstract," Frank said flatly. "It's real."

Allie's father put her to bed that night. "You warm enough?" he said. "Maybe we better get the afghan." He pulled it from its daytime place on the rocking chair in her room, all its colors bled into the dark now just as his figure was—a dark silhouette against light coming in from the hall. "The old afghan-istan," he went on, unfolding it. That was one of the jokes between them from as far back as Allie could remember, and she laughed, though she still didn't know there was a real Afghanistan; the nonsense syllables just pleased her. She touched it lightly, worked her fingers through the familiar loose weave as he settled it around her.

"'Sat good?"

"Um-hm—Daddy?"

"What, honey?"

"Are we going to move?"

"Well, we might."

"I don't *want* to move."

He listened a second more, and she felt his big hand move from the fold of the afghan to pat her side and squeeze her shoulder. Then he simply said, "I'm sorry," and leaned down, blocking the light from the door. "Goodnight, now." She kissed him back through the prickle of whiskers, getting the faint salt taste of his jaw—a sign of nighttime to her; his morning kisses were smooth and soapy-smelling.

"Is there an aquarium in Edgewood?"

"No."

Then all her bereftness and fear welled up. The sturdy little penguins would be clambering up their rock at the aquarium, looking for her; finning with their wings across their clear pool in search of her; gazing around with their shining black eyes for her, and she would not be there. The funny fish, orange and black and red and blue, with fins and tails rippling like silk trains behind them, would swim up to the glass mouthing greetings with their big pouty lips, kissing the glass as they always did—and she, their friend, would be gone. She would have stepped into some big unimaginable void like Wendy off the plank in *Peter Pan.* "I don't want to leave the penguins, Daddy. I want to be able to go see them. I want to see all the fish when I want to. I don't want to go away. I don't want to go where there's no aquarium!"

He had sat down on her bed by now to scoop her up while she cried into his shoulder. He rubbed her back through her nightgown. "They won't know where I am," she moaned, her body shaking. Every time she thought again about the wistful little penguins scanning the crowds in vain for her, the lonesome sea tortoise bumping his slow body against the glass without her there, her sobs would wind up again. Finally they subsided.

"I'm falling off the bed," she told her father sulkily.

At that he stood up, with a little breath of air blown through his nostrils, not quite a laugh. He kissed her on the forehead one more time and said, "I'm afraid you'll just have to adjust."

She watched him go. "Don't close the door all the way!"

He left it open a crack—less than her mother would have. She heard him open Fayette's door. "Goodnight, son." Goodnight. "What are you reading?" *Mrs. Coverlet's Magicians.* "Is it good?" Yes sir. "Well, don't stay up too late." Then Daddy's steps went into the kitchen and Allie heard him say, "Coffee, this late?"

And Mama: "I thought it might help me think. And we won't be getting to sleep any time soon, anyway, tonight." Clinking sounds, but flatter and deader than glasses—the sound of cups and saucers being handled. A pause. Then Mama again: "What was that all about?"

"She wanted to know if there was an aquarium in Edgewood. When I told her no, she cried."

Another pause. Then her mother, "I told you—lately she asks every day if we can go there. She's in a phase."

"I guess we could get her a little aquarium for her room. If we go."

"It's hardly the same!" said Mama.

"Shhh."

"Well, we have to decide. And there are going to be losses, either way. Don't pretend you can compensate for the things we're going to lose—you can't recreate the New England Aquarium with a bowl of goldfish."

"Let's go in the living room," Daddy said. "You're going to wake them up."

Why did grownups always assume you were asleep as soon as they said goodnight? Allie wondered. She beat the wall between hers and Fayette's room. They had made up a spy code. Shave-and-a-haircut, she knocked. That meant goodnight from her to him. Six-bits, came the two thuds returning his goodnight. The theme from "Man from U.N.C.L.E.," done very fast, meant that grownups were coming. But she wouldn't be needing that tonight. From the living room their voices lapped in a faint, ongoing murmur. First Daddy, for a long time, then Mama. Daddy, then Mama. Occasional phrases in a loud tone would stick out and then sink under the murmur again. "Such a *rat* race here—I mean the traffic, the fumes," mumble mumble. A rat race. A rat race? "—Danger of romanticizing—" mumble mumble mumble, "a few bright spots," mumble, "able to make a difference" in her father's emphatic voice, and then her mother high and very clearly again, "The big fish in a little pond thing, for you!" with a slight pause before the dip of the current of their mingled voices washed her separate one under again.

Big fish in a little pond, Allie heard. And for the words in her ear vivid images were created again. Golden fish and scarlet fish shimmered and swam before her eyes. Maybe she *would* get a little aquarium for her room in Edgewood. She would lie in bed and shine a flashlight on it every night. Her breathing got slower. Outside there would be small ponds. She pushed her fingers through the holes in her afghanistan as if she were parting fronds of underwater plants. Brilliant purple fish were moving up and down; the water carried them. Their lips opened and closed as if they were saying magic words to her. Spy words, passwords. The water was pale green and bubbled silently. She could move behind the glass in this pond. She was asleep.

2

WAY BENEATH THEM Louisiana looked dark, luxuriant, and green, like a carpet so plush it had sprouted—its nap threaded and flecked with water where the last rays of sunset glinted. As light drained out of the west, the bits of reflecting water below winked out. The sky went from darker to darker blue and then got black. A crescent moon came up. The plane, which had been hopping westward from Atlanta since five that afternoon, sank once again, deliberately as an egret, seemingly right into the swamp; but beneath the foliage it found the tarmac of the Baton Rouge airport, and a few passengers deboarded. Twenty minutes later it took off again. Far below them they could see a sheer sparse web of lights, like spittle across black velvet.

In the cheerful yellow tube that was the plane's interior, the stewardess passed by and gave Fayette yet another Coke. Allie was drawing pictures of her old neighborhood to give to Great-Aunt Amalie.

The crew announced the next destination to be Edgewood, Louisiana, and all the Texas passengers groaned. "Oh, I wish to God we wouldn't stop in these piddly places," complained an enormous woman, with diamonds in her ears big as those that patterned the snakeskin band on her husband's cowboy hat. "At this rate we'll never get to Dallas."

Aunt Amalie met them at the airport's only gate, introduced them to half the people who'd been on their flight, and bore them off in an ancient Buick. Before they got to the parking lot exit Frank asked politely, "Would you like me to drive?" and his aunt replied, "Oh, don't *you* start that!"

Her driving was crazy. Allie, wedged into the middle of the front seat, kept being thrown by erratic curves and wide turns into her father, and rolling her eyes up into his face. Then he would narrow one eye into a near-wink and purse his lips as if to hush her—before jerking his gaze in alarm back to the center stripe, which kept disappearing under the middle of the car. When they did look back at the roadsides they caught glimpses of low brick homes with big yards, where signs advertised taxidermy services, hairdressing, catfish; political posters tacked on enormous tree-trunks; a few gas stations still lit up for late business; and trailer signs with movable black letters arranged into moralistic quips—the trappings of the piney, hilly Bible

Belt. Then they crossed the Red River into south Louisiana. They saw the cluster of six- and ten-story buildings and chunky flat-roofed stores and warehouses that was Edgewood's downtown. Then, racing or dawdling according to the whim of Amalie's foot, they swept through a poor black part of town where an expressway cleaved to the fronts of tiny porches side by side, with their floors and railings slanting all different ways and disappearing back into shadow—and out to an emptier, dark highway, heading south.

That night they couldn't see much of Green Isle. In the flat darkness the only three-dimensional spaces were again unscreened porches, this time warm and lighted ones that jutted close to the road only at intervals, seeming independent of actual dwellings. Then they turned and drove for a minute through a grove of trees whose trunks materialized quickly in the headlights—"like in *The Lion, the Witch, and the Wardrobe*," said Allie, but no one heard her. And Amalie's house hardly seemed enchanted; it was just someplace into which they could finally straggle and set down their suitcases and duffel bags, with their sharpest impressions being smells—deep, long-imbedded smells of cedar closets and many noons of frying chickens and something else—mothballs? next Christmas's fruitcake, soaked in whiskey and wrapped tight as a mummy in foil, put away in some chest-of-drawers and forgotten? Less notable were glimpses of heavy furniture and drapery and lots of what-nots which the children took in wearily, already bored with the admonitions not to touch them that they knew they would hear. "I declare, I forgot to leave any lights on," said their great-aunt. She fluttered around them turning on odd lamps with switches they never would have found, getting glasses for ice water and forgetting to fill them, and pointing out various relatives who stared with pupilless doll-like eyes from delicately tinted photographs on walls and mantels. She vanished abruptly, only to reappear in a flowing robe—"housecoat"—with a glutinous-looking cream smeared on her face. Frank sat up with her for a while, but everyone else was ready to fall, or, literally, climb into one of the tall, testered, soft, cool-sheeted beds. When Lillian went to tell Allie goodnight she said desperately, "Mama, it's too *quiet* here"—and was asleep the next instant.

Allie was usually the first one of her family to wake up. She opened her eyes to a room flooded with white sunshine, climbed out of bed, and pulled on shorts and a shirt. She put on her Mickey Mouse watch and pushed her hair out of her face with a plastic headband. She parted the organdy curtains and looked outside. The dew on the grass and leaves looked thick; the trees seemed blurred with it, as if it stood in the air itself, yet the sun coming up behind made a rosy-yellow light in the sky and lay in sharp green bars on the grass.

She heard footsteps go by her door. "Fra-ank!"

Rap, rap, rap. "Fra-ank! I need some help from you-all. I've been hating to wake you up, but it's getting late."

"Oh, we're up," Allie heard her father call in a scratchy version of politeness. He woke up very slowly in the morning. Allie knew from his strained voice that his eyes would not be open more than slits right now and his hair was standing on end. "We're up."

"There's grits and biscuits and coffee in here, and fig preserves, I'll put out the mayhaw jelly but it didn't jell very well, but I remembered you used to like it so I said to myself I'd just put it out anyway." There was no answer from her parents' room. Now Great-Aunt Amalie's voice came closer: "Fa'te! Allie! Time to get up!"

Allie waited, perfectly still among the curtains, until the footsteps passed. Then she slipped to the door and turned the handle very quietly. She couldn't remember where the bathroom was, but luckily her mother was padding down the hall toward her.

"Morning, baby. How'd you sleep?"

"Fine."

"What time is it?"

"Six forty-five."

"Oh, it's getting late, all right." Mama was always a little sarcastic in the morning.

From the bathroom Allie went back to her room. She pulled the bedspread over the pillows and lay down on top of it, prone, propped on her elbows, with her head toward the door, watching it. In a few minutes her father went past, and she sped into the hall to join him. "Hey!"

He bent down and kissed her. "Hey. You been waiting on me?"

Together they went into the kitchen, where a very dark, straight-backed woman in a white shirt and slacks was frying bacon. Even her shoes were white, Allie noticed. The woman turned around when they came in. Daddy greeted her uncertainly and she grinned. "I believe you've forgotten me.—Bessie Mae Taylor."

"Well, hi, Bessie Mae. I knew your face the minute you turned around. I didn't know you work for Amalie."

"Oh, I been working for Miz Rand for nineteen years. She's real good to me."

"We've been here on visits and I've never seen you. Look, I want you to meet my daughter, Allie. Allie, this is Miz Taylor."

"Nice to know you." Allie smiled shyly at the woman. "If it was a holiday when you was here, probably I was off. Or either a weekend. Look here, have a seat." There was a table in one corner of the kitchen. "You want some coffee? I'll get you some."

"Oh, gosh, no, I'll get it," said Frank, fumbling at some of the cabinets. But Bessie Mae had a cup already set out for him and served him calmly, as sure and unbothered as if it were the most natural thing in the world. "Oh, and could Allie have one too?"

"*You* drink coffee?"

Allie blushed. "Yes ma'am. With milk in it."

"Better watch that, now. It'll turn you black, you know." Allie looked up at Frank in puzzlement but, with his face deep in his own cup, he ignored her. Meanwhile coffee was streaming into her cup from a white enamel pot Bessie Mae gripped in one big hand—a hand and forearm, indeed, the same color as the scalding liquid. She gave it a little expert dip and twist at the end so it wouldn't drip at all. Then came the milk from a bottle sweating with cold. And in her cup Allie watched the change from deep deep brown to tan. "Sugar?" said Bessie Mae.

"You bet."

Bessie Mae laughed. "Child, you a sight," she said. " 'You bet.' "

Allie's father laughed too. Then he said, "Do you live here on the place now?"

"Um-hm, sure do. You know that house that used to be the Johnsons'?"

"Sort of, yes, I think so—"

"Well, that's where we live at, me and my husband, Wallace.—Is this your little boy?"

Fayette had padded into the kitchen. "Yes, it sure is. This is Fayette. Fayette, this is Miz Taylor."

Fayette nodded and said "Good morning" with a bleary smile and a sort of seasoned, world-weary courtesy, like a jaded old diplomat. He took a seat, scraping his chair into Allie's. "*Ow.*" "Well, *move.*" They squabbled barely audibly while their father went on asking questions of Bessie Mae; soon plates of food appeared before them, and they quieted down.

"But you probably have children now too?"

"Um-hm, there's Wallace Jr., he's in high school, and Neva, and LaToya, and my little one Reggie, he's three ..."

As they ate they could see their great-aunt through a window. She had appeared beneath some sort of fruit tree, with a lanky black teenager dragging a ladder in tow. Now she was pointing and talking to him non-stop while he picked the fruit and sent it tumbling from his hands down into a sack Amalie was holding. Every once in a while, continuing one-handed to hold the sack open at the right height for him, she would reach out with the other hand and pick a few low-growing fruits herself.

"What's that they're gathering?" said Fayette, pointing with a jellied biscuit.

"Plums," answered Bessie Mae.

"How long has she been up?"

"Oh, since long about four-thirty."

"God, Daddy, are you gonna have to get up that early to run the farm?"

"Let's just say I won't, son. Don't say God like that."

"But you do."

"That doesn't give you the right to, now does it?"

"Oh, Mr. Frank, once you start trying to work this farm, you'll be more than God-din'," said Bessie Mae.

Frank laughed, toyed with his coffee spoon a minute, then decided to add, "You don't have to call me mister."

Soon Lillian wandered into the kitchen. Amalie came in with baskets full of flowers which (combined with a few sips of hot, turgid coffee) jolted Lillian into life; she jumped up exclaiming over each kind, and started helping Amalie put them into soak. Bessie Mae persuaded the McCains to turn over their dirty clothes to her. All of them suddenly realized they were stuffed with biscuits, they couldn't even finish the last one they'd taken; and with that the house shifted into another phase of the day. Fayette and Allie wandered outside. They heard their father saying halfheartedly behind them, "Brush your teeth—" but the door's slam muffled the directive enough that they could ignore it safely, so they did. They drifted behind the house, out of the shadow of the eaves and into streaming sunlight that already, at eight o'clock in the morning, made their arms and the tops of their heads hot to the touch, and yawned.

"Let's go climb that tree," suggested Fayette, "and that way we'll be able to see the whole farm."

"Okay."

It was a mimosa, but they didn't know that. Allie reached out and touched one of the flowers, a pink spangled feathery puff.

"Mmm, smell it."

"Yeah, it's sweet, hunh."

"The leaves are neat too."

The palms of their feet and hands reached the joints of the slender limbs easily. Way up they found places to pause, Fayette a little higher than Allie, and when they got settled they parted what they had to of the sparse, leafy fringe and looked down on Green Isle.

A whole vista lay beneath them. The mimosa blocked most of their view of Amalie's yard, but around it spread the orchard they had driven through last night, stopping neatly at the fenceline. Then there was the road they'd driven on last night; and the bayou, like a brown crayon scribble-scrabble running across a picture, with yellow-green bushes on both sides. On the other side of that was the winding, irregular line of little houses looking as trim and fragile as they had in the photo that had come to Boston. Between the houses viny gardens wreathed, and laundry on clotheslines blew like bright flags—overalls, underwear, dresses, sheets. A couple of tiny-looking kids with fishing poles walked down a dirt lane; someone's car poked toward a half-hidden church; a horse and rider rushed along a turnrow, kicking up dust.

"Wow, I bet I can see ten miles!" said Allie.

"I can see twenty where I am," said Fayette. But he sounded more dreamy than contentious. "This place is *great,*" he breathed.

And beyond all this, the houses and bayou and church and road, there were fields—rectangles and squares of different textures and different tints of green stretching away in all directions, encompassing and surrounding Allie and Fayette and all the rest of it as the sea surrounds a real island. Far out in the thickly leafing crops, sticking up like buoys or boats, were an occasional tin shed, a corral, a gleaming green tractor, a silo and barn or two. They could see to where the horizon curved, and the children felt they were standing on a vast encircling lens, with all of life contained within it and magnified.

Suddenly a door slammed. They heard their great-great-aunt's voice sounding as if it came from right below them. "Well, what do you expect me to do about it?"

Then there were some lower syllables answering her, which they could not make out.

Then Amalie's shrill tones: "Twenty-six dollars! I don't wear dresses that cost that much, and I'm *alive!*"

Swiftly, silently, Fayette was climbing one branch higher. Allie followed, though he frowned when she edged past him to reach a notch farther out on his limb. Through the mimosa leaves she could now see a black couple standing on the back steps with Aunt Amalie. The woman was wearing white tennis shoes and a light blue shirtdress and a scarf around her hair, and had a stolid look about her; her arms were folded. The man was in overalls. He was talking to Amalie and gesturing with a cap in his hand.

"Is Penney's the only place you looked? Now, Dottie, you could probably find it cheaper than that somewhere else... Where are you waking her? Because I'm gonna want to see this dress on her with my own eyes."

Now the black woman spoke for the first time, gruffly. They could hear her voice loud and clear. "At Claire's."

"At Claire's! Why not at Minerva's own house!"

"'At house it don't be fit to have folks in it. Them roaches"—she said it "rawches"—"them vines, big hole where the po'ch flo' be busted through. It ain't fit to live in. Much less to wake the dead in."

There was a pause, then Aunt Amalie said in a queer tone, "Oh, pshaw!"—just as Allie had read it in books, *p* and all—and the door slammed. Somehow the black couple knew not to leave. They stood impassively. The man started fussing at the woman, and now his voice was audible. "... No time to start that, here to ax a favor ..." Then the woman, "She be needing to hear that," and him again, "... time Minerva was alive, was when you shoulda been doing all like that. Cain't do her much good now ..." and then he fell quiet as the screen door opened and shut behind Amalie again, and she gave them some bills out of her wallet.

"Thanky, thanky," said the man, "I thank you, Miss Amalie," and turned away, replacing his cap, but his companion didn't say anything, and as they walked down the drive Amalie repeated over their heads, sharply, "I want to see it on her with my own eyes!"

Allie was looking at Fayette with her face screwed up and her head cocked, about to ask him something, the irritating way she did when she didn't understand something obvious in a movie or an episode of "Get Smart," but he said brusquely, "Move your hand, I need to step there," and started to go down.

She scooted over obediently and took a last look around. In a far field the same tractor she'd spotted a minute ago, now barely in view, moved in its little directed line along the horizon. She forgot everything else and watched it, fascinated. It made a slow, far turn, for a second seeming to hang off the very globe, and then came back within the circumscribing fields.

"Race you to the house," said Fayette, already on the ground.

She snapped back to the immediate. "Wait! You got a head start."

He waited patiently while she scraped and clambered down. They didn't comment any more on the scenes they had just taken in. They had already learned, as kids do, that some impressions must be guarded for a while, and it was tacitly plain that when the grownups called them in and asked what-all they'd seen, they should both reply, "Aw, nothin.' "

3

FRANK'S PEOPLE were north Louisianians—Scotch-Irish-Anglo-Welsh Protestants who had settled in Winn Parish and prospered, in the early days of the century, by razing virgin pine woods. They were the sort of family who started the town library and expected all their girl children to take piano lessons on the instrument that their one faintly aristocratic ancestor, the only literate forebear and hence the only one beyond two generations back whose name they even knew, had brought from South Carolina. Partly to preserve this whiff of distinction, their children were not allowed to say "nigger," only "Negro" as slurred as they wished. Yet with all this the McCains were vehement populists, like their neighbors. They peddled their business as a little man's enterprise and hated, deeper than scorn, the really big lumber companies that were taking hold. Their religion, Methodism, was a workers' church. Their manners and their self-regard were plain.

Frank's father, born in 1909, had been an earnest, intense child always enthralled by stories of his grandfather's travels on horseback to the circuit charges of his Methodist churches. It was mainly in an effort to recover that dramatic past that Pat McCain went to seminary himself. As soon as he was graduated and confirmed he married the daughter of the Winnfield pharmacist. At first he had a series of small-town appointments, and Frank was born in 1934 during his stay at one of the parish seats near the Arkansas border. The church had not disappointed Pat by then. When on Sunday mornings, aroused by black coffee drunk in solitude at dawn, he would glance at the sunbeams loosening a cover of frost on the altar window and read the account of Moses approaching Mount Sinai, he felt a powerful thrill that he identified as the Holy Spirit; and when at Annual Conference hundreds of hearty-voiced ministers gathered in memory of those among them who had died during the year and sang "And Are We Yet Alive," the thrills would multiply, stirring him so deeply that he never even attempted to describe them to anyone.

Then he had the south Louisiana charge of Frank's earliest memories, where his sister, Sarepta, was born in 1939. After that he was assigned to a church outside Edgewood and then was made District Superintendent of Edgewood. The Reverend McCain's Aunt Amalie and her husband, Hudson Rand, lived nearby, raising cotton, corn, cattle, and briefly potatoes and hogs on a working plantation not far outside the city limits. Frank grew close to his great-aunt and great-uncle. He had been grieving after the loss of his friends down on the coast, who had taught him to hunt, fish, crab, trap, and swim. The farm experiences that Amalie and Hudson could offer helped to fill the void the last move had made. Frank became a fixture on Green Isle—at the dairy, the office, the shop, and the corral, on horses and tractors, always in the company of two or three black children whose fathers worked for Hudson.

Then just after the war Reverend McCain was moved to a New Orleans municipal church, "a plum," his Conference brothers said. The family settled easily into the uptown parsonage. Even Frank, with his love for outdoor life, enjoyed the city. He could explore it by streetcar and on foot, and the alleys and quirky architecture, levee and haunted mansions, wharves, shifting crowds, and Audubon Park all intrigued him. In New Orleans just walking to school was exciting. He had the sense of being on the very lip of adventure; at any minute, one step might send him sliding right in.

But it was Pat, his father, who decided to drop in at the genealogical library at the corner of Camp and Tchopitoulas, which he had noticed many times in passing. The building was clean and airy inside, with a pleasant smell of musty ink. First Pat looked up a forefather of his wife's who had been a judge in Tensas Parish. Tracing backwards, he found another relative, the judge's uncle, whose name had been Frank. What do you know! thought the Reverend Pat; for he and his wife had picked out their son's name without knowing it had any family precedent. Then he looked up the Confederate Army records of his own grandfather on his mother's side. He found the volume he needed, and, with the leisurely feeling of absorption that comes when a whim is unfolding as one might wish, ran his finger down the pages of documents filled out in brown, spidery handwriting. His finger stopped. He read for a moment. His finger started to tremble. "Discharged; conviction, murder"! It said his grandfather had spent the last two years of the war in a Confederate prison in Atlanta, held on a murder charge. That was all—no other information to explain so bizarre an incident. Detained for murder by the officers of his own army! McCain was shaking as he left the library in the bright sunshine that followed one of New Orleans's torrential rains.

From this incident he gained much more than just a piece of unwelcome knowledge. The more he speculated on a motive for the killing, the more perplexed he grew. A lesson percolated down through layers of assumptions and habit: if his own grandfather had been a murderer, then surfaces in general were not what they appeared to be. Outwardly his life was much the same. He prayed more but with scarcely any satisfaction. He was a little sharper when someone came to him with a trivial problem and a little less attentive to the church's business affairs. He roamed the city more, looking at individuals in the crowds and wondering about their private sufferings as he never had before. His was not a holy sympathy—he knew that; it was idle and inefficient. From the walls of his study the fishy eyes of John Wesley stared accusingly down at him as if to say, "Yes, things are flawed, uneven, but what are you *doing* about them?" Yet McCain remembered, as he went with lagging heart about his rounds, that even Wesley had gone "unwillingly" to Aldersgate.

That June a famous missionary came to conduct a revival at the church. McCain's interest, which for weeks had been sulking in the mud of half-impressions and nebulous doubts, suddenly picked up. He found himself able to listen attentively to the man, who was just back from six months on an Indian *ashram* and was extolling Mahatma Gandhi. While his congregation listened with polite detachment, their eyes glazing over pair by pair like windows being shuttered at dusk, Pat McCain got more excited every minute. He thought he could detect a glimmer of sense in the ideas he was hearing—a concord with his recent confusion about appearances and identities, and a way out of his muddle of misgivings; an explanation for the maze of shadows beneath things, articulable, but still mystic enough to arrest and please him.

When the missionary insisted on speaking to black Methodists as well, McCain did the legwork to organize the occasions and went along to the Negro churches. The services slowly melted his apprehensions. He found himself enjoying the differences that distanced the familiar worship and so made it perceptible to him again. Psalms and liturgies were sped up to the rate of normal talking, hymns dragged at a quarter the tempo he was used to, and there was a colloquialism he liked, a pragmatic interpretation of the lessons that refreshed him. Gradually, after these impressions, he gained his first faltering insights into local black life. He was astonished that it was, after all, so real and big, so branchiated, happening with the haphazard grandeur of any people's life, a ten-minute drive away from his daily routine but completely out of his ken. The faces themselves intrigued him. He began to distinguish social strata. After the missionary left Pat continued to visit black churches and community meetings surreptitiously. He saw the same people over and over; sketchy hints of their character fleshed out as he observed and came to recognize individuals; bits of gossip about their private histories and trials added another dimension to his views. Somewhere inside him, almost reluctantly, as if his conscious mind were aware of the trouble it would bring him, the curiosity and the spectator's pleasure changed into certain knowledge of the injustice of blacks' subordination. Bewilderment and detachment dissolved like mist and left this conviction, rock-hard, and with it a cold, appalled anger at the extent of the effects of racism. He had a true calling now.

"Did you know," he would call to his wife after supper, as she stood at the sink washing dishes, "that as late as 1856, the *national* Methodist church was still condoning slavery?"

These new views of McCain's began to cause a rift in his church—a rift not between parts of the congregation, but between him and everyone in the congregation. White liberalism in the South was still an anomaly. When it did exist it was usually in the form of protest against only the more blatant kinds of oppression, like mob violence, not against the Jim Crow code itself. Pat was not overly ambitious. He concentrated on one vision, the joining of the segregated state Methodist Conferences. But the church hierarchy was not forthcoming. In the meantime, local congregations took Pat's version of the social gospel coldly at best and furiously at worst. They tore down his hopes. Even the most passive segregationists thought people like the Reverend McCain disturbingly radical.

And blacks cold-shouldered him too. Still a little surprised to find themselves veterans of World War II, and relating the atrocities of that war to their own persecution, they were seeking their own vents for a bitterness that had had decades to build up. No movement was definite enough yet for a new, unprecedented relationship with a white man to follow naturally—not even a white preacher who shouldered his way into the rear of the streetcar to ride with the "colored," and called joint meetings of blacks and whites when his mentor the missionary came to town. There was just no basis in history, or in the society around them, for trust.

Pat became too uncompromising to be a good pastor and too idealistic to stand the sidelong, painful advent of desegregation in the South. He felt sadly alone. His children were growing older, and he did not want to expose them any longer to the norm of racism, or to the vague threats by whites that had begun to come his way. He had been in correspondence with national church leaders for some time. Now he threatened to leave the ministry and pleaded with them for a position at the national headquarters. After a few months of wrangling, they gave him an administrative job with the National Church Board in New York—because they were sympathetic with his cause, and his record until New Orleans had been very good. In 1950 the family moved to a New Jersey suburb.

McCain was hurt beyond repair by the ineffectualness of his work in Louisiana. He had the sense of a great stage being set, on which, because of his age and color, he was destined to have no part. Later he read accounts of the civil rights boycotts and marches with passionate attention and kept a big scrapbook of newspaper clippings about them (which his wife would have given to the maid one day while cleaning out her closets years after the Reverend's death, had Frank not happened to drop by and stop her just in time). Pat McCain died of a heart attack in 1963. His widow moved to a tidy house in Shreveport and lived there happily, playing bridge and mowing down a line of successive "colored" yard men who never lived up to her standards, as happily as if she had never left Louisiana, as if Louisiana had not changed since 1950, in fact.

Frank finished high school in Glendale and then went to Rutgers on a scholarship. At a party in Manhattan his junior year, a classmate introduced him to two girls from Louisiana, new graduates of LSU who had come to Boston to work and savor the city till their money ran out. One of them turned out to be Lil Rabelais, from Edgewood. The two fell in love and were married in Edgewood a year later. After the wedding they went to Boston, where Frank started law school at Boston University and Lillian worked at one of the museums. Lillian loved urban life. And though Frank sometimes dreamed of returning to the South (half a bottle of wine could always prime him to talk about it) he was not motivated enough to put that notion into real terms. So, when he finished law school, he had shrugged and signed up with a modest Boston firm.

Fayette was born in 1957 and Allie in 1960. The McCains went home to Louisiana twice a year. As time passed they had learned they were not the inveterate Southern exiles they had believed; nor was Boston the beacon of enlightenment it was supposed to be. Frank especially got a little restless. His job was less than exciting. The future looked like a long dismal corridor of Atlantic winters. His children were piping words in Northern accents. Hearing that for a lifetime had been a gloomy prospect.

But now he was back. He was replanting the McCains in Louisiana. He was back with his lean, mobile, freckled face and boyish adam's apple and forelock of curling hair that would not lie down, his open, sharp blue eyes and his white teeth all framed by tiny gaps, and his slim, white-shirted body that would move through the crop-rows in high summer like an inquiring cursor combing lines of tiny print on a computer screen. Back with a *Progressive Farmer* magazine tucked under his arm. For support.

4

AFTER LIVING WITH Amalie for about a week, the McCains moved into the house still known to everybody on the bayou road as the Skinner house—a low ranch-style house that Aunt Amalie had been renting to the foreman she recently fired. Though Lillian chafed at its blandness and dark, low rooms, it did have a swimming pool, and there the kids and their Rabelais first cousins splashed happily into one another's acquaintance.

Lillian had a brainstorm soon after they moved. Why couldn't the children of the Green Isle farm hands come use the pool? She felt guilty, driving back from town with various nieces and nephews and her own children in the car jouncing up and down in anticipation of a swim, when she saw the black kids dispiritedly riding their bikes around their houses or sitting on their porches in the 97-degree heat. Frank shrugged when she asked him; he said he was busy feeling his own way around, and it was up to her; so Lillian herself walked up and down the road one dusk and invited everyone between ages four and eighteen to come swim in the morning. Aunt Amalie was scandalized. She had never pictured blacks in swimming pools at all—it seemed somehow unnatural—and she was especially horrified that Lillian let her own children and her brothers' children swim at the same time. But Lillian ignored the old woman. Finding out that Scrip Thomas, a teenager on Green Isle, had taken Senior Lifesaving at the Boys' Club downtown, she hired him to give basic swimming lessons and to supervise the other children, every summer morning. It was a beautiful sight. In a foreground of azure waters the children's bodies danced, ebony and tan and bronze and pink and mahogany, all banded in cheap bright spandex; and yonder in the distance there shimmered an impressionist backdrop made up of the dust clouds, churned up by invisible tractors, that masked these children's fathers.

During the swimming sessions Lillian often sat on the shady side of the pool and read, half-listening to the sounds of chatter and splashing and shrieks and Scrip's directives that wove around her in a steady rise and fall. Occasionally she would catch some child's comment that allowed her a glance into all their lives, limited but dense with meanings, like the view revealed by a tiny door opening onto a diorama. There might be allusions to uncles and aunts, including some central figure they all called "Cud'n Sister"; a sly, teasing reference to someone whose mother "got happy" in church the past Sunday, and that child's unflappable smile in defense; or one boy's account of the magical strangeness of his visiting relatives from L.A.—who had armed policemen at their school, and yet here were scared of horses.

Max Duval, one of the few children whose name Lillian was sure of, was diving for pennies in the shallow end with Allie one day, when another little girl sitting on the side asked if she could play too. Lillian heard Allie ask Max, "Is that your sister?"

"No!" said Max. "My sister *daid*." He hopped so vigorously in the water that he lost his balance and swayed for several seconds when he tried to stand up straight again. "She live up in the clouds. Preacher say she watching me all the time." He pointed up to the sky. Involuntarily Lillian glanced up too. The big pillowcase-white clouds of late July, veined with cornflower blue, moved at a snail's pace against the blue background of sky. Lillian looked back at the children. Allie's eyes were wide in her sun-freckled, chlorine-pinched face. "She was buri't in a lacy white dress. I seen her in her coffin. It had baby-blue satin all up inside it."

He hopped again until the girl on the edge of the pool stirred restlessly. "Let me go for some of those pennies!"

(That night Lillian overheard Allie ask Fayette what it was like inside a cloud. "Just fog," said Fayette. "You know when it's real gray and foggy outside and you can't see far? That's just a big old cloud come down real low to the earth." Allie stared and then said, "Nah-unh!" "Yes it is. Ask Mama." "I think you're wrong!" "Well, what'd you ask me for then if you weren't gonna believe what I said?")

Another day, instead of noise, it was the awareness of a silence that pulled Lillian's head up from *Time* magazine. The children were all gathered in an attentive crowd in the shallow end, with their eyes on the aqua slide that swooped up halfway down the pool. A little boy sat on top of it with a troubled expression on his face. Scrip stood in the water beneath it, squinting up at the child with his arms held out invitingly.

"Come on, Moog, you done it Thursday."

He just looked down at the teenager uncertainly, his hands gripping the edge of the slide.

"I'll catch you. I promise. Didn't I catch you Thursday? I don't know why you went up the ladder in the first place if you wasn't sure you could come down!"

"Sho don't!" declared the other kids.

"How 'bout if we help you down the ladder backwards?" called Lillian. "I know we usually have a rule against it, Moog, but we'll make an exception this time."

But still his face didn't change; his mouth looked crooked, and his forehead was wrinkled with consternation. He could only look doubtfully at the scene below him.

Scrip told Lillian, "I done everything from sweet-talking to threatening."

"Come on, Moog, it's not hard," said Max Duval. "Hold your nose like this so water won't go up into it."

"Unh-hunh, keep that water out your nose."

"Try this," said Lillian, standing up and walking close to the ladder. "Okay, Moog, I know you're ready to come down. You'll come down on 'three.' That never fails. Okay? Everyone else, Scrip, Reggie, Shelly, y'all help me count. Okay? *One ...*" All eyes were on Moog, his hunched figure looking so cleanly, delicately cut against the turquoise summer sky, his pink-soled feet splayed toward the sides of the slide as brakes. Everyone looked around at one another, smiling as they summoned breath for the next number. *"Two ..."* The count was a joyful shout. Afterwards it echoed for a moment way off in the woods beyond the fields. Then in the pause they could hear cows mooing. "Three!" And still Moog sat on top of the slide, his eyes going from face to face.

"Well," sighed a girl about ten, with her hair in little pigtails all over her head, and big glasses that made her seem old and wise, "we done tried everything else." She got up and stalked with dignity toward the gate. The back of her purple swimsuit was nubbly from her sitting on the concrete. The backs of her legs, thin and straight, had a capable, proud look.

"Where you going, LaToya?" said Scrip. Already a couple of younger girls, one chubby and one thin, had gotten up to follow

LaToya, walking single file. Now they stopped and looked back at Scrip. Their eyes traveled on to Lillian.

LaToya sighed and kept walking. "Gotta go get Rev'nd Dikes, I reckon. He Moog grandfather." Another dart of consternation shot across Moog's face, but he didn't move. Everyone watched the girls' figures swaying as they picked their way barefoot around the sticker patches and across a gravel lane toward the grove of cedars that surrounded the church. They waited. Some of the boys kicked restlessly in the water. "I want to slide!" "Can't nobody else slide with his big old self up there." "Old Moog he be taking up the slide all day."

Scrip muttered, "Rev ain't been this close to a swimmin' pool in his life. I don't know how *he* gonna get Moog down."

One of the children overheard. "He don't want to be close to no pool neither. He scairt of the water."

"Like my daddy," said another. "My daddy scairt of the water too."

"Mine too," said another. "Shoo. He can't swim. Him and my mama say, 'Oooh, Lordy, I don't see *how* y'all chirren be swimming up in that water.'"

Across the back pasture came a stout, erect man in a brown suit and hat, whom Lillian had seen getting out of his car at the church. The train of little girls had lost its dignity; they would leave that to the preacher. They wiggled before him, almost dancing with anticipation. From a few yards away he said, "Hello, Miz McCain," nodding and taking off his hat.

"You must be Reverend Dikes," said Lillian, rising. "It's nice to meet you." Her eyes sought out some bond with him, some amused isn't-it-funny-what-kids-get-into or of-course-it's-not-a-real-crisis sort of accord, but the man's broad face just continued to bear a troubled, uncertain expression identical to his grandson's. He hesitated a moment at the gate; then he stepped in saying, "What's the matter here?" His sharp-toed patent-leather shoes, now dusty, seemed incongruous on the concrete where so many lithe bare feet skipped and dripped.

Whoosh, splash! went Moog, and all the children cheered. Suddenly the slide was empty, and Moog was flailing in Scrip's arms as he steered the little boy toward the side. Everyone laughed, except Reverend Dikes—even Moog, as he blindly rubbed his face in an effort to get the water off it.

"Well, Moog been sitting up there half an hour, not coming down," said Scrip, "but I guess that settles that."

The Reverend shook his head and mopped the sweat off it with a handkerchief folded into a thick pad. "Y'all chirren be careful up in that water," he said.

"Yessir!" they chorused, still laughing.

"Y'all do what Miz McCain say. Moog, don't you be giving Miz McCain any trouble."

"Yessir!"

"Shoo," grumbled Scrip, as the preacher's figure retreated over the pasture, his straight back and enormous girth sailing buoyantly back across the dirt clods. *"I'm* the teacher. I coulda got Moog down myself, if y'all had a give me half a chance."

That night the Reverend Johnnie Dikes had a dream. He was in the bayou behind the church, yet at the same time it was the watering hole where baptizings were held when he was a boy, where he himself had been baptized. Multitudes were there, his present congregation as well as people now dead whom he had known when he was young; the sun blazed down, and the crowds, singing, pressed in from the banks. He was trying to baptize them all. Yet he could not stand up in the water. "In the name of the Father, the Son—" he would say, and then his feet would slip on the bottom, and again and again the baptismal candidate would slide out from his hands. In the dream he protested. When he tried to take off his shoes to gain some traction against the slippery mud, his bare feet underwater loomed huge before his eyes. He tried again. "In the name of the Father—" and still he lost his pastorly grip, still they spurted out of his hands like Ivory soap: first the Willis boy, then old Jasper Winger, then Mrs. Gwendolyn Page, whose big breasts nuzzled his palms and gave him a tingle even in the midst of his dilemma. "I baptize thee—" he gurgled, beneath the surface. The water closing over his head shrank the sun itself to a pinpoint. And the last images he saw as he looked frantically skyward were the bodies of his congregants, swimming above him, kicking, gliding, nonchalantly gathering their baptismal robes in one hand as they stroked, leaving little wakes behind as they propelled themselves to and fro—happy, and no more in need of his support than angels.

One noontime a couple of days later Reverend Dikes's big brown Lincoln drove up at the Skinner house. The farm children had just left, straggling down the road in a little band. The older boys came on bikes, but they rode as slowly as possible, dipping from side to side scarcely balanced, to stay even with those on foot. But the teenage girls, wearing long T-shirts to cover themselves, were gesturing and talking, ignoring the others. The littlest children scuffed along in plastic flip-flops.

Lillian was outside straightening up the poolside furniture and making a little sodden pile of shorts and barrettes that had been left behind. The McCain children and a couple of Rabelais cousins were still in the pool, reluctant to leave it although they were tired and puckered from the water and their calls to each other had gotten lower and lower in volume; they were beginning to ask about lunch.

Lillian greeted the minister in some surprise.

"Miz McCain," he said, "I'm here to talk with you about my chirren."

"Oh?" said Lillian. "Oh dear. Here, let's go stand in the shade. What's the matter?"

The two of them walked to the oak tree and perched on the canvas chairs Lillian had placed there. She looked at him quizzically.

"Miz McCain, our children come from a very different culture than yours."

"Yes," said Lillian, "I think I understand that."

"I don't know how to put this, but our children must grow up knowing how to live in two worlds. Two worlds, if you understand me, the black world and the white world—"

"Yes, yes, I know," said Lillian, flushing slightly, but looking Reverend Dikes steadily in the eye.

"They don't get something for nothing in the white world. They got to *earn* what they get in the white world. They got to work for it. It don't just come to them by being they natural selves. The Negro race has got to learn this.

"Now this swimming," said Reverend Dikes, "is give' to these children on a silver platter. White children spend they summers in swimming pools. Black children don't have those privileges. This swimming is *confusing* my children, Miz McCain, by suggesting to them that things are the way they are not. And that is why I'm going to have to put an end to these swimming lessons."

Lillian's forehead was crumpled into a puzzled expression. "But you just said they have to move in both worlds. I don't understand. Won't they be able to move in the white world better if they know this skill?"

"They won't get the chance. They won't get the chance to move *that way* in the white world again. And the sooner they learn that, the sooner they can start to deal with it."

"But everyone should know how to swim...I mean just for survival. What if they fall in the bayou? Or a lake? They need to know how not to drown. And anyway, it's just healthy. In all this heat."

"Miz McCain," said Reverend Dikes, "I hate to create any problems. You're new here, and I can tell you're a lady of God. You're actin' from your heart, but you just don't understand. The Lord has spoken to me about this. I don't want my chirren swimming." With that he turned, got back in his car, and drove away.

"It was the strangest thing," said Lillian at the supper table. "I'm just dumbfounded. What am I supposed to do now?"

She decided to continue the lessons anyway. Frank tried to talk her out of it—"You've got two powerful people against it, powerful people in this world, I mean, Amalie and this preacher; maybe you just shouldn't antagonize those two"—but the issue had become symbolic for her, a place where she shouldn't give way. The next lesson day, a Thursday, she unlocked the gate to the pool at eight-thirty. Ten minutes went by and no children came. They were sometimes late. At eight-forty, still no children. At nine she took a walk down the road. Bessie Mae was out sweeping the porch; her children, in shorts, rode trikes around the yard. One came silently out of the house and stood watching Lillian. "They won't be able to swim no more," said Bessie Mae, waving at Lillian. "Just got they hair done and I want it to last till school starts." She found Scrip reading sullenly on his front porch; he just frowned when she asked him where everyone was. "See can you figure it out," he said rudely. Lillian went on to the next house. "Oh, Max and Alfreda can't come swim down yonder. They went to spend the day with they auntie," said Claire Duval. And so it went, down the road: "R.P. won't be coming up there. He got to help his daddy...I just give a treatment to Shelly's hair ...Moog ain't here, I don't know where he run off to ..." She was home at nine-forty-five, drenched with sweat, her face pensive beneath its shiny layer of wetness. "Where is everybody?" hollered her own children. "They're just—out of commission," she told them. "Out of commission for the summer. You have the pool to yourselves."

Lillian Rabelais McCain had been born among the generation now dominating Edgewood and "came up with" them all the way—attending all their birthday parties and having them to hers, dancing on their porches as a teenager, and delighting them at college sorority parties with impromptu, wickedly droll cartoon sketches. Now this longtime local grounding paid off. Without any effort on Lillian's part, Edgewood just plugged her back in. It was as if she had never left.

And in this ready-made social persona, there was even some room for deviation; for Edgewood Rabelaises were indulged in nonconformity, even celebrated for it. Everyone knew the whole family was quixotic. Stubborn.

For years Lillian's parents had run a dance club out in the country while living on a tenuous base income from their farm. The only girl of five children, Lillian spent most of her youth in a round of chores, minding the boys while her parents auditioned new trumpet-players or picked up after the dancers who packed the club every night. She managed ably, and never let flag her spirit, humor, grade point average, or determination to leave home the minute she could. After graduating from high school in 1948, well ahead of her class, she moved to a boardinghouse in town and worked for a year. Then a little bit of oil was discovered on the Rabelaises' land. They stood in tall cotton. Long on dramatic flair and short on caution, the parents decided to give each child his fifth of all the revenues, outright, and the freedom to choose what to do with it. Lillian applied hers to tuition at LSU and then to that plane ticket to New York that led her eventually to Frank.

Her brother Tyler, our of law school by that time, had spent his bequest with characteristic quietness, here and there—part of it on care for his wife's debilitated father, part on setting up a home business for his wife, part on a house, "and *most* on Adlai Stevenson's campaign," Calvin Ray would proclaim, "back in the days when Tyler could do that." For Tyler was a judge now. Jules, also characteristically, invested all of his in stocks and bonds and local real estate. Gus's went to his degree in agriculture and his cattle farm across the parish from Green Isle. It was Calvin Ray who used his money most flamboyantly: he spent it on a year-long trip around the world, in fact, on the trip when he met his wife-to-be, who was touring the Scandinavian countries in her last summer before medical school.

Now Esther was an ear-nose-and-throat physician, and Calvin Ray hosted a radio show that started at four-thirty every morning. At that hour it had a definite agricultural slant. Whenever Lillian heard his program she pictured the farmers all over the parish who were Calvin Ray's audience: sipping coffee and pulling on boots, checking outdoor thermometers and starting their trucks and tractors; blowing into chapped hands to get warm, flinching away from the cold burning touch of seat belt buckles and metal dashboards, ducking back inside for one last cup of coffee while the engine warmed; all while her brother's sonorous bass voice, filled with rectitude and sympathy, crackled out of their old AM truck radios and the big old-fashioned Zeniths in their kitchens. He spoke of weather conditions, river levels, and farmers' aid programs that the "gob'nment" was trying to inflict. He gave the "bug report." He paused just long enough between words so that sleep-fogged, work-dogged brains would absorb his meaning. He was to the farmers' minds what coffee was to their bodies.

As the morning progressed he got more brisk and citified. By six or so the people in town would be stirring. The intervals between agricultural spots, ads for boll-weevil-killer and herbicide and bush-hogs, got longer and longer until, at last, at seven o'clock, the program was turned over to the national network for World News. The nature of Calvin Ray's program changed after world news, for the worse, in most farmers' opinion. This confirmed their suspicions that prolonged attention to the wider world was a mistake—it served only to dilute the issues that really mattered. For in Uncle Calvin's final half-hour he ran interviews of writers and dancers and Sierra Club workers and other eccentrics who interested him and made his pitch for the local arts organizations and for the Saturday Metropolitan Opera radio broadcasts. Most farmers turned him off by then. They did not recognize their early-morning ally in this latter-day voice, which spun forth so elegantly the multi-syllabled foreign names of singers and operatic characters.

Even Calvin Ray's house was a sort of contradiction. It was in a neighborhood of sedate streets, laid out around the turn of the century, which had once marked the little city's first suburbs. Now they spanned the oldest, most settled residential district, for the city had expanded, and no one—no one considered *anyone*, that is—lived right downtown any more. The houses in the innermost ring were all sixty or seventy years old. They were symmetrical red brick colonials or neat little white frame bungalows, each with dark green shutters and dormers and a chimney, or maybe a bay window to be different. All were separated a respectable distance from the street by tidy St. Augustine lawns about as wide as a solid croquet shot, and most had a few azalea beds, edged with monkey grass, across the front.

In the middle of these solid comforts was an angular house of redwood and brick, with a slanting roof that had a tree growing up through it. It sprawled so close to the street in front and to the neighbors' yards on either side that there was no room left for a lawn, and instead, groundcover had been allowed to grow wild, right up the trunks of the pine trees in front and the wall on either side. Through this tangle a few triangular and trapezoidal windows winked at the street, revealing parts of curious odd-shaped objects inside. These were strange fixtures and sculptures and musical instruments brought back from the Rabelaises' travels, which were placed around the big doorless spaces of the house.

In the middle of the living room was a simple round table about five feet across, made of small shining parquet squares of differently grained wood. Overhead a cone-shaped Danish lamp hung straight as a plumb all the way from the beamed ceiling. At this table much of the cultural life of Edgewood was spawned, and much of its political and social life dissected. Calvin Ray held court here with his ashtray and crossword puzzle and the remote control button for the TV spread before him. Guests came and went at ease, milling around for the pulse of gossip about Edgewood's art and musical circles, politics, schools, and family scandal, exchanging books and tapes and articles and recipes, and wolfing down Esther's sausage loaves, black-olive spreads, and baklava with Calvin Ray's good gins and bourbons.

There were certain regulars here, like Tyler Rabelais and his wife, Cynthia; Jane and Roger Hernandez; Dr. Aguillard and his second wife the flute-player. And people who were new in town—if they had a certain modicum level of wealth or panache—would also drop by at least once: Mrs. Delaney's latest foreign exchange student, the new pediatrician, the architectural historian up from New Orleans to look at old sites in the area.

And the Edgewood attitudes revealed by guests at this table were not unpleasant. They were mostly of Cajun *joie de vivre*—laced with New Orleans snobbery that eked its way upland and with the washoff of Bible Belt moralism from Louisiana's hills to the north.

5

IN THE MEANTIME Frank was out in the fields, riding in trucks and on tractors with men who knew more than he did about things he was supposed to be in charge of. He was keenly aware of his own ineptitude. When he tried to back up a trailer or use a swing gate to separate heifers from bull calves, he felt a dozen eyes on his back like lasers. But he kept trying. He had learned that things went better if he explored the farm without Amalie. Her tongue stung her employees into resentful silence. But if Frank trailed them doggedly through a day, jumping to help them when something came up that he couldn't possibly fumble, they would open up slowly, slip wisecracks his way and follow them with a cut of the eyes to see if he'd caught them, curse in annoyance, or with a jerk of the head give an explanation that wasn't essential—about the personality of some cow, or a preferred make of tool, or what a son of a bitch the ex-foreman, Skinner, had been—"Mr. Frank, I don't usually talk that way, but he really was"—which he absorbed gratefully, as a compliment.

He also spent hours in the farm office, poring over all the ledgers and files he could find. By harvest he knew without being told what was a good yield and what was not quite up to par. He had an idea which crops would be rotated how when it came time to plant in the spring, and he confirmed his guesses with Uncle Boy Hebert and Harlan Willis, two old-timers on the place.

Still, it was a lonely life in a way. He and Lillian socialized with other youngish couples in Edgewood and with her brothers and their wives, but Frank's work was so different from that of these doctors and car dealership managers and accountants that he could never discuss it with them—only tell them about it; and he developed a self-deprecating comic style for that purpose. The formality his workers first used with him dissolved pretty quickly—though the men called him *mister* and *sir* much longer than their wives and children did, and some of the older ones would probably never drop it. He made it a point to stop and visit with people on the place when he saw them outside their houses, listened hard to what they said, and tried to get their families straight. But he knew he was not completely included in his black employees' camaraderie and might never be. And other white farmers on the road shied away from him somewhat, whether because of his youth or different background or education or some other sort of mistrust, Frank was not sure. As a result of this mild alienation he drew closer to his family. He was home more often—in and out during the day, there for lunch now as well as the other two meals—and once he was there he was more talkative with them than he had been in Boston, when long freewheeling lunch conversations with other young lawyers had often taken the edge off his urge to discuss things.

In March 1969 Aunt Amalie had a stroke, and in late May she had another one, and died.

That summer the McCains rented out the Skinner house and got ready to move into Amalie's house—"the big house," Lillian lightly called it, the deep-roofed unkempt old structure that Green Isle's first settler had built. As Lillian packed away Amalie's candy dishes, china songbirds, and lampshades painted with roses, as she took down the dark oil paintings in ornate frames, she mused over her reaction to the old lady's death.

At first she really believed she was mourning. During the weeks between the first minor stroke and the fatal one, she had felt the shudder of pity that comes with witnessing an illness; she had sorrowed over Frank's and the children's loss. But as the summer wore on, she began to admit that she did not completely grieve the loss of Amalie as a person, or that at best her feelings were mixed. For Amalie had been a bigoted, querulous person who became harder to live with month by month. Her critical gaze and tongue had exacted their price. Lillian felt that her most passive awareness of Amalie's judgments (about the children's dress and manners, Frank's work, her cooking, their church habits, their friends, politics) was more than she should have to endure, and she resented it. Somehow even Amalie's most ridiculous observations, which should have been easiest to shrug off, had lodged and festered within Lillian, spoiling the part of her they touched, angering her if only because she had spent seconds of her life boiling over them and couldn't, or didn't, forget them. The sharp retorts she had struggled to restrain (she held back nine for every one that flew out) had taken their toll too, she knew—on Frank's spirits, on a foolish old woman's peace of mind. "You aren't going to change her!" Frank used to groan, and Lillian would mutter, "It just makes me so mad I could spit," and Frank would say, "Well, don't spit at *me*."

One day, gazing at the unfaded rectangle left on the wall of the entrance hall behind a gloomy landscape she had just taken down, a truth came to Lillian: deep down she felt relieved now. Lightened. She stood a moment staring at the wall, and then turned and walked slowly through the other rooms with a rising heart. Where she had pulled down the heavy velvet and brocade drapes that had cloaked the windows, a bare, clean expanse of light flooded in. Amalie had made the house into a dark, cloistered, oppressive storehouse of Victoriana; but all that remained of her taste was the simplest of the antique furniture—now stripped of doilies and shoved into the corners during Lillian's massive cleaning effort—and a couple of inoffensive light fixtures, which could remain. Lillian was creating something as spare and sunlit and open as a Hopper painting, a vessel reflecting sky and trees back outdoors.

When she saw Frank's truck driving up she remembered it was lunchtime. The children were in town for the day. She heard him walking back through the kitchen, questioningly saying her name. They sat down on the floor to open the mail, but in a moment she took it out of his hands, slid it across the floor, took his chin in her hand, and kissed him. She unbuttoned a couple of buttons of his shirt and then stood up and began to undress, very slowly, savoring herself. She never smiled but she laughed once as she pulled Frank up out of the jumble of his own clothes. The living room windows were of thin, wavy old glass, and the light coming in through it was wavy and speckled too, washing the shadows of its bubbles and tiny flaws over the two turning bodies. The smells of Windex and lemon oil mingled with those of sex, and after a few minutes, with the smell of snap beans boiling over in the kitchen. And still the two bodies lay there, each gently pinioned by various limbs of the other, absently kissing the softnesses and barenesses that enveloped them. The ghost of Amalie was very much banished.

Early one morning that fall, Frank was going over the day's plans and work assignments with Harlan Willis. "I'd like to start planting fescue in the far west fields and the old Worthington place," he said. "Where we had beans last year. Is William through doing the dairy pen so he could help you?"

"Yessir, he finished up late yesterday. He should be able to drive a tractor today. You want us to plow over there by the pecan grove too? Next to the highway?"

"No, not that. Those fields right near the house?—I'm'a hire somebody special to do that."

Harlan looked at him quizzically. "We'll do you a good job on that now, Mr. Frank."

"Hunh?—Oh, Jesus, Harlan, it's not that it could be done any better—I may do it myself, even. I've just got a plan I've been working over for those fields, well, not for just them. I want to start keeping them separate so I can have me a little farm once I deed Green Isle over to y'all ..."

"—over—?"

But Frank had a way of turning vague and abstract sometimes just at the crux of a matter, as if the person he'd been talking to suddenly wasn't there any more. And once he did that Harlan knew he wasn't going to get answers to his questions; nor was he importunate enough to press for them.

The area Frank had staked out for special treatment, or the lack of it, was about 120 acres extending from his house south and west. He started calling it the McCain place, and gradually other people followed suit. It came to look like a homestead that had seen better days. Frank liked it that way. He fixed gate latches with old dog collars and exhaust pipes with old tobacco cans. As if subconsciously wanting the place to fail he chose brindled, knobby-legged cattle. Oh, the place he retained for himself made money—not a lot, but after the first season at least, enough to pay most of the McCains' bills every month and leave their savings untouched—and to help out, Frank was studying for the Louisiana Bar exam, so he could handle a few cases on the side now and then, funneled his way by overworked lawyer friends in town. By shuffling some papers around he could make a fee or two as a cushion in case the bottom dropped out of the soybean market.

The other farmers in the parish thought the new set-up was the symbol of degenerate craziness, a reminder of the folly a man could fall to if his family ever moved north, or if he drifted too far to the left in his outlook. When Frank went to the farmers' co-op for feed and seed they greeted him in sober monosyllables, dropping their eyes. Then their tanned, seamed faces would inflate for a second as with suppressed laughter. They would readjust their bellies over their tooled belts and eye each other, or say "Oh me" and sigh and saunter out to their own trucks as if the foibles of the world were beyond them. They made cracks about the make-do appearance of Frank's place and eagerly scanned Green Isle's cattle for mutations and its beanfields for Johnson grass as they never did with anyone else's—not overtly, anyway.

Meanwhile, the Green Isle people came to treat Frank's own unkempt fields as a sister farm—if a slightly retarded sister—one they asked after caringly and helped when they could. The McCain place looked especially seedy in comparison with the elegant neighboring fields, which had become at least as lush and well-groomed as they were before Hudson's death and Mr. Skinner's coming. The Green Isle families were now beneficiaries of a mystery called a trust. The main changes it brought, as far as they could see, were Frank's peculiar removal to his own place, meetings he called at the church where he explained irrelevant things like profit-sharing and special dividends till their eyes glazed over, and tutelage he was giving to two or three of the younger men about taxes and bookkeeping and financial planning. He said Green Isle would be a corporation someday and they would need to know these things. The lessons were sometimes slow going. But despite its owners' ignorance of money, the trust had a lot going for it. It had no mortgage; the land being farmed was already paid for (many times over). There were sound business precedents to go by, at least since Frank's coming. And the farm was simply so huge that it tended, by the economy of scale, to be profitable. It was nothing new that Green Isle could afford expensive semen from Texas bulls to impregnate its sleek cows, and brand-new, spick-and-span machine parts of the highest quality.

With all these changes, the friendships between the McCains and the Green Isle families continued as they always had. They were long-standing, casual intimacies, still cast in old roles. Lillian took her best linens to Claire Duval for ironing. Every few months Ajax approached Frank for a loan; lately Lelia Thomas had been asking him to post bail for her son, Scrip, now a troubled college student. If Fayette and Allie got stranded somewhere without a ride, they still called Uncle Boy. Bessie Mae Taylor was their babysitter and once-a-week housekeeper. But after Aunt Amalie died she got to throw out her white uniforms. Now she could choose the clothes she scrubbed the bathroom in. Our emancipations are always partial.

6

WHEN ALLIE MCCAIN was ten years old, she found an old camera in the bottom of her father's closet. It did not bother her that the film chamber was empty. On afternoons when Fayette was at junior high football practice or busy with a girlfriend—lonely afternoons that would once have been filled with games with him—she stole through the big unkempt yard, aiming and shooting, clicking the shutter of her new discovery. Her face was blank, but she was so absorbed in her activity that an hour or two would pass before she knew it. Intently she framed shot after shot. Her mind was busy with dramas suggested by history or fiction or fantasy. "Now I'm with Lewis and Clark; I am the first photographer west of the Mississippi. I'm the first photographer to take a picture of this praying mantis, *Mantis allieansis.* I'm in Narnia—taking pictures of it to prove to the folks back in England that it's real—I'm in Lilliput, and this magnolia pod is the people's Mount Rushmore—"

Her father caught sight of her rapt in this play. "Would you like some film in that thing, Allie? I think it'll still work, and then you can make real pictures."

She rode with him to the camera store downtown and gazed at the shopcases of fancy tripods and lenses while Frank talked to the storekeeper. Then they called her over, and her father boosted her up to sit on the glass countertop and watch Mr. Grimes load the film. He showed her where light entered the chamber and told her how images were stored on the film. She looked from the camera to him with big, hard, gray amber-flecked eyes.

"Well, enjoy it, little lady!" said Mr. Grimes as he snapped the camera back shut and slung it around her neck. It felt heavy but she was proud of the weight. She stretched her neck to ease it and went to wait for her father by the truck outside, in case any of her friends from school happened to be riding by.

Then, impressed by her new authenticity, she went back and snapped the shots she had only pretended to take before. She took others as well: the cows, a little blue heron in the bayou, which flew as the shutter released, Mama rooting Bermuda grass out of her beds, and the dogs in various poses, scratching, snuffling, exploring a culvert, and sleeping. Two days passed before anyone was going in the direction of the camera store and could drop off the film for Allie. Then she started calling the store twice a day. "When'd you drop it off, honey?" said the clerk in exasperation on the second afternoon. "Tuesday," said Allie. "Oh, doll, it'll be at least *next* Tuesday before your pitchers come back."

When they did Allie was disappointed. The only one that was any good at all was the one of Mama furiously weeding. Daddy got a snort of amusement from it. She was on her hands and knees, glaring straight at the camera over a fringe of monkey grass, with a fistful of weed arcing behind her—all the better because the weed was blurred, and gave an impression of fierce motion. Most of the other prints were too dark. The cows were indistinguishable from shadows of the trees they stood under.

"You'll get the hang of it," said her father.

"It's an expensive hobby!" said her mother. "Ten pictures of the dogs?"

"Take a picture of me in my football uniform," ordered Fayette. He wanted to give it to the current girl.

As Allie's interest in her hobby grew, Lillian quit objecting to its cost and instead would compare the photographs aesthetically to paintings she had studied in college. Allie shot film, sent it away, and scanned the prints minutely when they came back. Sometimes she had another set made and would notice tiny differences in tone, texture, and quality that escaped others' eyes. It ate up all her allowance.

By this time Fayette had plunged head-on into adolescence and wanted nothing to do with her. She had suffered many phases of their relationship before—antagonism; friction; a resigned condescension since although she *was* irrevocably a girl, she could still be taught some essentials like football and poker to compensate; and sometimes friendly harmony—but never this absolute lack of interest. She would entreat his attention, first timidly, standing at his door laden with games and his favorite homemade milkshakes, then more and more boldly with the anger of someone denied the favors to which she has become accustomed. Fayette lent a consistently deaf ear. He had begun to drive and date and learned for the first time that the kitchen phone would just stretch into his room. He talked to girlfriends by the hour. Fretted with jealousy, Allie decided to eavesdrop on him. The boredom of that nearly killed her.

So she spent even more time by herself, exploring the farm in close detail, planning treehouses, designing shelters in imaginary scenes of Yankee invasion. She left with her dad whenever possible. Lillian had started raising flowers and nursery plants to sell wholesale; Allie would hang around the greenhouse until her mother gave her chores to do. Sometimes she went into Fayette's room when he was out, and out of those visits came her first photo group, "Fayette's Room." The tail of a squirrel he had killed hung lank beside his mirror, which had old school decals stuck down one side—that, with her own reflection shadowy in the mirror, made one picture. The wallpaper in his room was black-and-white houndstooth intended to look mod. On his rumpled bed were an open bag of Doritos and several books, face-down. In his closet were all his shoes from football cleats to three-toned platform dress shoes; she stood in his shoes, so long on her feet, and prowled among his clothes, and sniffed the aged sweat inside his hats—the engineer's work cap, the cowboy hat, and the Nazi army helmet that Uncle Jules had procured for him. She ran a finger down the cowskull on the wall where he hung his ties. And she took black-and-white stills of all these things. She considered taking the under-the-bed scene, a stack of skin magazines and an ashtray, but it wasn't worth getting him in trouble, and anyway she couldn't figure out the lighting. As it was, Daddy gave his amused snort when he looked at her work. "It looks like documentary evidence for a trial," he said. "It's the scene of a crime, all right," Fayette agreed. "My life is the crime." The books open on his bed those days were those of Kafka and Vonnegut.

To fill the rest of her time she would ride around with Frank when he was buying equipment or stock for the farm, or looking at real estate for speculation, or going to an auction or to visit a friend. Riding in the truck with the windows down she would chatter to him. She asked him questions, and he answered quietly, moderately, and thoroughly, his responses like a light cast around an old building: scanning the beams and skeleton of his knowledge, lingering on woodgrain, surfaces, and deviations from a type, but always in the end moving to those gaps in the subject that could not easily be explained—to the vaulted dark exterior that contained it.

When they left one of the highways that veined the parish for a back road, Frank would stop and let Allie get in the back of the pickup. There she sang softly into the wind, enjoying the independence of solitude so well anchored by the sight of her father, only a few feet away there on the other side of the glass.

After *Brown*, the LeBac Parish School Board had decided to integrate sooner rather than later. But its resolve went only so far. On the southern side of the river all-white schools were virtually eliminated, while all-black schools remained just that. In 1969 a local attorney sued the school board, and by late the next year the federal district court, with Lillian's oldest brother Tyler Rabelais on the bench, ordered parish schools to correct racial imbalances. This late measure of integration, stormily received in private, took place peacefully enough in public. A few threats were made to the School Board and Judge Rabelais, volleys of letters flew to the local paper, and the usual number of white children were hustled into institutions hastily raised outside the city limits; but for the most part the change was peaceful. Certainly nothing had happened to merit the attention of national media in the North.

Allie was ten then and Fayette was thirteen. Fayette was reading the papers and listening to family conversations to figure out what was going on. Allie had to be clued in by her parents, who impressed upon her easily enough where the right lay in this situation. But in the end they said, "You children decide what you want to do. If you believe you'd get a better education at St. Ignatius or Country Day, we'll find the tuition. If you want to stick with the public schools you do so with our blessing."

("You let your ten-year-old decide for herself?" said a friend incredulously, when she heard this story.

"They were bluffing," Uncle Calvin Ray told her drily.

"We weren't exactly bluffing," said Lillian, "we just knew what they'd decide.")

One might think that for the extended family of the one who had issued the order, compliance would be natural and a matter of course. But the community furor at Judge Rabelais didn't stop at family lines. The same genes that had produced him and Lillian and Calvin Ray had produced a stiff conservative strain as well, in Uncle Jules and Uncle Gus. Allie would never forget the half-lidded look of disdain on her first cousin Stovall's face as he parroted the words his mother had said in the car the day before: "I can't sacrifice my learning to the blacks. This is a free country, and I don't have to go to school with blacks."

But Allie and Fayette promptly said they would stick with the public schools. It was no big deal. Allie stayed at her suburban grammar school and then went to a sixth-grade center across the tracks. Fayette entered a fifty-fifty junior high next to an all-black housing project, where Allie would follow him. They would go back to the affluent side of town for high school. Sure, they had to ride the bus, but they were country kids and expected that anyway. It was no skin off their back.

"You can't change things overnight," Frank was saying after a late supper on the porch one night. He sat with his chair pushed back at an angle to the table, one ankle across the other knee, his face wrinkling as he worried a wadded napkin in his hand. "But you sure can't just flee. You can't run away to someplace neat and tidy like Glendale, New Jersey, and absolve yourself, and leave the mess for other people to clean up—"

Allie needed to know what absolve meant but she had sense enough to wait until later to ask Fayette. He was listening intently to their father.

"So?" he said. "So? Who are you to decide what his fight should have been? Maybe something bad would've happened to you, when you were just a kid, if he had stayed. And he wasn't black, after all. He wasn't the one wanting to sit at the front of the bus or walk into a white school. In some ways you benefited from his choice. I mean, who are you to congratulate yourself on what you did, and criticize him?"

Frank still had his head bent toward the napkin and soiled tablecloth, but he looked up at Fayette. "One thing, I guess, was just that I resented it at the time—resented going. So later I have to justify that resentment. There were a lot of things here I didn't want to leave when I was fourteen years old."

"Mama?" said Allie.

"No, not your mother. I didn't know her then. Just home, school, things I believed in. A belief the problems would be solved."

"He took you away so you could be who he thought you should be. But you had already started thinking for yourself. So as soon as you got it straightened out in your head, you came back here so *we* could fight the battle you believe in."

"Are you saying that's just as bad?"

"No, I'm saying it's just what fathers do."

"And what sons do is 'start thinking for themselves.' "

"Well," returned Fayette, a little defensively. But Frank just shook his head slightly, and smiled. He had reared his children to think and speak for themselves; of all the things they could manage, of all they threw themselves into with such cool fury, it was this independence of thought that he treasured most. In the people around him a lucky person found not "his own self back in copy-speech" but "original response"...that was Frost, he thought...Frank was quiet for a minute. Then he said, "I hated Glendale. The whole place was white. Everybody there was white and middle-American-Protestant—except for a few immigrants who came out from the city to get work as servants. The school was real good. Sarepta had to read things that I was never assigned in New Orleans. In Glendale it was assumed you were all headed for college."

They had heard this before. Fayette said, "Yeah, well, sit through eighth-grade Health and Hygiene a few days and you might wish you were back at Glendale."

"Why, is it that bad?" Their father flared with humor. "I imagine we could muster the tuition at Country Day, Fayette, or even St. Ignatius if you're unhappy—"

"Hell no. You know me better than that. I'm just trying to stop you from painting everything one color."

Such a conversation was not unusual around the McCains' house. Frank and Lillian's talk was like a big, loose net seining all subjects. It was assumed that Fayette and Allie could understand the matters that concerned their parents, and so they did.

Not everything Fayette and Allie were absorbing was social and political. They learned art from romping around the panels at local exhibits and literature from their parents' books and music from a '58 phonograph. The music came alive to them at concerts of the local Symphony Orchestra, held in the auditorium of the school they would both attend. Their mother was on the Symphony Board and Uncle Calvin Ray made all its executive decisions. This taught the children cultural responsibility, along with an inflated sense of self-importance. Not that the latter was all bad, if one unlearned it by the right age; it fueled a sort of brazenness, a cheap substitute for courage, that could prod a youth over the hurdles she needed to cross as tests.

They went to the Methodist church. Contrary to fashion they were most faithful to it in its tempests and lackadaisical when it was running along smoothly. Uncle Jules was the opposite. He periodically got furious with the church for some liberal preacher's daring: letting the teenagers have a slumber party in the recreation room—starting an annual "Arts Festival" at the church—having rock music as an anthem one Sunday—praying to "our Father/Mother God"—and would leave the church in a rage, returning to the Presbyterians or Baptists downtown, depending on how reactionary those churches were at the moment. Then Frank McCain would laugh, and sigh, and get mad, and go back to church in its defense. Once again the children would be scooped up on Sunday mornings, their grassy bare feet washed and stockinged and shod, to go hear the Methodists soft-pedal the social gospel. Fracases in the First United Methodist Church came along so regularly that for a few years in the late sixties they didn't miss a Sunday.

Their lives were free where other children's were regulated, and rigorous where others' were easy. Frank and Lillian treated chores as a common load, and the kids had specific responsibilities early. It was unpopular to be ailing in their household. Illnesses were dealt with briskly, not quite skeptically. If a slump came over any one of them between a Sunday and Thursday, it would always be treated with the comment, "Too much weekend?" After a disappointment, and the hugs and talk it generated, Frank and Lillian's last dictum was, "Oh, well, it'll build your character." ("I don't *want* my character built!" Fayette snapped once when he was nine.) The highest approbation Frank and Lillian gave of others was, "They rose to the occasion."

Yet Allie's early memories were like most children's, vivid, concrete, and intensely personal. There was a Fourth of July night when, after hours of dizzying play in the dark, so late that she had gone in to put her nightgown on and come back out, the family had all lit sparklers; a night when she had moved far away from her cousins and from Fayette—barefoot, treading lithely and delicately, turning and swaying, as if she were leading her sparkler, with her colored gown lifting around her calves; aware of her father watching while with white hissing fire she wrote her name in the darkness again and again, bedazzling even the fireflies. And there were timeless afternoons lapsed off into evenings lapsed off into nights when the cousins were together because their parents had gathered at one of the Rabelaises'. The grownups would be deep in talk about one of the recesses of Edgewood life or politics, under the warm lamplight that encased and set them apart, and the children, breathless, would play outside till the dark came too close. Pressing up against the windows, they noticed how after nightfall those outside the house could see in clearly, but those inside could not see out—the scene beyond them was just a dark mirror. Puzzled, wildly exhilarated by their chases and discoveries, they would rush inside themselves, to beg permission of some normally forbidden wish. "Can we have crackers and butter for supper? Can we have crackers and butter for supper?" Then some aunt or uncle would glance at a watch—yes, it was past suppertime—and say, absently, "Sure. Go ahead," before turning to join the others again with a jest or a long exhalation of smoke.

The murky issues that were always present didn't dominate the foreground of her childhood. She wasn't aware how prevalent they had been till much later. In fact her immediate life was stable and synchronized, with limits that were in the simplest natural sense quite beautiful. Its emblem might have been the pecan grove that surrounded her house. There, whichever way you looked—dead ahead, to either side, or catty-cornered—you saw long green corridors leading away from you: the trees were that perfectly spaced. As you walked the rows would come with you, changing, so that you stayed in the shifting center of a perfectly ruled design.

7

ONE SUMMER AFTERNOON in 1971, Mrs. Buddy Clark—Myrtle, to her friends—pushed open the door to the sanctuary of Edgewood's First United Methodist Church. Its weight surprised her, and she tottered a moment on the threshold, blinking at the juncture of the strong sunlight and shadow. It occurred to her that she had never pushed open a church door before. Always on Sunday morning the ushers were there to do it for her—Jim Rice and Henry Thomasson, lately—that is, for the past eight years—always with a wink and a bulletin and a whiff of spearmint and a "How you, Miz Clark?" for her, and usually a compliment, she wasn't past those, as she nodded and bobbed her head to either smiling side, maybe straightening her bent shoulders a fraction or arranging the loop of the bow of her blouse again as she entered. Think of that! She had never had to open the heavy doors of the church for herself.

But today she did, and she paused for a minute in the foyer, feeling the sadness well up in her heart. She didn't know where the lightswitch was but it didn't matter. The dark suited her mood better. Her whole life had taken place in this church, and she was here to bid it goodbye, for it was being torn down. The Sunday school wing was almost leveled already; the work crews had stopped for the day and now the sanctuary waited for the boom, its last service held, last wedding and baptism and funeral over and done with—but not its last meditation; for Myrtle, in her black low thick-soled shoes and support hose and the bifocals she had not replaced since 1963, was here to be quiet and think awhile.

Thousands of hymns seemed to vibrate in the shadowy air, all the ones she loved: "O For a Thousand Tongues to Sing," the staunch Methodist fight song, proud and sassy that it was about praise instead of sin and guilt like the Baptists', and "Come Ye Thankful People Come" at Thanksgiving, making her feel like a Pilgrim herself, huddled in a shelter from winter winds, and "Hosanna, Loud Hosanna" that called up images of her children, now in their fifties, as little clean-faced ones clutching their palmettos—and "Christ the Lord Is Risen Today" that always, since she was nine years old, made her heart rise despite itself and believe, believe, believe, and all the Christmas carols, and "Jesus Calls Us, O'er the Tumult, of our Life's Wild, Restless Sea." Oh, there was a galaxy of favorites that had affixed themselves to her over a lifetime of worship here. And now the best words and images, some knitted to well-known tunes, some buried like secret treasure in the second and third stanzas of obscure hymns, seeped out of the nooks and crannies of the sanctuary and paraded before her. The church was quiet but its very muteness, the brown thickness of its dark, seemed sullen, as if all these melodies roved in it, knocking at the edges of the silence and demanding to be heard again.

Myrtle took a step and then another. They were wobbly steps not because age had gotten to her; in fact her friends, who were all failing, or if not failing, like Imogene and T.I., had recently suffered falls, all looked to her and leaned on her as the strong, dependable one. It was she, Myrtle, who still inched her old Cadillac out of her garage every Sunday and went to pick up the others for Sunday school, settling in the drop-off space by the doors for ten minutes or so while the janitor Horace, whom she had referred to for eighteen years as "the young nigra," helped maneuver car doors and canes and walkers. No, Myrtle's steps were wobbly now with emotion, and she had forgotten to square her sloping back because she was overcome with remembrance. As she proceeded slowly down the aisle she thought of making that same walk with her father—on June 28, 1924, the day she and Buddy had married. Her passage seemed to cleave the air again, slicing away distracting images of the present to reveal the faces that had beamed as they watched her that day: of sisters and brothers and parents and friends long dead. She had worn her mother's dress—she had carried magnolias, she had insisted on that, though the day was so hot none lasted more than a couple of minutes, and she had had to send her little brother out at the latest possible second before she and Papa started their walk—had sent him out to the magnolia tree that used to be so tall and grand, that the church had cut when it added the Sunday school wing in 1926.

At the foot of the aisle she stopped abruptly. Here Buddy's nickel-plated coffin had stood, decked in all the flowers that showed the homage and love of his family, near and far, and the Men's Bible Class and the Association of Delta Businessmen. That had been in 1959—twelve years before. Here she had baptized their four children—how Darryl had howled!—and married off two. But it was the thousands of services in between the peak days that were getting to her now. During all those humdrum Sundays, as a dreamy teenager; as a newlywed, sometimes when she and Buddy had had a fuss; as a mother grateful for church sheerly as a time to sit down and rest *(Sorry, Lord,* she thought, *but You knew it at the time)* and as herself, now, sitting in *her* place on the right side, halfway back; somehow, in such moments, her life had happened.

She sank into the first pew. They had already taken out the hearing aids and, doubtless, installed them in the new church way out Jeff Davis Road. Well, that was all right by her. They had gotten by fine without hearing aids in the old days, and as far as she was concerned they could get by without them now, and without a lot of what they considered essential: most notably, the new building. Oh, she had tried to be supportive. She had listened to the ministers talk it up and she had given her brick money in the Aldersgate Class when all the classes had a competition to raise the most. Though she had not gone to the groundbreaking, she had driven out to look at the new church two weeks before, and sure enough it made her heart sink right down to her toes. She felt dismal. It was all modern—all fashionable and "contemporary" and uncomfortable and wrong, like a short short skirt or like social drinking or long hair on men. It wasn't going to have big majestic pillars and steps all across the front like this one. It wasn't made of dark red brick with white trim and a clock tower and it didn't even have a second story. It just looked sleek and plain, and its steeple swooped up in a weird way, not like any steeple Myrtle had ever seen—though goodness knew, she should probably be grateful it even had a steeple. It was going to have modern art inside, and she knew what that meant, nothing that you could tell what it was or would want to. And though people were saying it was going to have stained glass, it wouldn't be stained glass that made pictures of anything you could identify, not like the Jesus-suffering-the-little-children window overhead that she loved so much, with Jesus in a mustard-yellow robe and a pale, mournful-looking face patting a little boy with golden curls on the head. How she had loved that window, all her life! She remembered trying to make out its fancy Old English lettering when she could barely read! And how she loved the ornate old light fixtures, dim as they were, and the carved communion rail and the dark red carpet, frayed as it was.

She was not one to hinder progress. She understood why they had to move. Downtown Edgewood was not what it used to be, not like years ago when people came from all over to shop and do business there, from Cotton Boll and Devore and LaJolie and Flatsboro. Now everyone went out to these malls they had on the outskirts of town. All the young people bought and built out there. There were so many nigras downtown now, not up to anything but hanging around, loitering, planning crimes. She lived almost too far downtown even to suit herself; there were nigras in the next block. But she would never move from the house Buddy had built, and she was careful anyway. No, she knew the church had to move out, away from the nigras, and keep up with where everyone was heading. Understanding that, however, was not going to keep her from coming here to shed a tear or two for all that had happened to her within these walls. And it was sure not going to make her admire an altar with modern art all over it. That would be going too far.

In the sanctuary of the new church out Jeff Davis Road three people were grouped in companionable quiet. They were down near the front of the sanctuary, where a shaft of light came angling down through the gallons of height above them and splashed on the slate floor. The building was suffocatingly hot; the central air conditioning had been installed but not turned on. All the doors the three could find had been propped open with buckets of paint or plaster mix, but there were hardly any breezes outside to admit. The shirts of the two men, and Mrs. Delaney's blouse, were dark with sweat.

"Just makes me feel more authentic, is all," said the tile artisan cheerfully. He was a tall, lanky man with brown hair and a reddish beard, wearing jeans faded to a delicate eggshell-blue. He was working with patient, unhurried movements at a mosaic panel. All day there had scarcely been a variation in his steady motion. Since Martha Delaney had arrived in the early afternoon, he had scarcely seemed to need to rest his massive arms by dropping them to his sides, or even to shift his weight from foot to foot. "I can imagine I'm somewhere in the middle of Rome. In the Sistine Chapel. Michelangelo worked on that straight through the summers and you can bet he didn't bitch about the heat. We Brits are also blessed with hardy constitutions."

"You were born and bred with these luxuries, so you enjoy giving them up," said the other man. Slight, muscular, and black, he sat perched on a pew behind the craftsman, watching him with an intentness that seemed unrelated to his leisurely joking tone. "Those of us who didn't feel air conditioning till we were eighteen know what a valuable thing it is!"

"Ah, Paul, it's good to suffer. You need to, you know. You Third World artist chaps. Especially if you attain the liberation you profess you want. Then what other suffering would you have to paint about except a little physical discomfort?"

Paul Kalunge laughed. He picked up a tile from the small trays arranged on the floor and fingered it. "All I know is, if the Sistine Chapel had been air-conditioned, Michelangelo would have had it turned on."

Chuck Smith went on working unperturbed. "He had more clout with the ecclesiastical powers than you do."

Paul grinned and Martha Delaney clucked at their banter. The two of them were constantly ribbing each other in these dry, deadpan tones. Apparently they had worked together only once before, four years ago, on a project for a city hall in upstate New York, but the chords between them had lasted and deepened. Paul was now based in New Orleans and Chuck in Montreal. When the Building Committee had contacted Paul through another New Orleans artist whom Martha Delaney knew, he had arranged for the actual tile-laying of his design to be done by Chuck. They had been delighted to do the Edgewood church job together.

One reason Martha Delaney's involvement with the new sanctuary had moved her so deeply, besides what it meant to her as a worshipper, of course, was that the artists she had dealt with had all been so interesting to know. They were all so dear to her, by now. She had thought it the most wonderful coincidence that Paul and Chuck were already friends—even though they did kid each other about what one would think were the most sensitive matters. They reminded her of her own sons.

Martha was a plump gray-haired matron in a skirt and espadrilles. Her face was shining and her hair was wet with sweat and sticking to her face, but every once in a while she asked questions in a fascinated tone. She got up to wander around the room, fanning herself slowly with a newspaper.

"Paul?" she called. "What's the theme of the second section? I can't remember it."

"Temptation."

"Oh, right, the forty days in the wilderness. Is this like the devil here, part of a devil?"

"Mmm," said Paul. "A dervishy sort of devil, yes."

"You poured a lot of experience into that panel, Kalunge," said Chuck.

"Go to hell," Paul responded, and Chuck grunted amusedly as he worked on.

"I don't need to go to hell. This heat tells me I'm there."

"Oho, so even you are even feeling it a little."

"Someone who's really working is bound to feel it—as opposed to you dreamy sons o' bitches who never have to lift anything heavier than a pencil—"

"Brother, I could use a beer."

"Martha's having us to happy hour at her place when we're through. Aren't you, ducky?" Chuck raised his voice.

"Sure I am, sure you are."

A few minutes passed.

"It's no wonder you have trouble with women, Chuck, if you call them all 'ducky.' Did you check that patch on the second panel? Is it setting?"

"It seems to be," said Chuck.

"I don't know why those particular tiles are harder to anchor. I think they're slightly heavier. I think whatever gives these metallic tiles that shine, the bronzy look, also makes them heavy.—Excuse me, boyo, I don't mean to breathe down your neck."

"The bloody hell you don't."

"I'm still concerned about the lighting. It'd be all wrong if they installed those fixtures flush with the wall—recessed lights would be much better." Paul wandered up the side aisle to scowl and brood one more time over the boxes of lights that had been stacked in the back of the church.

Finally Chuck put down his putty knife. "Martha, what do you think the chances are of getting a beer *now*?"

"Now? Here?"

"Yeah. I'm dehydrating by the second."

"I can't give you a beer right here in the church."

"Nobody's around. What difference would it make?"

"My goodness, Methodists spearheaded the temperance movement in this country," said the matronly lady, beginning to grin at them.

"But there's a movement afoot to bring the arts back into worship. And artists can't survive without beer." They grinned back.

"Oh dear. Have you seen anyone around today?"

"Bob was here around lunchtime." Bob was the minister.

"He looks to me like he's had a few cold ones in his day," added Paul.

"Well," said Mrs. Delaney reluctantly, "you wait here."

She was back in ten minutes. The three of them settled down by the rear doors of the sanctuary where they might catch a breeze but were still within the shade of the building. Martha Delaney held out bottles. "Ah-ah," she said warningly as they uncapped them and started to drink. "Not yet. I just want you to look at it all. While you're resting."

They looked.

The mosaic panel stretched the length of the left wall of the sanctuary. Farthest back its colors were muted, almost monochrome. The human figures of Paul's design were perceptible, but interlaced in complex patterns. Their context was the life of Christ, and the themes of the images, moving from back to front, were blessing, temptation, service, and suffering. The pieces, thousands of them, tiny and jagged on their own, combined in huge sweeping, swooping curves that poured like a rearing surf toward the altar. Opposite the mosaic on the right side of the church was a series of stained-glass windows detailing the psalmist's images of the same themes. The thick, roughly cut, luminous small glass pieces showed expressionist suns and hills and planets and trees and fathoms of water. They, like the mosaic tiles they complemented, got brighter in hue as the eye swept toward the altar—which was a blazon of color. The communion table was a slab of marble supported by sculpted bronze clusters of grapes, wheat sheaves, and tendrils of vine. Above the altar itself was a huge plain cross wrought in bronze as rough as pine bark.

"It's beautiful," said Martha Delaney solemnly. The men gazed a minute longer. Then, spontaneously, together, they raised their dripping beer bottles to hers. The rush of shy joy they were feeling was the ultimate reason they did what they did. It brought them as close as they would ever come to understanding that odd piece of reportage in the fiction known as Genesis: how God, after seven days of creation, walked in the Garden at dusk and said, "It is good."

It was July 11, 1971. The new sanctuary of the First United Methodist Church at Edgewood, Louisiana, was really—though unofficially—christened.

8

AFTER A RELAXED DINNER with the Delaneys that night Chuck and Paul tried to go out on the town. Paul drove the yellow VW that Martha's husband, who owned a car dealership, had loaned them for their stay.

"You seem to be getting around pretty well," Chuck observed.

"You know I've been here a lot."

"No, I didn't know that."

"I never mentioned that to you? Martha and I were talking about it last night, but you must have been out of the room. I have two children who live here. They live with their mother's mother...So I'm familiar with certain parts of the town."

"I met your wife that spring we did the city hall, but I never knew you had children."

"Yah—we've split up now. But the children had been living with their grandmother for most of the year anyway. She can give them some things I really couldn't—a sort of stability—"

He had pulled into a gravel parking lot by a bar with a cocktail glass outlined in pink neon on its roofline. He switched off the engine and peered toward the door. Somehow neither man got out of the car.

"Well," said Paul.

"Shall we give it a try?"

Just then a couple walked by their car and entered the lounge.

"What color were they, did you see?"

"Nah, I couldn't tell."

"They *walked* like whites, though," said Paul darkly. They looked at each other and laughed. "Oh, hell," said Paul. "Let me think of another place we could try. We'll go to the other side of the tracks and see if it's just as impossible."

As they drove Chuck said, "You know, it might be perfectly all right. Probably would, in fact. But we wouldn't know otherwise till it was too late."

"Umm."

"It's always hard to know the bars in a new place. Which ones are touristy? Which ones are for bikers? Which ones dilute their whiskey? It's all trial and error."

"Oh, yes, in New Orleans I've twice gone into a bar for homosexuals without realizing it. A couple of months ago, the second time it happened, I had a date with me. Gorgeous girl...But she thought it was funny." Paul paused briefly at a green light, went on, thought better of it, and made a U-turn in the deserted street.

"It's really a coincidence that your kids are here. Is that how you got this job?"

"No, the committee at the church wouldn't know my mother-in-law! They heard about me through an artist friend of Martha's who's on the faculty at Xavier. Martha was in New Orleans for something and we met and hit it off and then she had me come talk with the committee."

"You must have come here quite a lot."

"I come up occasionally from New Orleans. This commission is great because I've been so much more often in the past year. And it's allowed me to meet people who have something to do with the art community here. There are some dedicated people here, for a town this size—and it's good to know what's here, for my kids' sake—"

"I hear they have a museum."

"Yeah, a new little museum. He-hey, now we're in Samtown!" Paul parallel-parked about a half block away from the door of a second bar, the Snake Eyes, identified by a big hand-painted sign with two dice on it. They were parked by a streetlight, and this time it was obvious that the people going in and out were black. He switched off the ignition. They sat there for a minute and then Paul said, "You know, we could just go to a package store and get a six-pack. We can drink it on the levee."

"That sounds equally suspicious to me. Someone would think we were homosexuals trysting. I've seen *Easy Rider*. Some cracker'd come along and blow our creative brains out."

Kalunge laughed. "Let's go in," he said suddenly. He paused halfway through opening his door. "This is not a wild place. This is a cozy little neighborhood bar. Best jukebox in town."

Inside Chuck thought the glances were palpable. He felt twice as big as he really was—taking up too much space. Paul went and jollied the bartender until he got a twitch of a smile out of him. They took two beers to a booth near the window and sat down.

After a few quiet sips Paul said, "No one's pulled a sweetchblade on you yet." He had remnants of his accent still, pulling at and softening his words. Rather than stinging him back Chuck just looked at him weakly, apologetically, and Paul felt bad. "I just meant it's more manageable than you think." Chuck was still silent and Paul went on, "As a matter of fact Martha told me they need a director of the little art museum here. I'm thinking about applying."

"Really!"

"Yah."

"I'm—surprised, Paul."

"Well, I think I'd like the work. I'm tired of teaching in these Catholic schools for the moment. But it would mostly be a way to be close to my kids. You don't know how it is with these kids."

"How old are they? Boys or girls?"

"Wait, I'll show you." Paul tugged his wallet out of his pocket. "One of each. This is Kimberly, she's seven now, and this is Ross."

The dim orange light of the bar, made of a neon beer sign reading backwards now from inside, fell faintly on the dim images held in Paul's fingers.

"Hell, you're a proper father, carrying the pictures around all this time and I didn't even know it. I wouldn't have thought you had this much respectable sentiment in you. Handsome children." Chuck handed them back. "They must take after their mother."

Paul didn't seem to know he was joking. "Oh, they do," he said seriously. "Yeah." He kept staring at them. "She hasn't seen them in two years, though. Can you believe that?"

"Bloody shame."

"Yeah. Actually, the little boy has some problems. He goes to the state school here."

"Learning problems?"

"Yah. Learning, behavioral. He's slightly retarded. I should take you to meet Glory tomorrow. Their grandmother. You'd love her. She would probably try to feed you. She'd take your insatiable appetite as a personal challenge."

"That sounds lovely. At least you'll get good meals if you live here. Since any one could be your last."

"Brother"—again, his tongue lingered over the word, drew it calmly out, not like an American black—"brah-ther, you think there's no racism in New Orleans? Montreal, for that matter? New York?"

"At least I could find a bar to drink in with a black friend, if I wanted. Without half an hour of getting up my nerve."

"Don't kid yourself," said Paul uneasily.

"There are just more alternatives in general in bigger cities. Besides, man, you're an artist, presumably you've got some sort of aesthetic sense—this is a singularly ugly town!"

"Oh, do you really think so?"

"My God. Fried chicken joints. Gas stations here, there. Shopping centers. Ugh. It's trashy-looking."

"All American cities look like that from the main boulevards. You have to get off the path a little bit."

"Oh, Paul, I'm just doubting that the structure of things here would let you get off the beaten path."

"I may find out."

Both men took long draughts of their beer looking over the other's shoulder. Then they stared at each other again, and Chuck felt jolted by Paul's face. His eyes looked wet, but they were unblinking, proud, as if the tears were flung out for a challenge. He had raised his chin and his face seemed cut out of something hard and glassy, buffed with blue and red and yellow tones in this light, the full curving lips reposing like a sculpture. He said deep in his throat, in a voice that almost started as a purr, "I'm glad you give a shit about it, though." With that his face split into a happy smile like a child's, the eyebrows flew up, as if something difficult had just been overcome. "I just didn't know anyone gave a shit."

"Why hell, of course I give a shit," growled Chuck.

9

Lil McCain had met Paul Kalunge briefly while he was in town to work on the mosaic, but after a few months passed she had all but forgotten about him. Then she learned in a disturbing way that Paul might actually move to Edgewood. She was making routine calls for the Symphony Auxiliary, trying to find someone willing to pick up a guest pianist at the airport. From one woman she got this curious response: "Not tomorrow. The Art Museum board is interviewing a black for the directorship, and Jimmy and I need to be there to walk out."

"That's ridiculous!" fumed Lillian, after she drew her breath in shock, gave an icy answer, and slammed the phone down. "What *blatant—!* I haven't encountered that attitude in years."

"What attitude?" said her children curiously. They had a game of trying to guess whomever Lillian talked to on the phone.

"I can't bring myself to discuss it. I'll tell you in a minute."

"Must have been some bigot," Fayette deduced. A few minutes later, hearing the story when Lillian started calling her best friends, they learned he was right. "Gross!" said Allie. The McCain children were well-schooled in all the right responses.

Lillian's best friends were a handful of matrons who, with a sort of demure saltiness, had managed to stake out ideological ground for themselves within the boundaries of Edgewood society. For home, church, and country they had deep apple-pie feelings, topped with a dollop of cynicism. They wore wool though they could have afforded fur, crossed the tracks to register black voters, sent their kids to public school, and often found themselves defending their sons' long hair to their parents and their parents' church habits to their children, while privately harboring doubts about both. They had recently all put McGovern stickers on the bumpers of their Buicks.

These ladies rallied their husbands and set off for the meeting at the Art Museum. Allie stood in the entrance hall watching her own parents leave. As usual when they went to a meeting, they were what her mother called "running late"; the haste gave an extra sense of urgency to their missions. Now her mother was standing by the open door, alternately muttering little comments to herself, rattling her keys, and cocking her head to hear how far along Daddy was in brushing his teeth. "'Be there to walk out,'" she said. "My Lord.—I think I'll go start the car."

Daddy was more cheerful. "Could be worse," he said, pulling on his sportcoat as he came down the hall. "We're lucky they're not sophisticated enough to be subtle about it." He kissed Allie goodbye, flipped on the porch light, and pushed the lock button on the front door in one quick motion, and Allie heard her mother saying, "What do you mean ..." as the two of them crunched across the gravel driveway to the car.

While their parents were at the meeting fourteen-year-old Fayette babysat, smoking Marlboros, drinking wine, and letting Allie look at his copies of *Playboy* for three hours, until they heard their parents fumbling at the door. "It's all right!" Frank called, walking through the house and turning out lights the kids had left on. Fayette was stuffing the magazines and bottle back under his bed and fanning smoke out his open window. Their father's voice, like a town crier's, was coming closer. "The crisis is over. He's going to get the job"—and he reached the climax of his tale as Fayette appeared questioningly in the door of the living room—"because they've discovered, in one of their eminently reasonable distinctions, 'he's not a *black*, he's an *African*.'"

The children could see that their parents had still not switched stages. At first their father was always tickled by such absurdities, and it would be several hours before his humor hardened into outrage. On the other hand, Lillian was clinched with anger and bitterness right now. By tomorrow her anger would have been channelled into all the remedies she would think of, and, like hot peppers melding into a piquant sauce, the pain of the story would have steeped into yet another dry, drawling satire to be told on her hometown. Now she stalked off to the phone. She had Mr. Kalunge's number in hand and was going to invite him to a dinner party in his honor.

Allie turned down an invitation to spend the night at her cousin's house lest she miss seeing him. She tallied up the things she knew about Africa. One: it was the place Uncle Jules said American blacks should be sent back to. Two: it was the theme for a weekend cabin in the country playfully named "Zanzibar," which the mother of a former playmate of hers had built. The house was actually pre-fab Swiss-villa in style, but the lady had decorated it in an African motif with baskets, cane chairs, and the poaching trophies of her doctor husband—elephant footstools, zebra skins, and water buffalo, hippo, lion, and antelope heads. There were also two wet bars, a TV and stereo, central air conditioning, and a black cook who, the day Allie visited the place, made Shirley Temples for her and her friend. Three: she had a vague visual notion of Africa, only the vaguest, from fragments of a Tarzan coloring book and the *National Geographics* in her grandmother's bathroom. These had given her the idea that an African would wear paint, earrings, and a loincloth like an American Indian.

"What do you think he'll look like?" she asked Fayette. She could count on him to give her a straight answer.

He pretended not to know who she meant. "Who?"

"Mr. Kalunge."

"He'll look like anybody else. He'll be wearing a suit and tie. He'll be black. He'll have an English accent."

"Oh."

"Why, did you think he'd have on feathers and a nose ring?"

"No," she said a little too hotly.

"You're just like everyone else. You've got all sorts of prejudices about Africa."

"I am *not* prejudiced!" she cried indignantly. She had known *that* word for years. On the playground the other day she shouted it (with reason) at a doughy little white classmate who threw down her end of the jump-rope, burst into tears, and said, "I am *not* pregnant!" Allie felt a pleasant superiority just remembering the incident.

But Fayette went on, "Like the people in England or wherever who divided up Africa. They didn't know anything about it. Sat in London with big old maps their explorers had made and carved it up into countries that didn't have anything to do with the way the African people already had it split up. Then they just took it over like we did the Indians here—"

"Okay, okay." She stopped him before he could get off on his Indian theme. Last month it was the Vietnamese. She had been riding with him in Daddy's truck, which Fayette was driving (illegally—he would not have his license for another year) to get cigarettes and wine at the 7-11, when, out of a desire to live up to the suave adult nature of the moment by showing herself able to discuss current events, she had remarked innocently enough, "I'm for President Nixon."

"Oh, Jesus. Where'd you come up with that?"

"*Weekly Reader.* They have this thing called 'Election Corner,' pro and con."

"So why are you for Nixon?"

"Well"—it hadn't sounded so lame in the sixth-grade classroom; there no one had disagreed with her—"I think he's been doing a good job."

"With what?"

"Well, with the war. I mean, we might win the war soon."

"Why should we win it?"

A flash of clarity saved her. "To keep out the communists!"

"What's the matter with communism? Do you even know what it is? What if the Vietnamese *want* to be communist?"

Weekly Reader had not entertained these questions. "But—I mean—"

"What gives us the right to go in there and decide for them they ought to have a democracy just because it's what we have?"

"A democracy has liberty and justice for all," she remembered. "I'm sure they want that."

"It's not a very good example of liberty and justice to be bombing their country to pieces when our Congress hasn't even declared war."

"Hmm." As usual he won the argument. Since then she had found out that her parents and Uncle Calvin Ray and Aunt Esther and Uncle Tyler and Aunt Cynthia were for McGovern and her grandmothers and Uncle Jules and Aunt Sadie and Uncle Gus and Aunt Mary Sue were for Nixon. She had momentarily confused the two camps into which her world was divided. She put a McGovern sticker on her bike the next day. Fayette was always having to enlighten her.

Now she said, "Well, anyway, I have to go. Mama wants me to pass the appetizers."

"Be sure you don't trip over Kalunge's spear when you do."

"Huh?"

"What are the appetizers?"

"Oysters wrapped in bacon."

"Ohh, bring me some when they're ready."

In giving directions Mrs. McCain had told Paul elliptically that she lived in the country. He drove out of town on the Baton Rouge highway, heading southeast, and turned off onto a smaller winding road as she had instructed. Now there were big weedy lots on either side of the road, with developers' signs in them, and then immense fields, planted with, he guessed, beans and cotton. He was not prepared for what came next: a high-mounted sign, decrepit and streaked with rust to be sure, but still—"Green Isle Plantation." "Oh, brother," he groaned, and chuckled. He was still keeping an eye on his odometer. The road was now running side by side with a bayou on the right. Then a row of houses appeared. They were small and white, with dark green trim; little cabins, really, perched on cement blocks, varying only in the assortment of cars in front, the angle at which the television antenna stuck out from the roof. A dark child hurried up the steps of one. He had almost gone the 3.4 miles—yes, there was the long drive to the left she had described, and sitting way back in a grove of trees was a house at least three times the size of these others. The impulse behind his chuckle was gone now. Rather feudalistic, he thought grimly. And this is the family that's supposed to be so progressive? Even Carmelina, the black matriarch who had been schooling Paul in local life, had grinned and shrugged her shoulders when she spoke of Frank McCain. "That man's my darling. Can't help it. He's a force for the good around here."

Why don't you persuade your darling to change houses with one of his serfs, Paul planned to say to Carmelina next time he saw her.

But the dinner party was not too bad. Frank McCain was a tall, freckled man with auburn hair and an affable manner. His wife was thin and dark, with the luminous eyes and lined face of a Goya portrait. The guests were selections (he didn't know how select) from Edgewood's art community and powers that be: two of Mrs. McCain's brothers, one a broadcaster on a local radio station and the other a judge, small and slow to speak, with a tanned face and crisp white hair; their wives, whom he kept getting mixed up; a big burly energetic man who taught art at the new public high school; a psychologist whose husband, apparently a rabbi, was out of town; and a last couple whose occupations he never quite identified—they seemed to be having babysitting problems and went back and forth to the phone during the evening. The house was old and oddly put together, as if it had been built in stages. It was furnished with faded quilts and rugs and baskets and ferns and squatty plain antiques, with books on every wall and a few good lithographs he asked about with genuine interest. There were no servants. Mrs. McCain managed everything, with the help of a skinny, big-eyed child who kept the door to the kitchen in full swing.

Allie noticed right away that the stranger did have on a coat and tie, just as Fayette had predicted. He was very dark. Against the crisp white shirt collar his face and neck almost gave off blue tones. But that was at first, in the natural light on the porch. Inside in the candlelight or when she pushed open the dining room door and a bar of light from the kitchen slid across the long table, his color seemed a deep, rich brown. He looked stern, imposing, with his drawn-looking brow and set jaw and old-timey glasses. But once when Allie was passing hot bread, Aunt Esther must have said something that tickled him, for his face broke up swiftly into a laugh, he looked droll and mischievous and his shoulders shook waggingly, so that Allie had to move the bread basket lest he bump it.

After supper all the grownups were a little drunk. Paul stayed longer than the other guests. The McCains wanted to show him around. They took him into the attic of the house and showed him the locust pegs and the mud and moss and deer hide mixture that served as plaster. "Slave-made brick," they said proudly, and to their credit ducked their heads in embarrassment, their cheeks pinkening in the stark electric light. Then they all took liqueurs and sat on the porch: an abutment into a night that yawed and hummed so with insect sound it could almost make you seasick, like the world around a dark, rocking carriage. None of them could see each other's face. When he got back to his apartment, loneliness was coiling in Paul again, the loneliness he called peculiarly American—though since he had experienced it only since leaving Africa at fifteen, it might be endemic not to his adopted country but to adulthood itself; he would never know. He turned off his lights and avoided his mirror and searched the AM channels till he finally got a late-night blues station, fuzzily beamed from Memphis, to combat it.

10

"WELL, HOW DID things look out at Green Isle?" said Carmelina when Paul saw her next, grinning so that the silver and gold caps back in her mouth showed. They were sitting in the hospital cafeteria, drinking from small thick green-rimmed crockery cups of coffee. Carmelina was in her white lab coat.

"Look? How do they normally look? The shackles and hound dogs were hidden, if that's what you mean. You didn't tell me it was a plantation."

"Why, it's not, any more."

"It looks like one to me. I even read it on a sign."

"Honey, it may look like a duck, and sit like a duck, but as of last year it quit squawking like a duck."

Paul stared fondly at her and started to laugh. They both laughed happily for a minute or so and then he said ruefully, "But I don't understand."

"Come here," she said. "Want some more coffee? I've got to be back at work in a little while. I thought you were gonna tell *me* something. But I can see I got some explaining to do."

"Shoo-er," he said. He still had a slow, strange accent, almost like a first-grader reading a primer; he pronounced more consonants in words than Carmelina knew they had. "But don't be late on my account."

"With all the *good* reasons I could be late? Unh-unh!" She was quick. Paul shook his head, beat. She grinned at him and shifted her weight in her chair. Even her belly gave an impression of firm, supple capability more than fat. And she was probably at least in her sixties.

"That plan'ation," she said, "has been gi'en back to the black folks who work it. Frank McCain made it into a trust in all of their names."

"Wait, wait. Start over, please, Carmelina?"

"Well," she said patiently, "It used to be owned by a man named Rand. This was back before the Depression—I don't know how long he had it. He had a lot of money from his daddy, I believe—timber money from big old holdings up in north Louisiana. You go up that way and you still see the name Rand on some lumber companies."

"Toward Natchitoches?"

"Natchitoches? No. Not so close to the river, not your big timber companies."

"Oh."

"We knew everybody out there. In picking time they needed extra help. Sometimes chopping time too. Oh, yes," she nodded at Paul's expression, "You don't see it any more, but the time we worked the fields by hand is not so far back. We're not even one generation away from it yet. We'd go out from town and they'd take us on for a week or two. And in a good pecan year, too, we could go out to Green Isle and pick up on halves for Mr. Rand. Most of the colored folks over fifty in this town would tell you the same thing. Mr. Rand hung on to the plantation, round about three thousand acres, all through the Depression and the Second World War and all, growing cotton, beans, cattle. He tried potatoes and hogs too for a while. Always made a go of it.

"The people on Green Isle stayed right there. Their people had worked that land for comin' on to a hundred-forty years. Some of their kids'd leave and go north or move to town, but lots of them were used to country ways and hated to leave their home. Mr. Hudson—that's what they called him, his name was Hudson Rand—paid 'em regular wages, regular for black folks, I mean, real low, and let 'em stay in their houses."

"Are those the same houses that've been there since slave days?"

"No. He put 'em up new in the twenties. They're on the same sites, though. So anyway, a few years back, Mr. Hudson had a heart attack and died. Miss Amalie tried to run the place herself for a while, and made a big mess of it. She didn't have the strength to do a job like that. The farm ran along about like always, but the business end of it went every whichaway. So she asked her nephew, that's Frank McCain, to come run the place, and he did. At first they lived in that little new house across the bayou from Miss Amalie. Did you see it?"

"I don't think so."

"I shouldn't count on you to notice anything! Well, Frank didn't know spit about farming, but he's such a charmer, and so polite and funny with the people on Green Isle, that they took to him and little by little he picked up what he needed to know, and him talking to them all the while. That's why I told you, I'm partial to that man; he'll talk with you and listen to you. You don't find that very much. And by the time Miss Amalie died and Frank and Lillian and their chirren inherited it all and moved into the big house—that was last year, right after New Year's—he had a plan all made up. He called a meeting, and he met and met all through the spring with the people on Green Isle. I'm surprised he didn't talk about it! He just made 'em into a trust, and all that money that old farm brings in is theirs now." She shook her head and bit her lip but beamed despite herself.

"Hunh," was all Paul could say. He shook his head and said it again. "Hunh."

Carmelina said, "You doubting Thomas. You *are* a Thomas."

"What's he going to live on?"

"He's keepin' a little land for his family, enough for them to handle themselves."

"White guilt," said Paul. "And anyway, I doubt it makes that much material difference, Carmelina, really. The structure there will be the same."

"It may be," said Carmelina, "and it's the result that counts. That's what I always tell my kids. So, we'll see. Anyway you can see why I was curious. I haven't been out there and I haven't seen Dottie Mathews in a while. She's my friend out there who tells me what's going on. I was hoping you could give me a little news about the changes."

"Well," said Paul. "You've always got an interesting story for me, that's for sure."

It was Glory Jones, Paul's mother-in-law, who had introduced him to Carmelina. The two were girlhood friends. Glory was plump, and like the fat that blurred the points and angles of her frame, her cheerful manner seemed diffuse and pliant and often hid her sharpness. Paul adored her, but it always surprised him when she revealed a particularly astute judgment. Recognizing his need for someone like Carmelina was a stroke of insight. When Paul moved to Edgewood to be near his children, whom Glory was bringing up, she saw the writing on the wall. New Orleans was one thing; it was a big city, and he had made out all right there; but moving to a town on the Red River was a different kettle of fish for anybody, especially for a black man from Africa. Someone had to orient him and school him in the lay of the land, and Glory knew she herself couldn't do it. Yet it was in her and her grandchildren's interest for Paul to be happy so he wouldn't give it all up and flee—maybe not just to New Orleans, but even worse, back to New York, or who knew where else, maybe overseas again where she knew how rarely they would hear from him. So she had musingly told him, almost as an afterthought one day, that he should look up her old friend Carmelina Pick. "I've told her who you are," Glory had assured him. "She knows who you are."

Who I am? Paul had thought. Which line? "He is a sojourner from Black Africa!" or "He is an artist," or "He is Eliza Jones's ex-husband"?

He had called Carmelina, and she told him to meet her at the LeBac General Hospital Laboratory. He found her perched on a high stool, staring down her nose through a pair of half-glasses at three test tubes that were swirling in her long, firm fingers. Her hair was pulled up to the crown of her head in a small bun, almost severe. Her brow was high and wide, her face long, the cheekbones drawn down to the thrust of a stubborn, jutting chin—a face with plenty of room in the jaws for a smile as sudden and enveloping as Louisiana heat. That day the woman and the man half her age had had their first snack and talk at the hospital cafeteria, where they were to fall into a pattern of meeting every week or so. So Paul's formal education about central Louisiana continued. To be taken under Carmelina's wing was all the entrée into Edgewood black society he needed. From her he was learning the threaded histories of many people, tragic or successful, whose common ground he had just set foot on.

Carmelina had been a girl of striking intelligence and sensitivity born in Edgewood in a day when black women prayed for their daughters to be dumb and numb. She had married at seventeen and while rearing her own three children went seeking work at the local hospital. She started in its laundry room, then switched and mopped floors for two years, and slowly, very slowly, moved up through a tier of jobs, till she was made assistant technician in the laboratory. Soon she was indispensable there. The hospital paid for her to go to school on the side, and now she was chief medical technologist. But science was not the only subject on which she had incisive views. She was steeped in Edgewood culture and history and wise to its politics, and as such she was a blessing to someone like Paul, who craved the inside scoop on such matters wherever he was.

When Carmelina got home that day her daughter was waiting for her in the kitchen. Carmelina didn't say anything, just heaved the sack of groceries and her big black zip-top imitation-leather purse on top of the counter with a glance at Miranda's face, which was downcast.

"Hey, Mama."

"Evenin', evenin', daughter."

"Don't you even want to know what he say, Mama?"

"I can tell by your face what he said."

Miranda started to cry. The tears, big perfect creations in themselves, slid down her soft flawless cheeks as if to trace their contours—the perfect flare below her eyes, the fashionable slight hollowness, then the curve into that modelled chin—the way a man's hand might: the way, doubtless, some man's hand had. And Carmelina knew what man. Miranda made no sound, but her lip flew regularly in and out like the wild, exposed heart of some creature being dissected.

"When are you due?" said Carmelina roughly. She was yanking pots and pans out of the cupboard.

"F-f-february."

Carmelina wheeled around and Miranda flinched, thinking her mother was going to slap her. She had slapped Miranda only once in her life, ten years before, but it had made an impression that lasted. Miranda had brought home an F on a paper in fifth-grade math—not even a test, just a little worksheet—and laughingly explained to her mother that she had added all the figures together, not noticing the directions to subtract or the poorly mimeographed minus signs. Her mother's hand had lashed out quick as a snake. While the girl covered her mouth and cheek, stunned, Carmelina had hissed, "We don't do thataway. We don't do thataway." Snuffling in bed that night, Miranda had wondered whether her mother meant "we" Picks or "we" Gilmores—Carmelina's maiden name—or "we" Negroes. Regardless, Miranda and her sister and brother knew that their mother held standards for them that allowed no careless errors, no shirking, no consequential mistakes. Now, this pregnancy was her worst nightmare of such a mistake. Ever since she suspected it, instead of feeling the new life growing inside her, Miranda had felt a palpable doom which was dread of her mother's censure—doom like the fertilized egg itself, fattening and organizing itself in preparation for all its later mischief.

But Carmelina didn't slap her when she wheeled around. Her face was so stricken she looked like the Indian on the extinction commercial, the redbone in her looks brought out by tragedy as it had been when Grandpa died—and she said, "I'm still prayin' Scrip Thomas won't marry you."

"Oh, there's no need to worry about that," Miranda said bitterly.

If only her mother had sat down at the kitchen table beside her and bawled. But Carmelina turned and kept slamming supper on the stove as if tears were only for salting mustard greens. She spat out her own bitterness in words. As high emotion brought out the redbone in her looks, it brought out black dialect in her speech, which was usually groomed white in the expectation her children would imitate and wield it in their trips up the ladder. "That Scrip not even the regular kind of bad man, the weak kind. Oh, no, I know his kind. He a bad man because he know too much—he got to hurt other people like he been hurt—you couldn't ever outsmart a man like that, you couldn't keep him in line, and he always be making you hope things-a be different at the last minute. *I* know *too much* about *that* kind of man. I *knows* too much. And I knowed enough all my life not to 'mongst with them—"

It was Miranda's father, James, who when he got home and took in the scene said, "You givin' us a grand, baby?" and stroked his daughter's neck and rubbed the hollow of her collarbones and then sat down and cried like a baby himself, awkwardly embracing his crying daughter as well as the two kitchen chairs scraped close together allowed—while his wife stepped out on the sloping linoleum they called a back porch, looking off at the red sun and blinking and thinking her heart was broken.

There were not many people in Edgewood born outside the United States, but those there were were viewed with great interest and no little pride, at least until their particular novelty wore off. When Paul had been in New York, all the non-blacks he met seemed to be first- or second- generation Americans with fascinating stories about their grandparents' immigration. But the South is not used to immigrants. There, children read in their social studies textbooks about the oh-so-familiar trip through Ellis Island and think they've never heard anything so weird. Southern whites generally have only the vaguest idea of their ancestry; they can trace their lineage back beyond Carolina or Tennessee only if some ancient relative happens to make genealogy her hobby and talks about it on Sunday afternoons. And southern blacks know only that their forebears were enslaved Africans. Identity in the South is rarely nationalistic—just racial, or for some, religious.

So Edgewood's few immigrants were celebrated. The prominent ones were several eastern Europeans, a Cuban couple, a fair number of Britons, and three Korean families. For a while after these citizens' arrival a magic aura had surrounded them. Then comment and speculation had dwindled, and the new Americans had been absorbed into the city's life without further surprise. Anecdotes about their background would come up occasionally, and at dinner parties every once in a while they might serve up some special dish of their culture, but for the most part the interest in them receded to levels held for everyone else.

Shortly after the dinner party the McCains gave, Paul retreated to such a fixed status. He was unfailingly present at local art show receptions, symphonies, recitals, plays, and board meetings of the Arts Council. He had a handful of devoted white friends who moved in the cultural set and usually joined him at these events. But for most people he faded into the background there as much as an inky-skinned person who wasn't a servant could. Where prominent whites gathered, many eyes would skim over him and pass on, kindly but hurriedly, as over any blatant fact that the looker assumed would be a source of mutual embarrassment—like the wheelchair of that disabled pillar of society Mr. Dove Schmidt or the enormous fatty bulk of the force behind the local ballet, Mrs. Sydney Crutcher, or the birthmark of the Lawsons' middle daughter, Jill.

For his apartment and studio he had rented half of the third floor of an old office building by the levee downtown, which was owned by Martha Delaney's brother-in-law. The fact that no one else lived in the business district didn't bother him. He had high ceilings, privacy, big windows that let in northern and western light—good for the painting he did on weekends and in the afternoons—and a view of the brown, turgid river. For space like this he'd pay three times as much in New Orleans and five times as much in New York. The Art Museum was four blocks west and south of him. Only six blocks or so to the east was the edge of the black section of town, where he could drop in at cafés and bars without a stir. His ex-mother-in-law and children lived in a black neighborhood two miles away, across the river, and he could visit them or other friends in his battered gray VW station wagon. It was a bizarre existence on the cusp of Edgewood's white and black societies—where he was sometimes accepted in the one because of some vague sense that he was exotic and in the other because of his skin color.

11

THE NEW GMC JIMMY burst upon the morning like a longhorn let out of the gate. The noise of its gears shook dew off the branches of live oaks, as far down the stretch of road as its junction with the new highway. People up and down the road paused with their forks halfway to their mouths and said, "Here comes Fayette."

Like a dark green thunderbolt it came into view. It was convertible, and its top was off. Fayette was driving. At his side and a little behind him, holding on to the roll bar, stood Allie. The Jimmy was overbrimming with flowers, the onlookers saw—then, in a streak, it was gone.

Allie, feeling like a general in the war movies Fayette urged her to watch, adopted the demeanor of such a man, riding cool and impassive in a victory parade. The blue summer morning arched above them, triumphal. The live oak branches were the arms of a throng that lined their way; shining kingfishers, darting in arcs from telephone wires on either side, were like coins flung toward them exultantly. And the flowers on the floorboards and seats of the Jimmy, soaking in old creased milk cartons—the snapdragons, roses, lilies, iris, verbena, and phlox—were their spoils.

On a morning like this, she could ignore these changes that had been cropping up here and there—sad, unsettling things. Prowling in Fayette's room recently she'd found a packet of condoms. In his bottom drawer along with the cigar box full of plastic army men from his childhood and the découpage picture she'd made him for his birthday, beneath the clip-on bow tie someone had given him for a joke (which was what she was looking for, she needed to wear it to school on "Tie Day" of "Spirit Week"; in junior high she still took part in such things). She knew what they were, all right. She froze and stared for a minute, then opened one and stared some more. Beneath her fascination a sad separate feeling spread out like a puddle. His girlfriend was just a face and a name to her, a cheerleader, "Cheri" embroidered on her cheerleader's collar in the back—"a lightweight," Allie had overheard her mother say to her father. Allie had stuffed the rubber deep in her pocket. It was terrible of her to snoop like this. Probably he would count them and miss it, but he wouldn't be able to do anything about it. And neither could she, at this point. She cut it up with scissors and flushed it down the commode, and went out of his room feeling older and enlightened and guilty, dismissing the pictures that rose up in her mind, too miserable to cry. His absence seemed like something tangible in the room. And just a year from now he'd be going off to college. She'd be left behind for good.

But today—today she put such things out of her mind. Today her heart was lighter, because this was the last day of seventh grade. No more squeezed hours doing farm chores and homework before and after school, no more missing the tides of light that came across the farm between eight and four each day. She could just be herself. They were on their way to deliver these home-grown flowers to a customer of their mother's who was having a big party that night and then to head back to school for an easy day of turning in books, cleaning desks, and shooting the breeze. Authority would loose its vise grip on the students. Somehow school had brought these changes on them, and today it would sink below the horizon.

They skirted the new part of town for now and headed down the brick-lined arteries of Old Edgewood.

"Damn," said Fayette briefly, "I didn't mean to come this way," just as Allie said, "We're going to pass Mémé's!"

Their grandmother was out watering her yard. By the time she recognized the two of them they were far down the street. Allie, craning her head backwards, announced, "She waved."

Suddenly they laughed. "Watering!" said Fayette. "It rained just last night."

"Poured," said Allie.

They laughed more. "She was probably out watering then," said Fayette. "Out in her nightgown, with rubber boots on, in the middle of a downpour, holding those hoses—"

"'Why, hon, I'm about give up on my yard, it hasn't had a soaking in so long,'" mimicked Allie. "Hey, she's gonna say something about how fast you were driving when we went by. Want to bet we hear about it?"

He resumed his silence. The houses of Edgewood fell away to either side of the Jimmy, in an alarming blur.

They found the Pilfords' home easily. The van of Mr. Charlie Woodward, the expensive yard landscaper whom no one used unless he was giving a really special party, was in the driveway. Luminaires already edged the curving monkey-grass-lined flower beds and the walkway to the house. As they unloaded the Jimmy the children commented politely on the house to Mrs. Pilford. Allie hummed over the flowers, speaking silently into their unknowing faces. She would never like them so much after they had been arranged in silver vases and cut-glass bowls, as right now, crammed together, their colors so vivid and new, so startling and abundant, with dew still on them and stink-bugs ready to crawl out of their leaves at any minute. Goodbye! she told them as she plunked them on Mrs. Pilford's spotless kitchen floor. A maid peeling shrimp by the sink smiled over her shoulder and made small talk with Allie when she went in and out.

"All right; let's go," said Fayette. They jumped back into the truck. Their doors slammed shut, one, two, like rifle shots. They made it to the junior high, where Allie got out, in four minutes.

That afternoon after school she walked to Theresa's and together they went to the Y for a swim. When Fayette picked her up, the Jimmy was full of beer. Silver and red beer cans lined the floorboards and were stacked four deep in the bed. They nestled around the spare tire and the tool box and rolled out from under all the seats when Fayette braked. *"God,"* said Allie—the interjection for eighth-grade girls that year.

"Eight cases' worth," said Fayette with pride. He added, "They're for a party tonight. Obviously, you're not supposed to say anything about seeing it."

"Say anything? Don't you think Mama and Daddy have eyes?" She opened the glove compartment, and two more cans tumbled out.

"What's your problem? They'll mostly all fit back under the seat. They've just rolled out. I have a tarp for the ones in the back. And you're going to leave your beach towel over the rest."

Allie balked at this. "I don't usually walk around in a wet bathing suit with no towel, you know." She was shy of exposing her breasts, which would be plainly revealed under the cold wet clinging nylon—small and flat and puckered like doll-sized Japanese umbrellas.

"They won't notice. Just say you forgot it at Theresa's."

When they got home she let the beach towel slip off her shoulders, glowering, and helped Fayette arrange it over the beer cans. Then she trooped miserably after him into the chilly air-conditioned house, with goosebumps standing all over her white, ungainly body.

"What are you reading?" said Allie to Fayette.

He answered her with the heavy bored tone of condescension that had become his usual. *"Invisible Man."*

"What's it about?"

"It's about this invisible man who marries this lady who is just as visible as you and me."

"Really?"

Now he was looking up from the book, talking glibly. "They have two kids, a boy who's invisible on his right side and visible on his left, and a girl invisible on her left and visible on her right. The two kids like to stand together and depending which way they do, their two halves either make up one completely visible whole person or one completely invisible person."

"That sounds pretty good."

"Yeah," he growled. "Leave me alone."

"I don't have anything to read."

"Have you ever read *Tom Sawyer?*"

"No."

"How have you gotten this far without reading *Tom Sawyer?*"

"I don't know. Does it have any dogs in it? I feel like reading a dog book."

"No, but it has a dead cat."

"Okay, I'll read it."

One day she went running into Fayette's room to ask him something before he left again. She slid in her thick socks on the hardwood floor and laughed when she bumped against his bookcase. He raised his head from his book scowling and then looked at her a minute as if he hadn't in a while and said, "Jesus, you're getting uglier all the time."

He had put his finger on it. She knew it was true; she had been suspecting this. Someone as repulsive as she didn't even have a right to the despair that flooded her.

She felt so ugly and clumsy that she held herself away from real contact with other people. Even her behavior was ugly. During the seventh and eighth grades she had a clique of girlfriends who believed themselves equally unattractive and at the same time superior to the boys in their class. She and the other girls read widely, hungrily, continually, for sexual knowledge. They must have combed thousands of pages of literature, some of it sophisticated and some trashy, in their quest for erotica. They would trade finds to familiarize one another with new terms and innuendoes. Often a teacher or a classmate would innocently use a word that triggered the girls' recall of some steamy or perverse act. Then they would choke in crude giggles, "cracking up," they said, their lightly acned faces turning beet-red from the allusions, while the teacher rapped her desk in annoyance.

Recently Allie had spent the night at Mémé's house and left a tampon thrown away in the bathroom wastebasket. Ruby Mae, Mémé's maid, walked through the living room a few minutes later and said, "So you's a woman now." Allie pretended not to understand. "I see you's a woman now," repeated Ruby Mae. "Oh," Allie said, blushing, "I guess so, yeah." But she knew she wasn't, they were lying, she and her body and Ruby Mae all three.

She faced her downright hideousness stoically. Though she knew in detail the syndromes of Freud's patients from a biography of him, and a range of sexual antics from a novel she found in Fayette's room, she never expected even to touch a boy's hand. If she herself shrank in disgust from the walls of her body, why would anyone else ever want it?

Yet adolescents are masters of duality, probably because they are learning to be adults—shedding childhood's ruthless consistency like so many baby teeth. So for months while she was utterly cynical about her own appeal, Allie nursed a crush she knew would never come to fruition. One of Fayette's best friends, the son of the local newspaper editor, was an Eagle Scout with a passion for ecology. He had light hair and blue eyes and his face and hands were tan all year long. He wore moccasins a real Indian had made for him. He was neat, compact, and self-contained, like a Swiss knife.

Christopher excelled at a new sport called orienteering and had won some national awards for it. From what Allie knew, it involved being turned loose in unfamiliar woods and navigating one's own way out as quickly as possible. She loved the vision of him moving slight and sure and golden beneath primordial pines—scanning the skies for his direction—picking up a bird feather to impart some fact about it to those less graced with knowledge. She took his intuitions of nature as a sign of his depth and sensitivity. She wanted to be some kind of girl guide to him, his Pocahontas in future expeditions. Together the two of them would roam the wilds of America and even the world, making love in tents and compiling photo-essays for *Audubon* magazine. Unlike other women, she would have the capacity to let him be, not to smother the precious, buoyant self-reliance she admired in him.

She fostered the infatuation as carefully as her mother tended a plant. At this point all her friends were doing the same. Few of them had real boyfriends with whom they actually spent time, but each had some cherished object of her fantasies, and bore patiently the tedium of hearing about the others' loves for the privilege of being able to hold forth about her own slight encounters in turn. "See, I knew he worked at Hang Ten, but I didn't know he worked on Friday nights, or I wouldn't have gone with my mother. And when I saw it was him, I was so embarrassed, I looked really gross, I could have died.

And he just looks at me, sort of checking me out, and then he goes, 'Well, hello!' "Each girl privately thought that all the others' crushes were merely that, silly and obviously doomed, while her own was blessed with small but significant signs of potential.

Allie's crudity at school and surliness at home were superficial. Beneath that her spirit seemed to be developing unruffled, making a smooth gradation from child to young woman with no repulsive adolescence of its own. The romance she cherished belonged to that inner world. Dreams about Christopher flowed in their own plane, and Allie never measured their distance from the course of her everyday life.

Her plans for after college were also remote. She wanted to travel around the world collecting endangered animals and breeding them in a giant natural zoo. She would photograph and film the creatures as well. It was offbeat but was still a child's dream, naive and pure, and with a child's trust she never fretted over its impracticality. Once she had conceived the idea she didn't question it much. It didn't really bear thinking about; she just happened to love photography and the outdoors. Everyone close to her had such sideline interests and she might as well call one or the other of them her vocation. She had school, she had the farm and Green Isle and the dairy to explore, and she had horseback riding, YWCA art classes, and occasional music lessons. Likewise Theresa had girls' basketball and gymnastics. Fayette had farm work and football and guitar lessons and trying to dig up Civil War relics with the metal detector. Mama had her flower business and her books, Daddy had books and his projects around the parish, Uncle Calvin Ray had opera, Aunt Mary Sue had doll collecting. So it went.

Then, the Christmas she was thirteen, her aunt Sarepta sent Allie a book on Margaret Bourke-White. Allie pored over it in the sated gloom of the rest of that day and in the vacation days following, and was smitten. She already owned a Time-Life book that explained technical terms and gave examples of good and poor shots. But this was different. It showed what a great eye could do. Suddenly Allie was seeing photography in a larger way. She realized that the childlike dream of collecting and photographing wild animals that had stayed with her was dead—like a dry, protective outer shell that rides around on an organism long after it has quit being part of essential growth.

Bourke-White's pictures engaged with the new depths in Allie and discovered them to her. Later she associated the very sheen and ink-smell of the pages with a humbling that marked her first stirrings of adult self-awareness. She was ashamed of the brazen carelessness with which she used to fling out the claim that she would take great pictures—and yet not ashamed, for that unmindful creature had existed in some other era, which she instinctively knew was past. Bourke-White returned her gaze to human life. Now Allie saw what one could *intend* with the eye and shutter, and with excitement approaching nausea saw the gulf between that level of intention and her own clumsy beginnings. The childish ambition melted. Bravado and illusions had of course not vanished completely. But the halcyon days of not really caring about what she would become, least of all doubting it, were over. Her ambition now was speculative and adult, morbidly self-aware, and dauntable at every turn.

From the school, parish, and local college libraries she took out all the books on photography she could find. If librarians made friendly comments about her obsession she would stare at them over the stack of folio books in her arms with the same hard, emotionless gray big-eyed look that she had turned on Mr. Grimes at the camera store that day nearly four years before.

She had always reveled in the visual; lately her mother had taken to telling people how even as a toddler Allie was unusually observant, squatting down to inspect the patterns and porousness of bricks laid out in a walk, or the veined bumpy surface of a caladium leaf. But whereas she used to pore over colors and patterns with an ecstasy almost mournful—what was it she wanted from this beauty but could not name?—she now saw and appreciated, and instead of being paralyzed was seized with the urgency of getting these images on film. The world was no longer unconnected, something she had to rush away from, into private fantasy. Whisker, hubcap, stained glass, or long plowed fields—everything needed her, like a witch or alchemist, to transform it into a satisfying oblong, selected from the rest of the field of the eye and framed by four thin white angular lines. *Holy,* her whole self breathed as she did it, *holy, holy.* The world mattered. A camera's potential consecrated it.

12

AT THREE O'CLOCK on a hot September day, Beauregard Senior High School seemed to drowse in the sun, like the drivers nodding behind the wheels of the big yellow buses lined up at the curb. The flag in front stirred and unfurled every few moments, scraping its chains against the metal pole. From the gym came muted, intermittent roars. The students were corralled there for a pep rally.

Allie had been at high school a month, long enough to be ambivalent about pep rallies. In the first place, she disliked having her art class cut short. Another student in the class had pleaded, "Mr. Haskell, can't we please stay in here during the pep rally? Just to work on our projects?" and Allie, too proud to beg the favor herself, had listened hopefully. But Mr. Haskell said no. At Beauregard, art teachers had to be careful. There was a long history of their infractions and firings.

In the second place the pep rally offended Allie in some way that was hard to pinpoint. It was a pitch for the sort of blind enthusiasm the cheerleaders called "spirit," which Allie suspected she lacked. She had not yet decided which was more embarrassing, to fake "spirit" or just not to try any display of it at all. The camera came in handy; she had gotten on the yearbook staff, and if she took pictures continually during the pep rallies, it had to be obvious to anyone noticing her that she could not be expected to cheer at the same time.

And yet—and yet—there was something rousing in these assemblies: that was the most baffling part. Here they all *were,* for better or worse. At Fayette's football games, Mama always got teary during the national anthem. Later she would try to explain that it was seeing the blacks and whites side by side: the players standing with their heads bowed and helmets off, Fayette's shaggy platinum-colored mane shining with the same mauve tones that the stadium lights gave to his teammates' Afros. Lillian's children, who actually attended the school, could not afford her sentimentality, but at times Allie thought she understood it.

Beauregard was the third public high school in Edgewood, built for the overflow from the once all-white high school in the old wealthy district and the once all-black school in Samtown. Because it had opened in the year of the rezoning, to Edgewood citizens it would always be associated with a certain power—a power seen as either splendid or malignant, depending on their politics, and one they could not have put into words but sensed nonetheless: the power of the federal government running down through narrower and narrower conduits of the bureaucracy, the last of which was the slightly arthritic hand of a janitor pushing open a set of double glass doors on an August morning.

By 1974 the splendor of the new building had dimmed a little. The carpets (green for language, humanities, and "business arts," blue for science and math) were usually littered with chips of paper. Formica on the lockers was chipping off. Grafitti was scrawled inside, sometimes rubbed over with a bleaching agent by summer janitors, which left a spot worse than the original scribble. The bathrooms stank of stale smoke and the toilet seats were pocked with holes where cigarettes had been stubbed out. The students were still an assigned cross-section of the parish, "white, black, Hispanic, Asian, native American, and other," as their registration forms said—a tide of adolescents, by turns laconic, voluble, fitfully angry, quailing with shyness or glaring with insolence, some walking to school, some driving, some bused, gossiping, dancing, eating potato chips, bickering, coupling, daydreaming, till the noise of their assemblage crawled up the stairs and buzzed in the girders of the prize-winning contemporary design of the roof.

Now Allie moved along the aisle in front of the bleachers with a straggling river of her classmates. They had been told to file in as discrete homeroom units. Instead they poured on toward the remaining empty seats impossibly mixed, steadfastly ignoring boundaries that the school computer had drawn among them. Mrs. Picou, the high-strung home economics teacher who was a stickler for such things, retreated to the exit door close to tears.

"P," roared the classes. "P-O...P-O-W-E-R, we got power (whoo) *Eagle* power—"

When the school had opened there was division over whether its mascot could be the Confederate Rebel. Spokesmen for the black community, finally joined by a handful of liberal whites—Allie's parents among them—won out in the end with threats and the first motions of a lawsuit; they would take it on up to the feds, and everybody knew which side *they* would come down on. The mascot became the Beauregard Eagles.

Allie was taking pictures as her classmates pressed her along. She used a 35-millimeter lens opened wide for available light. On the varnished blond floor to her right—which was throwing a problematic glare—cheerleaders hopped and skittled, their faces rosy with sweat and synthetic blush. Their pom-poms trembled and bobbed at the ends of their flailing arms, like ragged chrysanthemums. On her left Allie was passing rows of the most ardent fans: the wealthiest cliques in this public school, whites and a few affluent blacks, the incarnation of American teenage divinity. They stood and swayed, they punched their fists into the air on cue, their tongues rallied like clappers in a row of gaping bells.

"It's like the Seven-Minute Hate, isn't it?" said a voice in her ear.

"What?" She turned abruptly.

It was Jeanine Bass, one of her cronies in iconoclasm. "Orwell. *1984.*"

"Oh." Allie laughed. "Yeah."

"Whipping the blind fervor of the masses."

But total cynicism was just another out. It wasn't that easy, either. Now the broken stream that contained her was moving in front of the band, the percussion section. She saw a small ninth-grader who rode her bus, whose father dug up ferns in the woods to sell to Allie's mother. His hair flopped in his eyes but he was too intent on his cues to push it back. He chewed gum tensely while he counted. The bass drum boomed deeply, the cymbal crashed, and despite herself Allie was touched; a thrill quivered in her stomach and up the back of her neck. *Stop it!* she told herself. This is stupid.

Now they were passing the sections of the gym where the less devoted, faceless ones of the school always sat, farther from the center of action. Allie took one shot, then another. Her fingers were focusing and tripping the shutter nimbly, almost nervously, while her mind was busy in a wandering, aimless way. What was in those blank, dark eyes? The hunched, drab figures sat, with chins propped on their knitted hands, staring at the brilliantly clad ones in the middle of the gym—the winners, the skilled, the popular, "most likely to succeed." A group of tenth-grade girls stood up. They would never be in the limelight, because something was wrong. Allie could tell it by their frowsy blouses and the way their jeans did not cup their bottoms to the right degree of tightness, by the way they were a little too conscious of their purses, purses that looked like the hand-me-downs of older sisters. These girls put arms behind one another's backs and studiously attempted a can-can:

Two bits
four bits
six bits, a dollar:
All for the Eagles
stand up and holler—

One girl's glasses slipped down her nose, and their hair whipped one another's faces as they struggled.

Behind them twelve or fourteen blacks, boys and girls, were doing an intricate dance with a turning shake and a bump to the same jingle. They said only occasional words of the rhyme, mostly biting their lips in unconcern. They added a clap at a place in the rhythm where Allie would never have thought to, leavening the heavy predictability of the cheer.

Now the basketball players themselves were lining up on the gym floor, moving slowly with self-consciousness as they felt the eyes of their peers running over their loose-strung bodies. They came to a halt behind the cheerleaders and caught their hands behind their backs, feet planted wide, gazing without expression through the cheerleaders' wheeling arms and legs, as if they did not hear the high chant:

"We—are—proud of you, say we are prouda *you,* hey hey hey, we—are—proud of you—"

Whitman had written about it: "And these I see, these stores of mystic meaning, these young lives, building, building, equipping like a fleet of ships; soon to sail out over the measureless seas, on the soul's voyage—"

Yet the skeptical, aloof angels in Allie tried to beat down such references. There is a silent effusion that is only a different kind of pep rally, which some artists conspire in. She was leery of that one too. And part of her ability to endure school at all came from the fact that it interested her, it defied glib renderings at every turn.

All that year she kept herself circulating through the different levels of activity at Beauregard, moving within it as a scuba diver fins up and down and around the sides of a coral reef. She read widely, no longer for prurience but for closeness to the artists and thinkers whom the photographers of the '30s revered. A casual reference made by one of them would lead her on to another. She had that almost comically earnest determination that has always distinguished American thought—a determination that private ideals shall be fitted to public life—and so the world of the school, and the rhetoric with which it explained itself, constantly fascinated her. Sometimes she had to admit that she herself was what did not seem to fit. Maybe she would have fit in better in Bloomsbury, or in the Left Bank crowd of interwar Paris, or in the bohemian photographers' Group *f*/64, than at Beauregard Senior High School. The perversity of that idea was not lost on her: had anyone else but herself been so ludicrous, she would have "cracked up" at them.

Yet when Allie hated the school she hated it as only idealists can. Mornings after she had risen in the hard quiet of the farm dawn, immersed in her own moods, and had ridden the bus into town through silent working-class neighborhoods reluctant to wake up, she hated going into the crowds whose noise and smells insisted upon her attention. The smells were of greasy hair and unwashed gym clothes, cheap perfume and gum, and lunch cooking in the cafeteria—the noise a cawing like a rookery, slamming locker doors, hollered greetings, hormone-stoked chatter, and occasional outright shrieks. Elbows brushed against her, bodies shoved, fingers and hands reached over and around her: there was no withdrawing: this gathering, this education, ingrained in law and revered, would not allow the illusion of apartness, it necessarily pulled you in, involved you, made you duck and shove back and respond.

In gym class on one of her hateful days, dressing out, she would shrink back into herself from the touch of the clammy clothes, smelling of the condensed steam of yesterday's sweat trapped inside the flimsy locker. She put them all on, the prescribed zip-up knit outfit everyone had to buy, the white ankle socks and white "tennies" initialed with a magic marker in a certain color. Any deviation from this uniform was penalized—though again the rich and poor could be distinguished: those who had the money took the gym suits to a store to have their name embroidered in a curlicue script in white thread, and those who didn't purchased iron-on capital letters from the gym teacher at the beginning of the year—the crooked, glaring rows that resulted thus segregating the class a second time. Allie dressed fast, slipping out the swinging door into the girls' gym, cold and dank at this hour of the morning, and found her spot (also prescribed) on the floor. Other girls came out, some slowly, some somehow springing with energy, neat slim girls, others whose waves of fat sprawled around the elastic in their suits, smiling or sullen. Then fifteen or twenty minutes might pass, and maybe a senior aide would lead them in a few lethargic exercises while they waited for the teacher to come out and instruct them in some banal game, which they would execute without breaking into a run. The dress-in bell would ring, back they would got to the locker room, on would go the street clothes and back into the locker the slightly smellier gym clothes. Those girls having their period would describe their cramps. The bell would ring. It was time for Art.

Some time late in ninth grade a certain grace started to show in

Allie's movements, a grace which—falsely—conveyed infinite control. She developed a pared-down style of dressing that became her trademark. "Feminine-earthy-artistic-hip," her cousin Theresa termed it. Theresa liked filling out magazine quizzes that helped you label your personal style, but she claimed that Allie always fell between the cracks of the categories. Allie was thin, long-waisted; she moved with a suave, agile sureness—almost too sure; her hips swayed ever so slightly, describing the bell shape of a flower, when she walked. She had long, thick, pecan-colored hair with a halo of split ends permanently around it—creating the sensation that she was always out of focus, that one could never quite draw a bead on her.

About this time the cold war with Fayette abruptly ended. One day he came out of his room and said gruffly, "Want to come hear an album?"

"What?" She suspected a trick. He had been known to call her to his room, only to slam the door just before she crossed the threshold and laugh cruelly from the other side.

"No, I just thought you might like to listen to a little bit of this."

So she was supposed to act as if this happened all the time. "Sure." Just how do you go about it? she wondered uneasily as she went into the room, this time not as a spy and documentarian, but as a guest. The lamps made it inviting and familiar. "We sat around and listened to albums"—that was something older kids said and did all the time, not her, Allie. She perched on Fayette's bed and tried to be cool, careless, and interesting to him at the same time.

He put on the record and handed her the cover. Allie was relieved to have that to look at and lyrics to read. It gave her something to do. The album was Randy Newman's *Good Ole Boys.* She strained to make out the words over the rough clangor of the band.

"What's he saying?" she said.

"Shh, follow along." Fayette sang softly, slightly after Newman sang each phrase. "He's talking about a mentality, don't you see?"

"Oh," Allie said sagely, obediently going on with each line of verse as if she were in English class. She got restless after a couple of minutes and flipped the album cover back to its front. "See this picture? You know how it was taken?"

"Unh-unh, how?"

"Someone just steadied the camera and set the shutter on a real slow speed and ..." That was her territory.

The braces came off her teeth a month later. Fayette glanced up from the paper one day when Allie was trying on a new dress for Lillian, and remarked that she was going to end up "willowy." After sneaking off to a dictionary she decided to construe it as a compliment. Suddenly he started introducing her to his peers with a noncommittal air that might be pride.

13

IN THE MIDDLE of Allie's sophomore year Frank announced that he was selling the pecan orchard for lumber and a tract of land for subdivision—maybe commercial development. The family was shocked, but they could not talk him out of it. It was as if he had become someone else. He first told them about it on an unseasonably warm, humid night at the very end of December. The decision bewildered Allie. She went outside and lay down in the hammock under the live oak trees and pictured used-car lots on the front pasture. Stadium-bright lights would send a glare for miles. Fringed plastic banners would beat in the wind.

"What's he doing it for?" Fayette demanded of Lillian. "If it's money, Mama, y'all can quit paying my tuition. I know it's expensive. I can take out a loan or something. It's not worth it."

"No—no, that's not necessary, Fayette. If anything we're a little bit more secure now than we have been in the past few years. He's just got his mind made up about this. I don't know why."

"He wants to show he's keeping up with the times? Prove something to Uncle Jules?"

"It's his middle-aged crisis," said Allie.

"I don't *care* if he proves something to Uncle Jules. Since when has he gotten down on Uncle Jules's level?"

"I'm sorry," said Lillian. "I just can't explain it."

The farm had been getting less isolated. The public was encroaching there too. Telephone wires looped in the skies, and campaign signs whitened fenceposts and tree trunks. Every morning now the school bus came down a dirt road through the grove to pick up a handful of students. CITY OF EDGEWOOD trucks now graded the rutted gravel roads; green, white-lettered street signs popped up overnight beside them, perched over ditches swathed in vines. At night street lamps appeared, one and two at a time, in fields where no one had lived until recently.

The tree men came early one day in March. Theresa had spent the night because her parents were out of town. The girls were getting ready for school, Lillian was in her greenhouse starting a big repotting project, and Frank was out presumably on some other part of the farm—his truck was gone.

It was a foggy morning that smelled of fallen rain. Taking her coffee cup back to the kitchen, Allie thought she heard a sound of heavy motors approaching. She paused to listen and make sure, for it was too early for the bus. Theresa and she had some time yet before school. Then where a patch of fog had lifted, three trucks came into sight—rugged trucks painted paradise-blue, with a rolling black script on their doors. As they came down the dirt lane, the winches and ladders they carried rattled loudly.

Allie went through the house to her room. "Hey, guess who's here," she said, drawing the curtain from the window. "The tree men are here." The trucks had pulled to a stop at the edge of the grove, which started just beyond the yard, with no fence, even.

"What tree men?" said Theresa.

"You haven't heard about that? Daddy's having all this cut down."

"*All* of it? Why?"

"He's got money worries all of a sudden."

"That doesn't sound like him."

"He's been sort of weird lately."

"Haven't they all," said Theresa drily. Allie laughed.

She had counted eight men by now. Some leaned on the fenders of their trucks and some sat on the hoods and some paused with a foot on the bumper. They stretched and yawned. A few walked around the trees, picking up dirt clods to toss at one another.

"Close it," said Theresa. "I'm not dressed." She was standing by the dresser in her nightgown, with the lamplight silhouetting her body underneath. She bent over to brush her hair one hundred strokes.

"They're not close enough to see you," said Allie, but she closed the curtain anyway and turned and flopped down on the bed.

When she and Theresa were little they had played every day in the orchard. It was their own green world. Overhead the high branches, interlaced and vaulting, had led somewhere unearthly. Layer after layer of leaves stood out from the branches, like skirts that flatten on the air around a whirling dancer. In winter the trees were exposed and skeletal, ribbed across the sky. Leaves would bud out and grow; nuts formed and hardened through the summer and fell on the ground to be picked up and sold in the fall. At the harvest season there were locust skins on every tree, split and empty shells of the insects who sang on warm nights, which Allie and Theresa used to collect and pretend were treasured brooches, hooking them on their clothes by the dry brown claws.

"The thing about the trees," said Allie, "—the thing is, they just make up the place here. Know what I mean? I remember when we were little. We were always out under the trees. Remember what we called them—we called them 'the gates of fairyland.' "

Theresa giggled and stood up, staggering for balance on her nude feet. "Oh, we sure were little," she said. Her breasts lifted like widening eyes as she pulled her nightgown over her head.

Allie opened the curtain again. The men were surrounding one big tree. A few wearing spiked boots were swarming into its lower branches and others had raised a cranelift halfway to the top of it. "I think I'd better go take some pictures," she said.

"I'll be ready in five minutes," said Theresa, but Allie had already picked up her camera and left the room, and now Theresa saw her out the window, crossing the gravel driveway, striking out across the wet, muddy grass toward the tree men. "Yukk," said Theresa, and looked dubiously at her own feet in new low-heeled, open-toed sandals. She would wait for Allie on the porch.

Out in the grove the men had closed in on one tree. The man in the cranelift was in its uppermost branches, attaching heavy cables unwinched from the trucks. Lower in the tree the climbers started their buzz saws. The noise gnawed at the foggy air, getting louder in each machine with the pressure of the cut and then dropping back to a whine. Little limbs began falling to the ground. Allie clicked away with her camera.

One by one the sawyers returned to the ground. Now they cut a wedge at the base of the tree. The crew leaders would step back, look up, and point, arguing about how the cut should be made and how the tree would fall. Now that much of the fog had lifted, Allie could see its immature leaves on every twig.

The tree men jumped into the cabled trucks, started them, and gunned them forward. The cables strained and the motors sang high, but the tree held fast. Its leaves started to tremble, vivid green against the gray sky. One truck reared gradually like a horse on its back wheels, and another moved slowly sideways, leaving black scars of mud in the light cover of grass. The men killed their engines, nonchalant about it all. One of them lit a cigarette while others cut deeper into the base of the tree.

From the porch she heard Theresa calling, "You want me to lock the door behind me?" She was standing in the doorway, readjusting her belt.

"No, leave it." Allie headed toward her cousin.

"You ready? It's almost twenty till."

"No," said Allie slowly. "I'm not going to school today."

"Really? You feel bad?"

"No."

"Oh, you're *skipping!*" Theresa bit her lower lip, and her eyes moved doubtfully to the direction the bus would come from. "Well—" Allie knew she was wondering whether loyalty demanded that she too skip school. She was thinking of the eleventh-grade boy who had begun to stand around in the halls with her.

"That's okay. You go on." The grinding saws started again, blotting out any chance for normal talking.

Theresa winced and then shouted. "Where are you going to go? What if they ask where you are? What if your parents see you?"

"I don't know," said Allie, not even trying to be heard.

Theresa read her lips. She was still dismayed. The saws quit again. "I'm about to miss the bus," she said. "Oh shoot. Are you sure, Allie?—I've got to go. Look. I'll tell them you don't feel good. If they ask."

"You do that."

"See you, then," said Theresa. "Does this belt really look okay?"

"Yep." When she was halfway down the lane Allie could still see her yellow skirt gleaming against the mud.

This time when the trucks were gunned forward the pecan leaves shook more violently. There was a long, loud sound of splitting fibers. As the tree fell, leaning, leaning, it seemed to enlarge till it covered the sky. The outer branches broke first and cushioned the blow of the long hard trunk into them. The ground started reverberating and the acrid smell of crushed green pecan spread like a cloud, and Allie suddenly bolted. Dazed squirrels were running from the tree in all directions. A couple of times she had to jump sideways to dodge them.

The bus was just picking up speed again as she reached it, breathless. Mr. Chenevert came to a rolling stop and the doors flew open for her. "Yay!" said Theresa, waving her arms in a mock cheer that made the other kids glance sideways at her. "Yay! You made it after all!" Allie, white-faced despite her run, swung into a seat near her cousin. The McCains' famous mudholes nearly shook the bus to bits as it rollicked along toward the main road. One by one, on either side of them, the ordered rows of fruiting trees fell away, telescoping in the big sideview mirrors and vanishing to points with the muddy road behind.

That day at school was especially bloodless. When it was over Allie was glad to drop into a seat on the bus where she could stare out the window without having to think.

The day was still overcast. The fog had lifted only to a height of about ten feet, and everything underneath it had a green pallor and a stark-edged look, with the smell of spring flowers and mud on the wind. The bus inched through the neighborhood behind the trade school and finally pulled onto the highway.

They sped past the old truck stop, turned gay bar; the grouping of new subdivision homes; the lot with the junked school bus and shack; and the old brick commissary that dated from Reconstruction. The bayou was suddenly exposed behind a thicket of smelly weeds and broke away from the road, shining, widening, flat and clear at one point, then hammered with tiny points of light, then ringed like a target with waves where a fish jumped. There was the site of the secessionist governor's home, twice burned; there the line of live oak trees marching off to the eastern horizon where Green Isle began. On their right, now, was the church. Across the road Claire Duval waved and stooped to pick up her paper, with a tan dog frisking around her legs. Allie was sitting on the left side of the bus. She saw her father's Jimmy coming toward them. He must be looking at the crops too hard, for he was veering into their lane. She kept waiting for him to pull back toward his right, and she sat up so she could wave at him when they passed.

But Frank McCain didn't seem to be stopping. The Jimmy stayed firmly over the center line. "What the—" said Mr. Chenevert. "Is this a joke?" said Reggie Taylor. Frank's truck kept heading straight toward them. Someone screamed as the bus driver cursed and turned sharply off the road, bouncing over the shoulder and into the soft ground that sloped toward the bayou. Behind them Frank was pulling over, his brakelights showing red.

"What's the matter?" he called.

Allie jumped off the bus and ran toward him. "What's the matter with *you?*" she said as Frank climbed out of his truck. "You were on our side of the road. You nearly ran us in the bayou."

"I couldn't see," he said. He was crumpling his cap in his hands, crumpling and uncrumpling it. Allie heard the shame in his voice. "I've been having some trouble seeing. I thought I was in the right lane."

"Daddy!" she said in that appalled voice that girls reserve for censuring their fathers. "You'd better get it checked."

Mr. Chenevert joined them. "Hi, Mr. McCain," he said uncertainly.

"Hello."

"Are you all right?"

"Oh, yeah. Are you, though? Your bus—did you get it back on the road?"

It was no more than twenty yards away. "It's just right there," said Allie.

"So it is."

"Well," said Mr. Chenevert heartily, "I'd better get these kids on home."

"Daddy," said Allie one more time. "You might need glasses or something. You'd better get your eyes checked."

14

STORIES OF DEBILITATION are all alike. Afterwards Allie could never stand to hear them. Significantly lowered voices, significantly raised eyebrows, the words "They sent him to Houston...He was eat up with it, bad, real bad"—any of that was enough to make her leave a room abruptly. She hated them as she hated the reams of drugstore paperbacks and tabloids on the subject: *New Cures; How I Fought Cancer with a Positive Attitude, and Won.*

Frank's story started that March day when he had to admit the loss of vision that had been bothering him for a couple of weeks. He went to ophthalmologists and then to the single neurologist Edgewood had just been proud to claim. On Easter, by a weird coincidence, the darkness that had edged into his field of sight seemed to retreat. Late that afternoon he took the wheel of his truck again and under a pretense of checking the cows drove exultantly around the farm, letting the vehicle buck over ditches and slide through mudholes like a tiny mote in the whiskey-colored sunlight that flooded the farm. Even for Fayette the light-riddled imagery of the Easter liturgy was moving that day. But on Tuesday the shadow came back, bigger now like a waxing eclipse. From test results the neurologist reported a brain tumor. That explained the loss of vision and, the doctors said, might even account for sudden quirks in Frank's personality—like his insistence on cutting the pecan grove. The McCains cancelled the work order. No more trees were cut. Three raw stumps at the edge of the grove glared at the house like empty eye sockets. They were still burning the trees that had been cut. Their charred trunks smoldered on a bed of ashes that got deeper every day.

There were more CAT-scans; a biopsy and the pathologist's malignant diagnosis; then surgery, chemotherapy, and a long, long deterioration by fits and starts, while death worked patiently at prying away the gripping and re-gripping fingers of the family from Frank's life.

When Allie heard the diagnosis she thought she was coming apart at the seams, all her insides scattering to the winds and leaving only two eyes fixed on her mother's face, begging her it wasn't true. Already, in the thin superficial staccato of a news bulletin in over the wire, the bitter thought was forming: "I knew he was too good to last. It was all too good to last, we haven't had our quota of bad luck." But that was just intellect, speaking primly. Meanwhile in a vast separate realm of herself her emotions had started to regroup, slowly, into some disastrous shape like a hurricane on the weather map; and like that they were to strike home, in big lashing sledgehammer blows.

During those months it seemed as if time itself metasticized like cancer. Lillian willed a braking. She would avoid looking at clocks. The old year's calendars stayed by her phone well into the spring, and since her days were now filled with tending Frank and taking over a lot of his work, she could avoid her usual immersion in the progress of the seasons through her plants' cycles. She deliberately sought to lose track of time and to live languorously in preoccupation with the body, as she had during each pregnancy. But the growth inside Frank this time ballooned. Hours, days, and months accumulated, replicating wildly, intruding upon her strongly willed ritard and forcing her recognition.

Allie got home from school one day that May and found her parents in the living room, dancing. She stopped short in the doorway and looked on with disapproval. Her father could hardly walk now, his legs were wasted, and here her mother had him unsteadily turning out of step, while she clasped him around the back and lay her head on his shoulder. Allie stared accusingly at her mother's closed eyes and the dreamy little smile on her lips that Allie had once dubbed her "sorority-girl smile"—the one that seemed incongruous with her mother's usual pragmatism. As Frank's shaven head rotated, she saw a grin in his swollen face. But who could tell whether he recognized his daughter in the doorway or was just smiling as a result of some electronic twitch in his brain?

"Mama," she said, "I've got something for you to sign."

"Mmm. Can't it wait, honey?"

"Well. I guess." Her tone of voice made it plain that it really should not.

"What is it?"

"A form for next year. Eleventh-grade classes. You have to okay the electives."

"Oh—already?"

Allie walked out of the room. As she headed outside she heard, over the slam of the screen door and the record still paying, her mother calling: "Okay, I'll sign it. Where is it?"

"I left it on the kitchen counter," muttered Allie. She swore under her breath and stomped back through the new clover, to get to her favorite place to sit down. That summer Frank said he wanted to swim for exercise. He thought he had enough control of one side of his body that this would still be possible. The family, eager to fulfill any wish of his, set about trying to work out the problems of getting him to the Rolands'—now tenants of theirs in the Skinner house. Uncle Gus and Harlan devised a long ramp to get Frank and his wheelchair in the back of Gus's pickup truck. Then everybody else would pile in for the ride down the road. At the Rolands' they stood around awkwardly in swimming clothes, while two of the black kids on the place whom Harlan had enlisted showed up to carry the wheelchair down the wide steps of the pool into the water. Their smooth, young, dark bodies, whose muscles became pronounced and then smooth again with each concentration of effort, contrasted piercingly with the white indistinct flesh that everyone was learning to call Frank. And the odd wheelchair, silver-chrome, not sinister, not ugly, merely puzzling against the lush growth surrounding the pool and the swimming green and clay and blue tones of the horizon—out of place, expressionless, like something in a surreal painting—would roll and settle slightly in the limpid turquoise currents of the shallow end, as Frank pulled himself awkwardly along. Everyone else felt too bad to swim.

As the tumor pushed through the centers of sense and speech, his behavior got less and less predictable. The struggle to talk would distort his face. Then when he finally got something out the words would just be nonsense, disconnected fragments; sometimes he cried out that he hated you, with a venom that would leave even a perfect stranger—a night nurse—shook up for hours: Did everyone harbor hate like that deep in the brain? In the meantime Frank's long, muscled legs were shrinking; his flat stomach and slight biceps and freckled back all turned into an inert, rubbery, hospital-white material. It seemed to have nothing to do with human flesh as you knew it, yet looking at it you couldn't think of any word but that one: flesh. An ugly word.

Oh, the family rallied, and the people on the place rallied. They tried to stagger the inevitable moments when they crumbled, and to stand in for one another in helping the McCains. But how much can people do? Grown men cried when they saw Frank sick. Once, in August, Harlan called Lillian to say that he would like to visit. Lillian was apprehensive but said, "Sure. Come on."

Harlan was a thick stub of a man twenty years older than Frank. Anyone who had seen them talking six months before, contrasting the tall, jocular, energetic younger man with the stolidly gloomy Harlan, would have noticed all the advantages of vigor in Frank, and might have thought they personified the respective worldly power of their races: this white man, dressed in crisp khakis, so animated by the enthusiasm that his many securities licensed; this black man, wearing worn dark clothes, hesitant in assent and a little hunched in posture, as if basically dubious of his own worth.

But that day as Harlan was coming up the steps, Frank wheeled out onto the porch. His head was shaved, of course. His face was swollen from the cortisone, so that one eye was almost shut. He looked like a trick mirror distortion of his former self. Harlan dropped to one knee beside the wheelchair, to be on a level with Frank, and hugged his friend with one arm while shaking his hand with the other, and crying. Frank cried too. Lillian came to the door behind Frank and stood watching from behind the screen. The short, powerfully built black man, in his plain faded overalls, tractor cap in hand, now seemed to be the fuse of life itself beside her husband.

Fayette had finished the spring semester of his freshman year with grades that weren't bad, considering the circumstances. He planned to take off the next year and stay to help out at home. Everyone knew Frank would die that year.

All through that fall Lillian and Fayette met regularly with a lawyer. Allie just shook her head when they asked her to come. It angered her that they would do this. As if he'd already died! She knew Lillian had an obituary already tucked away in her desk, with a blank for the date to be filled in, which galled her the same way. Anyway, the lawyer worked it out with the McCains. After Frank died, his property would be half Lillian's, one-quarter Fayette's, one-quarter Allie's. A trust fund he had set up for the children's college expenses would continue. Meanwhile, Green Isle Trust would become a corporation. Lillian would take a seat on its board. That seat, and one for a farm loan officer they had known for years, and one for an ag science teacher at the local branch of LSU, were permanent appointments; the other four would be elected by the owner-shareholders—that is, Harlan and Corey Willis; Wallace and Bessie Mae Taylor; Claire Duval; the Reverend Johnnie Dikes; Alice "Sug" White; Clarence and Dottie Mathews; Josiah Thomas; Simon and Bernice Johnson; William and Neeley Sandifer; Benjamin "Hoodoo" Mathews; Johnnie and Velvet Taylor; Karo and LaShonda Willis; Almira and "Uncle Boy" Hebert; Ajax Sampson; Lelia Sampson Thomas; and their children.

15

ALLIE HEADED SOUTH out of town on the new Baton Rouge Highway and made the turn off it on two wheels, almost. These days, with Fayette taking time off from school, she and he were always arguing over the use of the Jimmy. Today she had won. When she drove it she pulled her long hair back into a rope and knotted it loosely. People shook their heads as they watched her go by, mastering the stiff, stubborn, noisy gears with a deft arm, as if there were nothing to it. She was the only girl in high school with a truck.

This was one of those times when everyone was saying Frank was sinking fast. Over the past few months there had been so many such lapses, when Allie had stayed home from school, ignored chores, friends, and projects, and practically laid out her clothes for the funeral, that after the last time her mother had said she would rather they continued as much as possible in the normal routine. That would be best. No one knew exactly how much warning they would have when Frank's death came. But for the past two nights her mother had slept at the hospital. Now Allie needed to get home to feed the cows, horses, and dogs, check for new calves or ailing cows before dark, clean up, and drive back downtown to the hospital to give her mother and brother some relief.

Surprisingly, Lillian's car was home, but the house was dark and musty. The day's mail was spilled across the kitchen counter. The disorder and closed-up feeling of the house seemed in keeping with the general chaos of things. Allie felt the edge of tension in her stomach that had been there off and on for eleven months now. Fayette suddenly appeared in the kitchen door, startling her.

"Hey! I didn't think you'd be here."

"I've been waiting for you. Where've you been?"

"School, stooge. Some of us still have it. Is Mama here too?"

"Yeah, she's taking a nap. I need to go check the cows."

"All right. I'll go with you. Let me get something to eat. How's Daddy doing?"

"About the same."

"All this food is old. Jesus. Look at this banana. It's almost fossilized. Really."

"Yeah, when're you going to the grocery? Look, I'm going to saddle the horses. I'll meet you at the gate to the fescue pasture."

"I'll be there in a minute."

She was anxious to leave the house and its reminders, the discord told by the unevenly drawn blinds and smell of neglected food. She changed just her shoes and ran outside in time to help Fayette saddle the horses quickly. They tightened the cinches in sharp tugs and mounted, like cowboys, without a pause—wheeling the horses around and down the fenceline to the back gate, which was the easiest to open without dismounting. They went at a fast walk for a few minutes until reaching the flat, hard-packed loam that made a sort of lane down the fenceline. Far ahead of them were clusters of cottonwood trees by the gulches, and second-growth woods they needed to comb.

"Got the notebook? A rope? The ear-tagger?"

"Yes, yes, yes."

"Then let's go." With a tightening of the knees, a kiss uttered close to the horses' ears, they took off. The horses' bodies flattened. Their upper legs seemed to fly out, poised in one extended lunge. Below the knees they were a blur of scrambling hooves. Slowly Allie's mare gained ground with Fayette's. Both riders leaned forward, parallel to the horses' necks. If they glanced down the earth came closer, sucked up and under each animal as if by a vacuum. The sun dropped and threw lengthening shadows before them.

The jolting, the pommeled dust and noise, the cold and smells of sweet horse sweat and leather and the jumbled scenery skidding by suited Allie now as any more sedate and cushioned environment could not. Maybe she would just let go—turn loose the reins. The sound from a slow-motion scream would trail behind her in the wind. She would fall backward, rolling spine to spine with the horse, her fingers grazing its smooth coat. Fetus-like she would curl as she tumbled over the lashing hooves behind, and laughter would shake out of her as she hit the ground.

Meanwhile the horses rushed on. Allie readjusted her grip on the reins and despite herself squeezed her thighs a little more tightly to the saddle. She did not really want to lose control. At most she craved the sensation of having come close.

In a hospital room several stories over the river and downtown Edgewood, Frank McCain gained consciousness. His eyes started open and his body began to jerk. The nurse at his side reached around him with arms pale as buttermilk, flaccid and liver-spotted with age, and clasped him gently. For a minute he was still, his swollen, distorted head rocking against her white-polyester-clad breast. She stroked the nubby hairs around his scar. Her big knuckled fingers were spread wide, as if to maximize their points of contact, as they patted and stroked him.

"There, Frank," she said. "There, now."

Others said of her, "She is so good with the dying." "She has a real gift," they said. With newborns she was clumsy and with minimum-risk patients irritable; to doctors and younger nurses she seemed dour, slightly stupid. But comfort flowed through her fingers to the dying.

A soreness settled in her lower back, the bedrail was pushing into her belly, and she ignored both. Frank McCain gasped and shuddered. Though he was wasted now, he had been big. The throes were powerful, more than the nurse's embrace could contain. The bedsheets writhed to the floor. The nurse's eyes were wet behind her slightly greasy, silver-rimmed glasses. They took in the signals on the monitors surrounding the bed—inept mechanical angels!—and went back to the more instructive struggle on Frank's face. She cradled the patient in her loose hug for twelve minutes, thirteen, fourteen, sometimes thinking of her own son and husband, sometimes not thinking at all, sometimes thinking clinically about the vital signs, and sometimes about the family and friends of this patient, whose faces she had come to know.

"Frank," she said in a minute, as the needles on the gauges dipped, his arm lashed out, and his eyes widened even farther, "turn loose, and go to God." She kept him firmly in her embrace.

He closed his eyes, relaxed, and died. Lillian was called at five-forty. She went to meet her children at the barn. They were coming through the aluminum gate when they caught sight of her. Fayette screeched the bolt back into place without comment, but Allie said, "She's got some news" and did not even wonder at her own certainty. They headed straight back to the small figure leaning against a fencepost. Their mother's colored shirt stood out against a background of yellowish scrub growth and gray outbuildings, which suddenly looked random in arrangement, and strange, with a washed-out pink sky behind them bleeding all intensity from the scene. The horses, not knowing dread, tried to run, and tossed their heads against the tight reins and snorted when Fayette and Allie kept them sternly held back to a walk.

16

IT MUST BE A SIN to picture the northwest pasture and think bitterly, "Heaven couldn't be as beautiful as this farm." Not only was it a sin, it was corny and sentimental and did not bear repeating to her brother; but it was what Allie was thinking the whole time they told her that her dad would reap in joy, bringing his sheaves with him.

Nothing they could tell her about the harvest reaped by the dead could match the one she knew about, which was on flatbed trailers along the roadsides now, the second picking of cotton white as sugar, as a cloud in July. Her father had loved the fruits of this life, here. He had not asked for transport somewhere else, with other types of bounty. Why should the church talk up his death as such a boon?

The funeral was being held in the small unvarnished Methodist church that had been Allie's great-great-grandfather's and grandfather's ministerial appointments, seventy years apart. Besides Lillian, Fayette, and Allie, the family who was there included Frank's mother and sister and Lillian's mother and brothers and all the in-laws and distant cousins. Friends who came varied from local farmers and farm suppliers to the entire Biracial Committee on which Frank had served; from a fundamentalist missionary to local Indians who had been in Edgewood and known Frank only ten months, to fishermen and executives he had rubbed shoulders with since boyhood; from nuns and academics to artists to a Vietnamese family whose three children had wound up playing in the symphony at Frank's instigation. Some of these had tanned, work-gnarled hands and some the smooth pale hands of administrators and managers. Some were grandmothers with laps calling for babies and some were restless young men. Most were white and many were black. All wore the same expression—troubled, grieved, and somber. Who had thrown the dice that planted a tumor in Frank McCain's brain, struck him and left them all still alive?

The weather was mild, for December, it was ten o'clock in the morning, and the church was full of a benign sunlight, lain gently over the heads and shoulders of the bowed people as if God felt sorry for them. The four square windows on either side of the church were open to cool breezes that came in smelling of cedar and wafted through the church.

The minister was new to the McCains, for they were still members of First Methodist, and the service was being held here because of the family ties to this place. Their own pastor was only assisting today. Fayette, who scorned religion, conceived an instant dislike for the minister of the small church. He was thirtyish, pale, and anxious, the type who kept his hair short in the front to appeal to conservatives and long in the back to appeal to "the young people." Fayette sensed his weakness at once. Ask, he told the bereaved crowd, and it would be given to them; knock, and a door would open. " 'Which one of you fathers, if your child asks for a fish, will give a serpent instead? Or if he asks for an egg, will give a scorpion? If you then who are evil know how to give good gifts to your children, how much more will the heavenly Father care for you'—"

Fayette spun a running parody in his mind. "Which one of you gods, if your manufacturer asks for life, will give cancer? If he asks for mercy gives a malignant tumor? Eat this prayer then, nongod—" Despite the pleasure he was trying to take in his cleverness tears rose behind his eyes and he resisted them angrily as well.

On the pew behind him, Harlan Willis's wife Corey unsnapped the big patent-leather purse on her lap and took out a handkerchief. She nudged it over Fayette's shoulder and when he glanced back at her, made a slight gesture with it toward Allie. His sister looked composed enough to him. But he shrugged and gave it to her anyway, and when she took it the tears started running down her cheeks. In the pew behind, Corey settled back with a troubled face. Fayette suddenly found it easier to be stoic himself.

Allie was in a maze of grief, and the latest minotaur she had run into was self-pity. It was real, not contrived, but it also served for the moment as protection, for it distracted her from facing the huge crater of loss itself. She contrasted herself with her father and berated herself for falling short of him on every count. In the variety of friends packed into the little church, she recognized the ever wider circles he had cast about him. This was his place, where he had made his resolves and beliefs into a living, whole, coherent thing—like a work of art, but without the frame, the borders; bleeding into the rest of experience at every edge. Heaven would be a poor foil to this place.

What more could she ever attempt that he had not already proven? What was left? She held his ideals, but her strainings toward them seemed to be a tangle of conflicting directions, not one concerted way of life. So this spare, tense crying—tears like water bled out of a cave wall—was for her father and what he could no longer be, and also for herself and what she was not.

Occasionally the minister shot helpless looks at the McCains. He did not know them well, but from local talk and from his dealings with them about the funeral he liked them. He approved their decisions, as far as he could tell: nothing major, but a cumulation of small things, like the father's involvement with losing causes in town; a certain plainness in living; the children's rather pointed independence; the mother's composure. They seemed not just alive, but embroiled in life, urgently, messily so. How could someone of his pallor console people like them? He was a city boy of what Fayette would call touchy-feely sensibilities who, being on the bottom rung of the Conference hierarchy, had to struggle along with a rural circuit charge at first. In shy dreams he thought he would revolutionize these sleepy country churches with the social gospel he had heard about at seminary, but not just yet; first he had to win the people's confidence and, as he told himself, "avoid missteps." Now, for instance, beneath the surface of his mind that was engaged in leading the funeral, beneath his concern for this hard-hit family, flickered the worry: What would his regular congregation think about the presence of so many blacks here today? How bad would the repercussions be?

He was speaking about the kingdom that human hands can strive to build on earth, and how Frank had contributed to it—his sense of justice, his warmth, his equanimity; his "lovely wife and fine children." Then he switched to rhetoric about the heavenly kingdom, where good deeds are rewarded and the dead consoled. Allie quit crying and gazed intently at him, frowning as she concentrated on each image. Fayette fixed the minister with a belligerent stare. Lillian, though her emotions had flagged, felt mentally acute, as if she were observing events in some deep dream. With a tinge of soreness she thought: "The kids'll be critical—but at least he's not trying to tell us it's the Lord's will."

From behind the McCains came a clear voice. "Yes, Lord." They were rattled just for a moment. It had been a while since they had worshipped with blacks, though that happened more often than it used to. After the next period of the eulogy the one voice was joined by others, less tentative but still decorous, polite-sounding, springing up unexpectedly like slender little shoots of growth. "Amen, amen—" "*Oh* Lord!" At first, astonishment showed on the minister's face. Then he quit fretting about how conspicuous the blacks were, possibly figuring that all was lost now anyway, and threw caution to the winds. As he connected scriptural metaphors with bolder and bolder strokes of his own, the interjections kept coming, supporting and lifting his message until all were woven together, billowing in the slight fresh wind like a semaphore of language being waved before the Lord. Allie raised her head and looked around with quick hope. Momentarily everything clicked: this stuff was real, it was everything else that was not. The people shared her sudden feeling of unity—which as soon as it was created threatened to collapse. At that point the minister had the sense to close quickly. He gave a short benediction, the pallbearers came forward, and in a succession that dazed the family the casket, flowers, and six straining men and boys glided out of view. There was no organ, but the church pianist launched into the closing hymn.

Time, like an ever-rolling stream,
Bears all its sons away.
They fly forgotten, as a dream
Dies at the opening day.

In the confusion of sunlight outside weeping friends pressed up against Allie and fell back. She was steered by her uncle's hand toward a shining dark car she had never seen before, whose doors stood open, blackly yawning. "Whose idea was *this?*" she thought, repulsed. Daddy would have laughed at the affectation.

Her passage seemed to part a crowd of mourners. "Darling," said a woman, "your father was a brave man—did so much to tear down these—barriers—"

"Hon, we all 'preciated him: what he done for us: he treated us all like sisters and brothers—"

"A real example."

Then came that other voice, which registered clearly at the time yet did not evoke a full reaction from her till later. A low, distinct male voice, that after a snort of irony said: "Yes: here go all the darkies at Massa's grave, cheering him on to white heaven."

"No," she said simply, halting at once. Her uncle's hand kept firmly pressing the small of her back, making her stumble a little.

On the way home she alternated between shock and a slow, building anger. Even if the implication were true (which it was not), even if it had so much as a grain of truth in it, who could be so callous as to sneer about a dead man at his very funeral?—in the hearing of his daughter? It went beyond a question of propriety. The issue was plain human kindness.

She looked at the small frame houses the car was passing. The porches of some were strewn with toys; one had a basketball goal on it; at least three had winter gardens beside them, and clotheslines with quilts and jeans and underwear flapping. Why, it was Daddy who had created a trust, and quietly deeded these over to the black families who had lived there for generations.—Now Venethia and Jackie Sampson came to the edge of their porch to wave to Allie, still dressed for Frank's funeral in carefully waved hair, patent leather Mary Janes, and petticoats that made their skirts stand out like lampshades.

Behind these doors maybe everyone was mocking the McCains as self-appointed diplomats across the color line, would-be peacemakers who still profited from the old wrongs. The jokes and conversations, working, voting, and school-bus riding she had been taught to feel so good about appeared to Allie in a different light. For from these joint ventures whites and blacks were still returning to home bases of huge discrepancies. Maybe the fake mutuality only made the truth more painful.

The barely undulating pastures were just showing their cover of green winter-grass, and farther away the cattle could be seen moving toward the water trough, necklaces of black dots against the green.—And her father was *gone*. The crater yawned again. She needed to beat a retreat, to make herself numb. After the next few hours she would figure things out: who had said this, and whom she would tell about it: and whether there were any truth to it. Why could she not simply refute it and go on? She had already contradicted the speaker, provided he had heard her (did it matter whether he had heard her?). If deep down she knew the charge was false, why didn't her verbal denial suffice?

17

Of everyone gathered at the house, only the immediate family seemed to be at a loss. Little cousins were running from room to room. Men and boys crowded around to watch football on the TV in the den, keeping the volume turned low out of respect for the dead. In the kitchen women with unfamiliar faces bustled around, wrapping ham in foil and removing pies from Tupperware plates to be returned to mourners on their way out of town.

Allie had lost all sense of time. She felt like a blank outline of herself, accepting everything that was said and done around her long before it would really register. Dimly she was aware that eventually, when everyone left, she would change clothes and get outside to reestablish herself, but now it seemed as if that hour would never come, as if time were a treadmill. In all the hubbub, with the house full of people and the driveway a hive of activity, her mind kept automatically jumping to seek her dad, as a buoy; just as when, knowing the electricity is off, one still reaches absently for the lightswitch. To keep beating down the habit was a constant shock and weariness.

Once someone—later she could not remember who; yet another of the dark-suited, country-voiced McCain relations from north Louisiana who had planted themselves soberly on the living room couch all weekend—asked Fayette what he would do now. To a number of people that question—"What are you going to do now?"—asked after a death still meant, "What is going to happen to *the place*?" and it was properly addressed to the next of kin who was male. Nobody had mentioned it recently. Even in her numb state Allie felt a little spasm of irritation, for hadn't they been managing without Frank, in effect, for a year? She looked at Fayette to see how he would field it.

Everyone else was looking at him too, and he was aware of it. He had jerked his tie loose the minute they came from the graveside, and sweat stood on his face and around his collar. He shook his head as if to clear it, in an energetic nervous mannerism, and then looked directly at the questioner and said, "Oh, I'm gonna run this farm."

Allie would remember later, with irony, that "I."

"By yourselves?" the friend, the relative, whoever it was, asked cautiously. In the plural.

"Yeah." Fayette nodded, sure. Allie noticed he got away without saying "Sir."

"In cattle, son, or in beans too? ..." the friend was saying, and Fayette answered, as coolly as if he had been planning the whole operation for months, "We'll keep the cattle operation and probably lease out for beans to Mr. Roland. I may plant some corn for silage too. We'll see."

"So the three of you'll stay right here."

"Sure," said Fayette, looking at Allie's and his mother's faces. Lillian McCain had been listening since her release from a clutch of departing guests. Her eyes were dry, but reddened around the brown iris, and the skin around the lids had a bruise-like color that sometimes appeared when she was tired. She looked quietly at her son, appraising him. "Us, well, and the rest of the family in town—I mean my uncles are always close by."

"Well, son. I want you to know how much I think of what you're doing. It's what your dad would have wanted. You're a man now, and you can handle what you make up your mind to. But I want you to think of me and Lottie Mae behind you, so you'll call on us whenever you need us, and keep in mind our door's always open ..."

But he had already faded away for Allie, into the background of the other moving guests. Obviously he didn't know the whole picture. Who cared what happened to "the place"? Their own place would probably continue much as it had, till hers and Mama's and Fayette's interest in it lapsed to nothing. And—maybe the old guy didn't know it—the fate of Green Isle had already been turned over to legal sorcery, and for better or worse was out of their hands. What she was wondering was, without Frank, what would happen to *them.*

During the afternoon she slipped outside to get away for a minute. "Look out!" came a sharp cry, and a football bounced against her knee. One of her nephews, Brad, trotted over to get it, smiling apologetically. He did not meet Allie's eyes. Jesus, thought Allie, pouring down a look of offended mourning that was not lost on him.—It's like a party out here.

But her grief was enough removed from her outer, active self not to be really affronted. Those words were merely what bereavement thought it *ought* to think. With no chance now to concentrate on emotions, Allie just kept acting, hoping that when the delayed feelings did arrive her bearing would have been appropriate.

It was no use trying to escape here. The whole crowd of Rabelais cousins was across the driveway, milling in the open space bounded by the garbage cans and woodpile, cedar tree, magnolia, and azalea island. They quit talking when she came up, darting looks of keen, curious sympathy at her and then averting their eyes in embarrassment. For many of them this was as close as death had ever come. They did not have a form of behavior on hand, as their elders did, for how to respond to the event, so they were very sensitive to any cues they were given.

"Hey y'all," said Allie evenly. Only Theresa continued normally with what she had been doing when Allie left the house—walking on her hands—while the children who had been tumbling around her in sloppy imitation now froze. Allie looked up at her cousin's bare feet moving erratically against the background of sky and branches and down at her face bulging with blood. Theresa stopped, oscillating slightly like a needle on a sensitive gauge, and brought her feet down slowly, finishing with a neat roll into a sitting position.

"Hey."

"Hey, Ree."

"How you doing?"

"Oh, I'm doing okay."

"I tried to talk to you in the house but you were always surrounded by about fifty people. Then I went back in your room but there were a bunch of people I don't know even back there. So I figured I'd just come outside and let you find me."

Allie nodded and stared at her cousin for a minute. Theresa's gaze of solicitude had furrowed her face into lines like a basset-hound's. Her dark curls trembled, her blue eyes were wet, but resolute loyalty kept her spine straight and high. Earlier she had "had her cry," as she would say, and now she too was set to take her cue from Allie—either to offer those pats and squeezes of sympathy that her less demonstrative cousin could never quite manage to return; or, if Allie seemed to be striving to set a normal tone, to chatter with her as flippantly as need be. Allie searched out this perfect willingness in Theresa's lifted, anxious face—like that of a retriever waiting to be thrown its lure—and as her faint scorn relaxed into affection, she suddenly felt like letting down. She kicked off her shoes, starting to talk, brushed aside leaves with her stockinged toe, and sank into the thatch-like grass, still talking. "There are lots of people here I don't know either. Coming up to me and telling me I look just like Daddy. Telling me they saw me in diapers years ago. Telling me Daddy was always so proud of me." Under the half-smile her voice caught and she dropped its pitch and pulled back the corners of her mouth to gain control, and ended up sounding more sarcastic than she felt. "One lady grabbed me on my way into the bathroom and goes, 'Alexandra Louise McCain! Do—you—know—who—I—am?' "

Their four-year-old cousin Correen, who had been listening open-mouthed, suddenly gave out a belly laugh. Allie looked at her and smiled. "That's right. And I just stared into her face—she had on a bunch of makeup and these glasses with little rhinestones in the corner—and said, 'No.' I guess I was rude."

"Well, who was she?"

"I don't know. Second cousin once removed or something. I don't know." Allie flopped back and lay with her eyes closed against the sun. "And there's some man up from New Orleans—you may have heard your mother talk about him because she was over here when he called—he knew Daddy at college or in Boston or somewhere, and is teaching at Loyola this semester. He called a month or so ago to talk to Daddy—didn't know he was sick, and we had to go through all that with him. So now he's up for the funeral ..."

"Oh, is that the one in the plaid pants?"

"Um-hm. Keeps poking around in the bookcases and catching me and saying, 'Frank had a great sense of the extended family. Do you feel your extended family is important? How long have you had a TV? I see you read a lot! Do you raise chickens?' Wanted to know if he could have half a grapefruit to eat, because he's on a special diet. We've got more food in the kitchen than I've ever seen, and he comes tapping my shoulder for a grapefruit—"

"That's the one who said I was blooming." Theresa giggled.

"Oh really?" Allie's lips curled. She kept her eyes closed but started to laugh.

"Um-hm. 'And you are—? Miss Theresa Rabelais. I'm so pleased to meet you. And how old are you? Fifteen?—and just blooming.' "

"Oh, Lord."

"He might come trotting by at any minute, going to look for the chickens."

"If he does, just pretend you're a flower."

"Yeah, I'll just b-loom right here," parodied Theresa. "How'd he get to be friends with Uncle Frank?"

"I don't know. I think he's writing a book on the South or something."

But Theresa's attention had waived. "You *spot* her, Katie!" she called sharply. Katie and Chevon, nine-year-old twin daughters of Uncle Jules, looked up guiltily, Chevon from a tumbled heap on the grass. Near them stood Ben, aged seven, the son of Uncle Gus and Aunt Mary Sue.

"I can't do it," said Chevon, superfluously.

"Sure you can't do it, without a spotter. I never would have learned it if somebody hadn't spotted me while I practiced. Do it like I showed you."

"Theresa Renee Rabelais!" cried Katie. *"Please!* I'm asking you nicely! I said *please* come do it again!" The little ones had gotten hold again. They figured that since Allie was with them now and was not crying as so many of the grownups had been, things were all right: death did not change all things, after all. Inside they were storing away images of this disturbing day for later reference, but for now they were impatient, even a little frantic, for proof that things were normal.

"Hush. Me and Allie are trying to talk."

"Oh, go on and do it for them and come right back," said Allie. "I don't mind."

Theresa wanted to yield. "You sure—?"

"Sure." Allie would not mind being a spectator for a minute, passive and diverted. Maybe that was why the men in the house kept the television on.

Theresa went to the space cleared of twigs and leaves where the twins had been playing. She pushed her sleeves back to her elbows and pulled her body up straight, focusing on some point in the horizon. Even barefoot, in washed-white jeans and a baggy sweatshirt, her body pronounced a coiled trained strength. The little cousins fell silent, even Correen, who had been absorbed in talking to herself while sorting and re-sorting some pecans she had found.

Theresa released into motion, springing backwards, landing on flexed hands, and flipping back a few more feet to a standing position. For a second longer she continued to focus on that nonexistent point, her arms lifted overhead. Then she dropped them, sauntered back to Allie, and dropped with exaggerated casualness into the grass.

"Hey, nice," said Allie. "Nice. That was good."

"Oh, well," said Theresa. "It's fun." She rolled her eyes and pouted self-deprecatingly, but there was satisfaction on her face as she settled back, resting her weight on her hands.

"Sure, fun, because you're good at it."

"Well."

"Did y'all change clothes here? You had jeans with you in the car?"

"No, we went by the house to change. Mama figured we were likely to be out here most of the day."

"She didn't want—want—want me messing up my dress and stockings!" said Correen.

The crowing of a baby interrupted them, and glancing up they saw their cousin Rory speeding toward them on fat toddler legs. In a departure from his usual shyness he made straight for Allie and plunged into her lap. Another first cousin, Stovall, was walking up behind the baby.

"Heyyyy!" The baby pressed sticky cheeks and lips into Allie's face but immediately squirmed around to lunge for Theresa. "Hang on, kid. What's your hurry?" To Stovall Allie said, "Did you tell him to come to me?"

"Nope. He wouldn't a done it if I told him to."

"That's right," said Theresa. "He's spoiled, aren't you, Boo?"

"Y'all ought to fix that swang over yonder," Stovall told Allie. "I set him up on the seat, but the board's rotted through and a little bit more of it come off while Rory was setting on it."

Allie shrugged. "That hasn't exactly been tops on my list of things to do." Her sarcasm rolled right off Stovall. Without a signal between them Allie and Theresa started to giggle. Then Rory clambered off his cousin's lap. "There he goes!"

"Aunt Mary Sue says when he gets like this you just have to wind him up and let him go."

"As long as he stays out of the driveway."

Stovall settled down beside the girls. He started pontificating about the funeral service. "Naw," he was saying, "in the Methodist church you don't kneel and you don't genuflect. But if you're Catholic and you go to a Methodist church you can genuflect if you want to; only they don't have kneelers to rest your knees on. And you have church, and we have Mass, and we have Holy Communion."

"We have Holy Communion too, only not as often as y'all," growled Allie, her eyes on Theresa.

"How 'bout niggers? Do they have Holy Communion?"

"*Sto*-vall!" This came from Theresa (and was for Allie's benefit). "Of course they do, if they're Christian. They have it just like other Methodists or Baptists or whatever they are. What'd you think they do?"

He grinned. "Eat each other, I reckon, like they do over in

Africa."

"What do you think Communion is?" said Allie, and lay back with the sun on her face and eyelids.

But Stovall just stared at her. Then he and Theresa went off into a patter of talk about how Ree had nearly added an extra "and ever" to the end of the Lord's Prayer; they almost had to sit by some niggers but Stovall's mama said, not at my own brother-in-law's funeral; one of the ones there was Fowles High School's junior varsity quarterback, whose locker was next to that of the boy Theresa had a crush on, who had said to her on Friday that his father had a ski boat and maybe they could ski sometime in the spring.

Mentally, Allie withdrew. Or rather, she felt distance settling in inexorably: like being at the ophthalmologist's with a series of progressively farsighted lenses being dropped between her eyes and the scene before her, so that with each click as a distancing glass fell into its groove, her surroundings fell away. She watched her cousins without listening to them any more. In fifteen years they would be having the same kind of conversation at Edgewood cocktail parties, frighteningly like their parents'. Instead of letter jackets and dances the talk would be of promotions and divorces. Its depth would not have changed. Theresa would be entrenched in subdivision life, one of the poolside Junior Leaguers whose expressions were all a tissue of local formulae: "Her mother was a So-and-so...He was a Kappa Sig from Tulane, married a Godchaux—as in sugar, not the department store ..."

How snide you are, she thought, bringing herself up short a little guiltily. Lillian sometimes remarked that Allie was an anti-snob snob, and when she did Allie's eyes would widen in mock horror as she said, "And where do you suppose I got that?"

She had to admit that Theresa's virtues, grit and steadfastness and the kind of pride that made her loyalties and enthusiasms unsquelchable, went deeper than a quick look would suggest. As a woman Theresa would be able to give others the support that Allie, despite her snideness, was relying on now. Her whole life she would maintain that toughness under a cover of allure, and it would serve her and her family and friends and colleagues—if she went that route—well. If she disappointed those who grew close to her it would be by the accretion of pettiness and tiny, brightly voiced deceptions, not by any major lapse during a crisis.

Maybe I'm jealous, thought Allie, of the ways she is that I'll never be, despite my cynicism and what I like to think is my real preference for my own outlook. Perhaps she envied Theresa's sailing into high school with such ease: "having *fun*," as she would declare when one of the uncles asked her how it was going, "I'm just having the time of my life!" Allie could never say the same. By and large high school irritated her. Or maybe she was jealous because she sensed an ebbing, again, not in Theresa's loyalty to her, but in her own influence upon her cousin, now that so many other friends had come into Theresa's life. Every time they spoke on the phone now there was background noise like a gaggle of prime-time teenagers. In Allie's own room the blue twilight would be coming in, seeping around the window edges, ricocheting softly off the big mirror and back into her own eyes, and muffling the clatter of supper being fixed in the other end of the house, as if to underscore new silences closer by. But from Theresa's house her cousin's voice would race down the line, the same old voice as always, only higher-pitched, a little startled, laughing a fake adult laugh, interrupting itself as if with stifled pokes and giggles: "God! Hush. So Allie—I'm sorry, Allie—so how is it all?"—then to someone else, scuffling—"(It's my *cousin.)* How's it going?"

We couldn't be a whole lot more different, Allie thought drily. Theresa was all dark curls and bounce and full curves, and Allie had hair like Spanish moss and was built like a rod. Theresa was a cheerleader whom Allie watched, appalled, from the sidelines. Allie wavered in tides of overawareness, art, design, literature, philosophy, in which the little cosmos that was high school seemed either embarrassingly trivial or painfully, obliquely emblematic, while Theresa cheerfully took things at face value. Allie could never decide whether Theresa sensed complexity and ambiguity but had some innate defensive system, like radar, that allowed her to sheer firmly away from them, or simply never doubted the world's coherence in the first place. Even Theresa's gymnastics were clean, set, and defined, cut-and-dried, like her very body, like her priorities. In fact, at the moment everyone but Allie seemed to be agents, creators, in charge of themselves. Even Fayette—"I'm going to run this farm." "And what are *you* going to do?" she asked herself, mimicking a dialogue that had not taken place, between some polite stranger and herself. "Oh, *me?* I take pictures."

Yes, that was it. She remembered now. This place would shrink to an appropriate size behind her. She would travel the globe seducing exotic and fascinating men. She would move light, with her camera on one shoulder, her lenses and film and batteries and a few understated clothes in a bag on the other. Palaces, guerilla camps, hostels, studios, concert halls, and laboratories would open for her like the door to Ali Baba's cave. She would enter, capture the time that passed within, and exit again, bearing the idiosyncratic light rays in her camera as in a sacred ark but leaving behind no imprint of herself. Even the suffering she now knew would be reduced to a mere facet of her mystique. A critic's line: "Her father died when she was sixteen—a sensitive, active man, the one who had planted in her the seeds of her unique social vision ..." For her photographs would not be just for news. They would not end up in last year's *Time* and *Newsweek*, tattered and pitiful in dentists' panelled offices. They would be timeless, the way she had it planned, documentary, sure, historical, but enduring, like Lange's or Hine's or Bourke-White's—and she would simply settle for nothing less.

"Allie?" Correen was squatting beside her anxiously.

"Hunh?"

"You see that squirrel? Way up there."

"Yeah."

"I'm leaving him something. Some pecans, right here. Because I think his father died. And when somebody dies we don't see them any more, and we do nice things for their children; my mother said. I'm leaving him these pecans, *right here*."

Allie laughed shortly. "Oh—" The child was breathless, peering with utter candor into her face. Correen was a special favorite of Allie's—they had the same birthday—and the little girl came near idolizing her in turn. Allie said, "Okay, baby. You do that."

Theresa and Stovall had broken off and were watching.

"Kids are pretty funny," said Stovall.

"Yep."

"Yep. Hey Allie, your mother's calling you."

She slipped on her shoes and jumped up. Her mother was at the edge of the driveway, waving. The football spiralled in front of her in another wobbly pass, and Brad came scrambling for it again with his smile of apology.

"Mémé's been looking for you!" her mother called. "And Ford and Louise are leaving; they want to say goodbye."

"Okay, okay." To the kids Allie said, "Bye y'all. I've got to go."

"Goodbye," said the little ones.

"Who're Ford and Louise?" said Theresa.

"Beats me."

"Bye.—Call me."

They watched her heading for the door, her figure slim and its curves elusive in straight black knit, catching the football expertly and returning a toss-out to Brad as she went.

Correen gazed as if the goddess were going back into the clouds. She caught her breath. "Bye, Allie," she whispered belatedly.

18

SEVERAL OF THE guests were still lingering when Fayette came to find Allie, his boots pounding on the floor, buttoning up a wool jacket, and said, "Come on. Let's go check the cows before it gets completely dark."

Allie changed clothes fast behind her closet door and was ready to go almost before he finished talking. Together they walked through the back yard and past the worn gray gate on a wheel and down the muddy fencerow, past the corral, without speaking. They walked a couple of feet apart with their hands in their pockets. The cold air and the quiet felt good after the close, noisy house. Streaks of color still lay above the western treeline.

"I guess we need the big flashlight," said Fayette. Allie could hear him scrabbling for it in the big wooden tool chest inside the barn. He swore. "It's pitch dark in here. I can't see a thing." Allie shivered a little, waiting outside, shifting from foot to foot. "You know, it'd be nice to have a light inside. Is that too much to ask?"

"Daddy was always saying he was gonna hook up those wires," said Allie. Their voices sounded plain and bald, in the spaces of the dark.

"Yeah—next week." Suddenly they both laughed, although their hurt was raw, it was a little too soon to laugh. "Goddamn Daddy," said Fayette affectionately, appearing with the big rusty flashlight. "Come on. Let's go."

They headed toward the northeast pasture where the cows were. It was their biggest pasture, partly wooded. In winter when the cows were calving they tried to comb it every day to make sure no cow was in trouble. Sometimes they took the horses; less often they went on foot. They had missed the errand these last few days.

"Have you got the ear-tagger?" said Allie.

"No, we can do that later, if there are any new ones."

The aluminum gate burned cold to their touch. "It's supposed to freeze tonight."

"Bullshit."

"It is. I listened to Calvin Ray."

"Since when has Calvin Ray predicted anything right?"

"If you don't cut off the water, I will. I don't want to be fixing busted pipes for the next week."

"You wouldn't be fixing them anyway, and you know it—I would."

Their low voices and footsteps rang out in the air, a tentative feeler of sound issuing forth, by its very thinness showing the size of the bowed, frozen earth underfoot, the arched night above. After the day's ceremonies and emotion, it was a relief to argue trivially with each other. Neither of them paid much attention to the actual content of their words; stronger than the contention was a bond of relief and peace between them, which the open farm smells and cold night in each other's company gave. Within the big silence their voices staked out a common, as the weak field of the flashlight, sliding and splashing over the rough pasture, paved a way in the dark.

"There they are," said Fayette. He played the light slowly over the sleek, huddled forms of the cattle. Their eyes shone green when the beam picked them up.

"Can't count them in the dark."

"We can try," said Fayette.

"There's that little whiteface I like."

"I'm looking for number forty-seven. She's due any day, and last year she had trouble."

"I think she's carrying twins," said Allie. "She's big as a house."

Together they moved slowly around the bedded herd.

"Let's just check the edge of the woods, where all those palmettos are—okay?"

The light splayed weakly into the forest dark.

"Hey, where're you going?" said Fayette.

"I have a sense where she is—" His sister's voice faded as she ducked under moss, behind a fallen tree, disappearing into the brush. He followed, making more noise. But he did not question Allie. She knew these woods and maybe even the animals better than he. All those hours he had spent on the tractor, bushhogging, plowing, planting, and fertilizing, she had spent playing nearby, exploring the woods alone or with a dog—those years she was too young to drive the tractor.

"Yeah, here she is," came Allie's voice. Fayette pushed through one last tangle of smilax and found them. The cow was breathing hoarsely. The sister and brother squatted down near her hind end. Fayette shone the light to check the progress of the delivery. The calf was already emerging, but backwards, hooves first.

Fayette swore. Only he could give four-letter words such reverence, thought Allie. He had always forbidden her to use them.

"I wonder how long she's been down."

"I don't know. Fayette, see—can you tell if the calf's dead?"

"I can't tell yet. There's not enough of it out."

"Did you bring a glove?"

"No," he said with irritation. "Did you?"

"No."

They were quiet for a while. Fayette lit a cigarette. The cow's breaths tore out jaggedly.

"She's pushing, but the calf hasn't budged," said Allie, after leaning forward for a closer squint. "What do you want to do?"

"Let's wait a while longer," said Fayette. "These things right themselves a lot of times, by nature." He moved to a tree a few feet away where a lower branch had broken and draped to the ground, and made a sort of railing they could lean against.

Allie joined him. "That's what Daddy always said."

And the fact of their father's death loomed up again, big as the bowl of darkness in which they huddled.

"The thing is—" said Allie suddenly, and too loudly, as if they had been in the middle of a conversation about it, "the thing is, I guess some people would say now he's just going to decay and turn into compost and dirt, and that's all."

"Sure," said Fayette. "Because that's the truth."

"I don't believe it," said Allie.

"Why? Why are you so sure there's more? Because you need to believe that. You can't face it any other way."

How, then? What *would* let her know that he was more than the dead earth underfoot, more than the death surrounding her in images as far back as her memory reached: cows bloated from drowning in the borrow pit; birds stilled from collision with the living-room window; dogs, armadillos, cats crushed on the highway, deer trussed on top of cars in the fall; soldiers dead in pictures on the news; Bourke-White's concentration camp series; the inert arm hanging off a stretcher that she had spotted once when they passed a fatal wreck on the way to Baton Rouge? She flicked through these images and posed her father against them, but could not consign him over to them. She was silhouetted against the faintest light in the tangle of dead vine and smilax in the thicket. Fayette saw the outline of her shoulders start to shake, and he heard her snuffling, a thin glaze of sound over the racked breathing of the cow.

"Hey, hey, it's all right," he said. "It'll be okay." He moved over to pat her shoulder roughly. Her face rubbed against his denim jacket. "He'll join the biological cycles now. The energy that was his body will be transformed into the energy of living plants and eventually other animals."

"Is that supposed to comfort me?" Her sarcasm was automatic—a response she had learned from him. What scared her was how plausible his version sounded. She closed her eyes briefly and saw loam, and wood, and bizarre little animated worms like those in a Disney cartoon. "Oh, Christ," she said.

Now with his hands back in his pockets, her brother turned back to the cow. Rippling clouds passed over the low moon and cleared it. Allie sniffed deeply.

"I guess what I meant," he said kindly, offhandedly, as he tried to peer under the cow's tail, "is: what have you got to offer as a theory instead?"

"Instead of what?"

"Instead of what *I* said—"

"Oh, cycle, decomposition, 'we are the grass' and all that." Allie thought a minute, then snorted. "Heaven, I guess. An all-white heaven!"

"What?"

"You didn't hear Scrip today? Right when we got outside the church?"

"No. I didn't even see Scrip."

"Well, he was there. I'm sure it was him." She told Fayette about the comment she had heard. He became absolutely still, down to the fingers holding the cigarette, jutting toward her. When she finished he blew out smoke and said, "That bastard!"

"I thought Scrip was in Texas, drying out."

"Yeah, but he's back now. I thought I told you Miss Lelia said he was back."

Scrip—he was never called by his real name, Earl—was a neighborhood legend. In his youth he had been a brilliant student and a promising athlete too; people said he could recite all of Martin Luther King's speeches by heart. Something had happened—whether it was when King or Malcolm X was murdered or when Scrip dropped out of college or failed to make the pros, Allie did not know—and now he was a creature of terror, invoked up and down their road to scare children into behaving: "You hush! I hear Scrip now, creeping up through the shrubs!" He would now be about twenty-eight, a tall burly man who, the last few times he was home, moved slowly as if he were in a stupor of drugs or alcohol. His mother, Miss Lelia, worked cheerfully and meticulously as a dairy hand for Green Isle and attended True Vine Missionary Baptist Church twice a week, where people occasionally lifted prayers for her troubles. Scrip sometimes showed up at the dairy drunk and with his pants falling down—so the stories went—threatening and demanding money from his mother. Once he ripped a phone out of the wall and threw it at her. He had a sister who taught school in Chicago.

"The son of a bitch," said Fayette. But he was still motionless, and his head drooped a little.

Allie shrugged.

Their father's practice of waiting for the natural course to play out was proving to be best in this case. They had waited out the calf's passage for an hour now. In five or six more minutes it was over. The calf lay in a bundle on the ground, with the membrane around it glistening in the moonlight, the color of a snail's trail. The cow got to her feet, the placenta hanging in ropes behind. She turned and began to lick the calf, her big sandpaper tongue pulling membrane away from its delicate nostrils and unprinted eyes. By instinct she unwrapped its senses; she revealed the creature; she exposed it. The woods were empty of sound except for the rasping, slow licks. Then the brother and sister could hear, beneath that, the steady lower breathing of a mass of animals. The other cattle had drawn near. They would come no closer to the newborn calf than this, but they were there. You could feel them. A welcoming committee.

19

SCRIP THOMAS lay in sleep that was like a heavy undertow. Three things kept pulling him toward consciousness, sun and noise and the knowledge of something crucial he had to face, but the cords were light and just as he nearly surfaced they would snap, and a load of sleep would roll him under again. Whatever this thing was he had promised himself to think about today, he had the feeling it was complex and would require sobriety to meet, and he dreaded it. Miranda got up at six-fifteen. For an hour Scrip dodged as her sounds, like a net dragging a river, sought to bring his body up from sleep: drawers opening, the screech of water pipes, and the light tap of cosmetics and brushes being set on the dresser, then the high, clean-sounding questions of the little boy being hurried through his cereal, then Miranda's heels and the final firm slam of the door. Scrip heard the house grow very still. There was only a faint murmur of voices from the living room; she had left the television on. Then the sunlight coming in through Venetian blinds got unpleasantly hot. Scrip tossed in the sheets. There was some reason, today, that he had to summon himself, some point to stirring: what was it? He dropped back to sleep. The patch of hot light mounted the long lump of his body, dropped, and traveled on across the bed. At eleven-twenty he was finally jolted completely awake by a loud screech from a winner on a game show. He got up, relieved himself, found a beer in Miranda's fridge, and held it unopened as he sat heavily on her couch, with only his gym shorts on, trying hard to remember what it was that made this morning different, why this day should matter.

A two-day-old newspaper Miranda had spread by the door where a leak always collected reminded him. "Civic Leader Dies," said the headline of an article on the front page. Frank McCain's picture looked at Scrip, jaunty and tousled and smiling like a Kennedy but with something in the eyes and brow self-doubting, a little puzzled, very unlike a Kennedy or for that matter most other whites in public images.

"Sorry, civic leader," mumbled Scrip, but now the thought was knocking more insistently than ever at his mind, scratching at the layers of film and fuzz that many binges of alcohol had cemented over the Wonder Boy's intellect ("First Area Negro to Become Merit Finalist," "Local Negro Wins Scholarship," "Negro Named Valedictorian at Edgewood High").

He had come in last night around nine, unannounced as usual. Miranda had pulled open the door stiffly and cautiously as she always did, trying to convince herself that it would not be he. Then she froze for that split-split-second, and told him hello in a voice that tried to be dry and denouncing, but had a quaver behind it, low and molten like the tremor before a cry or a laugh. As always he intended to swagger inside, but couldn't manage it until a minute or so had passed when he felt glued, bug-eyed as an infant, to her gaze. He had trouble surrendering to the helplessness she caused him. Tenderness wasn't within the realm of his control or his idea of manliness, and when it welled up he always had the sensation of being reduced to utter babyhood. The feeling humiliated him later, when he thought about it, and he always acted doubly arrogant after it occurred.

Miranda gathered her wits first, pushed open the screen door, and said, "Come on, then." He edged in one shoulder at a time, still looking uncertain and wild-eyed. All at once he dropped the paper sack in his hands and, quick as a big cat pouncing, kissed her. Would she ever be prepared for the rush of his kisses? All the nights he was gone—and there were many of them—for the few minutes after supper and chores and meeting Malcolm's demands for stories, hugs, cool pillows, and water and before her dunking in the oblivion of sleep, she would lie in the dark and go over Scrip's embraces in her mind. She recalled his scent and the pattern of his beard and the particular grip of his arms and thighs, and this bolt of speed whenever he first approached her as well. She concentrated so hard on the physical details that it seemed the vacant air around her would have to split open with her effort, and he would materialize. But somehow even rehearsing and expecting it each time was a far cry from having it really happen.

Before they had finished the kiss last night they heard the pad of the boy's feet in the kitchen doorway, and a disgruntled whimper. Scrip let go Miranda and said, "Hey there. Hey there, Malcolm, come see your papa. I brought you something." But Malcolm shrank against the doorframe.

"What, you still sucking your thumb? Don't you want to see what I brought you?" Scrip pulled a toy machine gun out of his paper sack.

"You know I don't want him playing with guns," said Miranda, cross but still breathless, so that her disarray diluted the reproach.

"All little boys play with guns," stated Scrip. "Here, son."

Malcolm came and took the toy and refused to give it up when Miranda sent him back to bed the next minute. He went to his pallet in the living room and lay looking up at his mother and his strange daddy, with one arm curled around the plastic M-67. By the time they closed the door, he was asleep. "He look just like a little revolutionary laying there," said Scrip cheerfully, as he wrapped his arms around Miranda again, from behind this time, nuzzling his cheek into her ear.

"That's what he learn from his daddy," she said, still in a tone of reproof. But she was wilting, melting inside, shedding deliciously layer by layer the habits of prudence and denial by which she kept her and Malcolm's lives afloat, forgetting the long conversations with her girlfriends over coffee in which she promised to give up Scrip for her own good; and they went quickly to the bedroom.

Twenty minutes later they had fallen into that space where nothing crushes or smothers or chafes. It was as if all matter, their bodies and the darkness and the walls and the space beyond, exerted itself equally on what surrounded it, making a perfect equilibrium, and cancelling everything out but one live little wire of consciousness. And Scrip was saying to Miranda, "I can get a job. This time. I've quit drinking. I haven't had a drink in two months, Miranda. I'll get a daytime job if I can so I can be here nights with you and Malcolm. I wouldn'a come back this time if I didn't know I could be good for you—"

"Shh, shh," went Miranda's lips into the hollow of his neck and shoulder.

"Why shouldn't anyone hire me?" Scrip went on. "I got *one* diploma—" and he was asleep.

For the first few years of his life Scrip had lived in a world as seamless and harmonious as an egg. As the baby of the first couple in living memory who were both Green Isle children themselves, and the first grandchild on each side of his family, he was destined to be well loved. Before he was even born an identity was created for him, solid as the pine cradle also made for him in advance by his Uncle Boy—and like the cradle, all he had to do to inhabit it was to slide from between his mother's legs and through the circle of waiting, indulgent, related, extended, crowing love, and claim it as his own. He grew up knowing how special he was and assuming that others did too. Despite the cockiness of the expectation, everyone he knew responded favorably to it. His elders, from blacks in the little community to its patrons the Rands, indulged and favored him with constant praise and attention. Since the boy was presumed from the start to be intelligent, everyone talked to him freely and without condescension. In September 1956 he started to the all-black elementary school that all the children on Green Isle went to then, a thirty-minute bus ride from the farm. He was the only first-grader who already knew how to read. It was plain to him he was the smartest one in the class. He was not surprised.

As he grew he learned that his color was supposed to handicap him, but the grim fact did not pierce through his ego—then. There had been no situation in his life so far where he could not shine and win and outstrip. Surely discrimination would be just another obstacle he would sail over. Surely white society would admit him when they learned it was he, Scrip Thomas, swaggering at the door—just as Hudson and Amalie welcomed him with fond tolerance when he dropped by their house on one of his expeditions around the farm, requesting a Band-Aid, a look through Hudson's magnifying glass, or a jar to put a molting crawfish in. From there he could go to his great-aunt's to watch a favorite soap and drink a Dr. Pepper with her; he could play on the smooth cement floor of the shed where the tractors and combines were parked and watch in fascination when they were taken apart for repairs; he could ride behind Josiah or William on horseback to the back of Green Isle, and slip off the saddle and wander in the woods, along the sandbars and big drainage ditches, till the end of the day, when he would make a long trek home. Everything in his small world existed either to charm or be charmed by him. Everyone he knew was a friend. Why would that ever change?

In this Eden Scrip was Adam, a namer. He pestered people till they gave him names for all the trees on the farm, car models he saw on the road, birds, fish in the bayou, wildflowers, snakes, insects, quilt patterns at his aunt's, airplane shapes overhead. He would ask questions till the adult he was badgering got to the brink of being fed up, and then scoot out from underfoot and on to the next point of interest.

One day way in the back of Green Isle near the river woods, he saw some birds whose name he didn't know. He described them to his father that night in hopes of learning what they were. In this way he had learned the log-god, the squealer, and the wild canary.

"Big ole tall white birds?" said his father, one eye narrowed over a big bite of pork chop moving to his mouth.

"No, sir," insisted Scrip. *"Gray."*

"You mean sorta bluish-gray."

"No, sir, ashy-gray all over, except for some red right on top the head."

"I ain't ever see a bird like that."

"Why don't you ask Harlan or Uncle Boy?" said his mother.

"Can I go now?"

"Yeah," said his mother, and "No," said his father at the same time. "Well, finish eating first," amended his mother.

Uncle Boy thought Scrip's birds were "cowbirds" whose height he was exaggerating and whose color he was lying about. But Scrip knew cattle egrets and these weren't cattle egrets or even any other kind of egret or heron that fished in the bayou. So he went down to Simon and Bernice's. Simon said he'd seen the huge gray birds every few years and had shot and eaten one once. "Tougher'n turkey," he said. "They real shy?"

"Yessir, I can't hardly get near 'em."

"That's them, then."

"Well, what are they? What do you call them?"

"I don't know what they are. I 'spect they some kind of crane."

Scrip went back to see the birds the next day after school and stopped at the Rands' on his way home. Even Amalie eyed him doubtfully on the doorstep. His pants were caked with mud from the thighs down.

Hudson gave him a bird identification guide and Scrip thumbed through it till he found the picture of the bird he had seen. "That," he said definitely.

"Sandhill Crane?" said Hudson Rand. "Oh, no, son."

"Yes, sir."

"That bird's rare." Hudson got out another book then. "Look here. It has never come to Louisiana. There are a few in Texas," he admitted.

"Lemme read that." After a few minutes Scrip said, "That's them. Look here, five feet tall, didn't I tell you they was tall? And red on the top of they head."

"It's just too doubtful—" said Hudson.

"Come on, then, I'll show you."

After that expedition there were two believers. Hudson called the Department of Ornithology at LSU. He was met with scoffing skepticism and finally was directed to an ornithologist near Edgewood, someone with the Forestry Department. "If Bill West says it's a Sandhill Crane, have him call us back." Bill West made the trip back into the back of Green Isle and came out certain the birds were Sandhill Cranes. Finally the university sent up a vanload of bird experts. They got out, wearing pressed khakis and camouflage jackets, with binoculars around their necks. Whether they had blond beards or short silver hair, they were all precisely manicured, with eyeglasses and soft voices and dull, impeccable grammar. And all of them, of course, were white. Scrip hung around sulkily, kicking the tires of their van and listening to their talk. Then Hudson pulled him into the limelight and said, "And this is the young hero who discovered the birds." Hero—he liked that. But they all looked at him quizzically and said only, "Well, let's get started." He sat between the front seats where the gear-stick was, and bounced and jounced way back through three enormous pastures planted in winter-grass. After entering the fourth he told them, "You better stop and turn that motor off. Now we oughta go on foot."

The men sat arguing for a minute. "They were back in the back of this pasture last time," whispered West. "You could see them from here."

"They there," announced Scrip in a stage whisper. He had already slipped out and gone ahead and come back. "There, just like always."

The strange, tall birds, gangling smudges of charcoal-gray, meandered in a herd on the other edge of the pasture. The closest one unfolded like an ironing board and flew over its fellows to the far side of the little flock, its wings billowed as if they were oddly jointed. The bird men had all stopped in a row, with their field glasses clamped to their eye sockets. "By George," said the old one. "By George, it's the Sandhills."

"So it is," said the middle-aged one.

"Gee whiz, that's what they are," said the youngest.

They tried to walk a little closer, but were too noisy. The birds flew back into the woods. "They gone downriver now," said Scrip. But the LSU men wouldn't believe him till they had pressed through all that underbrush themselves, cracking so many twigs and grunting so much that the birds wouldn't have stayed within a mile.

"Oh well!" said the men cheerfully. "We had a good sighting."

Then they got back into their van and drove away. And after that, so many people started coming, all of them as strange and joyless as these first ones, that the birds left altogether, and to Scrip's knowledge they had never come back to Green Isle. That's when he decided that if he had it to do over again, he would have just kept the special birds to himself—except maybe for Simon. As for white people, well, they really did appear to be as confused as people said they were. They had a long way to go.

It was a good lesson, Scrip was to think later in his life: white folks' passion for analysis and categorization chasing away the creature, life, itself. The white world was sterile, bland, infinitely delineated and acclaimed; his was warm, private, rare, and vital, but oddly dependent on the other for its validation and survival.

For the halcyon days ended fast. Scrip was smart, and he heard the condescension in the white librarian's voice when he stood at the tall counter trying to ask her a question. He was proud, and he hated moving to the backs of city busses. He was hot-tempered, and he flared at the white children who crooned "Nigger...nigger ..." at him in the dime store. The roaches in his parent's home repulsed him; when his mother sharply told him not to be a baby about them, he retorted, "Ain't no roaches in Mr. Hudson's house—how come? How come we got roaches and they don't?"—and she let down and cried. Oh, now he was getting older. In seventh grade he won a school essay contest sponsored by the American Legion. Two weeks later he was called to the office and told he'd won in the parish competition as well. And the next day he was called back and told the prize was not his after all. "Can't a black boy win it," his principal said with sudden anger. "The American Legion wouldn't have a black boy winning it—they give it to a little white girl across town—" That night Scrip coldly tore up his essay, which had been on patriotism. His mother cried again, and fetched it out of the wastebasket.

The incident fixed that principal's interest on Scrip. Whether it was due to the boy's bright mind, or whether any pupil who happened to be present when the man's anger surfaced would have received the same attention, Scrip was not sure. But the principal started calling him aside out of lines in the hall or off the playground. He would give him books to read: "Report back to me next Thursday after you finish this." They would talk in the principal's office. During these discussions Scrip rested uneasily on his chair. For him the office never lost its taint of reproofs and paddlings. But he learned that after he spoke for a few minutes, the principal would seize upon one comment of his or another, almost at random, as a springboard to take off on his own opinion of the book's themes.

The first time he saw Frank McCain, Scrip was fifteen. It was a Saturday in early summer and he was working at the shop—or, rather, watching while Harlan and William hooked up fertilizer spreaders to two of the field tractors. Miss Amalie drove up, and out of the passenger side of her truck jumped a man about thirty, with hair that looked deliberately tousled, and a khaki shirt and pants with no wrinkles, sweat, or dirt in their weave. His boots looked brand-new too. Frank McCain was introduced to the three of them as Miss Amalie's great-nephew. "He's the new manager of Green Isle." He shook hands all around. In a friendly tone he asked what the men were doing. As they showed him Miss Amalie said sharply, "Why was our fertilizer bill so high last time? Harlan, I told you-all I think you were spreading it too thick."

"I don't think so, Miss Amalie, it's just that it's priced so high," said Harlan.

"Look at that," she retorted. "Why, you've got the spreader valve gaping open. Mr. Rand never used to open it that much just to fertilize the new beans in the spring of the year. Frank, look here. You need to take a look at this."

"I was working on a problem like that last night," said Frank uncertainly. "In the *Progressive Farmer* handbook." He pulled a slide rule out of a holder on his belt and began to fumble with it, screwing up his mouth as he thought. "Let's see. How many acres are we trying to fertilize? How much fertilizer do we have? How wide is this tractor?"

Scrip saw Shad and Willis eyeing the slide rule doubtfully. Amalie Rand was the only person present who looked comfortable. In fact, she looked downright smug. She watched her great-nephew approvingly over his shoulder.

"Um," said Harlan. "Um, Miss Amalie, I knows this lever ought to be set just a little over the three-quarter mark, just like I have it."

"How do you know that, Harlan? It's just that you've always done it that way, and the fertilizer bills have been reflecting it."

Harlan looked at his feet and said softly, "I just been working in these fields for a long time. I got a feel for this here spreader."

"Pounds per acre. Pounds per acre index on a fifteen-foot spreader. Driving at twelve miles per hour. With valve openings of three inches. No, let's do it metric—Call that *one*, a whole—" Frank was saying. He mumbled and slid his slide rule some more. "Okay! Point seven-seven." He looked at his aunt. "These notches aren't too accurate, Aunt Amalie, I guess you should just set it a little over the three-quarter mark."

"You hear that, Harlan?" said Aunt Amalie.

"That's what the man *say*," cried Scrip. "Didn't you hear him? That's what Harlan and William say in the first place."

As a teenager when Scrip worked on the farm he often got paired with the old man William. He was sullen about it, for in the first place he hated any kind of work on Green Isle (except the brief stint of teaching swimming); and he felt sure that he was assigned to William because no one else wanted to be, because William talked all the time. William always worked the beef herd. He was a natural cattleman. During the day you rarely saw him off a horse—always a stubborn little paint William had picked out and broken himself, with herding instincts William could respect. He was sixty-nine, a tall, dark man with big wrists and hands, who wore not overalls but jeans, not a half-net tractor cap but a whitish-yellow cowboy hat slanted back on his long potato-shaped head. Working with him was like dancing to an endless record with a date you weren't especially fond of. He was tireless. He seemed to move all day with the same methodical motions, which at first seemed slow to a boy like Scrip or even a man of fifty, but after several hours had them flagging behind, eyeing that lean older man with sidelong envy. It was as if there were a pulse, not a fast one but a steady one, keeping William on his feet, his hands heading to the next task: as if he had a bottomless well of energy inside him, barely tapped.

And he talked. He didn't chatter, mumble, or pontificate: he talked. Not loud, not frivolously, not expecting any answer. He just held quiet conversations with himself all the time, without seeming to expect a response. He had lived on Green Isle all his life, "since the days we chop cotton by hand." He could describe buildings in downtown Edgewood that were long gone, floods and tornadoes and droughts that were just ghosts in other people's memory, gypsies and hoboes, shootings and wrecks, could talk about school, about women, John Wayne, staying healthy, cooking, Huey Long, slavery, hunting, the Apollo space missions, voodoo, Hitler—he had an opinion about everything. And he talked about the Rands and their weaknesses. About the foreman they'd hired, who had despised black people, who'd tried to treat them like the trees he loved to bulldoze. About Green Isle and its past and itself.

Scrip trudged up and down the tractor lanes, round and round the corral, back and forth in the horse barn after William.

"... I used to plow this land behind a mule. That was when you planted in January. Now, with these cultivators and all, you plants late. The beans be ready now all into December. That's how your season back up on you ..."

After countless hours of this, during which Scrip got less and less pouty and more and more attentive, a thought finally struck him: this land was *William's.* A piece of paper in the courthouse might say it belonged to the Rands, but that wasn't the truth. Once this occurred to Scrip he knew he was right and knew that all the ideas he evaluated for the rest of his life, if he were to accept them and abide by them, would have to fit with *this* one—would have to fall within the pattern it suddenly set.

"... Ground used to get so hot, time I walked this here, and down that way, I'd stop at the end of every row and dump my shoes out. My shoes would fill up with burnin' dirt. Right here where we're standing."

And he wondered: Was this why he was made William's partner? Had William even arranged it this way on purpose? Had he seen in the boy Scrip someone who could absorb his quiet, quiet thoughts of revolution, the deep running waters below William's stillness, and amplify them somehow?

20

IT WAS IMPOSSIBLE. Better not to have waked up. It was easier to wake up to a day void of hope than to have some shred of hope beckoning, disturbing you, making demands beyond your power to perform. That was what he must have instinctively known when he had tried to avoid waking up. Scrip drained the rest of his beer and turned up the volume on "Jeopardy."

It took him till three-thirty or four in the afternoon to get motivated to head out to Green Isle. He took a shower and had lunch—some black-eyed peas warmed up and a Pop-tart for dessert. He started to drink a shot of whiskey, actually pulled the bottle out of the cabinet and looked at it a moment, then remembered his new clean slate and put it back, and poured a glass of buttermilk instead. In his mind, beer didn't count. He watched some more TV until the time when he had to leave or else not go at all. He walked a few blocks from Miranda's house to the bus station where a one-time classmate of his, now a cab driver, usually spent his days, and persuaded the guy to ride him out to the Green Isle dairy. He could usually count on this man for at least one free trip when he was in town, and found an old joint deep in the pocket of his Army jacket to give him in thanks.

Afternoon milking was going on and the *thunk-a, thunk-a, thunk-a* of the machines almost drowned out the music from the AM radio Karo kept on top of the fan. "Hey, man!" he called. He heard a commotion from the cows' shower stalls, a cow bolted up the cement ramp, and then Karo appeared and clanged a bar down behind her as she entered her stall. He flipped a switch and a load of sticky grain plummeted into the cow's feed bin. Only then did he look in Scrip's direction. "Oh, it's you," he said in a heavy, bored voice, as if Scrip came around every day. No warmth. No handshake. No delighted questions.

"So it is," said Scrip, displeased and hurt.

Karo reached right behind Scrip for a roll of paper towels and methodically started cleaning the cow's udder. He was a medium-brown, heavy-set man in reflector sunglasses, a denim jacket, fatigues, and thigh-high rubber boots slimed halfway up with manure. He had a cigarette dangling from his mouth. He said, "If you looking for your mother, she's *not here.*"

Had this been the third or fourth day of his visit to Edgewood, Scrip might have started beating on Karo right then. They had fought before (as Scrip had with every man within five years of his age on Green Isle) and had once done considerable damage to each other before Boy broke it up. Scrip needed that release every so often. But as it was, there was not quite enough fresh disillusion within him to make him fight; rather, this vague hope was still hovering around inside, the same that had sent him out here to scout the situation. So he merely said: "What say, Karo?"

"Me, I don't say nothing. I *watch* my words. I don't be throwing my words around like bullets." Karo strode down to the other end of the milking parlor, pulled the suction tubes off another cow's bag, and with sharp, silent motions dipped each teat in iodine. He threw the screeching lever that opened her stall and slapped her flank as she ambled out.

"My, my, we mean today." The Guernsey chewing indifferently in front of Scrip seemed friendlier than Karo.

"Reckon you sit down and search th'ough your memory, you'll find something'll tell you how come." Scrip watched him, amazed. He was glad he had on dark glasses so the incredulity wouldn't show on his face. "*Recent* memory," added Karo.

Someone drove up outside with a spray of gravel. Both men glanced over their shoulders and saw Allie McCain getting out of her father's pick-up. She was in her usual jeans and sneakers and short-sleeved shirt. "Hey, Allie," Karo greeted her, in the tone of greeting Scrip had hoped for himself. "How you doing?"

"I'm okay, how about you?"

"Can't complain."

"Have you seen Josiah anywhere?—Oh, hey, Scrip, how are you? I didn't see you there."

"All right."

Allie's easy, absent manner had changed when she saw Scrip. She waited tensely for Karo's answer.

"He's over feeding the calves."

"I'll just go find him over there. He's got a fencing tool we need. Clarence is looking for it, I mean. He says Josiah was the last person who used it. Oh well. I'll go ask him."

"All right, then."

"Thanks, Karo. See you later."

Scrip watched her as far as the door. Then a gargling temper came over him and he grabbed Karo around the throat from behind saying, "Fuck you, man!"

Karo jabbed him in the gut with an elbow—if Scrip had really meant to be rough he wouldn't have left himself open to that. "I ain't go fight wi-chou, man," he said levelly. "We both too ole for that." He spun around, fast for such a heavy, stolid man, and faced Scrip, though the younger man could not see any expression in his eyes because of the dark glasses. "You can just take your own self and your nasty mouth off, because we don't want none of it. You and your type of trouble. Other people gots real troubles here without none of the kind you manufacture."

"You stick up for white people against your own kind? You don't have to be kissin' her ass—"

"I ain't." Karo went stolidly to the next cow, whom the machine had been milking dry for five minutes. "Ain't kissin' nobody's ass." Suddenly he grinned. "She ain't got a ass to kiss."

This was the opening for Scrip to make up. But he refused the good humor. "'Hey there, Miss Allie!'" he mimicked in a high voice.

"You better get on out of here now."

"'Oooh, Miss Allie, anything I can do for you?'"

"Least I ain't sunk low enough to be bad-mouthin' somebody at they own funeral. Where kinfolks can hear."

"Speak the truth," said Scrip, swaggering toward the door. He felt triumphant just to have his misdeed acknowledged. "I do. The truth shall make you free."

Nevertheless he felt lonesome as he left. It would be nicer to have struck the note of camaraderie that he and Karo had achieved a few times before. For one thing, he knew Karo kept a six-pack in the frigid room where the milk tanks were. Just one cold one wouldn't have hurt Scrip's new intentions. Furthermore it didn't look good to have to be walking down this road. The houses were spaced about thirty yards apart, and all together they made a long string. No one older than eighteen or so still walked from one to another. If he hadn't insulted Karo and needed to make a dramatic exit afterward he could have waited and they could have driven together down to the little store and then to Karo's house. They could have sat on the porch and waited for the other men to come. Much cooler to have a ride.

Scrip knew from Miranda's mother and from a cryptic conversation he'd had with William his last time home that when Frank McCain died Green Isle had become a corporation—theirs—black people's property—their own legally now as well as morally. This was the recollection that kept stirring in him. He wanted to be there for the new era. But he would have to prove himself anew to Green Isle. He would start by asking Harlan for a job. This would be tantamount to asking for forgiveness, reacceptance, of "the place" itself—the whole web of families there.

He hated farm work. He had hated it as a boy, hated the sun in the summer and the cold in the winter and the rains in between, all the weathers that he enjoyed when he was outdoors for other purposes. He guessed most of all he hated the tedium. But what he had seen that last month in Houston had shaken him, changed him, at least enough to know that he had to make a concerted effort to dry out and settle down. A job on Green Isle, where everyone had known him since babyhood, was all he was likely to get right now. He'd be lucky if even they still believed in him. By all outward signs, his early promise had stopped when he got his high school diploma. His truncated college record showed failure alone, rather than the education he had in fact gotten. His employment history had less continuity than his police record—not that his crimes were so bad or so many in themselves, a trail of charges for disturbing the peace, DWI, resisting arrest, simple possession. And he could never get good references; even close friends of his mother and the pastor, Reverend Dikes, who had known him since he was little were reluctant to recommend Scrip to anyone. Dikes had written him a letter that supposedly praised him but was in fact full of veiled wordy allusions to dark troubles in Scrip's life. Scrip still had the letter, folded and grubby, but he knew it was never going to do him any good. One look at it and any prospective boss would suddenly remember a very well-qualified candidate who had applied the day before and in all likelihood was going to take the job.

Scrip meandered down the road in a curious alternating gait—slouching for a step or two with his head hanging dejectedly, and then springing alert in belligerent defiance, until the tense pose would relax, bit by bit, and his head would drop again. At the Willises' house he stood still for a minute, then shambled across the board that spanned the ditch by their mailbox, and climbed the stairs to their porch. The inner door was open and he knocked on the screen door frame.

Corey came to the door in a pink-flowered duster and gray house shoes. She was soft and wide, and Scrip knew that when she smiled her chins rearranged themselves, like smug children, around her neck. But she didn't smile now. She looked anxious.

"Scrip Thomas," she said.

He continued to fluctuate between hostility and great wilting sadness, like a scrambled TV that zooms from horizontal to vertical warp with no pause at a normal picture.

"Where Harlan at?" he said rudely.

She bristled. "He off trying to get himself a little peace, which he ain't gonna have with you coming around!"

"Oh, *fuck* it, then," said Scrip, turning and stomping back across the porch. But when he got to the steps and put his foot out to start his defiant descent, it would not comply; it just stayed in the air until Scrip's body sagged and he sat with a plunk on the top step, his back still turned on Miss Corey at the door. She saw his head droop and his shoulders slump and maybe even quake a little as if he were crying. He had been a friend of Rodney's.

"Scrip, Scrip," Corey said through the screen. Scrip didn't answer. He heard the screen bang softly and then felt her patting her shoulder. "You not a little feisty boy any more. Get up and take account of yourself like the man you is. Come on now. Quit that ugly talk. Come sit in my kitchen and wait for Harlan."

She'd been right; his shoulders were heaving from his big gulps of breath. But he was not actually crying. He got up and followed her into the house. She stole looks into his face and saw that his eyes were all red where they should have been white.

Corey stopped suddenly and Scrip bumped into her. She had paused at the TV set, which had pictures of Rodney arranged on top of it: Rodney at his baptism at twelve, in his high school graduation cap and gown at seventeen, and in his Army uniform the following month, his bucktoothed good nature beaming from each of the junctures in his life. Corey fingered the doily the pictures sat on.

"He loved you," she said. "He really loved you. He 'as always trying to be like you. I bet you feel him sometimes, looking down from heaven and trying to steer you right. He always telling me, 'Mama, Scrip not a *bad* boy, he just get mad easy, and he so smart, Mama, he *so* smart, I love him, Mama.' "

Since Scrip remembered Rodney chiefly for his lack of smarts, the praise itself did not mean much. He had never paid much attention to Rodney during their childhood, and even if Rodney in his angel status did clamor at Scrip now, it was not likely that Scrip would heed him. So Scrip just said, "Huh!"

Corey led him to the kitchen, seated him, and at the stove began the slow motions of making coffee, talking all the while. Her voice dragged at a slow pace, nasal and exclamatory. He stared morosely at the patterns on the chipped formica tabletop.

She was talking about Harlan's heart condition and the "stress" on him ever since Green Isle had incorporated and he'd been made head of the board. She must have gotten that from TV. Her talk was a quaint blend of proverb and metaphor and platitude, all very black, and occasional white pop-culture jargon she got from "the stories."

Scrip had once had a friend in Chicago, the product of a rich black suburb of L.A., who was trying to expiate himself with a dissertation on black speech patterns. He would have given his eyeteeth for transcripts of her talk.

"And when Frank McCain died, he took it real hard. He love' that man like his brother, for all they differences...He going into one of his spells now, Scrip, honey. He about to get the nerves. I know the signs."

When Harlan got the nerves every year or so he went totally out of commission and dropped out of everyone's sight but Corey's. Usually he waited to get them till planting or harvest was done.

Corey put cups and saucers on the table and took the opportunity to look kindly, but shrewdly, into Scrip's eyes. "What is it you wanting to talk to him about?"

"I reckon I need a job, Miss Corey."

"A job on *this* old farm! *You!*"

"Yes'm."

They were both thinking of the other times he had tried to hold a job on Green Isle, once when he had supposedly planted a whole forty acres with no seeds in the planter, and then when criticized and mocked for his mistake back at the shop had hit Uncle Boy in the jaw; and another time, after another new-leaf vow, when he had gotten the workers excited about a new drainage plan they had tried that blocked up everyone's toilet for three days.

"This really it this time, Miss Corey. This a new beginning for me."

"The Lord give us a lot of second chances," she said, but guardedly, broodingly, not quite meeting his eyes.

"Unh-hunh, sure do."

"Even me and Harlan," she said. "Brother Dikes say the reason Rodney was kilt over there was becausa our sin. He don't know what it might be, but we do. Harlan and me can look in our own hearts and find that sin that had Rodney kilt over in Vietnam. And even after that, even after the Lord had to kill him, and punish us, he give us a new chanct."

He didn't give old Rodney much of a chance, thought Scrip. But he had heard all this before. He glanced at the woman and let his eyes run on, over the plaques on the wall, the fringed curtains, out the window to the pastures where big clouds were piling up like pillows, wrinkled and creased with blue. He tried to think of what he would say to Harlan.

"He were so happy going off that morning. Only seventeen. He told a story about his age. So excited to go sign up. Hadn't ever been out of Edgewood before. Harlan drove him downtown—"

Despite his effort to block them, Corey's words leaked through to Scrip. Rodney Willis, aged seventeen, black, poor, American, shot dead six weeks later in a jungle in southeast Asia; and a Baptist preacher had convinced his tenant-farmer parents there was a God who had done this thing deliberately, because of some obscure sin in their humble, straitened lives. Anger welled in him, dangerously. This was the point when he should stop his rage. He had finally figured that out. Why was he letting himself get riled up about this all over again?

"—but it's the Lord's will; and now, this grandbaby with the heart condition, I knows it's the Lord's will too, the Lord giveth and the Lord taketh away, I tells her mother all the time—"

"Can I go find Harlan?" said Scrip tightly.

Corey looked up in surprise.

"I can't wait too much longer. Can I go look for him?"

"He probably at the shop, honey."

"Thank you then, Miss Corey, I got to go."

She watched his lurching back from the screen door. Rude and ugly-mouthed he was. She knew he had talked bad about Mr. McCain right at the funeral. But in some men you excused the worst things—the way you wouldn't blame a person for biting you during a seizure. Somehow Scrip seemed more hurt than Rodney ever had. Rodney had never wrenched his mother by making her watch him suffer, not his whole life long; he was a happy boy; he never hoped for anything enough to make his disappointments great. Then when the news of his death came, and she tried to picture his last moments in that jungle, Corey underwent all the pain that he had spared her, in seventeen years, up till then. Her heart brooded and quivered and split with all the anguish that Rodney had never provoked while he lived, as if it had been storing up somewhere. But Scrip—Scrip seemed to be all the time suffering death wounds. So maybe he would die easy in a rocking chair. Maybe everyone had a set amount of pain he had to go through, and Rodney had to have his all at once...while Scrip was all the time hurting. Pity the mother who had to witness that, and be helpless.

That spring, life looked more passable to Scrip than it had in a long, long time, and he threw himself into it with all the fervor of a new convert. He left Miranda's place early, by a standing arrangement with his taxi-driver friend, and got back late, as if to make up for years of waste by double-timing his new application of energy. He liked the companionship of the other men and all their bullshitting and the role of the worldly, street-smart and book-smart one they expected him to fill. The labor itself was a mixed bag. He enjoyed the sense of physical well-being it brought and for a while that pleasure alone sustained him. But once he was back in shape boredom threatened to set in, and he tried to concentrate that much harder on what he was doing—mulling over every aspect of each task before him, inwardly describing it to some faraway third person, or trying to figure out a new, more efficient way it could be done. When he had a partner on a job he would raise knotty questions and argue whatever side of them the other man didn't take, while they both worked. With all those methods of staving off boredom exhausted he tried to make even the monotony a direct challenge, pushing through his tasks with a sort of savage determination and not stopping till he was finished. Watching him the others had a sense he was punishing himself. He would skip both breakfast and lunch till one day he passed out repairing a water line in the back pasture. Almira Hebert called Miranda and told her she'd better pack a lunch every day for that man of hers.

21

As Myrtle Clark backed out of her driveway and into the street, carefully looking both ways before she placed the old Cadillac back into drive, she began to hum a little tune, she was so happy.

Thelma, in the back seat, teased her about it: "Listen to that. Our squadron leader's in a fi-i-ine mood. You've got all us troops in order, sarge?" They called her their squadron leader because it was always Myrtle who organized and spearheaded their excursions.

"Seize the day," Myrtle replied goodnaturedly, as she usually did when anyone remarked upon her leadership abilities, especially when there was any inference that they verged on bossiness. "We're not getting any younger, ladies! Someone's got to take hold."

Take this very visit, for instance. If Myrtle hadn't urged and pushed and coordinated and directed, the four Colonial Dames friends would probably never have gotten together in Edgewood. If it were up to Phyllis O'Connell and Frederica Peters and Thelma Rigby

Lee alone, they would have just kept mentioning it and mentioning it in their round robin letters till it became more a formulaic phrase than a statement of real intention. Once, seven years before, Myrtle had nearly marshalled them into a spring visit to Edgewood; Thelma, who lived outside Atlanta, had actually had her plane ticket; but then Frederica, in Biloxi, had broken her hip, so they all had to cancel. Oh, Phyllis had driven down from Shreveport and spent the night once or twice, picking up Myrtle en route to the regular Colonial Dames meetings in New Orleans, which they did well to get to, she supposed, but this special get-together of the widows' foursome who had belonged to Colonial Dames together since the late '20s had never come to pass until now, azalea season, 1977, and then only because Myrtle had worked at it.

And look—they were having a ball. In her role as hostess and squadron leader, Myrtle had arranged their time well. Last night, after the girls arrived, they had eaten at the cafeteria. It was so dependable and you could see what you were getting. There they laughed and talked up a storm before they went home and put on their nightgowns and talked some more—like real girls. Then today was a Tuesday, which was really Imogene Rabelais's day to have Ruby Mae, but weeks ago Myrtle had asked Imogene to trade. So this morning Ruby Mae came to cook and serve a breakfast of eggs and bacon and her wonderful biscuits that everyone raved about. (Though everyone had declared she was splurging, no one consumed near as much as Frederica, who had eaten *seven* biscuits—Myrtle counted—and who tonight, doubtless, would be complaining that her "heart valve" felt queer again.) Then the foursome had gone to the antique show and luncheon sponsored by the Symphony Women. At the door Myrtle had realized that she had forgotten to transfer the tickets to her navy blue purse, and was initially mortified. But Janie Pilford had been sweet about it and let them in anyway; and, remembering by a sheer act of will her resolve not to let the unimportant get her down, Myrtle waved her hand airily as if to brush her mistake away, in the same motion herding her friends through the door. "Ladies," she told them, "getting old is a damned inconvenience sometimes!" and they chuckled. That Myrtle.

Then they had taken naps; they needed occasional breaks from Thelma's talking. And now, after naps, Myrtle was taking her friends for a drive to look at some of the antebellum sites in the area.

First they cruised west of town to Belle Acres, which sat serenely in a grove of redbud trees; then farther out that road they circled the Gregory place and the one slave cabin still standing by the levee. It was a mild spring afternoon and, though the lawns were still winter thatch, the sun slanted down through the branches of live oaks just putting out sharp yellow-green leaves, and of frothing white dogwoods, and lay contentedly on azalea bushes and masses of daffodils. The girls were enthusiastic, and Myrtle delighted in their responses, though she hit the brake each time they sighed or exclaimed.

She took a winding side road over to the other highway, and turned off onto the bayou road from there, heading toward Green Isle. But as they reached the first giant oaks that marked the beginning of the plantation, they saw the first signs of lively activity they had seen all afternoon. Negroes seemed to be gathering in one of the pastures. A bulldozer was at work, and there were many cars and trucks with Negroes with shovels and other tools in them pulling on and off the highway—"laughing and playing that music, the way they'll do, you know," as Thelma said. Myrtle braked and accelerated in confusion, torn between two deeply ingrained instincts, one to come to a dead stop when there was anything out of ordinary on the road and the other to flee assemblies of Negroes.

"What in the world are they doing? You know they are always getting together this way in Atlanta," said Thelma.

"They're just doing a farm chore. It's some sort of work project," said Frederica.

"Oh, don't be naive, honey, they're drinking and carrying on," said Phyllis.

Thelma went on, "In Atlanta, at least they try to stop the nigras from doing this on the roadsides by putting up these bridges in the air over the streets."

"Where do you suppose they get these cars?"

"Welfare," said Frederica promptly, and everyone laughed, except Myrtle, who was steering tensely.

"I know what they're doing," said Phyllis with inspiration. "Why, look what they're doing. They're taking down that gre-e-eat big old sign that used to be here."

"Why would they do that?" Myrtle veered a bit as she looked out her window.

"Who knows? I'll never forget when this was the main road, though—going home from Sophie Newcomb every time, that sign was a sort of landmark: 'Green Isle Plantation!' That meant you were getting close to Edgewood."

"Isn't that odd," remarked Frederica, mildly.

But Thelma shuddered. "I don't like to see so many of them together. You never know what they might be up to. Are you sure we should proceed, Myrtle? It may be dark by the time we're coming back."

"Of course," said Myrtle staunchly. "You'll love the smokehouse at Green Isle. It would be ridiculous to miss it. Courage, ladies!"

And the other Dames laughed. "That's our leader!" they said.

Lillian McCain loved the smell of dirt. She stood in her greenhouse surrounded by it, among sacks of sand and clay and garden dirt, compost and fertilizer and peat moss. As she worked a strand of hair fell across her nose, itching, and she finally stopped to push it away with her arm. The old digital clock she kept out here said six-fifty-two. It could be six-thirty-two, however; part of one digit was missing and she never remembered whether it was the "5" that looked like the "3" or vice versa. Well, it was probably later than she thought. She should go clean up for the quarterly Green Isle meeting, but she hated to tear herself away. Even though it was a simple enough project, dividing ferns, it had taken her a while to get started, and she hated to lose her momentum now. The big wooden planters spilling over with ferns brought in much of her business's income. All summer long they stayed rented out for weddings and fiftieth anniversary parties and banquets, while sale of the more flamboyant, less dependable plants—orchids, exotic lilies, summer annuals—fluctuated. Finally at five till seven she sighed, looking at the two granddaddy ferns she hadn't gotten to, and washed her hands in the big sink in her greenhouse, digging her nails into the Lava soap. Back in the house she realized she wouldn't have time to change into a dress; she switched her diaper-soft, baggy khakis for a skirt that matched the old shirt she was wearing, and instead of redoing the bun at the back of her head, just smoothed down the front of her hair.

She'd be late, but she wouldn't be the last one at the meeting. Sunset was just coming over the farms as she drove to the little church where they met. The spaces between pecan trees and fenceposts and parked trucks and shuttered houses were still three-dimensional, glowing a faint red before blackness swallowed them up. Lit windows gleamed in the dusk and through some of them you could see people moving in their suppertime routines. It had always been Frank's favorite time of day. That morning, engrossed in some habitual chore at the kitchen sink, Lillian had looked out the window and seen him walking across the far pasture. Or that was what she thought for several seconds, matter-of-fact and unsurprised, wondering if he was ready for lunch, before the shock of the present came back upon her and at the same instant she realized that he was dead and that the man she could see off in the field was really Karo, wearing Frank's favorite gold chamois shirt that Lillian had recently given him. Her heart pounded as her mistake flooded over her. Her hands trembled as she dried them in a paper towel. Now the odd sensation, the tantalizing sweet semblance of normalcy that a dream can give to some impossibility, was still upon her. She waited for Carmichael Boggs, the ag science professor, to turn and then parked by him, remembering again and then dismissing faint hints she had that he was interested in her, that his sympathy in these months was a little more earnest and pointed than just a friend's. She felt guilty for the fleeting thought, which had occurred before and was certainly mistaken. To make up for the presumption she greeted him a little more warmly than she would have otherwise.

Harlan and Reverend Dikes were already seated at the table in the little parlor. They stood when she walked in, and brought her a folding chair. After five minutes of chit-chat Ray Worley, the farm finance man, arrived, and they could get started.

Harlan opened the meeting and had Reverend Dikes give an invocation. Lillian felt a spasm of impatience. The man was so *ponderous.*

Harlan presented the figures from Mrs. Winkel, the part-time bookkeeper. All the while Green Isle had been a trust, the open meetings for the beneficiaries had served a sort of pedagogical function—and goodness knows they needed it, Lillian thought. Harlan had absorbed probably three semesters of accounting and one economics course since then. He had subtly changed since that day when he had cried on her porch beside Frank's wheelchair. He seemed to stand a little straighter. Or was it her imagination? He had always had power on the farm. Now he reported on the decisions he had recently made.

"Hirings and firings—well—we haven't had any firings—but I took on somebody new, well, not exactly new, I brung on Scrip Thomas again to drive tractors." Harlan looked down at his notes. "And Moog Mathews got work-study at school so he is now on a thirty-hour-a-week payroll. That's all I got to report."

"Excuse me, Mr. Chairman," said Dikes. "I have a matter I'd like to bring up. That is the property damage that was wrought over the weekend."

"Property damage, Reve'nd?" said Harlan.

"Yes, Harlan, I'm talking about a hole in the ground over there. It look like a earthquake hit over there where a certain *sign* used to be, and the motor on at least one tractor burnt out."

"Engine," said Harlan automatically.

"What's that?"

"You got a engine on a tractor, not a motor."

"Yes, well, nonetheless, we're talking some damage that's been done, and the ringleader of it all was none other than Scrip Thomas. And now you put him on the payroll."

"What's this?" said Carmichael Boggs. "Some of us don't know what you're talking about."

Lillian looked amused. "I thought something looked different this morning when I drove by, but it was barely light out and I couldn't figure out what it was."

"It's the old plantation sign," said Reverend Dikes. "They done tore it down."

"On Saturday," said Harlan. "We had some volunteers to assist us in uh—in uh—"

"In wrecking it," said Dottie Mathews. "And I don't see what your objection is, preacher?" She went to Rose of Sharon Baptist in town, she could afford to be disrespectful.

"My objection is that it was done summarily. Without the approval of this Board."

"Board ain't gotta okay every little thing," said William.

"I really don't see either what the problem was," said Ray Worley. "A few people wanted to do some physical improvements to the place, on their own time? I don't see anything wrong with that."

"See," said Dottie, "that sign been needing to come down. Green Isle ain't a plantation no more and it's been bothering some of us. Been getting under our skin to be so out of date and all. So we just got motivated to do something about it."

"They got a new sign ordered, I believe," said Harlan.

"Um-hm. Sure do," said William.

"I believe they do," said Dottie.

"Who's 'they'?" said Carmichael in an interested tone.

"I'll tell you who 'they' is," said Reverend Dikes. "'They' is Scrip Thomas, sowing the seeds of the devil, stirring up the people. And I don't like it one bit. Put *these* words *down*, Miz Mathews—*that* young man is headed for *trouble.* And the people are trying to follow right after him, like sheep. We've made some progress here that one hotheaded son of Satan can undo—"

"Scrip Thomas done had his trouble, preacher-man, and if you was any kind of a God's man you be able to see that." Dottie was getting her infamous thunder look.

"My people used to bind together to get things done in this

parish. Used to vote together. Last election, look what happened! They split our vote right up, and it's people like Scrip dividing it. Used to be some respect around here—respect for law and order, respect for property, respect for the word of God—"

"You shouldn't tell those big-shot white folks you can get out the vote, if'n you can't deliver," said Dottie. "That's all they is to it."

"Well, if they's no more new business—" said Harlan.

"This issue ain't going away, Harlan."

"Have you authorized the purchase order for a new sign?" said Lillian.

"Yes, I have."

"What's it going to say?"

"Corporation. Green Isle Incorporated."

"I was just wondering. Maybe if there are objections you could take up donations for a special fund for that, and avoid using the farm profits for something controversial."

"Miz Lillian, they ain't no objections over this sign but the one sitting across the table from you, and that because of jealousy."

"Go on!" said Reverend Dikes. "Go on with you!"

"This meeting hereby adjourned," said Harlan petulantly, with a wave of his hand. Well what do you know, thought Lillian. Something *has* come over Harlan the past few months.

22

THE MORNING AFTER the funeral the McCains had found that Lillian's brothers did more than watch TV the day before. They had also quietly whisked out of the house the hospital bed, wheelchair, medicines, carts, tubes, and bags that had been moved in around midsummer. Likewise the immediate family was supposed to try to expel the images of sickness that had become part of their minds' furniture, shift memories back into their proper places, and think of Frank in a context larger than the past eleven months.

Allie had known he was going to die for almost a year and thought she had gotten herself ready. But when it actually happened she found that she was not nearly steeled to the event. There was still a passageway of devastation she had to descend. As long as Frank had been alive, however barely so, she had relied on the simple fact of his being—his physical continuity. Right up to the end, she had navigated the rounds of her life according to a gut sense of his mere location, wasted as he was, in that bleak hospital room across town. Once he died she had to quit even this basic gravitation toward him. "For weeks he'd been hanging on by a thread," people were saying. She felt this metaphor applied to herself as well: after dangling by a slender thread she had slipped into bowls of pitch darkness. By then the months of foreknowledge might as well not have happened, so little had they been able to steady her for the new condition.

The rest of that winter and spring she saw everything in exaggerated terms. It was as if she couldn't perceive subtler shadings just then, and so she intensified the basic colors that she could see. The result was mostly melodrama. So in her own mind she became a tragic heroine, her father's death an event she thought she had successfully telescoped by maudlin formulae. She produced more pictures than she had in any stage before, and as she composed and framed them one by one and squeezed the shutter, she dedicated each to her father, her heart beating fast with the sense of pain and sacrifice. She was carrying the torch for him.

Even the other rival for her after-school time, the farm chores, had its epic side. Fayette's announcement about his intention to run the farm—something she would have been too doubting to arrive at—cemented his place on the pedestal where he had wavered for most of her life. She had always adored him as if his platinum hair were a halo, as if he really had taken on the glories of those personages he was always assuming when they played: "I'll be J.F.K. on PT-109 and you be the injured guy. I'll be Lee at Appomattox and you be the guy who holds my sword. I'll be the American double agent and you be the Russian." His announcement about running the farm fit perfectly into her hero worship. She thought it was noble of him to want to do. She decided to scurry around trying to be his helpmeet. How grand it would be to continue the work their dad had started! Typical of Fayette, she thought then, to rise to the challenge and turn a burden into something glorious. Together the brother and sister pored over maps of the water system, field-crop projections, and analyses of the soil mineral content that the county agent had made for them. With each managerial decision made successfully, their faces grew grave and beautiful in the sense of consecration to their father, their memory of how pleased he had been each year when the winter grass first showed or a new fence stretched neatly pinned across the horizon. So even their fights and bickering, over how chores were to be divided and who was to blame when something went wrong, had a higher purpose.

Of course that couldn't last. Later she would see this season as one of final innocence. She was fraught with romantic stirrings and exhilarations about the future, her surroundings, and herself. Even the grief that still hit her in bouts seemed pure and clean and unmuddled. In some ways she felt happier now than she had before Frank died—a fact which added guilt to her burden when the plummeting bad moods did come. But the illness that had been so hard was over, and she was growing into a marvelously live sense of her own suppleness. She shed her crush on Fayette's friend Christopher—shucked it one night in a single moment of reflection, as lightly and simply as she would an old coat that she'd been wearing too long, too late into the spring. Sometimes a happiness like fright or intense thirst came over her. Or, stretched taut with the exertion of some chore, she would be seized by the commonplace beauty of the farm. Something quicksilver, keen as pain, shot through her stomach and breasts. Then Frank's death seemed accounted for in the far-reaching order of things.

Jags of moody suffering overtook her just as abruptly, usually arriving late at night with a pressure inside her chest that crying would not relieve. Then she felt as if she were skidding toward an abyss, terrified, but digging her heels in and flailing her arms did no good. She was brought to the edge of Frank's absence. Once she cried her pain grew till it seemed she was grieving over more than his death itself, even the frail pitiful look his legs had had those last months, and the walls she detected between people, or the pitiful attempts at cheer on the evening news. It all seemed terribly sad. These spells would continue for a couple of days or so, manifest in moody blankness during her waking hours, a pain that seemed physical inside her, always threatening to well over.

At first her classmates either drew away from her or treated her with an exaggerated respect that made her uncomfortable. She knew that out of their own uneasy reverence for someone so marked as to have a father die, they shunned her. She was proud. She moved among them with a calmness just a little more taut than usual. Soon enough they forgot her distinction and it subsided into the same relief background as the facts of everyone else's life. The waters that had parted around her rushed back, closing, and as far as the social life of the school went she regained her sideline position—for which she was glad. Still, the loneliness of the weeks when she was scrupulously, delicately avoided stayed with her. Frank's death became just one more in a set of factors that alienated her from the normal teenage life of Edgewood.

So four, five, and six months passed. Spring rains came, and a rash of flowers by Easter, and in May a discharge of leaves that thickened the treelines and blotted the sparely etched horizons. In the first half of the summer the march of minute differences in sky and land continued. Old farmers could tell what phase of what moon it was, just by the thinness of blue in the June sky or the amount of dazzling white cloud drifting overhead in July. The nights were porous, steeped in dew, star-spattered, and ringing with insect song.

She was used to the seasons. In their kitchen, incongruous with the sleek, muted designs Lillian liked, a Farm Equipment Company calendar always hung by the phone. It had a picture for every month, none of which was appropriate to Louisiana: a snowy pond, a blooming mountain meadow, a one-room red schoolhouse, fall foliage behind a white New England church. The changes in the year here were subtler and would not have made good calendar pictures anyway—the presence and weight of the ground haze, the tinge of a magnolia pod and the volume of frogs' noise at night. But there were definite seasons in Louisiana. Lillian had a friend who had moved here from upstate New York and was always complaining about not having four seasons a year. But she was wrong—that was why, with a gravity out of proportion to the calendar's relevance, and surely out of keeping with their usual eye for absurdities, the McCains consulted its garish pages and marked on it their plans for the agricultural year.

But suddenly in July, the year seemed to stop advancing. Only the heat moved and grew, climbing to over one hundred every day, dipping into the nineties at night. The green days and black nights lost their quality of fresh elasticity. Now they chafed and frazzled the bodies of living things. Newspapers were skimpy, void of any news but freak accidents. Fights broke out among people usually placid. Others lapsed into moods of nervous irritability. Machines broke more often. The animals felt it too—the cattle rising early to browse for the least stiff, least withered grass and sinking down to rest before nine in the morning, the dogs erupting into snarls and fights. A suppressed hysteria prevailed.

It had been three months since the last good rain. People had finally gone ahead and planted beans and cotton, but much later than they should have, and without benefit of water except for a half-inch sprinkle the second week in June. The young plants were stunted and the pastures were scorched, a weak green only near the roots. At the

McCains' there was still a chance that decent hay could be harvested in the lowest pastures, near the bayou, where Fayette had dug some rough ditches to irrigate.

Farmers knew things were bad when even town residents became aware of their danger. At first all they heard when they went into the city limits was, "Lord, am I worried about my lawn," or "My swimming pool evaporates two inches every day." After six weeks of the drought, though, everyone became an expert on agriculture: "Wish we'd have us a rain. The crops sure need it."

This country was used to rain. It usually lay lush and green, swimming in fresh-fallen rainwater and traced with slow brown silted streams, which released changeable mists, which in turn condensed and showered down more rain: while fingers of sunlight in the sky parted and sorted the clouds, glancing through them to make rainbows like a blur of swiftly shuffled face cards. That sort of light, which dispersed and effaced itself kindly, was what the place was used to, not this cruel, changeless blaze of noonday, pressing like a headache on the hardened earth.

Now every day was like the day before it. The farm stirred and woke, and two feathers of cloud floated in a sky seared almost white. "Clear to partly cloudy today, with a slight chance of late afternoon or evening thundershowers," their uncle Calvin Ray would drone on the radio, while his listeners hushed each other up to hear better. "Highs today near one hundred and four, lows in the low nineties. The forecast for tomorrow remains the same. Slight chance of rain, decreasing through the end of the week. Barometric pressure stands at thirty-two point six; relative humidity fifteen-percent. Highs predicted to remain over the hundred-degree mark. At Simsport the river is dropping ..."

"Dry as a bone," went the saying, and now Allie felt she understood it. There was no way to squeeze water out of a blanched bone, a rock, a knob of dust.

That summer she seemed to harden some. She hardly spoke or smiled. Physically, even, she seemed to grow more taut. The result was seductive: she thinned out everywhere but in the bust and rear. Fayette noticed it with irritation.

She and her brother spun from one argument over chores and the farm to another. When Allie got furious she withdrew more than ever. She went out on weekend nights, usually saying she was spending them with Theresa; but Fayette heard rumors from his friends that she was going out with one of the more flamboyant derelicts of the senior class.

"I figure it's her way of rebelling," he said to Lillian, when they hunched over the kitchen counter talking about it one night. "But damn! it bothers me."

"Well," said his mother mildly, "don't you think she knows what she's doing? Don't you think she has her head on straight?"

Fayette scowled. "This guy is just bad news."

"What about the boy she went out with last year?"

"Which one, Jeff Carlton? I think he's just a friend."

"Oh."

"I think Allie's curious. I think she does a lot of things to be able to say she's done them."

"To say to whom? Not me."

"Well, maybe not say she's done them. *Know* she's done them."

Meantime the sphinx, innocent of such speculations, was working part-time at a photography store downtown—the same one where Frank had taken her to fix up her camera six years before. The job, along with the farm, left her with little of the kind of time she fancied she wanted most—long, uninterrupted hours for roaming around, practicing seeing, fine-tuning her judgment about light and shutter speed, or pondering her reading. By now pictures bulged out of both bottom drawers of her desk, and her closet had more negatives in it than clothes. Throughout her adolescence she had been taking pictures indiscriminately and with abandon. Black-and-white, color, portraits, landscapes, stills, and action shots all interested her. The world had urged itself upon her, and she was stirred by each image.

But this summer, like a well drying up, her photographic portraits stopped, the nature pictures stopped, the witty or interpretive scenes stopped. She started working strictly in black-and-white, and only with stark objects. She drew away from the curves and softnesses of animate things and toward the strictly functional. She immersed herself in books about the machine aesthetic of the thirties and forties. She did biting humorless pieces with boards and galvanized tin, cables, cylinders, and blades from the farm equipment and goalposts. Only Lillian voiced any appreciation of these at all. The aunts and cousins who chanced upon them usually changed the subject, and Fayette frankly said they were ugly.

There was a photography contest organized by a college in New Orleans. She saw the notice in a state magazine. She sent in a few of her best prints and settled back to wait.

She got nervous and edgy. The monotony of the days seemed to dare her to lose her grip. She made a long walk out of the trip to the mailbox every day and was disappointed every time that there was nothing from the contest, until she grew so cynical that each letdown did not even seem to add one hash mark to her existing bitterness.

The boy Lillian and Fayette were talking about was no one much. Allie had run into him at the John Deere place one afternoon and had had an amusing conversation with him. He fished around about what she did at night; she shrugged and agreed to go out with him, for the novelty. Last year she had gone out—once—with each of two or three boys from other groups at school for the same reason. This one, Luke, was from the redneck hood crowd at school. They drank beer in the cab of his truck, his lips tasted of cigarettes and his breath of beer, they danced to country music under a strobe light and his long lanky thighs nudged hers this way and that around the shiny floor, the pointed toes of his boots flicking between her sneakers. It was a cut of experience she wanted; she didn't feel anything, but she soaked in the atmosphere and images coolly. Part of her right now wanted to have as much as possible happen to her. She drove past the redneck bars with trucks on giant tires crowded into the lots. Why shouldn't she be able to be one of those people for a few hours, to brush through that little world just to be able to say she'd done it?

Her period did not come. In June she thought it was late, then finally gave it up. In July it did not come either. She thought of her body as arid, wrenched dry as the ground, so that no flow of the dark, life-symbolizing fluids could pass. Panicking she had to wonder, "Am I pregnant?" although she had not yet come close to sex. Still, she could already tell that the line between sex and non-sex did not seem as sharply drawn as she used to think. There seemed to be a blurry region there that astringent little information booklets given out in gym, and even novels, left out. At any rate, maybe she had cancer. There might be some inherited tendency from her father. Some tumor might be blocking release of her blood. In her mind she died, distributed her goods, and enacted a funeral—and continued to steal around the errands of her summer life, afraid. She consulted the image of her body in the mirror. It was thin, the legs and arms and neck freckled brown, the breasts and rear fuller than they had ever been, and it told her nothing.

23

EVEN A NORMAL summer wore hard on the tempers of Edgewood folks, and this year they were overheating right and left, like car radiators. Four-letter words flew around town like popped gaskets.

One hot morning Allie and Lillian were in the kitchen reading the paper, drinking coffee, and listening to "Good Morning America," the volume of which they would turn down to nothing any minute now when the bug-and-weather report came on the radio. Fayette came trudging in in his old high-school gym shorts and athletic department T-shirt, poured himself a cup of coffee, and told them he was going back to college in two weeks.

"Oh, I'm so glad," said Lillian with relief they hadn't heard from her in a while. "You don't think it's too late?"

"No, I'm gonna call down there at nine. I'm pretty sure I can still register."

"I'm so glad," Lillian repeated. "I really do think it's the right thing to do."

Allie pushed her bowl of cereal away uneaten. Even though they had fought so much, she would miss him. It seemed like desertion. And he looked so serene. "I assume you're leaving the Jimmy here," she said.

Instead of flashing back at her he said agreeably, "Yeah, I'll leave the Jimmy. I'm going to try to work part-time and get a used car in the next few weeks."

It peeved her that he wouldn't argue. "What do you think I'm going to do about this place?"

He looked at her with raised eyebrows and big surprised eyes. "Allie, you know you and I can't arrange our lives around running this farm."

"Well, why didn't you think of that eight months ago, when Daddy died? Now we're all into it, we've wasted our whole summer on it—why'd you pretend it was so important to do?"

"You didn't have to agree with me."

"I'm supposed to just go along with every whim of yours, and change my mind a hundred and eighty degrees whenever *you* do, without putting up a fight."

"We can talk about it—" Lillian put in.

"Sure we can. Wait a minute. We're missing the bug report."

"Oh, quit pretending like you care about the bug report," said

Fayette. How condescending he was. "Look, Allie, I don't think there's much of anything on this farm that I can do that you can't do."

It was a sort of compliment, so instead of retorting she groused into her coffee cup.

"And if it turns out that there is, that there's more heavy work than I can do on my holidays or on a weekend every once in a while, well of course we can sell it."

"The thing is," said Allie, "I'm just at the worst of it in all this. You two can just decide what you want to do, what you want to concentrate on, and go do it. I have all the pressures you have, but I can't even choose them."

"Let's put the place up for sale today, then," said Fayette smoothly. "I'll call Uncle Jules."

"And see it a subdivision. Over my dead body."

"Oh, Jesus, you're melodramatic. Quit making a federal case out of it. Maybe we *should* sell it. Maybe it's silly to hang on to it. Things change."

"You're the one who's been making such a big deal about 'responsibility' and 'not shirking your duty'!" She put on a pompous tone and swaggered in her chair.

"I *never—*" said Fayette.

" 'My estimate of the soybean market is blah blah blah.' 'Yes, you run on to the movie, I'll put the farm chores first and stay here.' You've been so full of yourself this whole year."

"Well, you'll be leaving home next year. We'll have to do something about the farm then. Mama doesn't want to fool with it."

"Don't worry about it. It doesn't look like your concern has been all that deep up to now anyway."

"I mean, all I'm trying to do is go back to school, make some progress toward my career, and I come in here to tell you and all you do is give me shit—"

"I'm not giving you shit—"

"Yes you are—what the fuck do you think you're doing? I won't be leaving any too soon." *Slam.*

Slam. The second exit was Lillian's, by another door.

Later that same day, two men were unloading chunks of granite from a pickup truck in the high school parking lot.

One was Jerome Haskell, the Beauregard High School art teacher, a potter and iron-worker. He had thick black hair and a thick black moustache, brown eyes, and a white, quick, beaming smile. A big, burly man who had played football in college, he scattered any notion that art was for sissies. All it took to do that was a few minutes spent watching him in rolled-up sleeves, throwing a pot, with the muscles in his huge biceps flexed, the forearms cording and relaxing with tension, and the big deft hands shaping the lip of the pot, smoothing its body, palming symmetry into its neck.

A friend of Haskell's was with him, the young pastor of the church where Frank's funeral had been—or rather ex-pastor, for he'd just decided to quit the ministry and would be leaving the parish the next week. The two of them were taking rocks into the artroom at the school. They had gotten them from the minister's grandfather's farm in north Arkansas, and Haskell planned for his Art IV students to carve it in the fall. High school students did not usually get to work in stone. Haskell was pleased that he could engineer the project for them. Despite the blazing heat in the parking lot he was whistling cheerfully as they worked.

On the Arkansas trip, and as a celebration of his decision to leave the church, the ex-minister had grown a stubbly beard. He was shirtless. His body was oiled with sweat, and sun glanced off it as it did off the windshield of Haskell's truck. The men made several trips in and out of the school. Then the principal drove up, parking his black Chrysler beside the pickup truck. He went toward the propped-open door near the artroom and ex-minister on the threshold.

"What are you doing?" he demanded. "What do you mean, coming in this facility in such attire?" He picked the minister, the one he didn't know, and fixed a stern gaze on him—that was how he saw himself, "fixing a stern gaze."

Jerome came out of the artroom and joined his friend. Both the young men stared at the principal, with astonishment showing through their sweat. In the pink, rectangular face of the principal, its edging of barbered, oiled hair, his smell of aftershave and peppermint lozenge, the suit and tie that spoke of hours spent in air-conditioning—in all this they both saw, wearily, a foe they were sick of facing: the antithesis of everything that meant life, like the glorious sun, and freedom, like the tumbling river near the quarry where they had swum after pickaxing the granite, and intelligence, for considering sex or God or art, none of which (they thought) the principal actually acknowledged as real. He was what they were afraid, with their every decision, of slowly evolving into. Something broke first in the minister. "Oh, go to hell," he said tiredly.

The principal's pink face flooded with red, as if the perma-press collar had become a rubber band and dammed up all his blood. "What do you mean—young man, just who are you—" he sputtered.

Now the minister was excited. He was grinning hugely. "Fuck you!" he went on, and added one more wild, breathless "Go to hell" for good measure. As for poor Haskell, all he could do was lean up against the sports trophy case in the hall, and shake his head. But the situation caught up with him. While the principal continued to sputter, a few chuckles erupted low in Haskell's enormous throat. "Hnh, hnh," he said as they rose, despite himself, and escaped. His friend noticed. "That was pretty good, wasn't it?" he said. He started to laugh himself. He had a high, whinnying laugh that pushed Haskell's bass volley along. "I said, 'Fuck you'—" the friend got out between peals, "I just told 'im, Jerry—'Go to hell'—"

But the principal told Haskell, "You're fired," and marched back to his office to write out the letter informing the School Board.

When Lillian hung up the phone from talking to Aunt Cynthia, and told Allie in a surprised voice what she'd heard, Allie burst into tears. She who used to pride herself on never crying (it was part of the basic behavioral code Fayette believed should be imposed on all little girls: *Don't Cry; Don't Flinch; Don't Tattle;* and *Girls Shouldn't Cuss, Goddamn It)* was now constantly breaking down in front of her brother and mother. "It's just my luck," she said savagely. "The one class I had that I could look forward to my senior year. The one thing I really care about. Oh, why does everything happen to me?"

"Oh, Allie, don't take it so hard."

"Everything happens to me."

Paul Kalunge, who had by now been director of Edgewood's little art museum for several years, would be the new teacher. He had taught art for several years in the New Orleans parochial schools. "Everyone says he's an excellent teacher," Lillian reported firmly. The night of Mr. Haskell's goodbye party Allie had cried so angrily she had literally thrown up. Lillian insisted she go to the party anyway. Her face looked thin and white, the cheekbones like knots beneath the skin, every freckle standing out in her pallor. She braided her hair in a single braid. "You look like you're all of twelve years old," commented Fayette on her way out the door.

"Go to hell," she said.

"*Allie,*" said Lillian.

The party was at Calvin Ray and Esther's and was in full swing by the time she got there. As usual she had her camera over her shoulder, like a discreet purse. If she continued to feel like this she'd be taking a lot of pictures, just to have the lens hiding her weepy eyes if for no other reason.

She knocked on the front door and slipped inside with a few yoo-hoos, and headed toward the living room where everyone would be. "My *Gawd*," she heard Uncle Calvin Ray's voice, "you tell me that Prudhomme kid has gotten out of med school? Well, Lord have mercy on us all. And keep an eye on his mamma. The *mamma*," he added significantly, raising one eyebrow by way of welcome to Allie. "Hello love."

"Sings?" he went on. "Hell yes she sings. She went off to Chicago and studied voice for ten years! Meanwhile her cousin back in that big house was getting worse and worse—but she used to pull herself together to ride the train up for Mamie's recital every year—" All his offbeat acquaintanceships ended up intertwining. There was hardly a family in the parish that he could not tell stories about in his droll, circumspect style.

Allie went to the kitchen counter, where Aunt Esther was beating up some sour cream concoction. "How're you doing?" asked her aunt.

"Oh, fine."

"Did you see what Jerome made for us? Go look at it, it's out in the workshop."

"Okay."

A small, dapper man, with a lined face and hesitant brown eyes, came up and said, "Esther, is there another ash tray somewhere?—Hey, Allie, doll, how are you?"

"Hey, Dr. Boggs," said Allie affectionately. They kissed. He was Mama's friend from the college.

"Where's your mama? Is she here?"

"No sir, it's just me tonight."

Esther came back with an ashtray. "Thanks, love," he said.

"Is Theresa here?" said Allie asked Esther.

"No. Now let me think, where did Cynthia say she was? I think she's at cheerleading camp. She'll be back Friday."

"Oh."

Allie went around the dining room table and out the sliding glass doors to where a brick patio spread out around a fountain sculpted by some Yugoslavian friend of Aunt Esther's. The night was warm. Rubber plants overhung the fountain, soft lights beamed out through the turquoise water, and the fountain's filter made a purring noise.

She sat in a chair almost overgrown by a hibiscus bush, where she could see the people inside as they talked and drank animatedly. She trailed her finger in the water. It was only then that she saw there was a couple already out here, sitting in lawn chairs. Their voices stopped, but not as if she was an intruder; they came to a closure, lapping like water growing still, and then there was a moment of silence.

"Hi," came a man's voice, deep, rather slow and dragging, English-sounding. "You've found the best spot of all."

"Yeah, it's nice out here," said Allie.

"If you stay," he said, "you'll be tempted to swim." He said *sweem.* "Except I think the water couldn't be any more liquid than this air."

"The water's nice," said Allie. "It's always about the same temperature as the air. When we were little we always used to play in it late at night." Sometimes the cousins would pretend they were mermaids. For hours on end, till their hands and feet were pale and whorled from the wet.

"Just a minute, I can't see you at all. I hate talking to someone I can't look at."

The man scooted his chair forward into the dim light, and she could see him, his strongly pronounced features, the gleaming porous face like the African masks displayed on Esther's and Calvin Ray's wall, she said, "Oh, hi, Mr. Kalunge, I *thought* it might be you."

The woman who had been with him took this chance to rise gracefully—she was black too, Allie saw. "I think I'll go back in now for a bit of cheese. It was nice meeting you," she said to Allie, in a lilting voice, and she was gone inside the glass door.

"I heard you're going to take Mr. Haskell's place."

"I don't know if I can do that. But I'll be teaching his classes."

"I guess I'll have you. I'm going to be in Art IV."

"You sound awfully excited about the prospect."

"I'm sorry. I'm just going to miss Mr. Haskell, I guess."

"Now are you Allie McCain? Is that right? Yes, he told me about you. A photographer."

"I guess so."

"And you're also some relation to Calvin Ray?"

"Yessir, he's my mother's brother."

"When you said 'we,' who was 'we,' playing in the fountain?"

"My cousin Theresa and I. And sometimes another cousin... We had read this book about some kids who spent the night in the Met—the Metropolitan Museum of Art? In New York?—"

"I've heard of it." He sounded amused.

"Sorry. They were hiding out, and after all the guards left they would bathe in the fountains there."

"Is Theresa Calvin Ray's daughter?"

"No. Her parents are Tyler and Cynthia...right there, the man in the red tie? That's Uncle Tyler."

"Right, and Cynthia is the blonde. I've met her. I still have trouble keeping people straight."

"Mama says you can live in Edgewood twenty years and still be new."

"That doesn't bode well. I've got fourteen to even reach that point."

The glass door slid open and Jerry Haskell leaned out. "Paul! I've been looking for you. Come here a sec. Hey, Allie."

"Hey, Mr. Haskell."

"Jesus, I'm not even your teacher now, and you still can't bring yourself to call me Jerry?"

"Well, hey Jerry, then."

"Listen to that, Paul, you better look out for this one, she'll take all sorts of liberties with you."

For the first time that day, Allie laughed.

Back in the living room she wandered over to a platter of fruit near a big chair nestled back against the wall, where books and catalogs and sweaters were usually piled up. Aunt Esther was sitting on a footstool, holding a gold-colored drink and looking bemused, with her bangs frazzled over her forehead and her legs tucked under her skirt.

"I almost didn't recognize this chair," said Allie.

"Oh, I know! I didn't either. Sit, sweetie." She patted the place next to her.

"Have you got something to drink?"

"Um-hm, wine." Allie waved it as she settled back into the crinkled, buttoned vinyl folds of the chair, and curled her own feet under her. "You don't mind?"

"Of course not. So how's your summer been?" Esther asked, and while her niece said the obligatory, "Fine," her brown eyes kept searching her face, to see whether it was true.

"Really? Really?" she said. "How about this school year? How does it look?"

"Oh, I guess it'll be pretty busy. I'll be working part-time—and probably there'll be some competitions, you know, art competitions, for the seniors to enter, at least, and the other subjects are supposed to be hard—"

"What about college? Where are you applying? Last time I asked you were thinking about the West Coast, I think it was Reed College—"

"I think I'll apply to Stanford," Allie heard herself saying. After she said it she sensed a little bubble expand around the statement, a perfect, wondrous enclosure, and she knew it was right. She was astonished.

"Oh, good, sweetie!" Esther was saying. Aunt Esther, with those smart eyes so full of light, so utterly surrounded with lines, could stroke people with pet names and still come off as so substantial. Her eyes, an extra watt brighter than a moment before, stayed on Allie's face, as pleased as if she had already gotten in.

"I've thought all along I want to go west," said Allie, "but I just finally realized I don't want to go to a little college, I want to go somewhere big, a university." And I mean *just,* she thought. As she was saying these things she was realizing they were true.

Aunt Esther was nodding. "I think that's wise."

"Somewhere really diverse, and challenging."

"Oh, you'll find it so stimulating. It's so open. And that campus is so energized—you'll have San Francisco—its museums—and other artists—you'll love it."

"I probably won't get in, you know, but that's my first choice."

"Oh." With a single onyx-ringed hand Esther brushed aside thousands of overachieving seventeen-year-olds standing between her niece and admission. "I know how those people think. You'll get in."

Allie laughed, a little doubtfully. But she was feeling better.

24

THERE WERE CERTAIN pairs of mourning doves she had watched all summer on the farm—one that was always at a certain place in the front road, another in the driveway, another near the fig trees clustered by the water trough in the back pasture. They would wait so long to fly away when you approached them by car or tractor that you usually hit the brakes at the last second, thinking you were going to run over them. Their feathers were a blend of opalescent gray and plum and charcoal-dun colors, like the expensive wool tweeds now on display in Edgewood department stores. Their wings look serrated, with their tails growing to a point like a sharpened arrow. When they cooed it was the sound of kids blowing over the tops of Coke bottles.

Allie had heard somewhere that they mated for life, that when one was shot its mate would not fly but would stay near the other, an easy second target. She looked at these paired creatures in their habitual places and thought of her parents. She used to hear them laughing in their bedroom late at night, after she had gone to bed—her mother's laugh rising, protesting against some outrageous thing her father would be saying, and his laugh like his voice steady, persistent, worming in around her mother's reserve like a tickling hand, and then a slur of giggles overtaking them both. This summer Lillian had grown thinner and paler than ever, so that blue veins showed through her skin, as if her skin were as light and inconsequential as her nightgown...It was easy to picture her mother in her nightgown, Allie realized, because she was in it so much, getting dressed for bed at seven-thirty, eight, seeking sleep, maybe, as the only drug she would permit herself to abuse. So that now late at night the house was the children's. They made the last rounds, locking up and turning off lights, themselves.

As the beginning of school drew near, unfamiliar Jeeps and pickup trucks started to crawl down the roads of Green Isle and the McCains' farm. "Who are these people?" Allie commented mildly.

"Dove hunters, I reckon, checking out their territory for next weekend," said Fayette.

"They can't come *here*."

"Sure they can. We've always let 'em. You must have forgotten."

"Our doves will just be sitting targets. There's no sport in that. You could just about run over them in your car. They're so trusting."

"Well, what are you gonna do?" said Fayette. "Lobby the Louisiana legislature against dove season? Good luck."

"Maybe I could put up some of those signs."

"Sure, that might keep people off *our* place. But you can't post the whole world, you know," he said patronizingly. "If you think it's worth it, though—"

She bought POSTED: NO HUNTING signs at a drugstore stacked high with leaning towers of spiral notebooks and binders. On her slow way around the perimeter of their land, she tried to hammer her resentment of Fayette into the creosoted fenceposts. But she wasn't strong enough to nail the signs securely; she had to go back for some super-glue and try that, and slopping a fixative on something, she reflected as she did it, is not as good an emotional release as hammering. Maybe that was the clue to "If I Had a Hammer." Theme song of the sixties. Now in the seventies people had chucked their hammers for super-glue. Or maybe this heat has addled your brain, she told herself. But this inward voice was a more cheerful one, and, walking back to the paved road to survey her handiwork, she was satisfied: the fluorescent orange message flashed to passers-by her determination to protect something that spoke to her, creatures alive in their own right. She had done what she could.

That evening she refused the pork chop Lillian had browned for supper and took more okra instead. "I've decided to give up meat," she said, pseudo-casually, looking at both her brother and mother and then back at her plate.

"Oh?" said Lillian, not missing a beat. "For health or moral reasons?" Wonderful Mama. It was so hard to startle her.

"Neither," said Fayette, pushing back his chair with the force of his legs as he stood up to go get more milk. "She wants to be *different.* Like Aunt Sarepta."

Allie ignored him. She was trying to control her temper. "Moral," she said. "I think I should be consistent about this. Why should I protect the doves if I then turn around and eat chicken?"

"My dear," said Fayette with a flourish, "you are living and working on a cattle farm. Maybe you don't understand the meaning of the word 'consistent.' "

"Are you going to eat fish?" said Lillian by way of a diversion.

But Allie just looked at Fayette, triumphantly. "Sort of like 'You can't post the whole world'!"

"Yeah, what about fish?" Fayette taunted her. "Crawfish bisque? Trout meunière?"

She hadn't thought of that, but she knew what she had to say. "No."

"What about dairy products and eggs?" her mother said.

"Oh, I think those are okay. Animals didn't have to die to give us those."

"What about those poor little vegetables that had to give up their lives when they were pulled up cruelly by the roots?" said Fayette.

She answered indirectly but coldly. "Is there any more squash?"

Of course he had a point; she was doing it partly to be different; she knew that in her heart. There were no vegetarians at Beauregard High that she knew of. The choice would be a statement, like her army surplus pants and simple Indian gauze blouses, the shock she gave other girls in gym when they saw she was braless. These things helped to remind her who she was. Different!

Besides, the challenge of the vegetarian diet appealed to her. She had been reading about Gandhi by way of Bourke-White, and now, to support her decision, she was piddling with the other parts of his philosophy that were convenient.

Fate, she thought. She had to work on the part about accepting fate. Amazingly, things had this relentless way of happening without regard to her will. "I am utterly unable to resign myself," she went around muttering, after her favorite Hemingway story. She wished Fayette would ask her what she was quoting because he was the one who had gotten her to read it in the first place. But instead, one morning not too long after Jerry Haskell's goodbye party, he just came out of his room in stiff, dark new jeans, kissed his mother and sister, told Allie, "You can keep *Viva Terlingua* for now," and drove off in a cloud of dust. He was taking the Jimmy for the time being after all. That too was inevitable. Allie would have to ride the bus.

So senior year was upon her. The golden dream of teenage America. It was supposed to glow with joy and ready-formed nostalgia, she knew from looking at old yearbooks. She had seen enough pictures of misty-eyed graduates to know that. Seniors got rings, portrait photos of themselves by a plastic tree, and early lunch bells. It was the last hurrah of America's strange adolescence, and before marriage and jobs and other fates overtook these teenagers, before the forces of stratification that public schools could curb only to some degree had their full, wanton play with them, the kids were supposed to have a ball. They would scream the last digit of their graduation year with a frenzy that told the other classes just how much fun they were having. In fact, they would be few in number by that time—attrition due to pregnancy, drugs, and simple weariness was high—and the survivors were nearly manic about their own staying power. To Allie, that was all that could really account for their roaring.

The ground haze now was chalky every morning, and thicker than ever. Flocks of cattle egrets had descended on the front pasture—a sign of army worms, Allie knew, but she wasn't sure whether to have it sprayed or not. The birds flying and resettling, flying and resettling all day, looked like a white sheet billowing over the grass. The weather was still sweltering hot, but goldenrod was budding by the roadsides, and to people who watched these things a dry dust, a tinge of red on the magnolia pods, seemed to predict fall. In stores chilled by air conditioning, signs announced Back-to-School sales.

Lillian took Allie shopping and out for lunch afterward, where they sat with paper sacks full of jeans and brightly patterned sweaters at their feet. These were the sweaters worn by dazzle-toothed girls in the glossy magazines that came once a month to the McCains' mailbox—Allie's Christmas present from Theresa last year. The features were called "Fall Football Weekend" and showed the girls scuffing up maple leaves with new Frye boots, while slim toothy white boys in corduroy pants looked on. This is what is supposed to happen to me this fall, thought Allie. I will not doodle in the margins of my math notebook. I'll wear the school colors on Friday. I'll do well on my SATs. I won't make fun of the drill team. Whatever happened at school, at least it would shake her out of her lassitude. She would discipline herself to photograph in the field for an hour every evening, and spend at least that much time in the darkroom.

Despite these good intentions, on the first day of school, sitting in homeroom with her schedule card in hand, she started to quail. The computer had put her in general science again instead of trigonometry. The principal was saying over the intercom: "If any of you notice an error on your schedule card, please fill out one of the forms your homeroom teacher has, and you will receive your corrected schedule on Friday. You are to go to all the classes as printed on your schedules until then. Repeat. No schedule changes will be made until Friday."

"Oh, great, I'll miss a week of trig right off the bat," said Allie. She went to the homeroom teacher's desk to get a form. "They really mean that? They won't switch you to the right class till Friday?"

"That's what they say. What's the problem?"

She explained.

"Look at that! If that isn't—! I tell you what, Allie, I'll write in the right class. You just double-check it with Mr. Blanchard. They'll never know. Which period is it?"

"Third."

"It says you have world history at third."

"I know, but there's another world history at fifth I can take, and fifth is where they have me in general science."

"Oh, I see. Here you go. Now keep it quiet."

"Thanks a lot, Miz Perdue."

"You takin' art again?" Traci Norton asked her from across the aisle.

"Yeah."

"Who do you have?"

"Mr. Kalunge. Sixth period. There's only one Art IV class."

"Who is he? He's new, isn't he? Is he mean?"

"He's an artist, yeah. I don't know if he's mean."

"Someone told me he's a"—Traci looked over her shoulder to see if the coast was clear—"nigger." Allie's eyes narrowed. "I heard he's not gonna give any A's. I heard he said he'd only give a A to Leonardo da Vinci. Man if I don't make a A in art my mama's comin' up to the school. I always made A's in art before I had Mr. Haskell last year and she come up to the school then."

"Did they change it?"

"No. But now if *he* gives me less than a A in art and doesn't change it—! Shit! That's the bell. Can I borrow your hairbrush?"

While students in trouble were being strong-armed to the principal's office, others would hear their outbursts flying down the carpeted halls, bouncing off the cinderblock walls and the fluorescent light fixtures: "This ain't nothing but a damn prison! How come you think they don't put any windows in here! It's just like a goddam reformatory—it could be a hurricane outside for all they ever let you see!" It was true that the school conspicuously lacked windows. Its architects probably thought windows would disrupt its long, sleek lines. Maybe boring, unbroken expanses of brick were faddish when the school was designed. Or maybe the planners had deliberately sought to make it easier to regiment the students by robbing them of outside views. The artroom was the only part of the school to escape this fate, and there they were, two wonderful oblongs of clear glass that started halfway up two of its walls and let in tree branches and neighborhood houses and the tops of school buses and nice lengths of sky. Lots of students signed up for art just because of the windows.

Allie would have taken art regardless of where it was taught—it was her only hope for the school year—but the classroom itself did please her. The high, solid, scarred butcher-block work tables and the misshapen metal stools, spattered with old dried paint, were comforting. So were the smells of temperas, wet clay, wood shavings, and paint thinner. As Billy Jones had said one day last year, when the Art III students were languidly sketching, "Mr. Haskell, I think we must get high off-a all these smells in here or something."

"I reckon that'd explain your behavior, Billy."

The art room seemed strange without Mr. Haskell towering over it, his massive head and walrus grin appearing in the cluttered back corner where the supply closets were. Mr. Kalunge had moved his desk way into the corner. He was sitting at a table when they came in, expressionless, with his chin in his hand, immobile except for his eyes searching out the face of each student who came though the door, and his eyebrows moving with interest as he did. Some of the students dropped their eyes. Some continued their own conversations. Allie nodded and said hi.

Once the tardy bell rang he suddenly pushed himself up from the table and took a ream of computer printouts off his desk. He shuffled through them a bit casually, and without any other preamble started calling the roll. He moved slowly but with a fluid sort of insouciance, as if his real power and speed were bunched somewhere inside his body, reined there because the walls here were too confining. When he called roll his voice was deep and sonorous, oddly accented, but not too loud. His forehead wrinkled inquiringly as he called each name and rested his eyes—now behind old-fashioned, black-framed glasses that sat crookedly on his nose—on each person who answered. He called Jess Aguillard's name with the pure French pronunciation and everybody laughed. "Aguillard!" corrected the class. His face refracted with his grin then; the shoulders shrugged. "Thank you. You're talking to someone who's spent more time in France than Louisiana," he said. But he got the slur in Louisiana right. He raised one eyebrow and went on. Then he thrust the printouts behind him, leaning against the table with his arms folded, and started to talk. The class settled back with half-lidded eyes and skeptical expressions on their face. They had already sat through a handful of tedious introductions that day, and they had a wary defensiveness built up from enduring the lectures of teachers whose strategy was to inspire terror on the first day. While they waited to be bored or intimidated they let their eyes skim over the new teacher's body. A slight frame, no taller than the tallest of them. Blocky shoulders out of proportion to the rest of him. Hush Puppy shoes. Golden-brown corduroy pants. A striped shirt rolled to the elbows, with its top button undone where the loosened knot of a necktie rested.

"I've been looking through your work from last year," he said. "You are all excellent artists." They waited. "By your own standards," he said. That figures, they thought. "And to some degree, by the standards of the art tradition itself," he went on. "To some degree. You are all more observant than you know. You have a greater innate sense of design and order than you know, of color and line and balance. Jerry Haskell told me this about you and I agreed once I saw what you've been doing. You've also all been a little too molded by your immediate surroundings—by what you think people expect of you.

"You're fourth-year art students now, and you've probably heard the story about Michelangelo's philosophy of sculpture—that the beautiful forms he carved were already in the marble, and all he did as an artist was to expose them, to release them, by taking away what was superfluous." He paused for a moment and then said, "Extra." Then he went on, "I see you, and myself, as artists in the same way. I want to spend this year taking away all that stuff that is extra—false standards and expectations that have been imposed on you. I don't mean imposed by other art teachers; I mean imposed by the society we live in. These impositions are really less than art. I want to help you listen to yourselves, trust your own eye and hand. I think you'll find that this kind of expression is more satisfying than some of what you've been doing.

"I don't mean we'll ignore tradition. We'll be studying art history all along as we work on our projects. But I won't be looking for right or wrong answers when you interpret great art. I'll be judging how much time and thought you spent with that certain piece, what kind of intelligence you shed on it for me. So there'll be better and worse interpretations, some more thought out than others or deeper felt than others, but no wrong ones. Okay?"

"Okay," said the class. Their eyes were round.

"Any questions?"

One girl raised her hand. "What will our grade be based on?"

"Oh." He shrugged. "I don't know."

She stared back at him for a minute, then dropped her head and pretended to be writing something.

"Anybody else?" Nobody else. "Now, specifically, what are some projects you'd like to do? What media would you like to work in? Yes? Yes, you, Mr.—?"

"Clint. Clint Johnson. I'd like to do some scratchboard."

"Fine. What else? Over here?"

"Are we gonna do any watercolor?"

"Yes. Your name?"

"Meredith Chaney."

He heard from several others, nodding. Then he went to his desk, again with that packed, nearly languid grace, and got a giant art reproduction poster that he tacked on the strip of bulletin board over the chalkboard. Allie recognized it as a still life by Matisse. "What do you see here?"

The class was quiet for a while until a smart-aleck boy sang out, "Why, a pitcher!" just as another anxious, cautious girl on the honor roll said, "Do you want us to *write down* what we think?"

"Yes, one thing you see is a picture. No, I just want you to speak out."

A few moments later the students started to mutter the names of objects within the painting. They were suspicious because their answers seemed too obvious. But Mr. Kalunge kept saying, "Fine, fine," until it seemed they had named every single fold and rind within the work. "Air," said someone finally.

"Air!" scorned someone else.

"Well, I reckon it's air in 'ere, even if you can't see it."

"Um-hm," said someone else. "Air be all around."

"Ain't nothing left, Mr. Kalunge," said someone else.

But he went on: "Okay, what else do you see?"

"Black lines," returned the speaker, sarcastically. "White space."

"Good!" said the teacher. "Anybody else?"

"Blue cross-hatchings."

"A green triangle."

Patiently, patiently, he received their remarks and egged them on for others, till they had exhausted not only the representational content of the painting—the objects within it, minutely detailed—but also its compositional content—mood, degree of abstraction, use of lines, spaces, shadow, repetition, contrast, light, pattern, statements. The process took the rest of the hour. He liked doing this orally as a class project, instead of in individual written responses, because he wanted to show the class how their thoughts could work in concert.

"How's Paul going to work out?" said Lillian over supper that night. They were in her room. They had started to eat in weird places, to avoid the empty feeling of the breakfast room, with both Frank's and Fayette's chairs empty.

"Okay I guess. He seemed sort of arrogant. Interesting though."

"How was he received?"

"I think people don't know what to make of him."

25

LATELY IT HAD BEEN a project of the Rabelaises to try to play matchmaker for Allie. Mémé would pass on reports about her friends' grandchildren: "His dad's a doctor and he wants to be a doctor too. He's on the football team. And, *my!* good-*looking!*—" Her aunts would invite her over just when distant cousins happened to be visiting and make illogical remarks. "You all used to play together in the playpen! I mean it!" "And what's your major, Kurt? History? What a coincidence, Allie is quite a photographer—" So Allie was not surprised, one night when she was invited to Uncle Jules's lake house, that there was a young man there—a newly hired assistant to Jules, who was a contractor and builder. By then she had had ample opportunity to craft her reactions to such set-ups, and could go through the motions almost cheerfully, of appraising the boy and avoiding any key involvement of herself. The most these encounters ever provoked in her was a glitter of sexual curiosity. Even then she was probably intrigued more by the notion of short-circuiting the linkage of supposed common traits and hobbies her relatives had so carefully laid, and connecting a little more shockingly, than by the young men themselves.

She went through the pleasantries, questioning Randolph and answering his questions in turn. He had grown up in New Orleans and graduated from Duke the year before. He had been accepted to medical school, but had deferred his entrance a year: "I want to work with my hands," he told Allie seriously, looking at his feet, but then shooting glances toward her as if to gauge her reaction. His *i*'s had a faint Yankee accent. She would never have guessed he was from Louisiana. He was tall and slightly stocky, tanned, with glossy brown hair splayed over his forehead, a moustache, and a dimple at one corner of his mouth that gave him a sort of lopsided sweetness.

"Won't you be working with your hands when you're in med school?" She couldn't help it. It just popped out.

"Sure, eventually. But I want to be in a different milieu for a while. I'm tired of studying and seminars."

"You want to be with the common people," she said innocently.

But he heard her undertone and surprised her by grinning. He had a second dimple that didn't show when he was straight-faced. "Yeah, you know? Gotta put in your time there. It's sort of a rite of passage. Gotta work on the docks or on a river barge or something."

"How'd you know Uncle Jules?"

"Well, my grandmother lives here, and she's a friend of your grandmother's. So my grandmother—"

"What's her name?"

"Clark, Myrtle Clark."

"Oh yeah."

"Anyway, she knew Jules and she asked him if he could find something for me to do. It was pretty shrewd; she wanted to figure out a way to get me near her all year."

"Oh, and I can understand why."

"Man." Randolph looked hurt, and shook his head. But at the same time both of them were laughing. "Do you think I'm that much of an asshole or what?"

"I'm sorry. I don't know what gets into me sometimes. So

anyway: are you living with your grandmother?"

"Yeah. I may look for a place of my own later, but it's nice to be saving money."

"You'll be interested in this, Allie," said Uncle Jules, who had just walked up, and put a hand on each of the young people's shoulders. "Randolph majored in *English.* Not biology or chemistry like you might think."

Randolph twisted his eyebrows into a rueful, comic expression. He sighed. "That's another thing you're supposed to do," he said, "not be a typical pre-med. You're supposed to major in English."

Uncle Jules did not understand this remark. Still, he saw that the young people were getting along. "Allie's always reading up a storm!" he said to Randolph. He squeezed both their shoulders and walked away.

After supper Allie and Randolph sat on the dock together talking. He would comment self-righteously or self-deprecatingly on any topic they slid into and she answered in a faintly sarcastic drawl—her inner self cagy, tense, poised as a cat. She didn't intend to cast any pearls before this type. But she saw that she had attracted him, that his pupils were wide with interest, his laugh rang out with a surprised sound when she made a joke.

The lake had a flat, dull sheen and blended with the sky into a single steely expanse. Wisps of mist moved over the plane of the metal-colored water. From behind them, up on the bank and partly blocked by trees, the orange anti-insect porch light of the camphouse glowed like a jack-o'-lantern. Faint music and the rumble of a roomful talking and laughing spilled down, emphasizing their removal. Their voices seemed to move steadily away from them over the surface of the lake, toward the huddled dark shape of trees on the other side.

They fell quiet, drowned out by the sounds of frogs and crickets and the human party like a din of static on a radio dial. She could barely see him; he hummed a little jazz tune but she had the feeling that it wasn't for her benefit, he would be humming it even if she weren't there. She was not at all surprised when he leaned toward her and started to kiss her. With vision and hearing indistinct, the other senses filled her consciousness: smooth lips, the wet, deliberate flicker of his tongue. His mouth tasted slightly of the peaches they'd just had for dessert. Heat flared all down her, in the tips of her breasts and between her legs. Yet she remained a spectator, as mute and unimpressed as the lake darkness.

Then he started talking again. "I'm just tickled to death," he said.

He had a light, buoyant way of talking with a mock country accent that she had already caught on to. They stood up and went to the edge of the dock and he kept their hands joined, pretending to dance with her for a minute. He talked about her looks. And brains too! And he had friends who said Southern women were overrated! No, he meant it. He had felt something when she walked into the lake house. She was so young! Seventeen. He had just turned twenty-two. She probably had tons of boys interested in her. Well, he wouldn't interfere. But in the meantime she put him in a really good mood.

He finished what he was saying and looked down happily. He didn't seem to require that she be exuberant too. He kissed her again and she responded, standing very still, taking note of the sensations he caused until she forgot to pay that kind of attention and for once her active and her spectator selves merged.

He called her the next night. And the next. She kept returning his banter, lightly as a ping-pong ball, listening to his serene chatter, and assenting when he invited her to go somewhere. To a movie. To his apartment. To a swimming party at a friend's. She wasn't sure why; there didn't seem to be any reason to say no. Yet she was realizing that they were far different people. Like skew lines in geometry—"not parallel, yet not intersecting; lying in two different planes." Not just because of the gap in their ages—for despite that, despite his New Orleans private-school upbringing, despite Duke, she felt older, darker and smarter and more complicated than Randolph. But by the time these differences sank in they were in a loose pattern of companionship. And though she usually held the reins of the relationship—they both knew it—power ebbed from her to him when he kissed her. It was then that he shrugged off his bounding good humor and proceeded to drive the point home to Allie that his whimsy and ebullience were not what she saw in clowning boys her own age, but were a man's traits, fully within his control. She liked him best when he used that power, turned her lightly as a top and left her a little dizzy for it. But she always resented it later, when she was back in command.

Allie's mother and aunts and grandmother were delighted with the liaison: how lucky they were that Allie had found someone suitable! They didn't mind that Randolph was a little older, for after all, Allie was not exactly your typical seventeen-year-old. Fayette had said nothing about it, other than commenting that Randolph "probably liked 'ranh-ranh music,' " which he refused to define. For Allie herself even the two strongest ties, of curiosity and sex, had begun to weaken, but not knowing what else to do for now she let the relationship drift on.

And she was happier. Her classes at school were interesting, and she realized that they probably had been last year as well, but with everything else going on she hadn't noticed. By October the Latin IV class was reading Catullus; it was a good thing the School Board had never done the same, or they would have banned it. The English IV class had scooted through Beowulf and was lingering over the *carpe diem* poets. "Gather ye rosebuds while ye may, Old Time is still a-flying ..." ran the singsong in the twelfth-grade honor students' heads as, like a little herd of calves, they bopped around the corner to trig. There they could stare till they were glassy-eyed at graphs of things like asymptotes, those curves that come closer and closer to some wrenchingly pure absolute without ever arriving. Then on to lunch, then "Free Enterprise," a new course required by the state legislature that provided comic relief, world history, and art.

"Not bad," said Fayette over the phone, when he called to find out how her schedule was.

"No. It's really not bad."

"Got any classes with Theresa?"

"Three. We have the honors classes together. But I don't see her much. She's dating some guy who goes to Edgewood and they spend a lot of time with each other."

"Where's she applying to college?"

"University of Texas."

"It'll never work. She hasn't got that poofed-up hair."

"Their gymnastics team is pretty good. She wants to go to the Olympics."

Allie got a letter saying she'd won the New Orleans photography contest, and there was a minor flurry of publicity—an article in the local newspaper, and a special announcement made at school. Though the attention from Edgewood at large pleased her and puffed her up, at school it embarrassed her acutely. She looked at the top of her desk when it was announced, turning pink, and finally raised her head apologetically. But her classmates' congratulations were kind and enthusiastic. "Way to go!" they said in the halls. They were proud of her. She didn't fit into any of the established categories, so they were making a minor legend out of her. When Dewey Barnes walked into Free Enterprise the first day and saw her there he had stopped short and said, "The Brain! Boy-I-tell-you, I know I'm in the wrong class now!" Allie looked at him and instead of getting irked suddenly giggled, and he giggled back and slouched into the seat across the aisle.

Poor Mrs. Andrews, who'd pulled the short straw of teaching this course, continued to erase the board wearily. "Don't worry, Dewey. We *all* have to cope with Free Enterprise," and Allie laughed again.

She was finding a new solidarity with her classmates. She had misjudged some of them, or they had changed. They weren't as one-dimensional as she had thought. They seemed older themselves, more tired, more worried, more critical, more droll. Walking up and down the halls she noticed that she knew almost everyone, people of all different types—from classes in all four years, from her bus route, from standing near the bench at football games when she'd been a school photographer in ninth and tenth grades and struck up conversations with the second- and third-string players. "Hey, Allie." "Hey, what's up?" "Hey. Nothing much. Hey." "Hey."

They would all be so *known* to one another by the time this year was up.

A summer's worth of dammed-up dreams hit her all at once. She dreamed that her father rose from his grave, not like Jesus but Frankenstein, and walked mummified around Green Isle—swathed in white cloth, with his arms sticking straight out in front of him. Children and dogs fled from him in all directions. Another night he was with her and Lillian, quite normally—they were going somewhere in the car. It was fall and Frank was carrying an armload of goldenrod and asters. They were in full bloom, fresh from the side of the road, dusty with pollen, fragrant, some pulled right out of the ground with their little purplish-white hairy roots still on them, crumby with dirt: she could see it so clearly. He extended it toward Allie, pushing it across the roof of the car before they got in, smiling and nodding and narrowing his eyes as if to say, *Take it, it's for you.* In the dream happiness ballooned in her as she reached out shyly for the flowers and tried to get in the car, and woke up thinking for a millisecond it had been true, that everything was all right and Frank, a vessel for all this feeling, was in the next room with Mama; then realizing, pore by pore, it wasn't true. Another night she dreamed she and Fayette were on top of a tower. She started to fall, terrifyingly. She had always heard that if you hit bottom in a falling dream you would die and in the dream too she remembered this fact, very calmly. She did hit the ground—but it changed into green grass as soft and padded as a cushy trampoline, and she and Fayette turned into babies, bouncing and rebounding into the air in slow motion. Abruptly the dream switched scenes to a giant ballroom. She met someone in the middle of it and everyone else there faded away. His arms took her in, light as air, and they started to kiss, one of those ethereal dream kisses where you and the other figure blend into one another like colored beams of light from two film projectors.

Every weekday her alarm clock rang at five-thirty and dragged her out of sleep. In the kitchen she would put water on to boil and fill the drip pot with coffee: crumbling, acrid, black as some rich loam Lillian might mix for her plants. When the kettle steamed she poured water through the grounds and covered the sweet brown foam that formed while she waited for it to drip.

She would raise the kitchen blind. The window over the sink faced east, and she could see the lightening sky, the sun casting ruddy streaks over the fields, and dirt clods and anthills and blades of grass backlit with yellow. The dogs were just waking up and even they were not lively yet—Troy curled in one of Mama's favorite groundcovers, just lifting his head at the noise of the blind, and Roscoe coming stiffly around the house, moving slowly, yet already drawn to the signs of human activity with a look of wistful sincerity on his face.

With the first drippings of coffee she went back to her room and pulled on jeans and a shirt. Her boots were by the back kitchen door—she'd get them on her way back. When she stepped outside, the cool air smacked her face softly like so many little waves, and at that minute of exit the house she was leaving would suddenly seem so close and stuffy by contrast that she wondered how she had slept in it. By this time she was already scuffing across the dew-sopped grass toward the shed. The sky was opening higher every second. She tugged one fifty-pound sack of feed toward the Jimmy (Fayette had finally brought it home) and tried unsuccessfully to swing another onto her shoulder. On a good morning she could relish these little demands, little rigors. She almost tripped over one of the dogs when he stopped in front of her to snuffle in a tuft of weed. "Dammit, Troy! Get out of the way." He looked up apologetically and ran on, with his tail windmilling.

The Jimmy coughed and died. She started it again, revving the accelerator, until eventually it gave in and started. She gave it a long time to warm up while fine-tuning the radio dial for Uncle Calvin Ray's daily program. Every morning she had to find it again because late in the day, when he was off the air, she switched over to country or top forty on other stations.

She would drive back along the road that went by the pastures, scanning the herd of cattle for any signs of trouble or sickness, trying to count them as she went. She scattered the feed and glanced over their salt and water supply. All of this took about an hour. By then the morning would be fully established, no longer hers alone. Traffic would have thickened on the highway. The elementary school bus would go by on its first run. She would go back to the house and scramble an egg or pour out cereal for breakfast, then carry it back to her room and eat it haphazardly while undressing for her shower. By seven-forty she was leaving the house for school.

One Saturday afternoon when she and Randolph were driving back from an excursion to a construction site of Jules's company outside the parish, a daddy-long-legs marched across the dashboard. Allie took it by a leg and scrutinized it until they stopped for a red light, whereupon she dropped it gently out the window. She was feeling particularly calm and confiding. "You know," she said, "this is probably sort of a stupid thought. But sometimes when I see things like this—just little things, bugs or even plants or animals—I get mad. I don't see how their bodies, I mean all their cells and organs and systems, can work so perfectly and keep them alive when my father's couldn't."

"Ah well," said Randolph, "everything is for the best."

She glanced over at him to see what he looked like when he was being ironic. But he looked perfectly serious. "Oh, come on," she said.

"I mean it. You know, you can't see it now, but even that happened for some reason, for some good that will come out of it—some higher purpose."

"So nothing bad really happens? It's just our imagination? That's what you think?"

"Well ..."

"I think bad stuff *does* happen."

"No," he said, "it just may be that the purpose isn't revealed to us yet."

Allie turned her head when he finished speaking. He didn't have time to see the twist of irritation of her mouth. She edged farther away from him, against her window, and they rode in silence for a while.

Randolph felt confused. He had lost something. He wished she hadn't scooted across the seat away from him. This truck was not really his; it belonged to Uncle Jules's company. Any time there was a chance of Allie's riding with him Randolph preferred this truck to his own and would finagle Jules into letting him take it. His own truck had a stick shift between two passenger seats that made it harder to do what he lightly called "playing around."

He said, "Do you want to go on back?"

"I don't care. Just drive. You're doing fine."

He extended his hand to her, palm up across the little gap between then, a good hand, square and able-looking, she had to grant him that, and she toyed over it with her fingertips—but in a preoccupied way. It could have been a table napkin.

Nevertheless he felt better. "I'm sorry you're upset about your dad," he began, sweetly and pompously, "but these things—" and she snatched her hand away at once. "Jesus, Allie! Sometimes you really act your age."

"Well, you sound like a *coach* or something. I can't stand it."

"Maybe you think it'd be easy to find someone who'd put up with your sulking. I can't stand a moody girl. And neither can most men."

"A *'higher purpose'* than my father's *life?*"

He was sulking now. His head drooped almost to his chest. They were at a fork in the road on the southern edge of the parish. There was no other vehicle in sight and Randolph had stopped. His tone was dogged and humble. "Look. I'm here and nobody else is so you may as well make the most of it too. Where—"

"I'll tell you where I want to go. I want to go somewhere *wild.*"

"Yes ma'am. Wild it is."

Pastureland and cotton-and-beans farms gave way to rice fields, and to swamps that had just been drained and cleared for planting. They would make sorry farmland. Big yellow bulldozers stood behind half-fallen trees, mired in mud. It would be weeks before they could be unstuck. After a while the trees thinned out again and the road changed surfaces, unrolling over open water with a cement railing cropping up beside it. There was space between the trees, and then they saw the spillway—a series of joined concrete ducts running roughly parallel to the road. Steadily and robustly, along its whole length, brown water was pouring in. It fell in a heavy curve, foaming dirty white where it splashed into the lower level. Even inside the truck they could hear the steady torrent as it fell.

"Look at that!" said Allie. "I've never seen it open."

"They've had a lot more rain down here than we have," said Randolph. "It never has been open until this year. They've never needed to use it till now."

"Yeah, I saw it on the news. Would you mind stopping? I'd like to take some pictures."

The rains had been so heavy that the bottomlands flooded. All that backwater needed somewhere to go, and the spillway had had to be opened. Already below them young trees were engulfed. The upper branches of light-green willows and cypresses struggled above the swirling water. White egrets marched along the spillway dam to fish, hundreds of them stalking with their heads alertly poised and bills ready to jab. To their left was the rushing, rising water; to their right was a hardwood swamp basin, with trees' trunks obscured by the gloom of their new leaves. It looked as if the trunks had been spun, thinning and hardening, out of the bulbous roots that stood in the black water.

Finally Allie said, "I'm out of film. You ready?"

"Yep."

"Thanks. Those should be good."

On the other side of the spillway, Randolph turned onto a dirt road that ran along a hardwood ridge. He turned off the engine and looked at Allie. His eyes reeled her haughtiness in like a fish on a line, turn by turn, and she felt resigned and peaceful as she followed.

She lay in his lap and he started kissing her slowly. After a minute the leaning bothered him and he twisted so that they both half-lay on the seat, trying to avoid the steering wheel as their heads revolved blindly. The seat was pitted vinyl and smelled of ancient, spilled, dried-up coffee and all the sweat that had rubbed through cotton work pants on thousands of warm afternoons. A seat belt buckle was pressing Allie's cheek. She opened her eyes as she pushed it away and saw the sifted dust and crumpled Exxon receipts pillowing her head and almost smiled. This was what she wanted, for the moment—to be ground into some compromising corner of the world, to thrust her nose and tongue and fingers into odd crevices, to shock and be shocked into something near devastation, to be irrevocably changed as the trees that had surrounded her home were. ("Lie back," he was saying tenderly. "Lie back, and I'll show you the skies." He actually said that, one of his well-meant romanticisms, and Allie thought, skies? It had to do with a lot of things that she knew of, but nothing to do with skies.)

Then suddenly he stopped. Just when the backs of her knees had gone liquid, he wasn't there any more. He heaved forward and lay on her stomach. "Are you all right?" he said solicitously, with his eyes closed, his face red and squished into her breastbone on one side. She didn't answer. In a few minutes he pulled himself upright and started to pick clothes up off the muddy floorboards. He eyed her and said, "You're a mess—I'm sorry" and started cleaning her with his handkerchief, whistling under his breath, cheerful and clowning again, as if she had been a two-year-old released from her highchair. She dressed quickly and was gazing out the window again when Randolph started the motor.

"Aren't you glad we stopped?" he said when they'd gone a few miles down the road.

"Why?"

"I think it's a lot better," he went on, as if he hadn't heard her. "You need to be real sure before you have sex. You're only—God!—you're only seventeen. It'll be a while before you know for sure what you want."

He had never entered her. It seemed more Christian to him. So these long episodes of play, confusingly undirected, had become a pattern—always a series of struggling embraces, not fluid, but like a jointed string of unrelated acts. They left her nerves drawn tight as cello strings. But she doubted her own judgment. Randolph was five years older than she and (according to his own anecdotes) a sexual veteran, while she had no reference except novels and movies for how these things were supposed to develop. So the decisions to go so far and no further were his alone. His reasons had to do with her age, he said, and with his wish not to "compromise" her. He did not consult her. She would lie beside him, passive, while he analyzed their relationship. Lately it had dawned on her that he always satisfied himself before he reached this stage.

"Have you come?" he would whisper tenderly.

"Yeah," she would say, not quite positive she was lying.

So now she kept silent more out of confusion than agreement. Inside she was full of questions. Why *not* have sex, if you did this much? Why had he held forth on a long monologue about "precautions" only a week ago if he intended to "stop" with her every time?

26

A GLASSY SEA: varying from the green of thick-cut curving Coke bottles, to the even, thin aquamarine of Mason jars, to window-pane clear. In the foreground, a man plowing with almost effeminate care, a daydreaming shepherd, a dog, sheep, a hawk. A sunny day, clear, ethereal, pure, and common as glass itself—a Tuesday, probably, that sort of day, a little after nine in the morning, that sort of feeling. In the distance mountains covered with white careless snow, and a little port town. But those two white, splayed legs flashing into the ocean—what did they spell?

Today Allie was in a fog of depression. She was relieved to get to the artroom and be able to look out the windows. As soon as Mr. Kalunge unveiled the art reproduction poster of the day she started scanning it automatically, looking for subtleties, the key choices in the act of composing that the other students were not going to articulate until they had laboriously tallied the other items in the painting. And today that was going to take a long time.

"All right. Fine," Mr. Kalunge was saying. "You've named lots of things. Sum them up."

The Art IV students were getting better. "A world—"

"A community, like—"

"Daily life."

"Where do those legs fit into 'daily life'?"

"Someone's swimming?"

"I'll give you a hint. The title of the painting is *Landscape with the Fall of Icarus.* Does anybody know who Icarus was?"

Allie did, but she would wait and see whether anyone else knew it. She had a loose quota system for answering hard questions: if she spoke out and were right too often she would have been known, justifiably, as a show-off, yet if she refrained too much her vanity suffered.

Someone must have taken Mythology the year it was offered as a mini-course. "Yah, Saundra?"

"He tried to fly into the sun and he came too close and it melted the wax offa these wings his father had made him."

"And?"

"Well, he fell, I mean, he fell in the sea, I guess those are his legs right there."

She looked from the painting to the sky, the gilded lace made by pecan branches against the sun. The students' voices lulled her like a chorus. The pattern of Kalunge's baritone against them, the rise and tilt of his questions and the stutter and whine of answers, was so familiar to her she didn't even need to attend to it. It was peace itself, pathetic because it was so homely: a bland background against which her own grief and anger pitched.

But the painting itself was expressing that. She looked far into it and was suddenly clutched by a recognition of her own familiar, mundane pain. Or was it rather the prettiness of the scene, so seriously wrought, that got to her? Why did the artist care so much? She wasn't sure. Her eyes filled up with tears and as she glanced away, toward the window again and away from the classmates who might notice them, she caught Kalunge gazing at her. He looked like a frame frozen from the movie reel of his habits, his automatically spoken patter of teaching—stepping sideways in part of the restless configuration he always paced off when leading this discussion. She saw that he had been about to question her; literally, his lips were parted. Neither of them looked away. All Allie could do was stare back, and after a moment—probably only a split-second—he shut his mouth, and went on to the next person, but she didn't hear the rest of the discussion.

The next day when she got to his class he put a piece of paper on her desk, saying, "I thought you would appreciate this." It was a poem written out in block capitals—"Musée des Beaux Arts" by W.H. Auden.

About suffering they were never wrong,
The Old Masters: how well they understood
Its human position; how it takes place
While someone else is eating or opening a window
or just walking dully along ....

In Brueghel's **Icarus**, *for instance: how everything turns away*
Quite leisurely from the disaster; the ploughman may
Have heard the splash, the forsaken cry,
But for him it was not an important failure; the sun shone
As it had to on the white legs disappearing into the green
Water; and the expensive delicate ship that must have seen
Something amazing, a boy falling out of the sky,
Had somewhere to get to and sailed calmly on.

Two or three days a week she stayed after school to use the darkroom. It had been designed as a broom closet but the art classes had persuaded the school administration to let them use it. The key to the darkroom hung on a bulletin board behind Mr. Kalunge's desk. Mr. Kalunge was usually still there when Allie left. If he left before her he would come and rap once on the door. "Ah—Miss McCain." He used "Mister" and "Miss" with the students, whether out of some chivalry that seemed to match his accent, or ironically, they could not tell.

"Sir? Just a minute."

"I'm leaving now. You want to bring the key back in the morning?"

"I'm almost through. If you'd hold on just one second."

She would emerge blinking into his face, which looked severe behind his heavy old-fashioned glasses, and would thank him in bright deflective tones as she gave back the key. She was never sure where she stood with him. Once he had laughed during one of these brushes in the hall, and said, "I only see you when your eyes are all twisted up against the light. I have an image of you as someone perpetually in a state of waking up."

"It's like when you come out of a movie," she said.

"Hmm." His speech was full of voiced, multi-syllabled murmurs and *oh*'s, which expressed ambiguous blends of approval, irony, or reserved judgment.

They left together the day he gave her the poem. She thanked him for it.

"I thought you—would like it."

"Do you want it back?"

"The poem? No, that's just a Xerox. I have it in a book. Several books."

She nodded. "My dad liked poetry a lot," she said briefly. Later, before she fell asleep that night, she wished she hadn't said that. It probably sounded like a bid for sympathy.

"Mmn." They walked to the parking lot together without saying anything more.

She paused inside the barn to give her eyes time to adjust to the brownish shade. It was a couple of weeks later, one afternoon after school. Instead of going to the new tractor that they had rented from the Mitchells down the road, she pushed aside a moldy hay bale where an oily funnel and rag were sitting, and went to inspect the tractor her great-great-uncle had bought in 1954. It was an International Harvester, once red, now faded to a clay-rose color by the sun and flecked with rust. An inverted tobacco can covered the exhaust. She circled the machine to look it over, breaking cobwebs with her knees as she went. On the far side she found a wrench that had been missing for months.

She was sure she could get it running again. First she would have to have the battery recharged. She found the battery compartment up on the flank of the tractor. Two wing nuts were holding the cover in place. But the clutch pedal and a sort of rod were obstructing it. How should she get it off?—Any instruction booklet or owner's manual was long since missing; Uncle Hudson had probably thrown it away at the very store. She scrabbled around in the tool box of the truck for the right-sized wrench and a can of WD-40. She sprayed the stiff, rusted parts till they dripped. Within a few minutes she had loosened the wing nuts. She set them in the tractor seat. It had once been vinyl, now torn or eaten away; the batting inside was spilling out; in 1967 someone had slipped a *Farm Journal* inside for padding, and its pages were brittle and yellowed.

Then she started to investigate how she might move the rod that blocked her from lifting away the battery cover. She found some more wing nuts to remove. But even then she'd have to bear down on the clutch to clear the way. So she mounted the tractor, scooped up the nuts and washers she'd just put there, and put them temporarily in the tobacco can taken off the exhaust pipe in front. She remounted and tried to push in the clutch. Nothing happened. Her weight made no impact on the part frozen so long by disuse. She pushed harder, frowning, straightening her leg. The rugged corrugated steel dug into the soft rubber sole of her sneaker. Her legs were not long enough anyway to reach those tractor pedals comfortably. Holding the wheel, now with both feet squeezed onto the clutch pedal, she pulled herself gradually to a standing position. The clutch went down about half an inch. She tried to jump and stomp to force it down. Great squeaks of resistance came from the rusty pedal. The dogs, snuffling in the strewn hay, jumped out, cocking their ears at the odd noise and wagging their tails good-naturedly. She swore, and sat back down in the seat, sweating. A spume of anger formed inside her. She could get madder at *things* than she ever did at people or herself. But alongside the anger rose her family obstinacy—cold, ugly, and stubborn, prouder even than the anger. She stood on the clutch pedal again. It was no different. She jumped off the seat for the wrench and gave it a couple of ringing sidelong blows. Old impacted rust flew. She hauled herself up to the driver's platform again, swiftly as a sailor pulls himself up into rigging, and crouched on the pedal one more time, both feet squeezed into the short space, rocking her weight back and forth. This time it gave, with a screech, to the floor. While it was down she moved the piston and pried at the battery cover away.

Inside, like the kernel of a nut, lay the battery. It looked corroded and she hesitated to touch it. With a rag she wiped it clean. Then she figured, Oh, well, I've gone this far, and lifted it out. Its weight astonished her. She took it to the truck, staggering, and practically dropped it in.

When she wiped her hands off on her jeans and looked at her

watch, it was five-thirty.

She whistled for the dogs and drove back to the house. Inside she dumped her schoolbooks on her bed and went to wash her hands and arms, calling International Harvester as she did so.

"No, ma'am, we don't take nothing after six o'clock."

"Allie!" called her mother from the kitchen. "Allie!"

She went to the door of the living room. "Ma'am?"

"Your brother called. He said to call him back before seven."

She was already at the phone. "Fayette."

"Hey. How you doing?"

"Doing all right. Mama said you called."

"Yeah. Why don't you think about coming down this weekend?"

"Oh, I don't know. There's a lot I have to get done here. Plus I'm already riding to New Orleans and back Friday. On a school trip."

"What for?"

"To see the King Tut exhibit."

"Tell you what. Why don't I pick you up down there, after you see the exhibit, and you spend the rest of the weekend? I've been wanting to get down to New Orleans anyway."

"I don't know—"

"I'm moving. You can help me."

"Again?"

"You didn't help me the last time."

"No, I mean you're *moving* again."

"Sure. What time are you going through the exhibit? I'll just wait by your bus. Get Mom to write a letter so they'll let you go with me."

"I think we'll be in there from eleven to one. Well, okay. That sounds real nice. I'll take you up on that. You know the museum?"

"Yeah. Good. I'll be there at one."

Headlights signifying parents dropping off their kids, and the big globes in the parking lot, glimmered in the fog at five-thirty Saturday morning. Allie parked the truck and went with her curious quick-swaying walk to join the others. The students looked sleepy, scowling, their faces raw-scrubbed and somewhat unfamiliar at this hour: girls with makeup glaringly applied, those normally in contact lenses now wearing glasses. Some people carried sack lunches, a few, books. Allie, cool as usual by some standard obscure to everyone but herself, had a duffel bag for the night and a copy of *Let Us Now Praise Famous Men,* which she had recently found under a seed catalog in what used to be her father's closet.

She milled around with the others, empty, wishing for coffee, joining occasionally in the chatter that seemed to creak with sleepiness and nervousness.

"My alarm clock didn't go off! God, I thought I was gonna be late. So I go in the kitchen and my mother's in there and I go, 'Mama, why didn't you wake me up—?'"

"Where's David Harley? Has anybody seen him?"

"He went home to get his jam box."

"I hope they bring us a *real* bus, not no school bus."

The telltale yellow of a school bus loomed out of the fog as if on cue.

"Can you tell who's driving?"

"Oh hell, it's that mean man drove us to State Choir Festival last year."

The rooms of the exhibit were blue-black, the blue of cobalt and the black of ebony turned into something breathable. Allie moved around the cases. Her classmates in tow were mere shadows. The room murmured with soft voices and the crackles of the guided tape tours seeping out of rented earphones. The gold and cerulean figurines, the masks and boxes of lapis lazuli gleamed like lasers in their twentieth-century showcases, clear cubes of light. How ancient these objects were, made for the unthinkably long-ago dead. Yet they stabbed the eyes with more vitality than the gray, living world outside the museum. Objects that the dead one might need with him in the afterlife. What should she have crafted for her father? ...

After a general twenty-minute scuffle in the gift shop the students were brought back outside. Fayette was chatting calmly with Mrs. Dupree by the bus. Allie—feeling smug with her duffel bag over her shoulder, conscious of her friends watching—produced her permission note from Lillian, which seemed superfluous by now, and walked over to Fayette's new car. "Hey, I like it," she said. It was a nine-year-old Triumph. "You have to stop every once in a while and put oil in it," he answered. They roared off toward to the home of "a friend" of his. It turned out to be a girlfriend—he hadn't told her and Lillian—a quiet, slender nursing student, with fine red hair that fell in loose curls on her shoulder, and pale skin. She and three other young women were renting a house on the edge of the Garden District. They all sat in the crowded living room, with plaster falling from the ceiling, and drank sangria. Maria's housemates smoked grass. Dismantled lamps—twelve or fifteen of them—stood around the room, with their old-fashioned shades, ruffled and looped and bowed like Mary Poppins's hats, piled in high stacks in the corners. "Oh," someone said when Allie asked about them, "we found those in the attic. We're going to fix them up. Just haven't gotten around to it yet." In the meantime light from bulbs cheaply covered with paper globes struck the unused shades softly, reflecting off the sheen of the satin, glowing through the muslin. Soon Allie lay on her back on the floor photographing the fanciful shapes.

After a while everyone was hungry. They made nachos and devoured them and went to a grocery store for the ingredients to make more. Outside the store the police were frisking a black man wearing army pants. Allie took pictures. "Jesus," said Fayette, "you're embarrassing me." Around midnight they went to a bar on Esplanade. "Just pretend you're my date," said Fayette, "they won't card you." Allie glanced at Maria, as if for permission; Maria suddenly smiled. "I *have* an I.D." They both laughed. "Why don't y'all stay?" said their friends. "I'm moving tomorrow," said Fayette. "Better get back." At two in the morning Fayette, Maria, and Allie piled in the Triumph, with Allie squished behind the two bucket seats, and headed out of New Orleans: pushing against its wet, swelling darkness that smelled of oysters and warm dripping leaves, till the upper speeds of Fayette's car scattered that atmosphere against their bare faces.

Fayette asked Allie about certain teachers, giving thumbnail descriptions of them to Maria first. Allie strained to remember the funniest stories. She mimicked Mrs. Andrews's deep voice: "Free Enterprise is something we *all* have to cope with!"

They giggled. "You ought to inscribe that, you know, and post it over the Green Isle sign. Sort of a warning."

"Oh, that sign is gone, remember?"

"That's right, that's right. They tore it down. Pretty wild."

"You know, there was that big scene about it at the business meeting. Dikes was furious."

"Yeah, Dikes likes things the way they were. He's had power, relative to everybody else, for some time now."

"Now, who's Dikes?" said Maria.

"Minister on the place," said Fayette, just as Allie answered, "Resident death insurance salesman."

"What?"

"No, seriously, he goes around selling funeral insurance to his people."

"I didn't know about that," said Fayette, shaking his head.

"Apparently Aunt Amalie used to shell out for funeral expenses herself. Mama said she was always complaining about it. But I'm not sure it's any better for Dikes to collect against the funeral fees."

"Probably not...So what's been going on on the place, Allie? Do you think it's working?"

"Oh, I guess. Everything looks okay from the outside. They screwed up last summer with the drought and the army worms, and lost a boatload of money. But we nearly did too, so I can't say too much about that. And I heard they're gonna be audited. They started getting notices of it and Harlan immediately got the nerves."

"Jesus, I don't envy that IRS man."

"That's what Mama said. She's helping them get ready for it. She said everything's in order on paper, but it's just real complicated, and every time she asks Harlan or William a question they get off into some long explanation she can't follow where they call everyone by two or three different names that seem unrelated—"

"Sort of like a Russian novel?" Maria put in.

"Yeah."

"Sometimes I'm not sure the old man did them much of a favor. You know?" Fayette looked in the rearview mirror and adjusted it, trying to see her face. Allie shifted. Her left leg had gone to sleep.

"What do you mean?"

"I think he just felt guilty. Didn't want to be in charge any more. Didn't like that position. Too paternalistic."

"Well, it *was* paternalistic."

"Yeah. But he turned it over to them without making sure they'd make a go of it. You know? All they had was a little bit of cumulative farming sense."

"They don't seem to be doing too badly. And they had him to ask questions ..." Allie fell silent.

"That doesn't help too much now," said Fayette. "And half the time he'd been there he was learning himself. There hasn't been a period of even a year when that farm was run by someone who knew what he was doing. Including Dad, Amalie, and probably Uncle Hudson. Hell, Dad got this syndrome from his own father. His own dad just couldn't take it down here, so he left. Wasn't any racial strife in New Jersey to deal with!"

"Not in his lifetime," said Allie. "But I can't blame him for going. The changes down here were going to have to come from somebody who didn't have white skin. He was ahead of his time and what could he do? Why should he be harassed when he wasn't even going to be able to do enough good to make it worthwhile?"

"Because you never know," said Fayette. "You may think you do, but he couldn't know for sure that he wasn't going to be able to do some good in the position he was in. He just ran out because he didn't like the flak."

"Well," said Allie vaguely, "that was a different situation from Daddy and Green Isle."

Fayette's returning silence was the last word. He started to whistle as he swung the car into the drive to his apartment.

The apartments he had lived in in Baton Rouge—two that first year, and one other one so far this fall—were indistinguishable. They had names like Wildwood Terrace and Buena Vista. From the outside they looked blank, more nameless than motels, with rows of big blind windows and numbered doors. They had flimsy outside stairs to the second floor. Inside there were always thin white unadorned walls, carpet, a colonial light fixture hanging crookedly over the dinette off the kitchen, a couch, a TV, a bed, and a bathroom. The quarters for the human beings were much less roomy and attractive than the parking lots outside, which were of new, shining black asphalt, patterned with yellow lines and speed bumps. The cars lining these lots were all like Fayette's, small and vividly painted. In flip-flops and cut-offs, carrying laundry baskets and textbooks and six-packs, the residents of these apartments went back and forth, their lives a succession of runs to the one-stop on the corner, the library, the car wash, the lab, the liquor store, the gym. They were a friendly bunch and resembled one another so closely that Allie wondered if some of them had moved from complex to complex with Fayette.

Allie's opinion of Maria had been going up every hour. By midnight it had risen from suspicion to real liking. She was casual but still attentive, not trying too hard with Allie, holding her ground with Fayette when he tried to railroad her, and calmly teasing him about it. Allie had never heard these dynamics going on between her brother and any girl. And they seemed to be sleeping together as a matter of course. Allie heard their voices murmuring on for a few minutes after their door closed, and felt a stab of longing to be entwined that way too, with someone she really liked; she tossed on the nubby foam couch, wondering when It was going to happen to her, until sleep wiped out that loneliness with everything else. The next morning she realized, sardonically, that the thought of Randolph hadn't come up once as an answer.

Saturday was a clear day in the seventies—a day that put the three of them in a good mood, a day for chiming along with Jimmy Buffet as they bounded along in their sneakers and rattiest jeans, carefree as pre-schoolers. They spent Saturday afternoon at the zoo and then out on the river road. Allie took pictures. Crumbling old brick chimneys rose out of the ruins of big houses, where the vast fields opposite the levee left off briefly, in embarrassed obeisance to something once grand that was gone and irrelevant now. They posed and played by ancient live oaks whose lower branches dipped to the ground and crape myrtle and huge magnolias with roots that plaited the ground. "Remember how Daddy was always spotting places like this when we'd go somewhere?"

"Yeah—he'd go, 'There's an old home-place' and you could see the yard and the chimney and we'd all start talking about whatever it was we'd been talking about and then he'd go, 'Now *there's* an old home-place!' "

"He got so excited about them. It was funny." Allie and Fayette eyed Maria to see whether she understood.

She was chewing on something. She held out a stained hand full of berries. "Look," she said, "a muscadine vine. Somebody really cared about this yard."

"At one time," said Fayette. He added in a redneck accent, "But sugar, now hit's just gawn with the wind!"

They wandered back to the car and the warmth of the sun and headed back for the city, stopping at a drive-through daiquiri shacks, and sped along Highland Road arguing about movies, making fun of radio stations, and singing intermittently.

"Shouldn't you be packing?" Maria kept asking Fayette back at his apartment. "I haven't got anything to pack," he said. They ate gumbo and po-boys and then went back and took two car-loads of his stuff to his new apartment. He was right: there wasn't much: the stereo, clothes, mostly dirty ones simply carried out in the laundry basket, and two houseplants, and a lot of books and his drawing materials, which were in a big leather portfolio he'd gotten for Christmas. A pot and pan, his beer mugs, a couple of water glasses from the 7-11. "King Tut had more stuff than this in his *grave,*" said Allie.

"Sister, I ain't no foreign king."

On the second trip Maria stayed at the new apartment—which looked just like the old one, except that the carpet was gold shag instead of short green and the floor plan seemed to have been flipped over—to get it in order, she said. They left a jar of mustard and some old cheddar cheese in the refrigerator. "There's one beer left—should we take it?" "Hell yeah," said Fayette. Allie held it and one last load of records in her arms and Fayette surveyed the blank walls and empty couch and table. "Pity the person who has to clean that bathroom after me," he said. "That's it. Let's go," and he unplugged the phone and followed Allie out, pulling the door shut behind them. They drove carefully over the speed bumps and tossed the keys in the twenty-four-hour drop slot outside the management office. It was after midnight. They went to the Phone Store and left the phone in the twenty-four-hour return depository there. His new apartment had a phone already hooked up. How foreign this would be to Mémé, Allie thought—dropping a phone down a chute at twelve-thirty a.m., with your belongings stashed all around you in the car. She watched Fayette on his errand under the brownish, energy-conserving, all-night lights in the parking lot. Life seemed eerie and impermanent, a series of brief starts and quick exits, neither of which made deep impressions. Then he was back, and they headed into the darkness on the other side of campus, where some friends of Maria's had persuaded him to move.

27

IN MID-OCTOBER Mr. Grimes closed his photography store and moved to Arizona where his daughter and her husband lived. Before he left he spoke to friends at the newspaper about Allie, and she was hired part-time in the photography department. It wasn't perfectly steady work; she was supposed to call in every afternoon to see whether any film needed to be developed or printed that night. Sometimes the regular day person, Vicki, could handle it. But Vicki's mother had cancer and had to be taken her in for treatment fairly often, and the volume of pictures being processed at the paper fluctuated anyway, so Allie never knew whether she was going to have to work one or five evenings in a given week.

The annual Arts Festival held at the church was to open at the end of October, and Allie was relieved that she ended up not having to work that night. She had two photographs in the exhibit: a coup, for it was a juried show with entrants from all over the mid-South. Her family was proud of the Festival. Lillian and Frank had helped start it the year the church moved to its new building. Last year they had hardly been aware of it, with Frank so sick. As she got dressed Allie tried to remember whether she'd even walked through the exhibit.

She pulled clothes off their hangers absentmindedly, trying them and casting them aside, and ending up in the sleeveless black knit dress she'd worn at Frank's funeral, scooping her hair off her shoulders and coiling it at the back of her head, leaving a few tendrils to wave around her dangling earrings. "Pretty," commented Lillian.

"Thanks. And you look *great.*"

Lillian blushed slightly. She was wearing a sweater in rich forest green, and a skirt with jewelly tones running through it; her hair was brushed to glossiness on her shoulders. "It's just that you haven't seen me in a dress in so long."

The church looked beautiful too, its pale bricks glowing above the little slope of the bayou, an expansive but sober building set among bare pecans and cypresses. Its tall doors opened and closed, opened and closed, and the yellow light that poured out each time some people went in gleamed on the droplets splashing up from the courtyard fountain—a thorny-looking bronze sculpture.

"We might have trouble finding a place to park," said Lillian.

"Good! That's a healthy sign for the arts here," said Allie.

The crowd inside hovered and hummed, moving like streams of big excited ants below the paintings: bold abstract and expressionist canvases that bloomed over the wide, shining hallways like exotic hothouse mutants of Lillian's; small prints studding the panels in the main exhibit room; feathery watercolors like a breath of fragrance, like harp arpeggios, diverting you when you moved by.

"Allie, I just love your work, darling—" voices were saying.

"Congratulations! Good going."

"Well, goodness! We haven't seen them yet," said Lillian. "I need to go see my daughter's work."

"Oh, *Mama,*" said Allie.

Her photographs in the show made up a pair called *Floors.* Both were black-and-white. One was of her cousin Correen playing pick-up sticks on the black-and-white-tiled floor of Aunt Mary Sue's den. The picture was taken from above—Allie had squatted on the bar—and its focus was the pile of spilled pointed straws, which made an interesting shape against the squares of black and white, a splash like a jagged sun. Correen was hunched at one side, half-kneeling, with one rubber-toed tennis shoe visible bent and unlaced, and her hair coming out of her ponytail band. The other photograph was of Mémé's maid Ruby Mae mopping Mémé's kitchen floor. It was a vinyl floor designed to look like granite, "or Heavenly Hash ice cream," Allie had pointed out to Ruby Mae, with flecks of black and charcoal and tan swirling on a whitish background. The center of interest in this picture was the mop bucket and the shining crescent of dripped water it sat on, playing nicely off the patterned floor. All of that was framed by a rough triangle consisting of the mop handle, Ruby Mae's arm, and the edge of Ruby Mae's body in its white uniform; so that the viewer was really looking through a window made by Ruby Mae's body holding the mop; the woman was visible only in part, fuzzily. Ruby Mae had gotten so irritated with Allie taking those pictures. Allie had had to jolly her along, sneaking up close to Ruby Mae and backing off, crouching, clicking the shutter all the time, wheedling and teasing, while Ruby Mae complained about her mopping being messed up and Allie getting between her and the kitchen TV set. But it had paid off. Now the photographer only glanced quickly at her work, to see how it had been hung—not wanting to be caught lingering there—and moved on, blushing.

They passed little widows and widowers from the old-age Sunday school class, peering and squinting up at id-informed oils; frizzy-haired, baggy-jeaned thirty-year-olds, come from retreats and studios all over central Louisiana, from day jobs at restaurants and parts manufacturing plants and night careers as artists, pointing at the art with rolled-up programs while they argued about it; well-heeled bankers and brokers and doctors and their wives, smiling graciously at each piece as if it were a friend, and discreetly writing checks for the more representational works.

Mr. Kalunge had a painting in the show, which Allie examined at length. It was of a beach, with the pebbled sand mottled in yellow and ochre and bronze and cream tones building up to a white that somehow looked blindingly hot; and the ocean in splotchy indigos, purples, and sapphire blues; and a crowd of people on the shore, people in different browns. When you backed up the people disappeared—you thought they were rocky outcroppings on the beach or something, and the whole thing gelled into fairly uniform spaces, like a photograph. It was only when you drew near the canvas again that you could see the brown and mahogany and reddish shapes as faces, very carefully and distinctly painted, and blurred body parts. Blurred? Allie looked again. Much of the anatomy was not blurred at all. She stepped back a foot, then forward a foot again. She laughed out loud. The people were entwined in lovemaking, joined like a tangled necklace of arms and nipples and legs and penises and belly buttons and breasts. A few of the explicit forms had been outlined with a stiletto or something in the wet paint; others were created by the subtle use of dark umbers and chocolate shading beneath lighter browns. But it was an optical illusion. Even after you discovered the faces, you could stare at them for several minutes without seeing the enthusiastically interlocked bodies around them. It was called *Dover South*. "Weird," commented a lady who had been standing with Allie for a minute or so. "Give me some paint and I believe I could do that!" She smiled brightly at Allie. It was a good thing she did not look at it any closer.

About an hour later she saw her teacher. He was talking to the Delaneys, drifting down the hall where Allie's photographs were hung, when she and Lillian walked up and made a small circle out of the group. He looked crisp and understated in a dark suit and white shirt. After a minute or two of small talk Lillian said, "Excuse me, Martha, but I've been wanting to ask you about the public TV station—"

"Oh, I'll tell you who to talk to about that," said Dick Delaney, and the three of them started discussing the topic animatedly. Allie tried to follow for a minute but got bored, and glanced down, scanning the trio in the polite manner of looking away from people whose talk starts to exclude you, her gaze roving to her feet and then across Paul Kalunge's face in the course of removing her attention. His eyes stopped her. They were fixed intently on hers—as if he were wresting her to him, but utterly quietly, and with his hands at his side. She couldn't move her glance on, around the room, as she'd meant to; she couldn't get past his slightly narrowed, brown-black eyes, so relaxed at the corners with something of a smile in them. She couldn't even look so far away as his mouth, to see whether he was smiling with his lips or just his eyes. Her face felt hot and she dropped her eyes, but despite herself they came up again, skittering up like a styrofoam float in a lake, and there his gaze was again and she was locked in it the same way.

"I like your photographs, Miss McCain," he said.

"Thank you."

"You've been holding out on me." They were still looking levelly at each other, as if their eyes were carrying on a separate conversation from their mouths.

"I told you I'm a photographer."

"Yes, but I didn't know you were good."

"I guess you wouldn't expect that from my other artwork."

"From some of it—from some of it."

"Congratulations on your painting. I like it a lot."

"Well, thank you. I appreciate that." Then he looked down for the first time, and folded his arms and shifted his weight, and suddenly looked back up at her with his eyebrows raised, and a pointed amusement in his eyes, but something sheepish there, like the sheepishness of a small boy, and something else newly released, and he laughed and said, "I'm glad you like it."

Going home that night she felt the same lightness, jumpiness, in her gut that she had felt that whole year her dad was dying. If the soul had a landscape, she was at a precipice again. But then the thing on the other side of the dropoff, which had to be avoided at all costs, had been stark terror; and now she believed that on the other side was joy.

The next day at school he seemed more withdrawn than usual. Allie called him over to ask some question about the cubist rendition of a bowl of fruit they were all supposed to be doing. He leaned over the table, propped on his fists for a moment to see the section of her sketch she was talking about. While he responded she breathed in the clean ironed cotton smell of his nearness, a tang of what must be deodorant, like soap just unwrapped; studied his shirtsleeves, white with a thin maroon stripe, with the loosely rolled cuffs looking crisp and cool against his dark forearm. When he pulled back, shrugging a conclusion to his remarks about the sketch, there was just a flicker in his eyes, something both amused and impatient, and she wondered in confusion whether he had asked her a question she didn't hear. He looked almost exasperated. Then in the silence that was following his answer he smiled with the corners of his lips only, and moved on to another student.

She left school undecided about whether to meet Randolph before going home. He had asked her to. She upshifted slowly as she debated.

She had responded favorably to Randolph at first. He was pleasant and different, self-assured enough to have interests beyond the immediate, which was more than she could say for the boys her age at school. He was nice, just as her mother and grandmother said. But lately she'd been wondering if his bright breeziness did not cover an even deeper insecurity: like California, tottering with all its aggressive sportiness over the San Andreas Fault...He had said he'd be at Tara Place, the latest atrocity wrought by him and Uncle Jules—a condominium complex designed and furnished with an Old South gimmick in mind. She found herself heading toward the place without ever really deciding to, as if her critical mind were detached from her actions.

It was on a large lot halfway downtown, where an authentically old house had been, which Jules and Randolph had razed along with two live oaks and six big pecan trees. They had a sign up now: TARA in big letters, *Furnished Condominiums for Gracious Living* in script, and a picture behind of some anonymous-looking bricks with Spanish moss coiling down. Allie parked by Randolph's car, which was alone in the lot. She sat in the truck a minute untying her hair from the rope-like knot she tied it in to drive, and glanced into the rear-view mirror. Then she shrugged, said, "Oh, what the hell," put her camera under the seat, locked up, and made her way across the mud.

She called him and followed the sound of his answer. He was just inside one of the second-floor apartments, whistling under his breath as he set shelves into a walnut armoire. "Hey," he said. He was hugely pleased to see her, though it came off as pleasure with himself. After kissing her he went back to his whistling and shelving. She stood digesting his smell and taste over again, and watching. He finished and dusted his hands and said lightly, "That does it for this whole apartment; thirty-five to go!" and then, "Now," and came to her for a real kiss, trying to make it a long one this time. "You got here just at the right moment," he murmured, and knowing he was thinking of it as just that, as sexy murmuring, she didn't answer. He stepped away and said, "You want to look around?"

"Sure."

He led the way, reaching back for her knotted fingers to hold as they walked through the rooms. They still smelled of fresh wood shavings and paint, with traces now of inlay and veneer from the old furniture that had been brought in, and over it all the heavy acrid scent of new carpet. She commented on bevelled mirrors and transom doors, a pie safe made into a stereo cabinet, tables with an artificial "distressed" finish ("Distressed that they aren't for real?" she said, and he laughed uneasily), ceiling fans, and even a punka in the dining room. "Slaves used to pull a rope like this, to cool off the white folks," said Randolph.

"Are you gonna reconstruct some slave quarters—say, behind the parking lot?"

Again that laugh. "I'll let you bring that up with your uncle."

Repenting a little of her snideness, she let herself sincerely compliment the curtains, which were white dotted-Swiss caught back with ties. He accepted the praise by pulling down shades to show her those too. She was polite. He was jovial. She opened cabinets. He opened closets. She noticed wallpaper, copied after antebellum patterns. He pointed out molding in turn. It didn't take long to go through the whole apartment. Predictably, he saved the master bedroom for last. He pushed the door open and took Allie by the waist as they went in.

They stood together in front of a huge four-poster cherry bed, bemused—Randolph by his guile and good fortune, and Allie by the unabashed neatness of his little plans: the parking lot, empty except for their two vehicles; Randolph working to finish the interior of at least one apartment; the little trailing tour through its rooms; the hush all around except for muffled traffic; and here this enormous bed and its brand-new, polyester, machine-made, faded-patchwork-look quilt. He rocked back and forth in his shoes. One side of her mouth smiled and she shook her head slightly.

"The bed's so tall we even had to get steps for it."

He swivelled her so that their bodies locked, and sought out her lips. She didn't want him, didn't want him at all. She kept thinking clinically and distastefully of mouth parts and saliva. In a minute he accused her, "You're kissing like a fish!"

She burst out laughing and withdrew. "Sorry."

Then he started saying sad, melodramatic things. "You've got lots ahead of you. You're going to make someone very happy someday. Maybe it'll be me. Who knows? I'll hang around as long as you let me—but it wouldn't be fair to keep you from going through all the things you need to, at your age. And if I ever get the sense you don't want me around, I'll just buzz away. But—you're special. You've got a mind. I want to know that when I get up in the morning, there's gonna be a woman with a mind across the breakfast-table from me."

As if there were no question that *he* was smart enough to eat twenty thousand breakfasts opposite *her*. "Maybe you should marry Jane Pauley," she said.

There was a startled pause, and then he laughed, a short bark.

"Randolph," she said, "I've got to go."

"We may get to come here a lot," he said. "This can be our little spot. Our getaway."

"I've got to go," she said again.

"See you tomorrow?" he said.

"So long."

28

THE SCHOOL ADMINISTRATORS had two ways of dealing with assemblies. They would either cut short every class by a few minutes and send the students back to their homerooms at the end of the day, just in time for the assembly, or leave everything the same except for a shortened sixth period. Allie hated it when they did the latter.

"All right," said Paul Kalunge in a heavy, bored voice over the sounds of students washing out their brushes. "Tomorrow you won't be able to work because there's some assembly at two-thirty."

"Aw, Mr. Kalunge. Awwwww."

"Assembly? What for? Is it a pep rally?"

"Naw, it's probably about the dress code."

"No, I know what it is. It's a band."

"A *band*."

Billy Jones rolled his eyes and grinned at Allie. "I know it ain't no group on the Hit Parade."

"Mr. Kalunge, can't we get excused from it?"

"You're welcome to go ask in the office. But I doubt it."

The next day found the Art IV students filing dolefully into the auditorium, which smelled of some plastic synthetic fiber in the stage curtains and of bagged gym clothes. As usual at such events Allie was irritated. Glancing at the stage she saw that the drum was painted red, white, and blue, and a cheery placard titled the band THE FOUNDATIONS. "Oh, brother," she muttered. She had a book with her, but she knew from experience that the audience lights would be dimmed. Of all types of rallies these were the worst. She was the last of her class to straggle in. She swung into her seat, and Mr. Kalunge took the one next to her. The classes started screaming their graduation year. "Eight eight eight eight eight eight eight—" "We are great! We are fine! We are seniors seventy-nine!" Looking around, she met Mr. Kalunge's gaze and rolled her eyes briefly, and he chuckled.

After the auditorium filled up and the principal spoke, the band entered. All five members had very white smiles and rosy skin and short, neat haircuts and wore white pants, red shirts open at the neck, and blue blazers. Unwittingly she heaved a sigh. Mr. Kalunge growled in his throat to her: "It can't last more than forty minutes." The first number was a sunny arrangement of patriotic and Christian lyrics with an imitative rock beat under it. It actually contained the word "groovy." "Clap along!" invited the lead singer. Allie sank deeper into her chair and wished she were elsewhere. Mr. Kalunge's profile was absolutely impassive. Around them rows of students bobbed in their chairs and snapped their fingers enthusiastically. Mr. Kalunge swung one ankle up to rest on the knee near Allie's. Allie fixed her gaze on his foot, and her eyes thanked her for their relief from the spotlit stage by gradually revealing the darkness around her. He wore his Hush Puppy desert boots and thick dark socks. There was paint on his boots. He fidgeted—and once seemed to incline his head toward her.

The band was crooning a low, saccharine number when the drummer stood up and took the microphone. He told the students he used to be a drug addict with long hair. He got so desperate for money to support his habit that he started doing stick-ups. He was arrested. In jail he found Jesus Christ and got a haircut. "And I'm here today to urge you—" Paul dropped his arm on the armrest between him and Allie. His fingers dangled off the end. Allie was leaning forward a little, with her hands slid toward her knee on either thigh. Their fingers were not far apart. The row was very dark.

"So, I just want to stand before all y'all and thank the Lord that I saw the light—"

Were his fingers moving too or was it her imagination? If she needed some defense later she could always call it an accident; she could jump a little and smile and murmur, "Sorry." Then she ceased to think. Their hands were moving as slowly as those on a Ouija board—and with just as much buried purpose. They touched hands and he secured hers unhurriedly. She turned it over so that their palms faced, in a quick instinctive sign of acquiescence. They laced fingers. They traced each other's nails and knuckles and fingertips. She kept her head turned blindly toward the stage. And now the droning testimonials and the trite songs went quickly indeed. Time had become a matter of the feel of Paul Kalunge's skin. Suddenly the lead voice was asking that everyone rise to sing, "God Bless America." One count after the rest of the school heaved to its feet, Mr. Kalunge and Allie rose to theirs. They turned their heads a quarter-angle inward and their eyes met fully—big, sober, and glistening, with the outermost layer of vision stripped away. He looked solemn as death.

"Will you have dinner with me?" he said in a low voice, the next afternoon. There was no brightness in the question—he looked almost grim.

She barely heard her own answer. "Okay."

"Tonight?"

"I'll have to—call my mother."

He did something with his shoulders that might have been a shrug. Then, as if curiosity got the best of him, he said, "What will you tell her?"

"The truth, I guess."

"Don't you think she might not like the truth?"

"Oh," said Allie, "I'll tell her I'm having supper with a friend of mine from my art class. Um"—in the past two days, he had become Paul and not Mr. Kalunge in her mind, but she still couldn't bring herself to address him that way—"where will we go? I mean to eat?" She tried picturing the two of them at various restaurants in Edgewood, places where her parents' friends often went, and couldn't.

He looked at her pityingly. "At my flat, if you don't mind."

When she knocked at his door her heart beat hard inside her chest; her whole body beat like a heart. In the hours since she'd last seen him she'd forgotten what he looked like. Lying awake the night before she couldn't reconstruct him. Then as the door opened suddenly there he was, recreated for her, and she knew all over again why she was here.

The flat was the second floor of an office building right downtown. Inside there was a spacious, bare feeling, at once restful and a little stark, like a modern art gallery itself, in fact. The walls were pale gray and the floors of bare wood. For furniture he had a small wooden table to eat on, a work table against one wall, bookcases of cinderblocks and boards on the other wall, and a trim gray couch and braid rug in between. In a huge bare space at one end of the room there was an easel set up, draped with a cloth, and some canvases leaned against the wall, facing it. Two huge picture windows had blinds but no curtains. Paul spoke enthusiastically of the light. In the quiet, and the bareness of the space, he seemed smaller and darker and his voice even more resonant than in the classroom. Allie felt drawn and distant. What was she doing here? All that had driven her was the recollection of her hand entwined with this man's on the armrest in the dim auditorium. Both she and he were reacting to that bond now. Their fingers had moved into another stage of relationship, where their minds and manners had yet to catch up.

She was wearing a long black jacket—really a cast-off smock of her aunt's, with deep pockets and no buttons to close it, which she loved because she thought it looked artsy. Paul hung it up for her and disappeared into the kitchen.

"Would you like a beer? Or coffee, tea? Or some whiskey?"

"Oh—tea. Let me fix it." He nodded toward a cup and kettle.

"What about you?"

"Tea." He had dumped some onions onto a cutting board. Now he looked straight across at her and said, "I am likely to get quite maudlin if I have beer." The sharp crack of onion smell crossed the kitchen. "So where did you get these aspirations of yours to take good pictures?"

"I don't exactly know...I used to fool around with a camera, and I always liked that. Then I read this book about Margaret Bourke-White. I always liked art and fooled around with projects and paints when I was little. But it seemed separate from real life. And then with photography—" Her voice got lost inside a cabinet.

"What do you need?"

"Another cup. Oh, okay, here. With photography, I can...have my cake and eat it too. It's an art form but connected with real life a lot closer than others. I can go out and see things and do things and have my camera with me and that's *everything*—"

"Isn't art always? Connected?"

"Oh—" She wondered if he meant the supper to go this way. Idea talk. She felt she was faking. "I guess." She smiled. "I mean it ought to be. Here's your tea."

A smile flashed over his face, and then it seemed to close and lengthen again, like a mask. He got meat out of the refrigerator and lapsed into silence again as he started to trim it. Allie looked at it in dismay. Well, she could just eat it. So what? Three months ago she wouldn't have hesitated. But what if she and Paul continued to—to do whatever it was they were doing? Eventually he would find out she was vegetarian, and he would wonder why she had eaten meat this one time. So she ventured, "Could you make mine with just vegetables?"

"You don't eat meat? Sure." But he was going to tease her a little. He shook his head. "Are you a Buddhist?"

"No-o-o!" she laughed. "It's just that it bothers me when animals are killed, and I figured it'd be hypocritical to go on eating meat if I felt that way."

"Ah."

"So what about your painting? Don't you try to make a statement with it?"

"You're amazing. You sound like someone I should have met in New York ten years ago. It just makes me want to laugh."

"Well, that makes sense," said Allie seriously. "My aunt lives in New York and she's probably ten years behind the times. No, I think she's stuck in the sixties for life. She's neat. She has this weird clothing store in Soho and she lives in Soho with this guy who runs a gallery... I really like her. But," Allie realized she was babbling and returned to the point, "if you had met me ten years ago I would have just been seven."

He didn't laugh as she'd expected, he just frowned and said, "I know. It's a problem." He put the meat back in the fridge—"I don't need it either"—then put water on to boil, watched it for a minute, and almost as an afterthought shook salt and a fillip of oil into it. "I may have a can of water chestnuts," he said absently, turning to the cabinets. His motions were tranquil, unself-conscious. Allie wrapped her fingers around her mug and watched him. No man had ever cooked for her before, she realized. Now the onions were browning and sizzling in a hot pan; the water chestnuts followed; then some red peppers that the long, dark fingers had just seeded and diced.The electric coil glowed. Paul added rice, turned the heat down, and covered the pot. She had thought he wasn't going to say anything more on the subject when he added, "I don't know what I think about while I'm working. Nothing is as obvious in my painting as it used to be. Or in anything." Meaning me? thought Allie. Probably not. He went on, "Someone in my position is supposed to think first of political things in his work. It's supposed to have a clear message. Clear as journalism."

"What do you mean, in your position?"

"Well, you know I was born South African." When he said *South Africa* his voice deepened and vibrated like something potent, hallowed—*Ah!*—and the last two syllables exquisite, quickly rolled out. "I left when I was ten. My grandmother smuggled me across the border into Rhodesia. I was small for my age," he added as if that explained the event.

"But—" her mind was darting, yes, it was not *why* she needed to know but—"where'd you go then?"

"She had names of some relatives in a certain town about twenty kilometers from the border. She had rehearsed it with me over and over. I headed there. A farmer helped me go—hid me in mealie-meal—that's something like flour. He had all the right papers...You see, she had figured out I needed to get out. She was concerned about my schooling and knew that I would have no future if I stayed. After my parents died she had taken me in, and there was a priest she worked for, who treated her as a friend, and used to talk to her a lot. She went to him to ask what she should do for my future. She was expecting to hear whether I should aim to work in a white man's store or drive a white man's truck. But this priest said, sarcastically, 'The best thing?

Get him out of South Africa.' He was being ironic, but once he said it she took it seriously. She clung to it even when he tried to take it back. If that was the best thing, that was what she was going to do. I was her only grandchild, the only thing that meant the future to her. I think once he saw her determination this priest went on to explain that I could have a life somewhere else, as I could never expect to in my own country...He told her it was quite impossible to get me out, though, that he had only been kidding." Paul paused and added, "He was an alcoholic, quite a souse."

"What a story," said Allie softly. "So your grandmother just managed it?"

"Yes. There was no one like her."

"And the relatives in—"

"Rhodesia. They took me in, they sent me to school, then on to better schools, other mission people helped me, it went on from there."

"You told our class once that everything is political."

"I did, didn't I?"

"And your painting is political, isn't it?"

Paul looked up at Allie keenly, and smiled. "Oh, to me it's political. Yes, by my own definition. The politics of the soul of Paul Kalunge! Before your very eyes. But the truth is—Allie—I'm not very good. I used to think it was good. I was good and I was bound to be great! But now I know I'm a very average painter. And lazy to boot."

She stared at him. Would something insidious ever happen to her to make her wake up and find herself saying that to a young, aspiring artist, about herself? And worst of all seem so unbothered by it?

"I hadn't really heard how you left. I knew you were African and I thought it was South African. And don't you have some children here?"

"Ah, you must do your research. A girl should find out these things." He looked directly at her. She couldn't tell whether he was being bitter or sarcastic or teasing her deadpan. "Ah!" he said. "But I didn't answer your question. Get two plates from there, would you, it's time to eat."

They ate on a table in one corner of his big central room, with a little reading lamp lighting their faces.

"And you've never been back?"

"No. Until the revolution comes, I won't be going back."

Revolution! If her Uncle Jules heard *that*—. "What about your family there? I mean besides your grandmother?"

"I was an only child, and an orphan. Fortunately, I guess." She inspected his face to try to figure out whether he was being bitter, but all she turned up was mild matter-of-factness. He suddenly reacted to her gaze. "You had better watch that, you know. Women are very susceptible to my story." It was only then that she heard what might be a jeer in his voice.

She was bewildered; her defenses rose, and she said in what come out as a sneer in turn, "What—you mean they feel sorry for you?"

"Ah-yah." Like a scrambled "yeah." He nodded and grew calm in an instant. They studied each other a minute.

"Then where'd you go?"

"I studied in mission schools through the equivalent of your high school. Then to London, Paris, Munich, always studying, sometimes in university and sometimes under an established artist. Then I came to the United States. I got a job as cartoonist for a newspaper in Harlem that some friends were starting. I finally took a B.A. here. I sold a few paintings, and I did some delivery jobs to get by." He was speaking rapidly now. Allie had the feeling he was getting tired of narrating. "I got married to a singer. She's the one from Edgewood. Of all places," he added wryly.

"Yeah, something—Jones, isn't it? I've heard of her."

"Yah, you should have. She toured a lot; toured in Europe and here. I'd go with her and paint or teach or manage galleries in one case, sort of riding her shirttails and her connections. We had the children, but she didn't really want to take care of them...She didn't want to have to give up any tours...So we sent the kids to their grandmother. After a couple of years of that we moved to New Orleans as a sort of compromise—I think I missed them more than she did, it was really due to my insistence that we moved closer. In New Orleans we were closer to them but still in a city. Of course, it was a Southern American city in the mid-sixties. But we made out all right. I love New Orleans...We got divorced. She went back to New York. I was just missing my children too much, so I looked for work closer to them, and this is what I came up with." He twisted his lips into a smile. "As they say in movies, 'You know the rest.'"

"Does she ever come back?"

"Who? Oh, Eliza? Sometimes. Not real often."

"Was that her that night at Uncle Calvin Ray's?—remember, you were talking to someone by the pool."

"Oh." There was a pause. He was quietly watching her face. "No, that wasn't Eliza. We don't get along well enough to go to a party together." There his tone changed, those words came out a little sharper, though the rest of him was always still. His voice relaxed again. "That was this graduate student from Baton Rouge. Some friends matched us up and she came to spend the weekend. She's from Cameroon. It's amazing how small people must think Africa is. They'll tell you about other Africans if it's a great coincidence to be from the same enormous continent, even opposite ends of it."

Allie nodded, not as amused as he was by this foible. "Do you see your kids often?"

"Several times a week. Their grandmother is a miracle. You would really like that woman. I'll take you to meet her someday. A goddess."

Allie laughed. "How old are they?"

"Um, Kimberly was born in sixty-four and Ross in sixty-six. They're—"

They said together, "Thirteen and eleven."

"I guess you are closer to their age than mine."

"Um-hm."

They looked at each other a while.

"Thank you for the supper," she said.

"I want you to come back, you know."

"I know." They continued this reflective gazing and Allie heard herself saying, "I want to."

"I've talked all about myself and haven't heard very much about you."

"I guess there isn't very much about me to tell."

"You talk deep talk for such a young girl." She didn't answer, but her eyes felt just slightly wet; she lifted her chin the barest bit. "You aren't a girl, are you?" he said softly. It was as if he was talking to himself. "You are a woman. Already a woman, and so young." He said *a* like its name, a full beat in the music of his speech, not the skipped-over *uh* of most Americans. He scraped his chair back suddenly, now saying in a normal tone of voice that sounded loud, "Where is that funny jacket you came with?" and disappeared in an alcove, and Allie cleared her plate. She stood for an extra second in the kitchen, feeling dizzy from his closeness, already knowing by instinct she needed to take in every inch of space he inhabited; mental pictures of him in this kitchen, alone and unself-conscious, in the morning, coming in from school in the afternoons, late at night, maybe humming, were going to occupy her for all the time to come that she could see. She turned around and nearly ran into him, holding out her jacket as he came around the corner. They stopped short and then he reached around her and settled it around her shoulders like a cape and kissed her.

She was trembling when they finished.

"Are you all right?"

"Yes."

"Scared?"

"No!" She denied it flamboyantly and corrected him, "I'm *excited.*"

"Allie—I hope you'll come back."

"I will, I will, soon."

"I'll go with you to your car." They went in silence, not touching, down the concrete stairwell. Their pupils shrank from its bright lighting. "Your truck," amended Paul, outside. "Do you think it's safe for you to come here?"

"Um-hm. It's a good place for me to come."

"Goodnight."

"Goodnight. Paul."

Standing at the driver's window he said suddenly, "I'm worried about you!"

"Oh, don't be," she said, puzzled. "Why should you?"

29

SOMETIMES YOU GET set against a thing and rage against it, and still in the morning and when you lay your head down at night it is there, and your prayers mildew and the taste of your food goes flat from it; but you can't sustain all those angers. Like water seeking its own level the oldest habit, of a qualified contentment, reasserts itself and after a long stiff stubborn siege one by one the furies fall, till one day without intending it you find yourself thankful for something—the paperwhites blanketing your yard again, a change in weather, just something; or after an even longer time, like a crick in your neck gone as suddenly and inexplicably as it came, the thing itself doesn't bother you and sometimes in the end you wouldn't have changed it if you could; you're downright grateful that you weren't able to stop it (though you don't have to admit that, not even to God).

So it was with Carmelina and that grandchild by Scrip Thomas. Malcolm became the joy of her life. He looked like her and no one else, and when friends commented on this Carmelina sniffed with pleased pride and lifted her chin a fraction higher. It had taken a while to reach this point. Those first few years, when Scrip was gone off who knew where, popping back to Edgewood and stirring Miranda up every time she'd begun to calm down, were hard. Carmelina resented what had happened to her daughter so much that she disliked even the baby. Rearing her own large family had taken her years, and she wouldn't have minded a good long respite from diaper-changing before she started in on grandchildren—especially ones that arrived this way, out of the bounds of wedlock and good sense.

Since she graduated from high school Miranda had had a good job working at Buckerman's, the ageless store downtown where Edgewood somebodies bought all their china and silver and antiques and even hardware. Half the white ladies in town were devoted to Miranda and wouldn't transact their business there without her. It was a good job with pleasant conditions and a kind boss and decent pay. Miranda didn't want to give it up just because of her baby. So she worked out a complicated schedule of care for Malcolm—taking him to a lady in her neighborhood from eight to three, and then having Carmelina pick him up and keep him till six-fifteen. For the first year or so of this Carmelina did what she thought was the absolute minimum for Malcolm. But by the time he could walk and talk, and wrinkle his brow and fix her frowningly with his big chocolate-colored eyes and assert, while still in diapers, mind you, "I can manage for myself, Grandmother" (none of these cute nicknames for Carmelina), she started falling in love with him. And then, once her devotion had been cemented a few years, Scrip came back and married Miranda in a quiet civil ceremony, and though she reserved her doubts over that for a good while, it finally did seem that he intended to settle down—he was working hard, he was polite to her, Miranda glowed, and Malcolm boasted about his daddy.

Even Scrip in and of himself was winning her over. Miranda watched drily one day when she and Malcolm arrived at her mother's and came inside the living room. Her mother stayed at the door peering toward Miranda's car. "Who you looking for, Mama?"

Carmelina turned her head almost sheepishly. "Thought Scrip might-a come along with y'all."

"No, he's working tonight. Since when do you dote on Scrip so much?"

"I never did dislike Scrip, daughter; I told you, I just knew too much about how hard it is for a man like that to tame down." Carmelina came on in the house, latching the screen door behind her. "I had a article to give him tonight. I guess I'll have you give it to him."

"He hasn't been reading very much. He's so tired when he gets in. He still reads while I'm fixing supper but after that he goes straight on to bed."

"He's probably read more already than most folks do in a lifetime."

"Grandmother, can I have some Coke?"

"Of course you can!"

"Mama, I don't want him drinking all that Coke. He'll be up till midnight not giving me any peace."

"Why then he can just spend the night with me!"

"Yeah, Grandmother! Please!"

"I got someone I want Scrip to meet," said Carmelina.

"Really? Malcolm, hold it with both hands."

"Um-hm, my little African friend."

"Oh, the artist man."

"Yep."

"Scrip knows a lot about Africa," said Miranda vaguely. "He was all into that one time...Isn't this lamp new? ..."

So one Saturday late in November Carmelina made chili and hot tamales and invited Scrip, Miranda, Malcolm, Glory Jones and her grandchildren, and Paul over for supper. When Scrip met Paul he held on to Paul's hand after the handshake, then clasped it vertically in the black power shake, and then back across again. "He-hey!" said Paul.

"Hey, bwana!"

"He-*hey!* Have you spent some time in Africa, brother?"

"Nah, but 'black is beautiful,' you know. There was a time when we learned all that stuff."

"Négritude," said Paul musingly, still smiling and gripping Scrip's hand. "Even here."

"He took a African name," said Miranda, glancing quickly at the two men.

Malcolm had been staring at their hands. "Daddy, what y'all doing? Do it to me, Daddy."

"Okay, give me your hand...Now like this...And back like this."

"Y'all come on and sit down now. Get you a beer now."

"Ice cold, man," said Malcolm. "Hey! Lemme show Ross."

"I've had a lot of names," said Scrip. "Had my real name and my nickname and a African name. And one time the fuzz wanted to give me a false name. The fuzz ..."

They had fanned out into the living room, carpeted and dark-panelled but still somehow not cozy, as if some of Carmelina's severity had infected it too. A man who looked close to sixty got out of a recliner in a corner, spilling newspaper pages out of his lap, and greeted them: Miranda's father, tall, slim, genial in a quiet way. Miranda and Scrip settled on opposite ends of a plaid sofa; Paul took a low armchair near the TV, which was on without the volume, showing studio wrestling, and the children flitted in and out of the scene like moths. Glory had already trundled into the kitchen. The group in the living room was silent, and they could hear the clanging of pot lids and Glory's voice intermingled with chuckles and squeals—"So I say—oooh, *girl!*—what you talking *about!*—just don't put none-a them hot peppers in mine—"

"So," said Paul. "About that other Movement. Were you involved with that one too?"

"Some. I was in Chicago during the riots. I didn't do anything really—what you might say—constructive."

Miranda looked over at Scrip, for he usually didn't talk this way, with big words and seriousness, to someone he'd just met; he spoke this way less and less to anyone, as a matter of fact. She thought it was good for him to talk naturally like this, as he used to back in high school when she first knew him. At the same time it always disturbed her to hear him allude to his bad days. Even if he didn't go into detail it brought back a nightmare she had suffered vicariously: bouts of drinking; his first failures at school; the pulls on him this way and that by his increasingly disgusted college advisers, his new friends, and—over long distance—her and his mother; street violence and debates about it; longer and longer spells of drunkenness, punctuated only with trips on drugs whose names he rarely knew; idealism and old sanctified longings and commitments that campus speakers would set blazing one more time, before everything clouded over again.

Her father had picked up his newspaper once more, gently, as if he hoped no one would see.

"I knew the issues and the personalities. I followed it close. But—you might say—it kept washing over me. It was stronger than me. I couldn't stand up in it."

The artist was listening intently. "Do you think that was due to the way the movement was run, their attitude toward the rank-and-file—or to conflicts between the leaders?"

"No. Mainly I think it was because of what was happening to me at the time."

Malcolm darted into the room, picked up the remote control button off the coffee table, and ran the TV channels all the way through and back, full circle, to studio wrestling.

"Children, y'all come wash up!" called Carmelina, and he ran off again. Ross had tagged into the room after Malcolm, much bigger than the other boy, heavy, stolid, big-headed, and not a fraction as quick and bright-eyed; now he picked up the button, zoomed the volume up, and slowly, one by one, changed the channels. The grownups, who had fallen silent, just watched him.

"Oh, you don't know how to do it," said Kimberly, seizing the toy from her brother.

"Come wash your hands!"

"Come on, Ross, let's go wash up." She wrapped her long thin arm around her brother's shoulders and bustled him out of the room.

After supper, while the women were doing the dishes, Scrip and Paul went onto the porch—ostensibly so Scrip could smoke, and where the darkness veiled what little self-consciousness remained between them. It was one of those muggy nights that Louisiana Novembers sometimes produce. To get histories of one another they had used the halting, staccato questions of people who have sensed a rapport in each other and need information to back it up; now they could cut to the quick of what mattered—well, not straight to the quick, but less obliquely than men usually do with each other.

Paul said, "Carmelina has told me some things about this place where you work."

"Oh, Green Isle? Yeah." A slurp of coffee. "It's interesting."

"Do you think you'll stay there? Help run it, maybe?"

"Yeah, that's what I'd like to do," said Scrip. "I still got some problems, you know, problems that need ironing out—that I need to stay on top of. But once I get them worked out I'd like to hang out—stay on at Green Isle. Not for the farming part, that's kind of boring. But the business part, managing, you know, watching the market, analyzing what's happening with all our—resources, that's something I think I'd like to do."

"They need you, don't they? From what Carmelina says."

"Oh, now I'll tell you a little something about the way this farm works. You got these few old guys everyone listens to. But they, you see, don't think they know shit, which in effect becomes the same thing, because they back down when it comes to a crunch. And then you got some younger guys think they know everything. But it's unique, man—black-owned, group-run—and it's a fascinating business, close to the earth, you know, organic, and really tied to the economic trends of the country—"

To Paul's mind the younger man was trying a little too hard to persuade. But he sipped his coffee, and watched, and listened, and questioned a little more, just the same.

In the kitchen Carmelina was getting happier and happier. She even laughed her rare laugh, a cackle that got on Miranda's nerves, as Glory went on and on about some old bird who went to her church and was getting married for the fifth time. Carmelina would rather clean up than cook any day; it satisfied her to get rid of all those scrapings and leavings and return the dishes to their pristine, arid condition, so clean your thumb would skitter and squeak if you drew it across a plate. And it pleased her that she had given this supper party that folks had enjoyed, specifically the two she had thought of bringing together who were now talking up a storm on the porch. She had done well.

Miranda was the opposite; she liked the table-setting and cooking and serving itself—and got tired of washing up. And during this particular clean-up she got crosser and crosser. She tried to figure it out as she moved around the kitchen rubbing dishes and glasses and pans with a dishtowel that was already wet through and through, stepping out of the way of Glory's and her mother's big happy hips as she put up the clean things. She sincerely wanted Scrip to have people he could talk to, who understood him and were at his level mentally. But now that someone like that had come she felt left out. That must be it; she guessed she was a little jealous of this man Paul and of the two men's visiting out there, so comfortable, so heedless in a way. And how she herself disliked resentful women! She got even grouchier realizing what was going on with her.

But she knew just how Scrip would look now, leaning forward eagerly with his forearms resting on his knees, his hands still raised to gesture toward the other person, his eyebrows raised and his eyes nearly bugging out of his head. Subtly, with all the benefit of his intelligence, he would be presenting himself in a certain way: victimized bright boy, prodigal hero, deposed prince come wandering back to his kingdom. It got on her nerves just to picture it. There was a little truth in all those images, but that wasn't all of it. She could imagine the wonder dilating in his listener's eyes and felt exasperated that they would just take it all in, without a grain of salt, apparently. Well, she could give them salt if they wanted. She had gleaned hers the hard way.

30

THE NIGHT BEFORE Christmas, Paul was at home trying to pretend that it didn't matter to someone of his mature beliefs that it was a holiday, that he could paint as usual. He was all set; his brushes and paints were neatly laid out and he'd uncovered his current work, *Blue Figure No. 3.* He had a cup of coffee on a plant stand behind him to keep his adrenalin going during those stages when creation alone couldn't swing it. And the radio was on low, but his favorite Baton Rouge station, which usually played classical jazz, was playing holiday announcements over and over and over again—"Edward Talley and Sons Hardware, Incorporated, sincerely wishes you and yours a very merry Christmas, and all the blessings of prosperity in 1978"—interspersed with the sole Christmas carols the station owned, "Jingle Bell Rock" and "I'll Have a Blue Christmas Without You." So he was finding it hard to get in the mood of his work. He stared at *Blue Figure No. 3* for a long time and finally said, "Bleah," and sat down on his work stool. That was still officially within the work mode; he used that stool for studying his paintings and for resting when he'd been on his feet a while. The day before he had changed a dominant line in the painting, and now he saw it ought to be changed back. He spent about twenty minutes redoing it and then, before he was really through, lay his brush down and said, "Oh, shit," very wearily, and went over to his couch—definitely out of the work mode. He opened the blinds and sat on the arm of the couch, looking over its back and out the window, where he could see blue and red and green and orange Christmas lights shining, and the big tinsel Santas over the middle of the downtown streets and the garlands around the light poles and across the broad shiny swath of the river more lights, and the small lights by the airport runways that were always there, blue as Bunsen burner flames.

The lush-figured, aloof *Blue Figure No. 3* wasn't nearly as good company as a real female. One in particular. He was in the middle of a series of blue figures. They were conceived as an expression of the best of all his women, that band of angel women whose indulging, caressing, teasing, and enfolding charged and recharged him day by day—women with his grandmother's softness and his mother's strength and Carmelina's queenliness and Glory's staunch pragmatism and Eliza's curvaceous flash and verve. And Allie's mind and straightforwardness, the droll earthy sideways wit with which she approached things; her clear gray eyes that widened a little bit with relief, or something like it, when she saw him, and wrinkled at the corners when she was amused; her eyelashes the color of cinnamon, her mane, her veil of hair shimmering like something radioactive; her evenly warm, smooth body with its small breasts, its round high rump and flaring shoulders, sensitive as film, responsive to his every breath, so that the first time he held her it felt exactly right, sturdy and quiet and surely notched into his as if their bodies had been cut out of a single chunk of stone, like Rodin lovers. She wouldn't be thinking of him tonight. There was a church service and then a family supper, the annual Christmas Eve gathering. She had painted it for him in words, comically sketching the assembly of neurotic aunts and uncles and children home from colleges and far-off jobs, everyone wildly flaunting the new haircuts and weight losses and boyfriends and clothes and vocabularies that would tell their relatives they were *different* now; little rituals and habits sending the figures in mad patterns around the family circle, like inexperienced ice skaters...a funny scene. "I'll have pictures," she'd promised. At any rate it would be absorbing her right now, she would feel wrapped in, included, it wouldn't be a time for her to think of the incidental quirk in her life that he was: uninspired stump of a man in a madeover warehouse room he called a studio.

Usually on Christmas Eve he stayed at Glory's and helped her do Santa Claus for Kimberly and Ross. But Eliza, who he'd heard had a new boyfriend and must be in a fresh spasm of motherliness, had flown the kids to New York. He felt dismal about it. It would have been a thrill to show them his New York, to hear Kimberly's reaction to all that splendor and spectacle. He could have done it, of course, any time...It was just so expensive. Oh well. They'd be back next week. Glory had asked him over to eat with her and some of her widow friends, but he had declined. It shouldn't matter so much. He was already supposed to have Christmas dinner with her tomorrow.

And in the meantime his painted women, for all their lusciousness, were flat and stale, just marks on paper. Or else why didn't they appease him, why did they leave him feeling empty and sorry for himself and too aware of the silence of his rooms—he, a man of thirty-eight who had lived alone for most of his life?

Someone knocked on his door and he jumped. "Hallo," he called, getting to his feet. "Who is it." It couldn't be her—

It was Scrip Thomas. Looking as if he felt ridiculous, and subsequently looking ridiculous, with a six-pack of beer in his hand—not just cans, but something bottled, German, mountainsides on the carton, a bedraggled bow on top—"Come in! Hallo, man, how are you! Merry Christmas!"

"Merry Christmas. I've been going around to share a little Christmas cheer with my friends. I was down this way." Scrip pulled a knit cap off his head. "It's getting cold out there."

"Well, thank you. Come on in."

"You haven't got company or anything?" He sounded as if he were hoping Paul did. "I didn't know if I'd catch you."

"No, no, I'm just sitting around." Scrip stepped inside. He looked a little wild-eyed, and his hair was pulled out of shape from the cap, with fuzz sticking to it. With a visitor here the room seemed to draw in a little bit, the lamplight got brighter and cozier, and the night scene outside looked even more austere. I guess I really did want company, Paul thought. He grinned. "Just here getting into a funk and dreading having to take a drink alone. Here, give me your coat."

"M'randa went to Midnight Mass and I didn't want to go, so I told her I'd come by and see you."

It didn't exactly fit with his first explanation, but Paul said, "Sure. Sure. Sit down. Is it midnight already?"

"No, Midnight Mass starts at eleven. I don't mean to bother you or anything, if you're in the middle of something."

"No, really."

"This is a nice place. I like this."

"Well, let's break into these, what do you say? Will you have one with me?"

"Sure, yeah." While Paul scrabbled in a kitchen drawer for a bottle opener ("No tweest-offs for those Germans!" he was saying) Scrip examined the canvases. "I guess you really are an artist!"

Paul gave his noncommittal, lilting "Mm-nnh."

"Sometimes I wish I had something like that, you know, like painting. If I had that I'd know what I was supposed to do next. I'd have a *cause.* It must be great, man. Not that it's easy," he added hastily. "I didn't mean it comes easy to you."

"Well, it's nice," said Paul. Now he was putting on a tape: Ella Fitzgerald. "Even though you have to do something else as well. It's nice even to have the—the delusion you can do something that might matter. Or even if it doesn't end up mattering, might please someone."

"Yeah!" said Scrip. "That's what I mean. It's more than I can say."

"Oh, come on," said Paul.

"No, really. What I'm doing now doesn't add up to shit. It *is* shit a lot of times. Literally." He was sitting on the edge of the couch, with his elbows on his knees and the fingers of both hands interlaced around the beer bottle, his head bowed. He grinned at his joke, but when he looked up at Paul the smile had disappeared. "If I'd seen into the future when I was sixteen and known I'd be doing this, I'd have blown myse—that is, like, taken the first exit right there, with pills or something. That'd a been *it*."

Paul was very still, listening. "I thought from what you said the other night that you liked it, that it was interesting you."

"Ah, no. Not really, man. I try to pretend it does. It's nothing but a sorry operation, a place with a sorry history that a lot of old men are going to fuck up, that should be fucked up. I don't want to be part of that, man."

Paul sat staring at his own beer bottle as if he hoped to see a genie in it. "How'd you get your name?" he said.

"My name? What do you think? Come on, take a guess."

"Ah—"

"Oh, you'd never guess. Don't know those American Nee-groisms. When I was a little boy they started saying about me, 'This one gonna out-scrip all the others.' Soon they were just calling me Scrip."

"Out-scrip?" said Paul tentatively.

"Sure, man, sure. My whole identity, born in a mistake, a ignorant Nee-gro mispronunciation if you will, a—" Paul looked as if he still didn't understand, so Scrip, with an air of exaggerated patience, spelled it out: "Outstrip. Only they couldn't pronounce it right."

"Oh!" said Paul.

"You wouldn't believe where-all I got names from. I got my real name, Earl, from my daddy. I got my last name, Thomas, from some white slave-owner slum way back. I got my ignorant Scrip name. I got my African name I took in college, Emeka. I was Black Muslim for a while so I had a X. Then I started having some differences with the Black Muslims and apparently that got around. The cops came to me to see if I'd go undercover for them doing investigative work on the Muslims. Said they'd give me a false name when I was through to protect me and send me wherever in the States I wanted to go! I said not no but hell no, buddies, I got too many false names as it is."

Scrip took a big swig of beer and glanced at Paul to see how this recital had gone over. Suddenly both men laughed together, uproariously. They shook in their chairs, holding their beers to keep them from spilling.

"So what do guys like me do? Even if we try to dry up, go straight, not get out of control, what do we *do?* Work for IBM? Sell computer software? Try some of this jogging shit? I couldn't do it, man. You know I couldn't do it. I couldn't do that crap even if I did go back to college. I look at little Malcolm. What's he gonna do? You know what he's most interested in? Clothes. What kind of jeans he has on and stuff. Can you believe that?"

"You were talking about art. Maybe he'll be a fashion designer."

"Or just a dumb consumer, like most of us."

There was a pause while the men drank beer. Paul got up and went to the kitchen and Scrip said urgently toward his back in the open refrigerator door, "I'm too smart to be happy being a tractor driver my whole life. Or a garbage man. Goddamn it. Or a janitor. You know?"

"Or a bureaucrat," said Paul mildly. He came back with two more beers.

"Yeah."

"Aren't there ways into the power structure for you? Even little ones? Couldn't you do something political locally?"

"Oh, come on," said Scrip. They were quiet for a minute. "I been reading all these books, stuff from college. I wouldn't have them at home except one time when I was in trouble, I was in this county detox program in Illinois, my mama came up and packed up my room where I'd been staying and she brought all these books home. Anyway I been rereading them. Talking about the power structure, about the way social change could come about in America. It's most likely gonna be slow. I'm not sure I believe in a revolution here any longer. It's gonna come through the existing structures. And some forces we don't expect. Redistribution of wealth. New alignments of power groups."

"That's what I'm talking about. You aren't going to need the machine guns here, brother! I'm talking quiet stuff, slow stuff, smart stuff."

"Nah. If I could really start over that's what I think I'd like to do—try to get into the power structure here and see what I could do from within it. I like leading people, trying to get them to take up my ideas. It's too late for that now, though. I been in too much trouble. If I'd kept myself the way I was in high school I might could have done it. But people like me, Paul?—there's nothing out there for us."

"Yeah." Another long pause. Paul said, "You need to be born again." The words sounded so funny in his slow, meticulous accent. Now his grin came, mischievous and dazzling, scattering the somber planes of his cheeks and chin. "That's what the American politicians do! You got to get religion, Scrip—then you can run for some office."

Scrip groaned. "Jesus."

"See? A good start."

"Religion. You know what the church has done for the black man in American? Trompled him. Fire-hosed him worse than the police in Birmingham. I mean the black church, too. I know more fat-ass preachers drive big cars and wear diamonds—! I know more widow ladies give their rent money to the church—! Religion—shee-et."

Paul said, "Brother, you are too smart to be happy, period!" They laughed and Scrip's eyes shone with a little bitterness and Paul went on, "The fact is you're never going to be happy at anything, because you're too smart—you just know too much. So you may as well accept the fact you're going to be unhappy. Then you can just look for something to do that you think is worthwhile. And that supports Miranda and Malcolm."

"Worthwhile. And supports Miranda and Malcolm. Sounds great," said Scrip. "A whole life without being happy? Why should I have to resign myself to that? Everybody else in America has the right to be happy."

Paul shrugged again. Both men knew they were bullshitting; but to admit it would be to lose any distance they had gained. They were like spiders, spinning their own rope as they advanced. And so as they sipped beer the men kept exchanging glances that were fraught with certainty. Ironclad meaning. That is the secret of beer-drinking: You may be comic or grim, but you must never question the freight of your statements. "Here's to the pursuit of happiness!" exclaimed Paul with a sudden grin, raising his bottle.

"Pursuit of happiness!" said Scrip.

"You Americans amuse me," said Paul. "You are so indoctrinated with this belief in your rights. I hear these kids on the playground: 'This is a free country! You ain't got the right to tell me what to do!' Even the cab drivers in New York—'Hey, you mother, you got no right to park there!' "

"Are you happy?"

"I don't know. I'm not American, so I don't think about it. Have you ever been happy?"

"I don't know." Scrip thought. "Yeah, I guess so. When I was little. Well, that's not all. I'm happy most times with Miranda."

"She seems like quite a woman."

"Yeah, she is. You know Miranda doesn't need me to support her. She's one who's gonna *make* it in this world."

"She is?"

"Anybody made it with *me* so far *sure* gonna make it. No, really, she says she's gonna open up a little store someday—a little retail store—"

The world was a friendlier place than it had been an hour before. The lights outside looked warmer; the force of friendship seemed invincible before any dread that could intrude, or any suffering that already existed.

"Is that snow?" Paul asked. "Do you see snowflakes, or am I just seeing things? Look under that streetlight."

"I think it is snow. Or at least sleet."

"We might have a white Christmas here in Edgewood."

"Depending on what you think of religion, you might say they're all white," said Scrip drily. "Oh God! Speaking of which! What time is it? I'm supposed to pick Miranda up at twelve-ten in front of the Cathedral."

"You'd better jump, brother," said Paul. "It's twelve-thirty."

"Where's my coat?"

"The wolves around here might get a woman like that. You'd better go claim her."

"Thanks, Paul."

"Thanks for the beer."

"So long."

31

ON CHRISTMAS NIGHT the McCains' house was quiet, sleeping. Snow lay on the house and yard like a cape, unfamiliar but pleasing, under which everything slept the light sleep that contains the awareness of some change. If the dogs outside, or the mice or the fluffed-up wrens in the eaves, awoke for the least second, they would have only one sensation: *Snow—?* giving pleasure before they turned again into a delicious sleep.

Allie wasn't asleep yet. She lay on her right side with one arm encircling her pillow, her knees drawn up as if she were jumping into a pool. The arm resting on her legs relayed the picture of their shape to her mind, and she saw the long curving thigh, the tiny planes of the kneecap, and the smooth calf as if they were not her own—as Paul might see them. Abruptly she flipped over to her left side and nuzzled her cheek into the cool cotton skin of the pillow. Then she lay on her back, musing about the feel of sculptured hard bone under her nightgown; her fingertips rode the belly and ribcage to her breasts. She raised her arms and stretched them, making her splayed fingers arch like her backbone, and flopped slack on the mattress. Then she turned back the coverlet with one smooth motion, and swung her feet to the floor.

Now she appeared behind the leaves and blooms in the mirror. Her skin was pale in the blue gloom, like the side of a fish. Her form passed quickly out of the glass. She went to the window and pulled open the curtains. As volumes of moonlight reflected from the snow poured in, her room got many shades brighter. Filmy squares of light slid over the bed, floor, and dresser, and shadows of bottles and trinkets were suddenly thrown on the walls, like a skyline of a town with minarets.

She remembered snow from other Edgewood winters. This was the first snowfall of her life that was ankle-deep and had lasted till night without melting; and it was the first Christmas snow ever recorded in Louisiana. The town was drunk with excitement. Everyone she'd seen all day had a flushed, dreamy, big-pupilled look. On top of the holiday satiation it was just too much.

That morning she had walked in the snow through field after field, admiring it with a continued, private, untaught thrill. She took three rolls of pictures and would have taken more if she hadn't run out of film. Besides the snow itself, lining, defining, reshaping every object, there were all sorts of new things it did with light and shade that changed the landscape she had plundered for so many other photographs. It sparkled like sugar; some of the packed crystals glinted like mica, or rhinestones, or diamonds, suddenly dimming during each footfall, and passing the glint to other points of lighted ice. It was so white it was blue. A painter would have had to use soft blues to show it, and soft pinks too where the earth had warmed through. The whitest white is blue, she had thought, snapping away. But the blackest black is blue too. Paul's skin in some lights is so black it is blue. Blue is the whitest of white and the blackest of black together; white so white and black so black they are not themselves; they meet in blue, blue is the mediator, which is why I like twilight so much—when the air is like clear water, with a drop of blue ink dripped into it, and stirred, before nightfall.

It made her cold now just seeing the pecan trees lined with snow, the doghouse roofed with it, and the pear tree heaped with it—not made to hold it, losing branches from the weight of it on every premature leaf. Back in bed pulling the quilt over her she thought of the bridge that had been closed at two o'clock, after three wrecks. Glory Jones lived across the river. She figured Paul had been there for lunch and couldn't get back now. She'd sneaked off to call him before she went to bed, and there was no answer at his place. A sort of fear came over her to think how right now they were separated—not just by convention and circumstance, which she was used to, but physically, forcibly. The image of the deep brown river, with its clay bluffs floured by snow, lasted a minute in her mind. She returned to the thought of him. She thought of him always. Beneath everything else, not latent or dormant or even like a melody in counterpoint but steady and prominent, was the awareness of him in her mind. Even in his absence a mass of detail about him was so finely knitted in Allie as to embody him almost. Her captivation did not distract her from her experiences apart from him, but strengthened her participation in them: she wanted to live because he did. Often she pored over the sexual moments of their intercourse, but the rest of the time the mere thought of him, just the knowledge that he existed, accompanied and stabilized her.

Did she love him because he was forbidden? Because he was her secret and black and over twice her age? Maybe so; if she had heard about the affair as a third person, that was what she would have thought. The risks of being found out were exciting, and it flattered both her and Paul to know that the other one took them. And part of the intensity had to come from the fun of defiance. The relationship was a flagrant, deliberate rebuttal of Edgewood's social codes, of racism Allie had been taught to hate and of presumptions about herself—about her as a teenage girl—that she had learned to hate on her own. But she didn't think about these things when she was with Paul. He was not a certain age or color then, not even in moments when she listened to him recall things that happened before she was born, or stroked the nap of his hair. The only gap that mattered when they were together, she could honestly say, was a galvanizing rather than a sundering one, the gap between male and female.

She could not imagine him as anything but himself. Still, the question occurred to her whether she would have loved him if he had been an American black rather than an African. Maybe she was just like those people at the museum, in the incident when she had first heard of Paul. Maybe his exotic quality suspended racism of her own. She had asked Paul wistfully about that dinner party her parents gave to support him: "Do you remember me from that night?"

"Oh, sort of," he had said, deliberately vague to tease her. "But you little honky kids all look alike. And there are so many of you."

Little honky kids in his voice sounded funny, with the consonants all softly tapped, the last word stretched to *keeds.* She laughed at him and then abruptly got serious. "I remember *you*—"

"I bet you do."

On nights she had to work she was through at the paper by nine, and would go to Paul's right afterward. Sometimes when there was no work she lied to Lillian and had all evening with him that way. Usually he'd been painting when she got there and the smells of acrylics and turpentine lingered in his rooms, engulfing her along with his presence when he opened the door, so that later in her life a whiff of them stopped her short with a reflexive pang. When he closed the door and held her she could feel through his shirt how, despite the strength and mass of his arms and chest, he trembled. His jaws were smooth; he shaved in the evenings now, he mentioned once, and it took her a minute to figure out why. Even with everything else this surprised her: a grown man shaving for her!—They would sometimes drip a pot of coffee and sit by the windows to drink it, or look at his work or hers for a while, and move pretty quickly to bed.

Sexually too, she could hardly fathom him. He would raise himself from some delicate homage of her body, and propped on bulging arms would say, "Tell me what you like." "I don't know," she would say, stupidly, shyly, or, "Everything." Then he would move back with a control she adored, long hands following the powerful arms, making every gesture an opportunity for some deliberate caress. She was silent, other than that, even when she took the active lead and made love to him. She adored him. While they played one another her face was rapt, intent, flickering like someone about to laugh with joy; her eyes were inflamed, till some touch of Paul's made them close. "Oh, God," she would say then. "Oh, God."

She ached as she went home in the dark, and she would shift in her seat and feel pleased, and a little bereft, and mysterious all at once. She would sing roughly to herself. Then she fell quiet. It seemed he was there with her. He could hear her. He observed. He knew. She gave a short laugh at this foolishness. She counted the hours till she saw him again.

"You're late," Lillian would say.

"There was a lot of stuff that had to be developed."

"Does someone go with you to your car?"

"No, Mama, I told you, I'm there by myself. But it's parked under a streetlight, not very far outside the door."

"Maybe you should bring Troy and Roscoe with you."

"They'll just snuffle all in the car and smell it up by the time I get through." She was in the refrigerator, pawing through the meat tray, the hydrator tray, the cheese rack. "But I don't mind," she added. "I'll take 'em, tomorrow night."

"There's some fresh pineapple in that blue plastic thing. No, on the top shelf."

"But I can't take them tomorrow night. Tomorrow I'm going to work straight from the Art Club meeting." The pineapple dissolved in her mouth. Cold. Golden. Sometimes she felt her very tongue could discern the color, golden.

She had never felt so strongly about anything. The clinical detachment that she had learned in her family, the habit of skepticism she picked up from Lillian, were scattered by the feelings this man evoked from her, not just in the communion of his bed but every time she walked through the artroom door and saw him across the room. Her heart and mind and body seemed aimed in the same direction for once.

Though Edgewood would disagree, the only wrong she felt guilty of was deception, and that was just an unfortunate by-product of their other circumstances. She would have liked to be truthful about things, but it just wasn't possible. Still, she didn't spend much time consciously worrying about being found out. With everything else to think about she had little attention left for that. Suppose Mama talked to Mr. Brooks, and found out there was only about ninety minutes' worth of work for Allie to do every night—but Mama never talked to Mr. Brooks. Suppose someone saw her truck parked behind Paul's building by the levee—but no one she knew ever went downtown at night. Suppose Mama found the diaphragm she had bought from a clinic outside of Edgewood. Allie could say, "It's for future reference," or, "All the girls are doing it—someone dared me to," or, "Randolph insisted I get one. That was all he wanted from me." That'd be funny. Maybe she would just come out with the truth: "I love Paul Kalunge. I adore him. So what?" She would go on with that great maxim of her culture: "Can't you see how happy it makes me? How can it be wrong if it makes me this happy?"

She didn't harbor illusions about a future with Paul. She was not foolish enough to picture the two of them driving a station wagon around Edgewood. Sometimes she imagined living with him in Berkeley or New York, some big progressive city where no one would blink an eye at an interracial, intergenerational couple, but she didn't truly think it would come to pass. At the same time she believed she would never love another man. She didn't know how these thoughts would be reconciled.

What she did believe was that Paul knew what he was doing, simply because he was an adult. Her upbringing had spared her many delusions about adulthood, but she still believed that adults had a plan for their actions—that everything had happened to them before so they never had to figure it out anew. Paul had twenty-one years on her—twenty-one. She knew there had been many other women. Doubtless not anyone else quite like her, of course!—but they definitely had existed. He would mention them in passing as if she weren't supposed to care about them. "A girlfriend and I were at the Guggenheim, and—" "This woman I was seeing had taken it upon herself to teach me to ski—" Surely out of all that head start he had gained knowledge enough to have a plan, to see to it that this was all unfolding to a pattern. He didn't even have to tell her the pattern. She just needed to believe it was there. Along with the other trusts of the relationship went this basic, blind trust that was never alluded to—her trust that he was guiding the attachment.

She wouldn't have dreamed that Paul was making the same mistake about her. When he looked into her eyes and saw the studied coolness narrow and crinkle at the edges, heating in a split-split-second, it was plain she knew entirely what she was about. She looked so much surer and calmer than he *felt*. It was not that he thought she'd done this before—she had told him that, and it was obvious anyway that for her this was that first, pristine happening—not just sexually, that had little to do with what he meant—it was like her first opening of a new, sacred book, her first gingerly stepping onto a sanctuary land. No, what he thought was her sheer, firm control must come from some knowledge he had always sensed in the women he adored, some utterly sure, warm wisdom that enclosed him. Surely she didn't have any expectations from this thing. He had never led her on to any hope that would hurt her—had never told her he loved her, wasn't sure when, or if, he realized that himself.

So in fact he had no plan for the affair at all. When he was forced to think about it he knew it would end when she left for college. He went from meeting to meeting, painting, speaking, brooding out of the big surrounding fragrance that this girl had become to him, and tried not to think about her leaving.

Sometimes Allie grieved over the things she couldn't do with Paul—go to a movie; sit across from him at some restaurant like people in a magazine ad, with her hair coiled on top of her head, her knees touching his under the table, wineglasses glinting in the half-darkness—. But every once in a while they did go way out in the country, where they wouldn't see anyone they knew. Allie would take her camera along. She tried to get him to sketch, but he'd shake his head. "I'm not a sketcher. I just look."

"Come on," she'd tease. "Don't you think your art is connected to the world? Better get out here and affirm those connections you're always talking about."

"No," he'd say, "I'm in your mode. I'm just after pattern and contrast, you know." The closest he would come to doing his work outside was picking up a bone or seed pod that had some shape he liked.

As the year passed, her landscape photographs got better and better. More than any other genre they expressed her mood this year. If she could just catch that expanding quality of the sky—that infinitely alluring, elusive look of the edge of the woods just below the horizon. Clicking, clicking, walking, sidestepping, rewinding, and clicking, she would work at a view, then turn to Paul and laugh just because she felt so good, and see a slow smile coming across his face too.

Once in February they inadvertently ended up near the upcountry Mardi Gras celebration. They saw the line of riders from across a stubbly field. Paul's VW was pulled into a tractor lane. Allie turned toward him, her face pink in the cold wind. "Oh, let's go!"

"What is it?"

"You didn't see the article in the paper on Sunday? It's the Mardi Gras riders. They must be almost through. They start early in the morning and ride all around from house to house, on horseback, and try to catch a chicken at every house to put in the big community gumbo for that night. Only of course they've been drinking all along—"

"Are you sure it's not part of the Klan? That's what it looks like from here."

She giggled. "Come on, really, it's a spectacle. You'll like it. I thought you liked Mardi Gras when you were in New Orleans."

"There you could get lost in the crowd. I think I'd be a little too visible here."

"I'll go take some pictures of it and you can stay in the car. We can at least follow it a little way and see if there's a good place to park the car."

"You drive, then."

Against the straw-colored fields, clumps of purple and scarlet and green and gold stood out—the riders, lurching along before a slow procession of other trucks and tractors that were doing the same thing as Allie and Paul. "I'm going to head 'em off this way," said Allie. She bounced the VW along a tractor lane parallel to the riders' route, and parked the car by a culvert, waiting for the riders to come. Paul slouched down ill-humoredly in his seat. Allie got out and sat on the hood, slipping her lens cap in her pocket. Then she walked a few paces away from the car.

The sound of hooves got closer, and the strains of music, fiddle and accordion, from the band that was being pulled in a trailer behind the tractor, and catcalls and yells and honking from the drunk wagon. The captain's horse passed Allie, prancing sideways just as she snapped. But at least she was in focus now, and she swung back to frame a face, ghastly in white pancake makeup with the eyes starred and the grinning lips reddened. Now she got the swirl of a green, gold-fringed cape, now a rider standing upright in his saddle, now a leering mouth, a wig, a beer can. She let the camera fall around her neck for a minute, eyeing the rest of the line to figure out depth of field if she tried to get the whole thing, then swung her head the other way to see if it'd be better to get the ones who'd already gone by. When she looked back a bay was upon her and an arm was swooping down for her. "Hey, baby, wanna ride with carnival!" She looked into the snapping eyes in the white-painted face, laughing her assent, and sprang without thinking about it. Only one of her legs made it over the saddle, just barely, but still the horse was trotting on. A hand on her thigh and another at her waist on the other side squeezed, levelled, patted her, stayed put. She was laughing and shrieking. She barely caught a glance of Paul's car, half-hidden by weeds, as she passed. The rider's hands moved up her ribcage and briefly cupped her breasts. "Yeeee-anh!" he yelled. "Baby, you made me drop my beer back there, but I think it was worth it." Allie had abruptly quit laughing. She realized what she was going to have to do, and immediately squelched any further thought about it: she twisted, swung her right foot back over the horse's neck, skimming its ears, and pushed away as she jumped. She landed on all fours—or what would have been all fours, if one hand hadn't flown automatically to protect her camera from hitting the ground—and scrambled up as she felt gravel from another horse's hooves skitter in her face. The rest of the procession went by. She heard her rider yelling, but turned her back on it, crossed the ditch, and walked back to Paul's car. She didn't see him till she got in the driver's seat and he rose up from the floorboard.

"Hey, there you are," she said. She felt a little shaken up, but said cheerfully, "That could have gotten out of hand."

She had never seen such contempt on his face as when he looked at her—on anyone's face. She started quaking. "I'm sorry, Paul."

"Just drive."

"I'm really sorry. What's wrong?"

"Just drive us out of here. You're in the driver's seat, you know. It'd be hard for the nigger to duck while he was driving, so he'll just stay under your control, but he requests, ma'am, that you get him the hell out of here."

His venom caught her by surprise, and she knew what pain she was going to feel and dreaded it before it could really register. In a couple of seconds her insides began to fall away layer by layer, as if they were scalded, exposing deeper and deeper membranes of herself. She tried to say, "Don't use that word!" but couldn't speak, and a long sniffle came out instead.

"What the fuck did you think you were doing? Did you set out to humiliate me? Or merely put me in danger?"

"I didn't mean any harm," she said through clenched teeth, with tears still sprouting from her eyes. "Here, you drive."

"No, let's not have any illusions that *I'm* in control."

She pulled over. "No one's around, just drive." She got out and went around to the passenger side, got in and sat with her knees pulled up under the big gray coat Aunt Sarepta had sent her from a used-clothing store and her arms wrapped around them and her chin on them. In a minute she said, "You're not mad because you were afraid. You're jealous! You want me in your control, not some other man's. You're just trying to say it was racial so I'll feel guilty."

He didn't answer. She was sure she was right—not in her behavior, that had been bad judgment, a silly whim gone too far, but in sizing up his anger. She kept stealing looks at his profile, and it didn't change, except to look more irritated when back on the main highway they got caught behind a car, a rusting bottomed-out Chevrolet with fishing poles sticking out the windows, that he could not pass. Allie, self-righteous and hurt, stayed hunched in a ball but turned her head away from him in case she started crying. How could this be happening with *him*—

This stretch of road ran alongside bayous and by straw-colored fields that looked drab and flat this time of year. Then there were several small towns in succession, the kind recalled later as one long stop at a red light with plenty of time to examine fried chicken franchises, lean-tos of corrugated metal that served as bait shacks, car lots, brick storefronts, and gas stations selling boudin and hunting licenses on the side. The sun beat down on it all undiscriminatingly, as if in pained boredom. On the windshield it blazed so that every nick and flaw—the pocked dust of winter and each past swipe of the wipers in a faint muddy arc—showed up plainly, across everything they could see. "I wish I'd brought my sunglasses," murmured Allie, forgetting for a minute they weren't speaking. She had a headache.

Outside the city limits of LaJolie the slow Chevrolet finally turned onto a dirt road and Paul sighed, accelerated as if freed, then sat up straight, arching his back to release it from the press of the sweaty seat. In a few minutes he said, "I guess this is a waste of time, Miss Allie."

For a stricken moment she thought he meant the whole thing; then she saw the contrition in his face and caught on—he meant their argument. "You're right," she said.

He pulled her close and said, "You're terrible."

"I know."

When they saw the eight-miles-to-Edgewood sign he said, "Want to come over for a while?"

"Yeah. I want to. But we're having my grandmother's birthday dinner. It starts in half an hour."

He stopped on the shoulder of the highway at the McCain place road and even though there was another car coming kissed her attentively, slowly. She still felt anxious—that someone would see them and that some residue of their quarrel was left between them. When she pulled back he was studying her face with the purest expression she had seen on anyone. It wasn't the look of ruffled pleasure or urgency or questioning or longing or mischief or desire; it was neither hot nor cold, grave nor joyous. It was simply the rare look of someone absorbed in *seeing.*

"I—" she said. "I—"

He shook his head and his self-awareness came back instantly with his smile. "Better go."

She nodded, wheeled, and started down the road. A few yards away she turned again and half-waved and extended the hand toward him, then her other hand. He raised his hand off the steering wheel and pulled back onto the highway.

32

ONE FRIDAY IN MARCH there was nothing to be done at the paper, and Paul's kids were spending the night with him, so Allie looked forward to a quiet night at home. Someone who had had a big party and rented ferns from Lillian had given her a quart of leftover crawfish bisque. She thawed that out and Allie made a salad for herself with some fresh lettuce Uncle Tyler had brought by earlier. After supper she took a long hot shower, washed her hair, shaved her legs, and put on a new eyelet nightgown she'd already gotten for graduation from her cousin Elaine. It was chilly for March and Lillian started a fire. Allie sat close to the hearth, poring over a book on Cartier-Bresson that she'd ordered from the state university library,

She was deep in Kashmir when she heard the dogs outside. She steadily ignored them through another overleaf. But Lillian went to the back door and then called: "Allie!"

"What," growled her daughter.

"Allie!"

"Ma'am!"

"Oh, there you are. The cows are in the yard—they must have gotten through that wooden gate, finally. Can you do something about it?"

"Oh, great," Allie said to herself. "Oh, that's just great." To her mother she said: "Can you call Moog or Karo?"

"I'll try. But I think LaShondra said they were going out to a big concert at the fairgrounds tonight."

As for Ajax, it was no use calling him; every weekend he took off to see his girlfriend in Mississippi, and was lucky to make it back on Monday mornings.

Allie threw her book down petulantly and rose, going to the bathroom to get a pair of clammy jeans out of the dirty clothes basket, grimacing as they slid over her smooth, lotion-perfumed legs. "Well, that's a hell of a note!" she announced as she stomped her heels, one at a time, down into the bottom of her stubbornly yielding boots.

When she shouldered her way out the back door, there were the dogs, miserably huddled because they did not like thunderstorms. They raised their heads gratefully at her appearance. "Phew," she said. "Y'all stink. Come on." They bumped against her legs gladly and followed in a close clump.

It was absolutely black outside, as if the whole world had been plunged under a cameraman's drape. Rain drove down in airless torrents. Every minute or so a crash of lightning flared in the east and the dogs would quake against the floorboards of the Jimmy—for there was no question but that they rode with Allie tonight. Things were much better with the dogs there. They would listen to all complaining, as Mama, beyond a point, would not. As Allie started out the driveway she saw Lillian, oddly shaped in a light-colored gown with a thigh-length rain tunic thrown over it, emerge from the kitchen door. "I'll be right behind you. I'll take my car. You just tell me what to do when we get there."

"Well, where *are* they?" said Allie. "How'd you even see them out here?"

"I heard them bellowing. And in the lightning bolts you can see them. They're heading for the highway. But if they get into my daffodils, so help me, Allie—"

Allie closed her window. "You shouldn't have planted your damn daffodils in the one place the cows always tromple when they get out," she said crossly to herself and the dogs both. "Even if they wanted to stay out of it, which they have no way of deciding, how could they on a night like this?"

Roscoe flicked his eyebrows anxiously, catching Allie's irritated tone, and settled his chin on her boot on the accelerator. Immediately she had to brake for a cattle guard and he, sighing, had to remove it.

In the next burst of lightning she could see that the herd was about fifty yards away from where the daffodils were planted and heading straight for the highway. She roared up the rutted, gumbo-like road to outrace them, backed the truck at a right angle to the direction of the oncoming cattle, and jumped out to do what she could on foot. It would be a matter of turning them all around—moderately hard to do in daylight, and next to impossible in this wet, pitch dark—and heading them back to the far east pasture along a fencerow and ditch. Then there would be a short gap where they would have no solid barricade to flow against. Would they scatter into the yard? She would have to open the back gate as wide as possible and hope that the lead cow had enough sense to start inside. With a good lead cow you had it made.

There was Mama. "What do I do?"

"Park by me. Try to block that space. But I need your headlights more than the extra length of the car, so don't park sideways, park backward and leave your lights on."

Allie had been chasing cows ever since she could remember. Only when she had inexperienced friends out and something like this came up, or when she and Fayette tried to direct Mama in helping them, did she realize what a delicate art it was. Stupid as they were, cows responded with some consistency to movements and voices. But even their foolish consistency was inconsistent. People used to working with them needed a sense of just how close and hard to push them and when to drop back; of how wide an arc to make in a pasture when approaching a stray, and at just what pace to urge her back to the others. They had the horses to use for a routine roundup or move of the herd, but in unexpected cases like this one, there was just no time to catch and saddle horses.

Now in the lights of Mama's car she saw the big quarter-sized eyes of the lead cow coming toward her, shining green like a cat's. "Yah!" hollered Allie, stretching wide her arms, waving a long stick she'd picked up. "Gi'back, y'ole mama cow—" This always sent her cousins and town friends into hysterics. "*Gee*-onh, mama mama mama mama mama, *hey* now, y'ole witch—"

The cow had come to a slogging, surprised near-stop. She turned her head back uncertainly. Through the diagonally slashing rain Allie tried to see into the bovine mind. What she imagined was dark and blurry, like a black and white channel poorly received on TV. The cow turned and Allie's hopes went up; then she suddenly jerked forward again at a fast clip, and bolted down the side of a ditch, exactly where Lillian's car had been unable to reach. The herd poured after her.

The rain had not slacked up any. If anything it seemed to be coming down harder, whipping in opaque gray sheets across the weak cones of light her headlights produced. But Allie had to reach the highway before the cows did. She accelerated, felt the wheels start to catch and slide in muck, eased to the firmer side of the road and accelerated again. Now headlights were coming toward her. She quit accelerating. The headlights drew near, past her, and stopped; it was a white truck, a truck with stripes, that would be one of the Green Isle trucks; oh—Scrip Thomas. "Which way'd they go?"

"Across the highway, I'm afraid."

"Oh damn," he said, "oh, *god*-damn."

"You mean—they're y'all's?"

"Yeah, they ours. You thought they were yours?"

"I just got out here. Yeah. Wait a minute and let me get out of here and I'll meet you up on the highway."

"Let me turn around."

"Don't get stuck."

They heard the screech of brakes and the thump and the cow's scream, it seemed, all at once, as they reached the highway. Then the next, and the next. "Head 'em back, head 'em back," Allie heard, and she was already out of the Jimmy—"Stay, *stay*," she screamed at the dogs, slamming the door on them. Headlights were everywhere, pointing in crazy directions, and a red glow from taillights where there should have been no taillights. Here came another cow slogging toward Allie and she took off her hat and waved it, yelling, moving sideways with the halting, uncertain cow, till the cow finally turned, down the ditch that gradually sloped away from the dangerous road, and turned the rest of the herd with her.

Three cows were so badly hurt they had to be destroyed, two cars were damaged, and four people had to be treated in the emergency room.

Scrip had forgotten to turn on the juice in the single-strand electric fence around the new fescue pasture.

"Well, you sure fucked up *this* time," said Karo bluntly.

And Scrip sank down, down, down, into a blue-purple oblivion. Beer was too slow and he bought whiskey and went down in a spiral, in his and Miranda's bed, rising only to lurch to the toilet or to jerk open the door for his son with a face so terrible, so red-eyed and bristly and stretched out of shape, that the boy would flee. In fits of wakefulness he would hear Miranda on the phone: "No, you can't come over here. I don't want to get into it wichou, Mama...Obviously, Mama, I can't keep it away from him. If I could don't you think I would?...Oh, *damn* it to hell!—"

He knew, when he floated up toward sobriety again, that these were his deserts: he had failed Green Isle so many times before. But the irony of being turned away, the one time he really meant his plea for a new chance! And had *shown* them he meant it, for months! The picture from Houston that he had successfully pushed down all this time would rise to his mind's eye again: the young kid sprawled across the floor of an apartment stairwell, with his belly blown open by a close-up blast from a sawed-off shotgun—a kid Scrip knew casually, who as a matter of fact had been sleeping with a girl Scrip had introduced him to, stopping in unannounced to buy a few lids from a guy Scrip had told him about. He was blown away because the dealer had simply gotten jittery, waiting for Scrip to make a pick-up he happened to be late for. By the time Scrip arrived on the scene it was obviously a bust gone amok. He tried to saunter past, then realized he should gawk like a bystander, was picked up and charged anyway, but, again by a fluke, he had no evidence on him at the time and they couldn't make the charges stick. Still the kid's image hovered before him: the purple high-tops with gold laces, the pale jeans with their heat-whitened crease down each leg, the thighs showing tight and hard under the cloth, then—that mess where a middle should be; or starting from the top down: the 'fro, the smooth amber face, the eyes bugged as if in a question, lips curled back, an odd lavendar color, the collar of the shiny silver jacket, black T-shirt, and then—that hole, that bomb-hole where a kid's smooth abdominals should be. It was a kid he knew, not just personally but many times over. He had hung out on a thousand street corners in Scrip's life, played a thousand games of hoops, jay-walked a thousand late-night streets at the same time Scrip had with his high-tops squelching on the pavement, eyed a thousand women Scrip was with and murmured appreciatively when they passed. In short it was everybody Scrip knew—it was a brother.

The dealer was picked up, too. His charges stuck. Scrip wasn't sorry about that. It turned out the dealer had some reason to be jittery; he had on him, besides the marijuana and Quaaludes intended for Scrip—chicken scratch to him—some amphetamines that were part of a huge amount drained systematically out of a mall pharmacy inventory over a period of fourteen months. His arrest didn't keep Scrip awake at nights; the big guys knew the consequences and if they were unlucky enough to reap them, tough luck. But what did was the death of the kid, who had been punished—erased—in Scrip's stead. Talk about who should reap consequences—Scrip himself had many yet to suffer, if only justice were absolute. That day for instance. If he'd shown up three minutes earlier, he'd have walked into the bust or the gun barrel or both. Scrip couldn't account for it.

It wasn't that he thought any god was looking out for him. He'd never been able to understand it when people attributed close calls to providence anyway. It was just that a more innocent life had been taken in his place—sort of like Rodney in Vietnam. That blown-away kid was a simpler, better person than Scrip had ever been. He lived with an old great-aunt and a younger aunt or sister or somebody who had six or seven kids, though she was only twenty-five and had fled a husband who beat her up, and whatever the kid made got split up among them all—in their casual acquaintance Scrip had picked up this much. He had a baby girl by someone he didn't see any more, but he still walked the baby to the Headstart Center most mornings. He was a good kid. The kind old people in the neighborhood said hi to. He might have turned out all right. Not great, not stellar, but all right: not like this aged, bleary, twenty-eight-year-old, this alcoholic steeped too long in his rages and self-disgust, this letdown of his people, this Scrip.

33

MYRTLE CLARK AND Imogene Rabelais ate at Preston's Cafeteria together every Wednesday. That was the morning they both got their hair done, and they enjoyed being out in public before the blue paled. They wore low square-heeled pumps and carried patent-leather purses—no gloves or hats, though, because they knew those were "out" now—a fact they occasionally pondered together.

As they waited for the line to move them close enough to read the vegetable plate and the luncheon special posted behind the silverware, Myrtle told an anecdote she repeated on about one out of every four times they ate there. "When my little granddaughter was visiting me once I told her we could go anywhere she wanted to eat. And she said, 'I want to go to the cafeteria!' And I said, 'Why?' And she said, 'Because they have all different colors of jello, and you can pick out whatever color you want.' "

"Heh heh heh," said Imogene. Now she could tell her grandchild-cafeteria story, which Myrtle had likewise heard before. "That reminds me of once when Fayette was little. He kept talking about how he wanted to go to Preston's and kept talking about it. It was when they lived in Boston and people don't have cafeterias in Boston and he remembered going with me before on another visit and it had really made an impression on him, you know. Well he got to pestering me so I took him about mid-afternoon and got him a Coke and a cream puff and me a cup of coffee and he looked around just as terrible and mad till I said, 'What's the matter?' And he said, 'I want to come back when it's *crowded!*' "

"Heh heh," said Myrtle. "Well, it looks like they got their shortcake out. Finally. What are you going to have? That haddock looks mighty good."

"Oh, I think I'll just have the vegetable plate."

"Well, I usually just eat vegetables, but I think some fish'd be good for me. I have to watch my salt and fats but I think I could stand some of that haddock."

Some minutes later, when they were settled at their table with their trays dispensed of and their dishes arranged around their glasses of buttermilk and iced tea, Myrtle said, "It's hard to believe that little boy Fayette is getting married."

"Ooh, I tell you." Imogene buttered her cornbread, looking not particularly incredulous. "Isn't it though?"

"Where are they going to live?"

"I expect they'll get an apartment till Fayette finishes school. I don't know."

"She's in school too, isn't she? When does she finish?"

"Oh, I think she's a year or two behind him. Maybe not, though. He was off for a while."

"And it's just going to be a small wedding."

"That's what Lillian tells me they want. And a reception at Maria's grandmother's home, which probably means it has to be small. I declare. I hope they let me look at the guest list so they don't make any big mistakes."

"I'd love to send them some of my caladiums to set around in the church or the house. If you think they could get them down to New Orleans and keep them cool. You know I've only lent them out of town once before and I never got those back. Had to buy new bulbs the next year. That was that bad Regnier boy." Myrtle's caladiums were an old Edgewood tradition; summer after summer they had leafed forth for the town's brides. No one ever turned down the offer of their loan.

"Well, I'll ask them. To tell you the truth I mentioned it earlier and they didn't say anything. Maybe Maria doesn't know what caladiums are. I hope not."

"Maybe she misunderstood."

"I tell you though," said Imogene around a bite of ambrosia, "I can hardly think about the wedding right now, Jules has got me so worked up about moving."

"Oh, is he still after you to move?"

"Yes, he's got it in his mind now and there's nothing gonna shake him from it. 'Mother, Tara Place has this and that, it has a recreation room and a music room, it has a nurse and a nigra man to look after your car, you can have your own kitchenette if you want—'"

"Well?" demanded Myrtle. "Are you going to?"

"Oh, I don't know. I'd miss my yard. He says I could have a window box but it's not the same. Though when I think about the watering I don't know if I can make it through another summer moving hoses."

"Stan and Alma sure like their automatic sprinkler system," said Myrtle.

"Honey, for that price I could buy *two* condos at Tara Place."

"Well," said Myrtle with satisfaction, "Stan keeps trying to get me to move, but I don't think I could go through with it. I've lived in my house for forty-three years and I don't see any reason to quit now."

"Well," echoed Imogene. "I expect I'll do it. I've dealt with Jules before, and when he gets like this it's easier to give in to him than to keep saying no. I don't know how I managed to raise somebody like that, but I did."

"Jacques was always hard-headed," said Myrtle solemnly and kindly, and Imogene peeped at her from behind her powder compact and giggled, and both the widows laughed as they counted out change for their bill.

"Do you still want to go to Buckerman's?" said Imogene in the parking lot.

"Oh, yes. Wouldn't miss it. I can still get home in time for my nap." Which they both knew meant her stories, the two-to-three-o'-clock hour containing Myrtle's favorites.

As they entered the store the bell jangled over their heads, and smelling the wafts of floor wax and furniture polish and oak cabinets and faint potpourri that meant they were about to spend money satisfactorily, they breathed deeply and happily.

Miranda Thomas came out of the office, smiling as she greeted them. On the job Miranda exuded a sort of cool capability that reassured and encouraged her customers. She, too, made them feel good.

"Hi-do, Miranda," they both said. "Miranda! What happened to your eye?"

"I ran into a door. It was the stupidest thing. I had my head turned talking to my little boy. What can I do for you?"

"Goodness! When did that happen?"

"A couple of days ago. It looks worse than it is, really. Are y'all looking for something in particular?"

"Well, my little grandson is getting married," said Imogene proudly.

"That's right. That's Fayette, isn't it?"

"That's the one. They were in here picking out patterns Saturday, I think."

"Yes, let me show you her selections." They followed the tall, swaying woman past miscellaneous wares and through the felt boxes of sterling in big glass cases and back where the walls were lined with Lenox and Wedgwood and Royal Doulton behind glass, to the antique table set with the current brides' patterns.

"Oooh," said Myrtle, faced with the dinner plate, "isn't that pretty."

"Sort of plain," said Imogene critically. "Let's see the every-day."

"These young girls like things plain," said Myrtle, to cover the subsequent disappointment of the every-day. "It's kind of modern, isn't it, Miranda?"

"Some of them think it's very classical," said Miranda sagely.

"Classical," said Imogene. "I reckon. I wonder if she let Fayette have a say-so."

"Is she picking out sterling?" said Myrtle.

"Well, I've offered them Jacques's and my sterling, but they haven't said yes or no yet."

"No, she didn't pick out sterling. Just stainless." Miranda read from a card.

"That's odd," said Myrtle. "Unless they're going to take your sterling after all."

"That must be what—" Imogene started to say, when a crash from the front of the store startled them. Then they heard swearing and as if that weren't all bad enough, the expression that crossed pretty Miranda's face nearly have scared the nitroglycerine patches off their bosoms. And here came this big black man, grizzled over like he hadn't shaved in a while, but young, saying terrible things about Miranda and falling into cases of china and crystal.

"Oh, God in Heaven," cried Miranda, and the man came right for her—the ladies backed away too shocked even to scream—and grabbed her arm still saying terrible things. Already they heard a siren, but the man didn't seem to hear it. "I give up. I just give up. I give *you* up!" Miranda was saying, and then she fell out in a dead faint and the man dropped to his knees beside her in all the broken glass and started crying and the police got there and hauled him off. It was better than a thousand hours of the stories, and it sent Myrtle to bed for a week.

34

THE ENVELOPE CAME. It was thick, as people had said it would be if the news was good. "Dear Ms. McCain: Congratulations ..."

When people get older and exclaim about how fast time is passing, it's not really the swiftness of days they mean: on a given afternoon the clock drags as slowly for someone forty as for someone fourteen. What is different is that the changes just get more gradual.

Older people have to look at the calendar and, in a way, hand over another year without receiving any sense that they have grown dramatically in return. But no seventeen-year-old has reason to begrudge twelve months' passing—to her they've brought change enough for a decade.

Allie could hardly believe what had happened in this year. She felt she was a million years older, that if you were any deeper or more knowing than *she* was you'd keel over with age.

The summer her father was sick they had sat frozen for hours in the living room, not bothering to turn on lights when dusk finally came, letting the TV run out its thin ribbon of programming while they stared away from it in different directions. During the weeks of evenings spent that way political conventions had come and gone—for the most part affecting them about as much as a patter of rain on the windshield, a buzz of voices coming from a banquet room you're passing and have no connection to, that was all. If all had been well they would have been excited about Jimmy Carter, as Lillian's friends were at the time. But as it was they watched dully and didn't really see. Finally on the night of the acceptance speech it was the music that cut through their apathy: brass and percussion, in big long strange loops of sound—ascendant, celebratory, but somehow sad. Copland, *Fanfare for the Common Man.* "It was so beautiful," Allie had said wonderingly—the first words spoken in that room in several hours. She looked at her father and his face was shiny and silvery in the TV light, as if snails had tracked it up and down. "Especially when you know you don't have much time, Allie," he had said. "Everything just seems more ..." He didn't complete the thought. From over in the wing chair she lived in that summer she didn't say anything; just watched the screen turn into a big glob of blue and brown, shimmery at the edges, the way the earth must look when you draw away from it very far.

That was the closest she came to talking to him about his death. That reticence, too, grieved her now, as she walked around inside this wound that was still trying to close. They should have talked about it more, experts would have told the McCains. Everyone knew you should be more "open" and "upfront" than you were naturally inclined to be. The McCains couldn't fail to know this, for Aunt Mary Sue kept dropping by and leaving books about it on the table in the entrance hall, where they sat unread, buried deeper every day by piles of coats and newspapers and hospital bills. Denial was normal, according to such books, but after a certain number of weeks death should bob up into the general conversation. Yet this family of verbal jugglers, debaters, punners, and tongue-lashers, of children who had talked at twelve months, had still failed to tackle the subject. What language—as the hymn went—would they borrow? That of soap operas, college seminars, self-help parlance? "Say, Daddy, why do I want to reject the idea of your mortality?" It wasn't their style. As if by instinct they resisted, resisted, and tried to shove death under the surface of life, like kids treading a ball underwater. So Allie was left with glancing allusions and this one remark by her dad about the way a piece of music made him feel, those days when he was locked inside his own skull with a tumor. And she still wasn't sure, if they all had it to do over again, that it could have been any different.

Now time had changed again, time was flying, and she could feel her father's remark in a different way. The date of her leaving loomed on the horizon, compressing the months she had left and making her anticipation of them more vivid, more poignant, more austere. "Everything just seems more" ...something. Blues were bluer, greens greener, the big Disney spread of the sunset sky hurt more. There was another silence going on too, the silence between her and Paul about what this affair meant—if anything, she thought in bitter moments. The silence of love countering the silence of death. So in response to the thick envelope from Stanford—partly to stave off the rush of time, partly to create a chance for Paul to consecrate it—she arrived at the idea of spending graduation night with him. She had never spent a whole night. There had always been the pressure of the clock chiming back in, always some place one or the other of them was supposed to go next. When they brushed against one another in the artroom, with their yearning marshalled behind steely faces, Allie had the sense that she was jerking along in perpetual motion, something fluttering, damned, like a bird on a long flight, and that she would not come to rest until when she was alone with Paul. Only then would she be able to stop, like a child at play, crying: *Time-out!* The quiet of his apartment enclosed them perfectly. It filled with a seamless time of its own. As the year gathered momentum, moving toward graduation, crowded more and more with meetings and tests and parties and projects for both her and Paul, forcing their trysts farther and farther apart, she longed for the time-out even more. Paul teased her and still she planned carefully for graduation night and focused on it. She would expand the impeccable pause that was their affair—expand it as far as she could.

On graduation night Allie parked between Rick Jasper's old Dodge Dart and Lee Lee Shannon's brand-new Cutlass Supreme, and with her robe over her arm crossed the football field. The sky was swiped with pink, thick as cotton candy, and beneath it the grass where all those predictable games had been played was oddly bright—though it was natural, not artificial turf—as if it had some other-planet light of its own. The seniors' gowns, shimmering violet, added to the strangely tinted scene a lurid iridescent color like that of spilled gasoline or purple grackles. She walked with her cool, sashaying walk through the class—369 of them—grinning, saying hey to them. A distinct feeling of unreality came down over her, as it used to at times when she was growing up, like at the fair, or in a crowded store.

"Hey, Allie—"

"Hey, T-Bone."

"Allie, what say."

"Nothing much, hey."

"Hey, Janet, you're looking great."

"Terry! What's up."

"Hey, Allie."

The faces looked odd over the same dress, beneath the same foolish-looking mortarboards. But they looked so nice, the guys well-shaven, the girls well made up. A few of these faces she had been with from kindergarten. She saw Theresa and gave her a hug, and then found the people she would be next to in line.

"Hey!"

"Allie—you excited?"

"Sort of."

"Who'd you come with?"

"I rode my motorcycle—that's why my hair probably looks like shit."

"No, it doesn't, really."

"No shit?"

"No shit. Besides, we all have to put on these hats—"

"How're you gonna keep yours on?"

"Hell, who am I next to?"

"I think, me—"

Mrs. O'Gillvie was heading their way, and their classmates on one side had become more defined—a sinuous line rather than one giant cluster. "Thompson, Mike...Thompson, Sherry...Hebert, Patrice... Williams, Banister...Hi, Allie...hm, McCain—Breaux, Hugh ..."

"What time do you have?"

"Close to eight. It's time."

"Your folks here?"

"Yeah. My grandparents and shit."

"What are you doing afterwards?"

"Me and Rhonda got a hotel room, at the Sheraton. You oughta come by."

"No, I mean after school—"

"I've got a job offshore. My uncle got it for me. What about you?"

"I'm-a go to LSU-E for a while. Get my nursing degree."

Already the people around her were separating. They seemed old. Adult. Deciding what they would do because they wanted to do it, not because it was required. Allie felt confused, pained for a moment. She could remember when Brian, the one who was almost married to this Rhonda, who would be working offshore for probably the rest of his life, who would have a beer belly and maybe a kid by this time next year, had thrown up in the middle of their reading circle in second grade...The thought made her laugh and regain her grip, and now the line was moving.

Just as at every pep rally, the mediocre band music moved her deeply despite herself. The bass drum seemed to boom inside her own gut.

"You can sure tell the seniors aren't playing with the band tonight," muttered Hugh Breaux behind her.

"Pomp and Circumstance" flowed imperiously around them. The chords sounded dwarfed in the outdoors, under that vaulted pink sky. The graduates filed past one goalpost and, slowly as a viscous purple liquid, filled the phalanx of dun-colored folding chairs that waited for them.

Reverend Johnnie Dikes of Green Isle gave the invocation. Then the class president, Denise Peters, stepped forward to welcome the crowd. Someone passed a joint down Allie's row. She took it from Hugh Breaux and inhaled deeply: her first taste of marijuana: a communion. She passed it on to Rhonda Sharp.

After the ceremony she went by the class dance for a few minutes and talked to some of her friends and danced with one or two. Then, with her heart pounding, she headed to Paul's—parking by the telephone pole downstairs, as always, climbing the concrete stairwell with its peculiar smell of building materials, and knocking quickly while she readjusted her hair over her shoulders, her belt, her shoulder bag. When he opened the door he looked away from her face at once, and backed up, inviting her in but not touching her, and over his arm she saw Scrip Thomas sitting on the couch. She flinched—as much from shock that anyone else was in their sanctum, as that it was Scrip.

"You know Scrip Thomas, don't you?" said Paul. He looked

apologetic.

"Yeah. Hi." Her displeasure was clear. Tonight of all nights! she thought.

Scrip grinned and she imagined she saw amusement in his face. He was glad he rankled her.

She sniffed and looked around sharply until she saw the small brown cigarette in Paul's hand. "Not you too!"

"Ay-yuh—we're having some of this. Would you like some? Or would you rather have a glass of wine to celebrate?"

"A glass of water," she said frostily.

"Celebrate what?" said Scrip. She wondered why he thought she was here. She knew he and Paul had become friends. Had Paul confided in Scrip about her? How would he have put it? She didn't even know how he thought of it within himself, much less how he might mention it to someone like Scrip.

"Allie just graduated from high school," said Paul. He came back from the kitchen with Allie's water and passed the joint to Scrip, who looked at it critically. "She now belongs not to the public schools of Edgewood, Louisiana, but to Stanford University."

"No shit?" Scrip breathed deeply.

"What did you mean 'You too'?" Paul said suddenly to Allie.

"Oh." Even in her exasperation she laughed. "People were smoking weed all during the ceremony. It was sort of—nice. Funny."

"Old Edgewood's coming around," said Scrip. "When I was over at Edgewood High, a little Mogen David was the worst thing you could sneak around with. I know it's a long way from that now."

"Lordy. All the ringleaders were probably my other Art IV students," said Paul.

"Yeah, you've been encouraging them to loosen up and drop their inhibitions all year and they're finally catching on," said Allie.

Scrip laughed.

"Give me some of that, please," she said. She took the cigarette from him and sucked in a long breath of air.

"Look at that, look at that. A natural."

But she was disappointed—it didn't seem to be affecting her. It was way past the time Scrip should leave. This was her special night with Paul. Why wouldn't he leave? Why wouldn't Paul tell him to get out?

The three of them continued to pass the joint, and Allie studied Scrip while he talked to Paul. He was wearing a navy blue jogging suit with white trim and white sneakers. He was clean-shaven—his face had sagged since the days of his picture in Uncle Luke's high school yearbook, he looked older, the fine chiselled features of his high-school self were now smeared, and his eyes, though animated, were reddish around the edges. She had heard from Mémé about his scene at Buckerman's. As a matter of fact it was a wonder to see him looking so good now.

"Anyway," he was saying, "so I was telling you. So the ladies got this League now. The Green Isle Beautification League where they plant flowers all in the hole where the big plantation sign used to be. They have cake sales and shit trying to raise money to buy a sign. Place nets thirty thousand a year—*nets* that—but they won't buy a sign with the Green Isle profits because Dikes opposes it. Opposes it because it was my idea to start with. See, I'm getting popular now. Getting power out there. So I'm in jail, right, overnight for losing it with Miranda down at Buckerman's, fined the damages and all that shit, I just backslid a little bit, you know? And the League ladies come down to the jail bringing my bail money. That just sort of did it to me. I heard their voices out there and I kind of rallied. I stand up and I call out, 'Ladies. Ladies,' I say, 'those funds are to pay for the Corporation signpost—not my bail.' 'Now Scrip honey,' they say, 'just sit tight. We brung it down here to get you out, and that's what we gonna do.' 'I insist,' I say. 'I done wrong, ladies, and I'm ready to suffer the consequences.' 'The Lord give us all a second chanct,' they say. 'You our leader, Scrip, honey. We need you.' I started crying, Paul. Felt like a new baby all over again."

"'Sat right!" said Paul. "*I* be damned!" He shook his head softly from side to side, looking at Scrip.

"So I'm back out there, Paul. I'm on top again. The court had asked Miranda if she wanted an injunction against me. I told her she should. I've done some terrible things to that lady in her life. She told me about it, looking at me, and then she said, 'No. I don't want it.' Malcolm says, 'Daddy, you're well now, hunh?' And the people—they love me. Are you believing that? They want to do things. Want to start a day care center and shit out there. We're getting moving out there. You know Claire Duval? Well, *you* do." He addressed Allie for the first time. "Claire says, 'Scrip, you giving us a new leaf on life.' New leaf on life! Made me laugh. But for her to tell *me* that—!"

Allie burst out laughing. The men turned their heads inquiringly. "Scrip's sounding like you," she told Paul. "He's talking with an African accent. And you said something Southern a minute ago." She was giggling helplessly. "Y'all are switching."

As they exchanged glances with one another a long, long time passed. For ages Allie sat on the couch watching them. She had quit wondering when Scrip was going to leave. She just kept looking at the two men. It was pleasing just to look at them, Scrip sitting on a straight chair turned around backwards, tipping it toward Paul, and Paul on the end of the couch she was on. If she could photograph them now she would know just how to do it. The picture would win prizes. It would contain the very essence of friendship. Look at the triangle of interest Scrip's arm formed reaching out to hand the joint to Paul, formed with the back of the chair and with Paul's torso leaning forward to take it. Look at the smooth, polished planes of their faces, all those browns and red-browns and purple-browns where the light buffed them, the shine off their eyes. She would organize the picture around their eyes and brows and foreheads. She would capture them as they were, she would get the particularities of their friendship, that disclaiming gesture of the palm of Scrip's hand, on her film and on paper: she would nail it down, get it.

Then there occurred a blank in her mind. If her consciousness was a continually running film, some of the freeze-frames that composed it had stacked up, like slides getting jammed in a projector. For a little while she was aware of just blankness.

Suddenly she was on her feet over near the door and all the frames she'd missed rushed before her eyes. She saw what she must have been doing those few seconds before. She even heard words she'd spoken a minute ago. She was getting the camera, urging the men to stay put, slipping back for the view of the scene she wanted. And now she was taking pictures. Six, seven. "And by Paul's easel," she said. "Scrip, you sit on that stool." Eight. "Now look straight at me. Don't smile." Nine. Save some for later that night.

Now Scrip was going. She and Paul were telling him good night. She heard her voice, bright, tripping, circle down the stairwell. Paul closed his door gently. His face loomed very big into hers. "I'm sorry," he said. His back muscles, little individual hillocks on either side of the spine, suddenly reminded her of turtles: little baby hard-shelled turtles resting just beneath the surface hard warm sand, along a furrow. She ran her hands over and over them and the silly thought made her giggle into Paul's collarbone. "You look wonderful," he said. "Happy graduation." He lay his cheek against his hair. "You've got to let me go, so I can go open a window," he said. "You sure don't need to be breathing any more of this smoke." Still to each other while Scrip's footsteps clattering downstairs got fainter and fainter, and the outer door clanged open and shut. Then they were solely each other's again, in the tower they had created.

Myrtle Clark always watched a little bit of TV before she went to bed. She had more options of what to watch now that Buddy was dead. He hadn't let her watch any shows that starred black people. Used to, his rule had extended even to any network that used blacks even in its commercials or on its news hour, as well as the products advertised by one of them. But soon by that rule there were no acceptable networks left, and he hated to give up his Ford once Bill Cosby started sponsoring that, so he changed the policy to cover TV shows only. But now that he was gone Myrtle could watch "The Jeffersons" to her heart's content.

Imogene had given her some strawberries that someone brought her from south Louisiana, and she hulled them while she watched the late news, and washed them and put them in the refrigerator. She always tried not to go to sleep too early lest she wake up in the middle of the night. If she went to bed later when she was more tired she would usually sleep the whole night through. At ten-thirty she went around checking the doors to her house and speaking to her deaf old poodle. She had only one phone in her house, back in her bedroom, so that if anyone broke into the front of her house they couldn't take any other extension off the hook. She put on her nightgown and housecoat and house shoes and washed her face and put cold cream on it. Then she went to bed.

At one-twenty she heard a noise and opened her eyes, and a hand clapped over her mouth. She screamed, and tasted the salt of the coarse skin crammed back in her mouth. The light in the room was dim and the shape over her seemed only massive and dark, she couldn't see much of it. Something cold touched her throat and a voice was saying, "I'm gonna kill you, bitch, I'm gonna kill you," the breath beery and stinky and hot over her face. Fingers grabbed and squeezed her old flesh. A body was on top of hers, a heavy body, a man's body, twisting and grunting, rank. She whimpered, the cry of an animal. She felt the scratch of his whiskers as his face sank suddenly into hers, and passed out just as he raped her.

Each turning and stirring during the night woke Allie slightly, and when she realized every time it was Paul's skin brushing the edges of her sleep, his arms enfolding her, a hot sweet airy disbelief came over her; she felt spongy as a honeycomb, weightless, shot through with light. His leg lying across hers scissors-style was so heavy and alien to her sleep she could scarcely rest alongside it. Dawn came early. She'd thought she might go to a picnic breakfast on a sandbar of the river with her classmates—they would have been out all night carousing, where Lillian thought she was. She had told Theresa she'd be with her boyfriend, and Theresa, thinking she meant Randolph, had promised to cover for her...As the first light came into the room she woke up. But she couldn't bring herself to get up and dress and leave him. She lay on her side watching Paul sleep. His whiskers were stubbly and whorled in patterns darker than his skin. She fell asleep again herself. The next time she woke up she slipped out of bed and crossed the room—looking back to see his eyes wide open. Then he closed them again and said sleepily, pretending to be grouchy but succeeding only in not smiling, "Where are you going?"

"Never mind." She got her camera off a chair where it sat piled up with her clothes. As she crossed the floor he looked again. The late spring sun, surprisingly hot for its weak look, washed Allie in a yellowish cast, the shadows flitting over her breasts and ribs and navel and pubis like the greenish-gray shade of thin new leaves.

"Oh, now your eyes are open again," she said disappointedly.

"I'm sorry, I was watching you."

"I wanted a picture of you asleep—"

"Mmn." He let his lids, red with light, settle over the vision again. There were a couple of clicks, then Allie said, "I doubt they'll be any good, you're faking."

"Come here," he said.

But instead she went around to the other side of the bed. She stood by the window, a huge block of light, thinly curtained because it overlooked only the river and levee and a street that had no view inside here. It was this sun-warmed, bare feeling she got from being at Paul's that sustained her reveries later, as if she, and everything, were pared down to their best essences here. She stretched, luxuriantly like a cat, and was quiet a moment. She sneezed a little dry sneeze in the sun. "Paul?" she said. She looked, and this time his eyes were full on her, liquid, reflecting that window. He was half-sitting against a pillow, very still. Then she shook her head.

"What?" he said.

"I don't know."

"Come here to me," he said.

"I wonder if I could ever take a picture of you looking at me like that. So I could always have it."

In a minute he said, "No. Because I couldn't look into a camera lens the way I look at your eyes. Which is why painting will always be superior to photography."

"Oh, bull—!"

"Oh, yes. If I re-created your eyes and face from memory the image would contain every time you've ever looked at me, or I've thought about your look. All that much more than just a photograph."

"But you don't," she said. "You don't try to paint like that anyway. You paint more abstract things than that."

"Allie," he said, a tone deeper. "Come here."

That time she placed her camera on his bedside table, slid under the sheet, and fit herself over the smoothness and warmth of his body.

35

A WEEK LATER Allie stopped by her grandmother's to visit. The TV was turned up loud and Allie winced at the noise. She knew Mémé was getting deaf. They sat down and shouted greetings at each other through a used car commercial, and then "Crimestoppers" came on.

"On Friday, May sixteenth," a police sergeant droned, "at approximately twelve-forty-five a.m., a black man climbed through the kitchen window of a residence on East Madison Street."

"Why, this is about Myrtle!" said Mémé.

"What?" hollered Allie.

"Hush." Mémé turned up the volume with the remote control. On the screen a tall, lean black man pried up a window and disappeared into the house.

"Have you ever noticed how everyone you see on 'Crimestoppers' is black?" said Allie.

"The suspect entered the bedroom where he awoke a seventy-six-year-old woman who owns the house, threatened her with a knife, and raped her."

"Mm, mm, mm," said Mémé.

"There are bound to be plenty of crimes here committed by whites. But they never show those."

"He bound her and left the premises bearing jewelry and household silver."

"It was her mama's julep cups," interrupted Mémé.

"Really, I wonder how they find black actors willing to do these scenes."

"The suspect is described as a bearded black man about 180

pounds. Anyone with knowledge of this crime should call three-seven-five-STOP. All information will be kept confidential and you will be paid for your assistance. Thank you."

The Reverend Johnnie Dikes switched his TV set off and sat in the darkness of his living room. "All we like sheep have gone astray," he murmured. He kicked his recliner back to the upright position and sighed as he got up to go to the kitchen. Opening his refrigerator he suddenly stopped; the full beam of the light inside lay on his stout figure; he stood there letting all the cold air out into the room, staring at the milk cartons and ketchup bottles and orange juice as if they held the portents of some divine message. He closed the door slowly, forgetting to get anything to eat.

Thursday night after a particularly boring deacons' meeting, he had lain down on the couch in his office for just a moment to rest before starting home, and had waked up three hours later. So at about midnight he was stopping at the 7-11 for a carton of ice cream—Julie and the kids loved it when he got them up in the middle of the night for ice cream. Scrip Thomas had come in for a pack of cigarettes. "Rev!" he had said—a nickname Dikes hated. He preferred to be called his full appellation, in hushed tones. Scrip had said, "You in here to buy you some skin rags?" Johnnie was confused until Scrip pointed at the magazines behind the cashier, the ones with cardboard blocking the middles of voluptuous white women on their covers. Scrip had a grin on his face that was positively wicked. When the clerk glanced at them a little nervously, Scrip had leaned way up close to Dikes and started whispering in his ear crude things, vile, lustful things. "That's the real heavenly power, ain't it, Rev? That's your kind of Rapture, Rev." Dikes backed away into the potato chip stand but Scrip pursued, twisting up close to his ear and whispering, "Don't *love* that whiteness—*screw* it, before they screw you." Dikes jerked back and said, "Go to the devil!"—something he said only when he was very upset. Then Scrip had burst into laughter and said, "Got to you, didn't I?" Sauntering out the door he had called over his shoulder, "Just a joke, Rev." Dikes had shuddered, getting his change from the clerk, and said, "That man is crazy." "I believe you," the clerk had said. "You have you a good night now. And look out for them crazies!" Joke, ha. Johnnie Dikes could take a joke. But what he was thinking now was, that wasn't a joke. That man—he had seen it since he was a youngster—had violence and lust on the brain. Hadn't Dikes been the one to go over to the dairy and try to subdue him when he was drunk and threatened to expose himself over there, years before? He had no hard and fast evidence about Scrip and this particular crime. But maybe the police ought to know about Scrip, a man who would wander around in the middle of the night—the same night someone was raped—talking about sex and racial violence.

Dikes sat down heavily at the kitchen table and tried to pray. But his brain was moving too fast for prayer. He felt hot and fluttery the way he had before his heart spell, as if he had just had three forbidden cups of coffee. He would ask the Good Book what to do. That was what his grandfather had always told him. He went back into the living room and pulled it off the coffee table, flipping it open and stabbing a finger at the page where it fell open. "When thy right hand offend against thee, cut it off." He reread the passage. Hadn't he tried to pray Scrip through, many a time? Hadn't he knelt with Scrip's mother, good hard-working sister in the Lord that she was, and prayed to be able to forgive him, prayed for a conversion of the heart? Where would his people go with this sort of man amidst them, stirring up hate and undoing the slow progress that Dikes had been able to make for them with his white, vested politicians? You had to court the white man, not fight him. He wouldn't lie—he wouldn't say he knew for a fact Scrip had done that rape. If thy eye offend thee, pluck it out. "Three-seven-five-STOP," he muttered, and went to the phone.

That night Scrip Thomas had called a meeting at Green Isle, down by the bayou on the beat-down grassy place where the men played baseball. It would be his second "teach-in," to prepare the community for Juneteenth Day, he said. The moon was full and low and orange-yellow, but in case there wasn't enough light Scrip had parked his truck and his mother's facing one another with their headlights on. He would jump them off tomorrow—he'd just look at the run-down batteries as a price of his calling. Scrip had built a rough platform out of planks, like a raft. His figure on the platform, washed with bright cones of light from either side, was dark with a blurry radiance like some stellar object brought back in satellite photos.

The people thought he was crazy, but more than a dozen of them had shown up, out of curiosity. They were sitting in rows made of a variety of porch and yard chairs, and some of the younger ones were on blankets on the ground.

Suddenly into the yellow-white glare enveloping their Scrip, blue bars intruded: blue bands of light like fan blades cutting across it. And then the people saw the new set of headlights. And then the black and white doors of the car. And light hitting off the epaulets, the shoulder badge, the trim on the cap, the buttons, the gun of the policemen coming Scrip's way. They never turned on their siren.

Scrip's voice trailed off. His hands fell to his sides.

"What's this? What's this for?"

The people couldn't hear what was said in the conference taking place in front of them. Scrip stepped back from the policemen, shaking his head wonderingly, his palms moving up and out from his body in a great shrug, and like dancers the policemen stepped with him. They kept talking and finally Scrip held out his wrists with a gesture of bewilderment, and he was led away, out of the light, and the police car backed up, and the blue light beams like helicopter blades withdrew, and the taillights shrank into red dots on the highway leading to town.

The fluorescent lights of the police station were not usually flattering, and on Myrtle Clark they looked positively ghastly. She came in leaning on the arm of an officer, her body bent like a Z, and she shuffled along in tiny steps. She was wearing sunglasses that sat a little crookedly on her face, and around them the flesh was powdered white as snow, except where grim lines in it showed.

A detective and an officer led her slowly down a labyrinth of bleak halls—typical of the cinderblock maze her life had suddenly changed into—and into a grubby anteroom. It was painted the weak, dirty, pale green of institutions of a certain vintage. A couple of tired-looking posters on crime prevention curled from the walls. One wall had a partition of glass that went from the ceiling halfway down and was now curtained. They sat down in chairs upholstered in split, cracked vinyl that showed yellow foam inside.

The two men briefed Myrtle about the line-up she was about to see. "You realize, Miz Clark, that the men in the line-up won't be able to see you. You can see them, but they can't see you," they said. She nodded, but flinched anyway when they opened the curtain. "Now remember, they can't see or hear us," said the detective quietly.

"Don't you need to take off those dark glasses?" said the officer, and she shook her head vehemently. Her head moved from side to side. Abruptly she said, "That's him."

"Which one, Miz Clark?"

She pointed with a shaking, crooked finger.

The two men exchanged glances. "I thought you said he had a beard, Miz Clark."

"Ah, but he musta gone out and shaved. That's how they'll do you." Suddenly her face around the glasses bunched into new, gray, even deeper groves and her mouth jerked downward even farther at the corners. "That's him, all right. Can we go? Can we go now?"

"Sure, we can. Let's go now. Take it easy, Miz Clark." The officers led the sobbing woman away.

36

ON FRIDAY AFTERNOON of that week Allie was trying to call Paul. The phone rang and rang and rang. The sound had a desolate quality. Finally, slowly, she lowered the receiver toward the hook, but just before she actually hung up one of the burring rings was interrupted, and she heard his low, dry "Hallo."

"Paul. Hi."

"Oh, hallo." The pleased uplift was still in his voice.

"I was about to decide you weren't there."

"I wasn't. I was over at Carmelina's. Heard the phone as soon as I got downstairs."

"And you're not even winded."

"Well, that's because I didn't run. I figured the hell with it, if it was someone who really wanted me they'd keep trying."

"And I did. Do. So I guess she's pretty upset?"

"Yeah. Who told you about the arrest?"

"Harlan, first," said Allie. "Then Hoodoo came by, and Karo and LaShondra together. It's funny. With everything else he's done, they don't really seem to think he was capable of this."

"No. But the worst thing is, the woman—what's her name?—the victim—"

"Clark, Myrtle Clark."

"Yah," said Paul. "Today she picked Scrip out of a line-up of suspects."

"Oh, Jesus. That's it then, isn't it?"

"I don't know. Miranda says there's some question about the legality of it. Mrs. Clark has been saying all along the man had a beard. And of course Scrip is clean-shaven. The police think he could have shaved after the crime. But all of that is another question—the quibble is that these police officers apparently talked this over with Mrs. Clark during the line-up. Scrip's lawyer is going to claim they prejudiced her."

"But we saw him that same night, and he didn't have a beard. I remember noticing. He'd been looking so scruffy the past couple of months. Scary."

"Yeah. I was talking to Carmelina and Miranda about that, trying to figure out whether that would be of any use to him as an alibi. But it's just our word about the beard. And when we saw him it was still several hours before the crime happened, so it doesn't do Scrip any good. They were asking me if I noticed anything unusual that night—"

"Even *they* were? It's like they were doubting...What'd you tell them?"

"I said a woman who was unusually beautiful came into my bed, but that other than that—"

"—Oh—"

Then his voice got impatient. "So what'd you call about?"

After the flurry his tenderness brought, the shift seemed abrupt. She said almost shamefacedly, almost whispering, "I wanted to see what you were doing tomorrow afternoon."

"I'm taking Ross to the zoo."

"Oh. Okay. Well, I was sort of planning the day. Just thought I'd check with you—" She could pull back with her voice, too—she could herself be as crisp and matter as if she were discussing some flower delivery for Lillian—she'd show him.

"Sorry," he said.

"Maybe Sunday," she said, "Or even Monday, now that school's out," and when he just said, "Mm," added quickly, "Well, tell Ross hi for me."

"I will."

"Talk to you later."

"Bye."

The newspaper building was hot—they turned the thermostat up on weekends—and deserted, except for a couple of reporters trying to get their stories in before the last absolute deadline. Allie trudged up to Photography, her sneakers squeaking on the floor, and was greeted with the familiar blink and buzz of the fluorescent light she flipped on, the familiar sour smell of developing chemicals. There were four rolls of wedding pictures to do for the paper—you could tell it was June—and the one roll from graduation night to do for herself.

She sighed and went into the darkroom. She would do the wedding pictures first. She unwound the roll with practiced, accustomed fingers that worked nimbly even without eyesight to guide them. She turned on the infrared lights to a dull scarlet glow, like a cheap stage set of hell. She started the newspaper film in its developer, and then turned to her own roll, set aside.

These should be her graduation night pictures, plus the Kertesz imitations she'd taken from the bridge at dawn the next morning, plus pictures from the class brunch where she'd stopped on her way home, the morning after graduation. She had high hopes, aesthetically, for this series, but emotionally of course she was more involved with the ones of Paul. She didn't have a real good shot of him yet. And she would be wanting it next year.

For the next two hours she worked in silence and red-edged darkness, always keeping the newspaper's film a little ahead of her personal roll. Usually she didn't mind this part of her work, though to some it might seem too pedestrian or mechanical. The pseudo-scientist in her liked measuring out the various fluids, the cook in her liked the small skills of wrist and thumb, the knack of patience and timing, required in getting her result. She fancied herself a labor technician: delivering images out of a womb where they'd been resting, insulated and safe. But today something was bothering her. It was as if she knew she had forgotten something important. Or as if she had been thinking over some problem but was distracted before sheved she was trying to remember what it was.

Finally, with her roll in its last wash, it was time to unwind the local news photos and the brides, whose veils and dresses looked amusingly like widows' weeds in this negative form, she always thought. She checked the squeegee tongs carefully before wiping the strips as she hung them up. Her first week at work she had scratched a whole roll of film by using gritty tongs; Mr. Brooks had not been happy. Maybe that was what had been bothering her—the thought like a piece of grit itself. But now that she had remembered it and taken care of it she still felt uneasy. The brides leered down at her with black, Halloweenish teeth, as if they knew something was wrong. Now she unrolled her own exposures. In the long strip of images she could trace graduation night and the next morning: first the seniors' caps like byzantine tile in the crowd shots; the skeletal lightness of Scrip's and Paul's black faces; the sheet like ebony in the bedroom pictures; the lighter sweep of the sandbar background at the picnic breakfast that Friday morning.

Now her edginess grew to a big pit in her stomach. Her fingers were trembling a little. She left the brides overhead, but put her own negatives into the film dryer to hurry them up, and went outside to wait and think this through in Mr. Brooks's office.

She knew she had exposures of Scrip Thomas at Paul's apartment on the night of May 16, the night of Myrtle Clark's rape. In one picture there might even be a clock. Paul kept a clock on the wall behind his work-stool, and she thought some of the shots might include it. It had been around eleven o'clock, hours before the rape was committed, and Scrip was clean-shaven in her picture.

If she were right, and among her pictures there was one that clearly showed his face earlier that night, it could prove Scrip innocent. Or at least make it harder to convict him. But what about the informant who had called in to "Crimestoppers"? That person must have something on Scrip—something she didn't know.

In that case it wasn't worth getting involved. For if Allie turned in this picture, she'd have to give an account of why she took it—why, which was easier than where, and when. What reason could she give for being at Paul's? "Oh, lots of the seniors run by their teachers' houses during graduation night—"

"Okay, Miss McCain, which of your classmates were with you?"

"None of them—"

"Where were you the rest of the night?"

And would she have to give up the rest of the roll? She wasn't worried about the street scenes, but the pictul looking up sleepily from the couch, where he was reading the newspaper in only his shorts—or looking straight at her with narrowed eyes, a three-quarters angle so you saw the shape of his cheek and jaw, a portrait so big and a gaze so close and open and somber that you would know the context of the relationship in which it was taken—and the one of him lying in bed the next morning, his skin so dark against the white sheet. Could she surrender these to the court? It would be the surrender of everything, their whole relationship and the person she thought she'd become, all her arrogance and secret joys.

After fifteen minutes she went back into the darkroom. She made a contact sheet of her roll. She looked at it with the magnifier. Scrip and Paul showed up clearly, with the clock visible behind them, showing eleven-seventeen. Sandwiched between the public graduation and the public breakfast the next morning, the print had to have been taken that night. It was evidence. She took her negatives and the contact sheet, locked up, and left.

37

THEY SEEMED incredulous that he would ask for paper. Their eyes narrowed to slits and they cocked their heads, peering at him through the bars, as they tried to gauge for what bizarre motive a monster like him might want paper. "Just writing paper," he told them. "Blank." It took them a long time to come up with half a dusty legal tablet. He sat down on his bed with the tablet on his knee and wrote, in a column, *King & co.* And opposite that: *The Cause! justice.* Under *King & co.* he added *Malcolm, Bonhoffer, Gandhi (S.A.), Mandela,* and as an afterthought, *Thoreau,* each time writing *justice* in the column beyond the name. And then in smaller writing under Thoreau's name he put *me.* Then his hand stopped, hovering in the air, and he flung the pen to the floor, ripped the page off the tablet, and threw it down too. He put his head in both his hands, curling into his own lap like someone in the air raid defense drill position, and rocked back and forth like someone who got bombed anyway, trying literally to hold himself together.

38

SHE KEPT THE NEGATIVES with her all that night and the next. She still didn't know what she was going to do with them. She couldn't sleep or eat much. Her jaws and her shoulders and her chest felt tense and tight. An innocent man was in jail and only she could get him out, she thought. At a loss to herself she could get him out. A loss of what? She'd be leaving this place soon anyway. She would still live, even with her family's trust in her scattered, even with the orderly design of her Edgewood life broken down. Many people had had to live without that—had never had it in the first place. Look at Paul.

But this was a man who had insulted her, a man who had hurt those who loved him—just as her disclosure would hurt her family. What was his life next to hers, really, when you got right down to it? She was going to do much more with her life than Scrip was with his. She needed to keep her world intact for her own strength and nourishment. Out of the wholeness that came from preserving what was dear to her, other good was going to come. She was certain of that. *She* was at stake, with all her promise! And what assurance did anyone have of Scrip's worth? Even his biggest admirers, his wife and her mother and Paul, doubted it.

Maybe her photographs wouldn't be evidence anyway. In the wee hours of Saturday morning she had drifted through the house looking through her father's old law books, but she couldn't make head nor tail of them and wasn't sure in the end that she'd even been looking under the right section to answer her question. Would it be circumstantial evidence of Scrip's innocence, or an alibi? An alibi, she thought. It had been so long since she'd watched TV or read a detective story.

So Allie vacillated. At times she would decide to turn over the negatives. She would go down to the police station and tell them what she knew. The order of the exposures was an important part of the proof, because the graduation at Beauregard High and the pictures from the seniors' brunch would pinpoint the night in question. She would have to bring them all. Where was the main police station? She looked it up in the Blue Pages.

In other moments she longed to be rid of the whole problem. Maybe she had made it all up. She could just ignore it. Oh, if she could just redo that night, not take those pictures, *something*.—But she had. Before this twist of circumstance, she saw now, her life had been so simple and enjoyable. Why hadn't she realized at the time how free from complication it was?

On Saturday she couldn't eat lunch; she might throw up if she did. She showered and washed her hair and put on clean shorts and a shirt. When she walked to the old Jimmy at one-thirty the burnished sun lay on her head like folded hands pressing down.

But instead of going toward the highway and downtown Edgewood, at the end of their driveway she turned back, into the farm. She drove as far as she could toward the river and got out and walked. For once she wasn't wearing her camera, and she felt oddly light, unencumbered, with its weight off her neck; but she carried a folder under her arm, and in her opposite pocket was a box of matches. She walked steadily. There was a faint path made by some animals that she followed, stepping over logs, ducking around briars that briefly pricked her khaki shirtsleeves. As long as she was walking she didn't have to think too much. It was snake season now. She had better just concentrate on that. Then the underbrush thinned into a stand of young cottonwood trees, and she came out on the sandbar, first clay gulches and low, clinging plants underfoot, then just the pale sand. She still kept walking downriver for a while, but more and more slowly, till finally she came to a stop and sat down.

She pulled out the negatives again and stared at them for several minutes. It was a beautiful day: sunny, with just the beginnings of the summer's heat in it. The riverside breeze nosed her hair and tried to bend the negatives, but she held to them firmly. She pulled out her box of matches and lit one. The breeze blew it out. She swivelled and lit another, cupping her body around it. She held the match close to the negatives till her hand started to tremble. Then she advanced it till it touched the corner. She wouldn't be able to undo this action. There was no repairing it. Again there would be no going back. She jerked the match away again and dipped that corner of the strip of negatives into the sand. Part of an exposure of the brunch was gone, that was all.

Then, deliberately, she lit another match. She brought it toward the sheet of negatives and lit it. She watched the flame dance on its peculiar fuel, licking the page faster and faster now, consuming the saving images, nearing Allie's hand, till she dropped the burning sheet on the sand and watched it extinguish itself.

Paul was finding the zoo even more depressing than usual. It was his least favorite outing with the kids. He had tried to talk Ross into doing something else—park, museum, lake—but no go. The afternoon had clouded over into a listlessness that seemed endemic to certain Saturdays, whether in summer or winter. The animals paced in their cages or sprawled torpid near coiled hoses, opening their eyes long enough to stare balefully at the zoo visitors as if to dispel any notion they were napping in contentment. Ah, friend, he breathed within himself, don't think I don't know what you've lost through this captivity! He stopped when Ross wanted to stop and bought the sticky drinks asked of him and walked on with his son, answering his barely intelligible chatter, glancing at the other little groupings of people who kicked at the rails and moved past him on the walks. There were times when everything in the world seemed infused with such a heavy sadness, a withering lack of the interest that either purpose or anarchy would provoke—just boredom and inertia.

"Stop it, son," he said, restraining Ross's arm. Ross was throwing popcorn at a grizzly bear. "You're going to make him sick." Ross pointed at another child, a towhead in shorts and an Astros cap, who was throwing popcorn unchecked and who smiled smugly at the father and son. The bear lumbered across the front of his cage. He sat and dragged one great paw down the wire mesh, making a low, twanging noise. Ross crowed. The heaviness in Paul's chest was concentrated. The bear, too, seemed restless and despondent. He dropped back to all fours and hauled himself to the corner. "I don't care what he's doing. The bear isn't supposed to eat popcorn. Come on."

"Rain," said Ross.

"I know. We'd better get back to the car."

Allie called just as the two of them were finishing bowls of ice cream at Paul's apartment. It was the wrong choice for that day; the cold food sent chills shivering through him.

"Paul? Can I come see you?" He was not surprised at the tightness of her voice; it fit the atmosphere within him.

"Well—in a couple of hours."

"I'm really—I have something to talk to you about."

"Sure. Come on."

"I guess Ross is there with you."

"Yeah."

"You're taking him home soon?"

"Yah, at five."

"Well, I'll be there after that."

Her eyes were giant, smudged underneath with darkness. "You look—" he said.

"What?"

"Hollow."

Even in his hold she didn't relax. She pulled back, though his arms still wrapped her waist loosely, and said, "I've done something terrible." She started to shake. He made her sit down with him. He held her hands to keep them from shaking, though she tried to pull them away, without realizing it, to gesture while she was talking. She told him what she had done. Sometime during her talking he lay her hands quietly back on her lap. His face drew into its long mask; his chin jutted slightly forward. When she finished he was quiet for a minute. Then a tear came out of his eye and slid down his cheek. The rest of his face didn't move. "Excuse me," he said and got up and crossed the room and went into the bathroom for a Kleenex. He came back and sat down. His tears were coming faster now and soon the Kleenex was a wet lump. "You'll have to excuse me again," he said and left the room again. Back at her side he said her name. They kept looking at each other, their eyes swallowing each other up. "What have you done?" he said. "You can't just do things like that."

"I know," she said miserably. "But I did."

"If you were uncertain, why didn't you at least hang on to them till you talked to me about it?"

"I don't know." If he would just touch her!

But he got up and went to the window. "I suppose the only thing to do now is to go and tell them what you told me. At least it will be your word against the tipster's. We know he was innocent, so they can't have any hard evidence against him either."

"I know." Now she spoke faster, eagerly—now that he was talking of practical things that could still be done. "And I was thinking. Mémé said Mrs. Clark was with her when they saw Scrip out of control at Buckerman's that day. That could be why she got him mixed up in the line-up. I need to tell them that."

He kept looking out the window. "But who knows if that will help. And your pictures—they could have done everything."

"But Paul," she said, trying to keep her voice steady, "they would have shown—I told you, they would have exposed everything about you and me."

He shook his head and half-turned and said very quietly and wearily, with disgust, "Don't you understand *anything*?"

"I guess not." She said. She was crying now.

"Get your keys. I'll follow you to the police station."

The police sergeant at the reception desk looked exasperated before they even opened their mouths. He glanced back and forth from Paul to Allie with an ironic expression, and Allie felt a flash of anger. She wasn't used to being a couple with Paul in public.

"We, um—" she started, and then corrected herself, "I want to talk to somebody about Scr—Earl Thomas's case."

"Thomas?" said the sergeant. "You haven't heard? We found him in his cell just a couple of hours ago, dead. Hung hisself with his belt. I thought you were reporters, as a matter of fact. Things haven't slowed up around here since we found him. Nope, he's a suicide, Miss."

They had scarcely been at Paul's apartment five minutes when he said he had to go on to Carmelina's. He called Glory Jones and Allie heard him say, "Mama Glory? I have some bad news.—Oh. Oh, I didn't know whether she would have called you.—Yes, I was out.—Never mind, I'll tell you later.—Me too. See you out there."

Allie, curled up under his quilt like a little fossil leaf, called him in with a question.

"My God, don't be an idiot. Of course you can't go with me."

"Do you mind if I stay here till you come back?"

"No."

He started to leave, but the quilt's buckling and shuddering with Allie's breaths touched him, touched the quick of him, and he went back to the bed and sat on the edge of it, scooping her to him. He kissed her softly all around her hairline. "Be sure to drink this whiskey I've poured for you." His sternness was kind now. She looked at the shot glass standing on the bedside table and nodded. He kissed her gently on the lips. "You'll be all right," he said.

"I know," she said. "I know I will. That's the trouble."

39

SHE LAY AGAINST the pillows in Paul's bed and sipped the straight whiskey, every few minutes a sip, and watched the color drain from his walls and the dusk come into the room. She fell asleep for a while and woke up without knowing where she was or how she had gotten there. It was completely dark. She recollected herself enough to cry out, "Paul?" but there was no answer, and no light showed through the bedroom door from the rest of the apartment. When you don't know what else to do, you get your things together and go home. It is an old instinct. There you will find your own bed to lie in and your own ceiling to watch. Allie knew she needed to make herself eat, too. She felt a little shaky just going down the stairs.

She told Lillian she was sick and was going to bed. Lillian swept her hand over her forehead, looked into her eyes, and said, "Yes, you've probably overdone it." She was too exhausted to snack, wash her face, or brush her teeth; she stripped and left her clothes on the floor and got in bed. But when her head sank into the pillow she knew she was awake for the night.

After a great while she thought, so this is how you learn things.

After a great while longer she thought, everyone is always out on their own. No one should count on other people, for in the end we will all be left absolutely alone in a great darkness, all supports kicked out from under us, all threads of connection broken. Everyone ends up wheeling and spinning in a big void, like in those dreams of falling. The reason those dreams scare us so much is that we know they end up happening. It is our fate to careen through empty space that way, and any pretense that there can be companionship in it, that anyone will sacrifice to help you, that love will make a difference, is a lie. Daddy lay in there consulting with a tumor in his head and Mama lies in there missing the hell out of Daddy; I lie here missing the hell out of Paul and Paul lies in his bed missing something that came before, something he never was able to have, homesick for a place he can't go; Miranda and Glory and Malcolm lie missing Scrip, because Scrip lay in jail missing any hope at all; and no one can lessen anyone else's pain at all. The best we can do is feel it ourselves, the worst is to shaft each other directly the way I did Scrip—forcing the end a little sooner than it would have come otherwise.

Whoever had said it could be any different? That was what she wanted to know.

She could still hear Paul's voice. "Don't you understand *anything?*" Well, maybe not then. But she understood now. She had no more illusions. She knew. She knew, for instance, that she would lose Paul, and that her foreknowledge would not lessen the pain of it. The summer would go by with their passion unshaken. But every time he pulled out of her body, every time they said goodbye, and later with every long-distance phone call that did not go through, she would lose the whole man over again. And even in this, this thing born out of themselves alone, they would each be powerless to spare the other. People were not allowed to cross those acres of empty space. There were no exceptions.

She went back, deliberately, over the first inklings of her liking for him. She thought of a few dozen conversations they had had. She remembered jokes. She arrived at this month and projected the void of the future again: Paul would break away from Edgewood, no less than she would. He would leave and move back to New York. There would come a day when she would not know his address.

She tried not to think about Scrip.

At daybreak she got up, washed her face, put on a nightgown, went in the kitchen, and had a piece of cornbread and some chocolate milk. She brushed her teeth and went back to bed, and slept until eight-twenty. Again she woke up, and again the hours stretched before her like a desert.

"Feeling better?" said Lillian.

"Yes."

"You still look sort of tired. I have some sad news. Scrip Thomas apparently killed himself yesterday in jail. He was being held on that rape charge."

"Oh, God."

"Yes. I don't know about the wake or the funeral yet."

"Poor Lelia."

"Yes. Poor Miranda," said Lillian. "I had to use the Jimmy this morning and found your camera on the seat."

"I guess I forgot to bring it in."

"Well, it's in the entrance hall. You had a phone call, too. I didn't tell you last night because you seemed to be feeling so bad. Randolph Tate called."

"Oh."

"I think he'll call back. And Fayette and Maria are supposed to be here by eleven. Elaine and her boyfriend and Jeff are coming out for brunch. I thought it'd be nice to have a visit before y'all get all involved over at Mémé's."

"That's right. I'd forgotten about that."

"I'm just going to put out some banana bread and fruit and cheese and let everyone help themselves. Pamela and Stovall might come too. You can ask Theresa if you want."

"If that can all happen without me," said Allie, "I think I'll go to church."

"You're still planning to help with Mémé's move?"

"Of course." Allie carried her camera back to her room and set it on her desk. She looked at it there for a minute and then dug around on the high shelf of her closet till she found its case. She put it in the case and up on the high shelf.

Then she got dressed for church. It was not that she retained illusions about church, any more than about herself or anything else, any more. But she had to be somewhere this Sunday morning. And she did not want to chat on the porch with her older cousins and Fayette and Maria and their friends.

She got there early and sat way back in a corner where she could see the whole length of Paul's mosaic. With any luck she would be inconspicuous and no one would try to talk to her. It was at times like this she wished she were Catholic and could sit in a big shadowy anonymous cathedral where no one, not even the priest, knew who she was—instead of among hearty Methodists with their bent for "fellowship."

Back in that other life of hers, before yesterday, she had loved Methodism. Or loved the vision of it her father gave her: of those early days when the Anglicans banned Wesley from their grand churches, because he preached to the working class. Of missions into jails and slums. Of women ministers preaching throughout England; or Wesley firing off letters to Parliament condemning munitions factories, condemning the slave trade. And then in America, later, she had visions of those slightly crazed, wiry horsemen galloping through the wilderness, with Bibles and beef jerky in their saddlebags—galloping to the fringe, the edge, the unmapped frontier, with the message of grace. They were the scouts, who despite their mania had a deft, pragmatic touch, a bourgeois respect for an order and comfort they would never pause to know in their lifetimes, and an intuition for seeding it. They had the genius of organization. While they were dashing on, always farther into the twilight of the west, they left behind, among a vast well-ordered network of ordinary people, the dazed sense that even the clumsiest efforts toward perfection were somehow blessed. But now the fleet scouts were gone, and it was settled people who made up the Methodism of today: recyclers of the corny jokes about beating the Baptists to the cafeteria; guardians of the attendance registration forms and huge air conditioning bills.

Fayette quit going to church long ago. He thought it was made up of hypocrites who never intended to change their ways at all. Why else would the weekly confessions be so formulaic? During the Lord's Prayer he used to chant the Pledge of Allegiance, and when Lillian opened her eyes and glared at him he would hiss back: "What's the difference? You learn them all when you're about four years old and don't know what they mean." In the end it had been easier for Frank and Lillian to let Fayette stay home.

There was a stir behind Allie and then a flurry at her elbow. She looked up, startled. Mrs. Clark was maneuvering her wobbly way into the pew, with a walker. Her eyes had livid purple and yellow-greenish bruises around them, like a Mardi Gras mask, but she was smiling.

"Excuse me, honey!" she whispered, though Allie was already obligingly scooting down the pew as best she could. But Mrs. Clark said, "No, don't get up! I'll sit on the *other* side of you." Mr. Thomasson, who was helping her, eventually had to let go of her arm, and Mrs. Clark sank into her seat with a big plop that could have incapacitated her even more. "Ooof!" she said. A cloud of Youth Dew wafted over Allie.

The girl smiled vaguely, trying not to make eye contact. But an elbow nudged her side.

"Hand me a hymnal, would you? I just had to get back," said Mrs. Clark. "You wouldn't believe how much I missed my church. I've been—ill, Allie, and as I lay in my hospital bed you know what helped me most? Just trying to picture that big old sun down there on that wall."

"Yes ma'am." The prelude was winding into its last predictable chords.

"And there it is! Red, and gold, and all! I knew if I could see that again, I'd make it."

"Yes ma'am." Now the ministers were coming in. This time Mrs. Clark fell quiet.

As their congregations got richer, Methodist ministers had dropped their plain black robes and instead affected something called an alb—a long tunic, tied at the waist with a rope, which was supposed to symbolize holy poverty. The ministers' shiny shoes stuck out underneath and they would hitch the alb up at the belt, which might need to be a little longer this year than last, and their hard plastic eyeglasses, with fashion frames, gleamed and glinted over the monkish garb, making it look a little less than authentic; but never mind. Today the ministers of the First United Methodist Church at Edgewood wore red stoles over their albs, because it was Pentecost. The congregation rose to its feet.

Jim Norton, the associate minister, took the microphone, twining his fingers around it. The soft track lighting blazed upon the diamond rings on his hand. "This is the day that the Lord has made," he said.

At length the congregation answered, like a big sullen wave rolling back: "Let us rejoice and be glad in it." The organist launched into the hymn.

"But you'll be leaving, won't you?" whispered Myrtle Clark. "Let's see—Imogene told me. Out to California, isn't it? When are you going?"

"Soon," whispered Allie. "Excuse me." She stood up and slipped past the old lady, out of the pew and up the aisle, through the richly colored, sensuous spaces of light cast by the stained-glass windows, out the doors at the back and into the world of street, sky, branches, signs, cars, and passers-by. She took a deep breath. The scene looked complete, as blind and seamed and inscrutable as a finished jigsaw puzzle, daring her to take it apart again.

40

FAYETTE AND MARIA were coming home partly because the aunts were throwing a shower for Maria on Monday, and partly because Mémé was moving to Tara Place and everyone was expected to help her. Uncle Gus had sent word that the Jimmy would be needed at noon. As Allie got close to Mémé's old house she saw cars and pickup trucks lined up halfway down the block. The yard was full of teetering stacks of boxes. Dressers and hatracks blocked the front sidewalk, showing sun discoloration and dust and scratched and peeling finish that no one had noticed before. Hatracks and bedframes leaned against the porch posts. Inside, Allie saw that people had brought food as for a funeral. Mémé wandered around in a haze, looking smaller and more bent than usual.

"Where's my car? Has anyone seen my car?" Allie heard Aunt Cynthia calling. "Hey sweetie," she said to Allie. "Have you seen my car?"

"I just heard someone drive up in it," hollered Jeff. "Oops, no, that must've been Allie. Hey, Allie."

Stovall emerged from the hallway. He was covered with grime.

"Where have you been?"

"In the attic. It must be a hundred degrees up there. No, what I was saying was, Uncle Calvin Ray took your car over to Tara Place, Aunt Cynthia. I think he took the houseplants in it."

"The houseplants weren't ready to go," called Sadie Rabelais in an irritated tone from the back of the house.

"Well, I have to go get Theresa at gymnastics practice. That's all. I'm late already. Where's your camera, Allie? I told Mother I thought sure you'd be taking pictures."

"Oh, it's at home," said Allie. "Look, I'll go get Theresa. I have the Jimmy right here."

"Doesn't somebody here need the Jimmy? They were clamoring for it earlier this morning."

"No," said Jeff, "that was for getting the refrigerator out to Jules's lake house, and he ended up finding a company truck to do that with."

Allie asked her aunt, "Now how late are you? She won't have gotten a ride with somebody else?"

"Oh no, she was specifically going to wait. Besides, they usually run late, so that's one reason I wasn't rushing. That's sweet of you, darling. It's at the college. That first long building on the left. And y'all come straight back here, okay? Theresa promised her grandmother to go through some old clothes and so on."

"Theresa gets to look at old clothes, and I end up moving boxes in the attic," complained Stovall.

"It's rough, it's rough, boy," Allie told him. "No equality."

She listened to country music all the way out to the college—nasal, predictable songs so clichéd they made a parody of love and sorrow. So when she pushed open the heavy steel door to the gym, the hush hit her in the face like a brick: a taut hush composed of minds concentrating on many tasks, of suppressed grunts and gasps, of the whisper of chalked hands and feet against bare wood, the squeak of trampoline springs, the slap of weight against vinyl. The room seemed shadowy compared to the glare of light outside. Girls in white leotards with red and orange diagonals slashing their waists and upper arms hurled themselves quietly into dim air; edged along rims of wood and reordered their bodies into strangely balanced sculptures; rushed with surprising speed toward goals invisible to viewers; and made themselves into a counterweight to the varnished plane of the floor. The coach, a slight bowlegged man dressed in nondescript shirt and pants, moved calmly among the gymnasts.

It took her a while to see Theresa, but she finally spotted her starting her routine at the uneven parallel bars. There was that curious short run and jump: the "mount," Allie knew to call it: the well-pronounced muscles of the thighs working, the duo of tendon cords flashing at the back of each knee, the extension of Theresa's long arms, the further tightening of her round breasts and flat belly. Then this machine became a pinwheel of color that spun around the bar for several seconds. The bar bent slightly in the middle from the maneuver; you would swear Theresa's abdomen did not touch it during most of the spin. When she came out of it, raised on straight arms, the eyes in the chiseled-cameo face looked steadily ahead as if they had not moved the whole time. Yet all the while she was dipping toward something. And suddenly she curled around the bar again, only one wheel around it this time, before her rear end went straight up toward the ceiling, the balls of her white feet touched the lower bar, the hands released somehow and snapped to at a new point somehow, and she was hanging from the top bar. The feet, neatly held together, toes pointed, aimed through the space made by her arms and trunk, sought the bar, and insinuated themselves around it as her body followed, curling slowly upward. A quick wrap around the bar, by her knees, and that perfect profile was transported by you for an instant. Then there was a slow rising above the high bar and a flip dismount. Allie joined the smattering of applause that came from a semicircle of other girls.

Theresa walked to the side of the room, breathing heavily. Sweat glued tendrils of her hair to her face. When she saw her cousin she grinned.

"Well, hey! 'Dyou come to get me?"

"Hey. Yeah. That was great."

"Oh, well. Thanks." She bent to pick up a towel. "It's hot in here."

"Yeah, even I think so, and I haven't been doing what you have."

Theresa suddenly looked at her sharply. "I knew you looked different—where's your camera?"

"It's at home."

"I'd like some pictures of that routine. What's the matter, is it broken or something?"

"No, I just didn't feel like doing it, today."

Theresa shrugged. "How was graduation night? I saw you across the room at the dance."

"Oh, it was okay. Did you have fun?"

"You weren't with Randolph, were you?"

Allie paused. "No. How'd you figure that out?"

"I'd like to say I put a bunch of clues together from the way you've been acting. But really I ran into him the next day at the mall."

"You didn't say anything to him about it?"

"I didn't have the chance to. Hi, Kathy." Theresa raised her hand to a ponytailed wraith slipping by. "He asked me how you were doing, so I just put two and two together."

"I know I've been sort of a shit to him."

"You think you'll keep seeing him?"

"No. Not a chance. But at least I feel bad about it."

Theresa pulled on a T-shirt, then sat down on the floor to put on sneakers. In a minute, still looking at her shoelaces, she said, "So who *were* you with that night?"

Allie looked at the shoelaces too, and finally answered, "I don't think I can tell you right now. I may be able to, but not right now."

"All right." Theresa stood up. "Come on, I need some water." They walked toward the hall. "By the way, I never thought taking pictures was something to do because you *felt* like it."

Allie became a little indignant. Just who did this girl think she was, preaching like this? Did a spin around a wooden bar give Theresa the right to nag? But she was too dispirited to retort. She watched in silence as her cousin leaned down to the water fountain, holding her hair back with one elbow crooked up, tilting her face a little to catch the halfhearted spurt of water, so that the faint freckles showed on the otherwise perfect ivory skin. The heart-shaped face looked moony and its dimples showed lavender in the fluorescent light, while the lips slurped thirstily. When Theresa stood up, releasing her hank of dark curls, the cousins faced each other, not smiling and not quite hostile. Then Allie's expression because a little shamefaced. Who is this girl? she thought.—This girl is somebody different from who she was the last time I really thought about it, which was probably two years ago, is who she is. Beneath her sting of pride was the realization that Theresa was right. Allie had always respected photography as a discipline. Anybody could do it when the impulse was there; but only the toughest looker could keep up a watch with that third eye when it was less than fun, when it showed a vision less than sweet. And she realized that, outside the span of her own attention, Theresa had learned similar lessons; had obviously learned some of them better than she.

"Let me run home and get my camera and come back," she said impulsively, "and you can do your routine again."

"Nope," said Theresa, "you missed it. I'm not doing that again today. You screwed up."

Allie's eyes widened. Scraps of conversation, some she had held with other people and some she had never held with any living person, worked themselves loose from the bottom of her mind and unreeled in slow motion. *Here-go all the darkies...Bad things really can happen...You screwed up someone's life...You were sulking, so you missed that shot and you can't ever get it back.* "Touché," she said slowly. And then, in the slightly peeved tone of someone waking up late to a workday morning, "Well then, at least come with me to pick it up. You've talked me into it now. We'll stop at Green Isle together on the way to Mémé's, and get my camera so I don't miss anything there, at least."

"Don't do *me* any favors," said Theresa lightly, unwrapping a piece of Juicy Fruit from a pack she had just stuck out toward Allie. But her strong, springing walk, her touch on the steel door going back into the gym that swung it open like magic, charged the flippancy of the words with something more important. "And we're stopping at McDonald's on the way too. I'm starved."

"Okay, okay," said Allie. They had found the rhythm of banter again. "God, you're still eating meat?"

“God, you’re still a vegetarian?”

Theresa scooped her gym bag off the floor by the bleachers. The next set of doors they exited together, coming into the sunlight almost cheerfully.